"Just when I thought we had solved all your problems, you look ready to cry again. What is it, Paula?"

"Some news my daughter brought. My ex-husband has grown a beard and joined a rock band. And he's dating a twenty-five-year-old . . .

"Paula, he is a classic case of midlife crisis. This has nothing to do with you." He studied her with a new intensity. "But he was a fool to look for anything else when he had you."

Derek's kind words were Paula's undoing. Her tears spilled down her cheeks unchecked. He enfolded her in his arms, and the warmth of his touch and the compassion in his voice allowed her to vent her emotions at last.

"Nothing has turned out right," she whispered. "Why did it all go wrong?"

"It hasn't gone wrong," Derek told her gently. "You are only at a crossroads. Taking a new direction is always difficult." He stroked her hair, then kissed her softly. He pointed high above them where a wafer-thin moon hung in the black sky. "Make a wish," he told her.

"I wouldn't know where to begin."

Derek's husky voice wrapped her in warmth. "Then I'll wish for both of us," he said, as he pulled her toward him for a deep and thrilling kiss.

THAT SPECIAL SUMMER

LINDA SWIFT

ZEBRA BOOKS
KENSINGTON PUBLISHING CORP.

ZEBRA BOOKS are published by

Kensington Publishing Corp.
475 Park Avenue South
New York, NY 10016

First Printing: January, 1994

Printed in the United States of America

*"For Bob,
With special thanks to Ann LaFarge,
Jim Finn, and Boni Heck"*

One

Paula dropped her garment bag onto the narrow bed and looked around the cubicle that would be her home for the summer. Besides the bed and its duplicate on the other side of the room, there was little else to see. A three-drawer student desk whose oak surface was dotted with white circles, permanent reminders of transient former occupants, and a straight-backed chair were the room's only other free-standing furniture. On the opposite wall a pair of sliding wooden closet doors flanked each side of a double built-in chest.

Paula surveyed her spartan quarters with wry detachment—just bare necessities. She should have known, but she had not lived in a dorm when she was in college thirty years ago. Surely it couldn't have been that long since she, solemn and resplendent in black robe and mortarboard, had clutched her coveted diploma and, with a head full of newly acquired learning and grandiose dreams, gone out to meet the world. What had happened to that girl she was then? How had she become the woman who stood here now, feeling as empty as the room around her? She resisted an overwhelming urge to pick up her garment bag and run.

"Hi! Welcome to Winthrope Hall."

Paula turned at the sound of a soft voice behind her, and saw, just outside her doorway, a girl with pale blond hair and a shy smile who shifted her stack of thick textbooks from one arm to the other. She continued, "Since your door was open I thought I'd just stop and say hello. I'm Sharon Swafford, your next-door neighbor."

"I'm Paula Howard." She glanced at the girl's armload of books. "Looks like you're getting a head start on studying."

"I'm a graduate assistant in the Speech Department. I'm preparing material for the summer program."

"Oh." Paula looked at the unassuming girl before her with new respect. "Where are you from?"

"South Carolina. But Alabama has one of the best programs in the country for the

8

speech-impaired, so I'm very lucky to get a chance to spend a summer here." She glanced at Paula's garment bag. "Are you bringing up your luggage?" At Paula's nod, she added, "Let me put these books in my room and I'll go down and help you."

"Oh no, you don't need to do that," Paula protested. Was the girl feeling sorry for her because she was obviously older than most students here? Paula was determined to blend in on campus as unobtrusively as possible, so she waved a hand in dismissal as she stepped into the hallway and closed her door.

"I really want to," Sharon insisted. "It's a long way from the parking lot. If I help it will cut your trips in half. I'll just be a minute."

"Well, okay," Paula answered, grateful for the generous offer in spite of her misgivings about the motive that prompted it.

In the heat of the noonday sun the glistening asphalt was soft beneath Paula's sandals as she trudged toward the back door of the dormitory carrying the final load of her possessions. Sharon Swafford walked behind her, arms piled high with blankets, pillows, and a boxed coffee maker balanced on top.

"Whew, the temp must be a hundred in the

9

shade today." Sharon eased carefully through the door Paula held open with her foot.

Paula smiled. "It gets worse. Even in Tuscumbia. And we're farther south here."

"Tuscumbia? Is that your home?"

"Yes." After a moment Paula added, "At least it was."

They were on the elevator now, rising slowly toward the top floor. "You're not going back?"

Paula shook her head. "I don't know."

"New job prospects?"

"No, not yet, but I'm looking. For a job and a new place to live. I'm," Paula hesitated, making a concerted effort to form the unfamiliar word and speak it aloud, ". . . divorced."

"Oh, I'm sorry." Sharon looked embarrassed. "I didn't mean to pry."

"It's okay." Paula shook her head. "I'm just not quite used to it yet."

The number above the door registered eight and the elevator opened to release its passengers. They crossed the lobby and headed for the front wing.

"Thanks so much." Paula rescued the teetering coffee maker and Sharon deposited the rest of her load onto the only bed with empty space remaining.

"Glad to help." Sharon's eyes swept the

jumbled room. "I think you have an afternoon's work here."

Paula glanced about her. "It's pretty dismal, isn't it? The decor, I mean."

"It will look different when you add your lamps and throw rugs and things."

"I'm afraid I didn't bring any." Paula hesitated, then confessed, "I've never lived in a dorm before, but a trip to Wal-Mart ought to take care of that."

"Sure." Sharon turned to leave, then stopped. "Have you gotten your meal tickets?"

"Yes. When I checked with admissions this morning."

"Good. And can you find Gaither Hall and the cafeteria?"

"I think so," Paula told her. "I have a map of the campus so I surely won't get lost."

Sharon looked at her large leather-strapped watch. "They stop serving at one, so you'd better hurry. I'd go with you but I have work to finish, so I'm skipping lunch today in favor of a granola bar. See you later." And with a wave she disappeared into the hallway.

Paula looked around her as she hurried across campus, marveling again at the sheer enormity of it all. What am I doing here? she asked herself. It had seemed like a good solution to her problems when she had applied for the grant, but now that she was actually here, she was filled with doubts about her decision to come. It was one thing to read about the university in a brochure but it was quite another to find her way around the sprawling campus and cope with all the unfamiliar rules and regulations.

She could have enrolled at the extended campus in Tuscumbia but the grant program had only been offered here. Besides, she hadn't wanted to stay on in the house or even the town after Quent walked out on her. But to suddenly find herself in the middle of a large university after being out of school for thirty years was intimidating. What if she couldn't fit in, couldn't make it? She had probably set herself up for more failure and humiliation—and she'd had quite enough of both already.

Gaither Hall was farther than it appeared on the campus map. Paula glanced at her watch and ran up the steps that led to the noisy lobby of the cafeteria. The din of voices, scraping chairs, tinkling glasses and clanging silverware reverberated beyond the large room. A smorgasbord of smells assaulted Paula's nostrils as she gave her ticket to a student seated at a small table by the door. She suddenly realized that she had not eaten anything for hours.

With her mouth watering, she selected bowls of grits, black-eyed peas, kale, and apples, chose a meatloaf entree and a corn muffin. When she reached the end of the long counter she made room among the dishes for a large glass of iced tea. She lifted her heavy tray and began searching for a table, but as she turned the corner which brought her to the open seating area, Paula collided head-on with a man returning an empty tray.

"Oh," both said together and stopped. "I'm sorry," they spoke in chorus again and each stepped sideways in the same direction so that they were left with trays still touching.

"Want to dance?" The man grinned for a moment, then looked dismayed. "I've sloshed tea all over you."

"It was my fault," Paula said quickly. "I should have been looking where I was going." She felt the cold liquid seeping into her white knit top.

"Here, let me blot some of that off." The man balanced his empty tray in one hand and took a white handkerchief from his pocket. He reached forward to swipe at the dripping material, suddenly realizing that his hand was reaching for her breast and stopped in midair. He blushed, cleared his throat, and mumbled, "Just a minute." Deftly depositing his own tray on the nearby conveyer, he took Paula's and thrust the handkerchief toward her. Mutely, Paula accepted the crisp white square and dabbed at the spreading stains.

"I really am sorry." He looked at the tray he held. "There's tea and ice on all of your food, but now the line is closed so I can't get you anything else."

"It's okay." Paula reached for her food but he didn't turn loose.

"Damn. What a mess. It was really very clumsy of me to bump into you like that. I'd like to pay for cleaning your blouse."

"No, that won't be necessary. The stains will come out when it's soaked for a while," Paula assured him with more confidence than she felt. She gave the tray a slight tug and the man let go of it.

"Well, if you're sure." He looked at her without conviction.

"Oh yes." Paula turned away and headed for the nearest vacant chair she saw.

The whole episode had occurred in only a few minutes but it seemed to Paula as though she had been standing there dripping tea for hours. What a way to start her first cafeteria meal. She supposed this sort of accident had happened before but she wished it hadn't happened to her. It was just one more thing to call attention to the fact that she was not an average student. And then she realized that the man who had bumped her wasn't either. His hair was shorter than any of the male students sitting near her now and it was graying at the temples. And he'd had a terrific tan.

Well, Paula Howard, she said to herself as she broke a piece off the soggy corn muffin, for someone embarrassed enough to sink through the floor you made an awful lot of specific observations. But no matter. With thousands of students on campus it was unlikely their paths would ever cross again. She suddenly remembered his wet handkerchief wadded under the edge of her plate. She picked it up, saw the small blue initials in one corner. D.V. David? Donald? The V was harder. Vance? Vaughn? Vincent? She really should have remembered to offer it back to him, tea-stained or not. And now it was too late.

Leaving her shirt soaking in a small plastic pan of cold water, Paula pulled on a black tee shirt and set to work unpacking her belongings, a job made easier because she had all the closet and drawer space normally shared with a roommate. A private room was the one extravagance she had allowed herself. It was going to be difficult enough adjusting to life on a big university campus without the added stress of living with a stranger.

With the last piece of luggage stored away, she considered the drab room. A fleeting image of her own house crossed Paula's mind—pastel walls with matching window treatments and floral upholstery that tied it all together to create a serene ambiance. Determinedly, she turned her thoughts back to the present and what she might do to convert this dreary cell into a cheerful sanctuary for her summer stay. She would go shopping today before she became involved with classes and had to devote her attention and energy to academic matters.

Paula picked up her purse and as she closed her door two women approached from the direction of the lobby. "Excuse me," she said. "Do either of you happen to know where the nearest shopping center is?"

They shook their heads and the thin one who wore her red hair in a sleek bun explained, "We only arrived from Jamaica yesterday so we've no idea where anything *on* campus is located, let alone off campus."

"Are you planning to go there now?" The bronze-skinned woman was dressed in an emerald green jumpsuit with matching scarf tied in her short Afro curls.

"Yes, if I can find my way."

"Would you mind if we go with you? I'm Louise Montgomery, and this is my friend, Ruth Valcourt. We have no transportation and we've been hoping for a chance to buy a few supplies."

"I'd be happy to have company. And I'm Paula Howard, from Tuscumbia, Alabama."

"Ah, Helen Keller's home," Ruth said quickly.

Paula raised her eyebrows in surprise. "You've heard of her, in Jamaica?"

"No, I . . ." Ruth stopped, shrugged, went on. "Her reputation is global, isn't it?"

A look Paula could not interpret passed between the two women, then Louise smiled at her. "Come on, we'll ask directions at the desk in the lobby."

Two hours later, arms filled with bulky packages, the three women returned.

"I didn't mean to buy so much," Ruth Valcourt was saying as they stepped out of the elevator, "but when I see such an abundance of everything, and at such low prices, I just can't seem to resist."

"Is it difficult to find items you need in Jamaica?" Paula asked.

"Sometimes it's almost impossible," Louise explained. "But my family has a condo in Miami. One or the other of us is constantly coming or going, so we can usually get what we need from the States. Our biggest problem is getting it through customs, unless it's something we can wear." Her eyes met Ruth's and they laughed, sharing a secret joke.

Then Ruth added, "Sometimes she comes home wearing a lot of clothes, especially for the tropics."

They had reached Paula's door and as she struggled to produce her key from her shoulder bag while still holding her purchases, Louise asked, "Would you like to walk over to Gaither Hall with us about a quarter past six? We wait till the crowd thins out a bit and avoid the long lines."

"Fine," Paula told her. "I'll be ready."

Paula looked with surprise at the time when she heard a light knock on her door at six o'clock. Perhaps they had changed their minds and decided to go earlier. But when she opened the door, Sharon Swafford stood there.

"Hi, Sharon. Would you like to come in?"

"No, I just . . ." Sharon looked beyond her at the transformation she had wrought during the afternoon. "Wow. You've been shopping, haven't you? It looks great."

"Come on in." Paula stepped aside to let the girl into her room. "It's all Wal-Mart specials. Do you like it?"

"It doesn't look like the same room! I love these colors."

Paula had bought blue floral spreads and accented them with deep peach throw pillows and colorful Dhurrie rugs. A blue pottery lamp for the desk and peach and blue silk flowers in an interesting wicker basket on the chest added a final touch.

Sharon suddenly remembered why she had knocked. "I was going to supper and I thought you might want to go with me."

"Well, thanks, I really would but I've already said I'd go with your neighbors from the other side. Do you know them?"

"Not yet, but I'd like to. Do you think they'd mind if I came along?"

"Of course not." Paula checked the time

again. "They'll be here in a few minutes if you want to wait."

"Sure." Sharon sat down on the nearest bed, took off her glasses and rubbed the bridge of her nose. "I was so tired I almost skipped supper in favor of a nap. I'm beginning to think a synonym for graduate assistant is slave." She smiled. "But I'm still not sorry I came. I just need to gripe about the work load I'm under. I don't see how it can get much worse when classes begin tomorrow, but I'll bet it will."

A second knock at the door interrupted Paula's response and this time when she opened it, she found Ruth and Louise.

Paula looked around the still-crowded cafeteria and realized that being seated here at a table with three women she knew gave her a sense of already belonging. She should have realized there would be people of all ages from many places attending summer classes at a large university. But somehow she had envisioned it to be like the small local college where she had been a student in the early sixties. She focused her attention back to the present.

"My husband and I own a Coca-Cola plant

20

in Kingston and we've been on the island since early in our marriage. Our five children were born there and two still attend the American School where Ruth and I work."

"What do you teach?" Sharon asked.

"I'm a counselor and Ruth teaches special education classes. Her husband is a doctor. One of the few really good ones the city has, I might add."

"Thank you." Ruth spoke with a soft French accent. "And I have a son who is studying medicine in the States."

"Now what about you, Paula?" Louise turned to her with an expectant smile.

Paula took a sip of iced tea before she began. "I have a son in India, with the Peace Corps, and a daughter who is a flight attendant. I came here from Tuscumbia, as I told you. And I'm . . . divorced." The word came easier this time. In Tuscumbia she had not been forced to actually tell people. In a little town, everyone just knew.

Sharon broke the small silence that followed. "And I live on a farm near Spartanburg, South Carolina, with my parents and six younger brothers and sisters. I'm a speech major, working on a master's in communication and," she took a deep breath and said with an impish smile, "I'm not married but I'm open to the idea."

"Then we'll see what we can do to help you," Ruth told her. "There ought to be plenty of eligible bachelors around here."

"But don't consider anyone who isn't completing his doctorate" Louise added, "or you'll end up putting your degree on hold and helping him through school."

"That's true," Paula agreed. "I had already been accepted into a graduate program when I married. But my husband transferred to another school to complete his engineering degree and I took a teaching job instead. Then I had a baby and I never did get back to school." She stopped, suddenly aware of a small resentment she had not even known she harbored all these years.

"It's happened to most of us," Ruth said. "We sublimate our goals for our husbands and our families. And somewhere along the way we forget who we were or what it was we really wanted out of life."

"Hear, hear," Louise broke in. "These discouraging words may change Sharon's mind about a husband. And that would be a pity because she will never have better waters to fish for a great catch."

"True." Ruth smiled at Sharon. "And there's

really nothing as wonderful as the cry of your firstborn. Or making a home for the man you love."

"Not to mention ironing his shirts, and tending the baby, and cooking supper every evening?" Sharon asked

"You wouldn't have to do any of that if you lived in Jamaica," Louise told her. "We have housekeepers and nannies to care for the children."

"Wow. I think I could become accustomed to your lifestyle very easily," Sharon answered.

"But it would be more difficult to acclimate yourself to our culture," Ruth paused a moment, then went on. "The poverty, the lack of sanitation, the scarcity of food and medicine."

"Not to mention the difficulty of finding an outlet mall or a big department store." Louise shook her head. "And now that I'm surrounded by both I won't have time to shop."

"I hadn't thought about all those things," Sharon said. "I only had visions of wide verandas and a breeze blowing off the ocean and sandy beaches in the moonlight."

"We have all that, too," Louise smiled at her, "and brilliant red and purple bougainvillea spilling over the veranda balustrade and exotic birds calling to each other from the rustling palm trees. Doesn't that sound romantic?"

"And we also have lizards running over the veranda floor and mosquitos buzzing around and hurricane season and . . ." Ruth stopped, taking another direction. "But just listen to me. I'm sounding like a person with no romance in my soul, and nothing could be further from the truth."

"She's right about that," Louise agreed. "Why, she and her hubby still hold hands and make eyes at each other in public like a couple of newlyweds."

"That's the kind of marriage I want," Sharon said.

And so did I, Paula thought. She and Quentin had that for a while. When did it all go wrong? And more importantly, why? But she had asked herself these questions too many times for counting and the answers always eluded her.

Paula turned off the shower and reached for her towel. She preferred a leisurely bath in the evening but the only available tub was already in use and she hadn't wanted to wait. She pulled her terry robe off the stall door, then opened it a crack, hesitating a moment before she stepped out.

"Next." A student she didn't know slithered past her into the stall, already peeling off her long tee shirt.

Paula picked up her toilet bag and made her way to the row of lavatories where other students in different degrees of undress performed a variety of nightly chores. As she waited beside a plump blonde—wearing only panties and a bra—for a chance to brush her teeth, Louise Montgomery stepped out of a toilet cubicle.

"Got caught in the rush hour, did you?" She smiled at Paula as she joined the others waiting for a lavatory. "I guess we forgot to warn you not to wait till bedtime to bathe because it's bedlam around here."

Paula nodded, feeling terribly out of place in this very public bathroom. She would certainly make an effort to find a more private time to use the facilities.

Paula stood in front of the oak chest, absently patting moisturizer on her face. She missed her marble-topped bathroom vanity with its lighted mirror. It was going to be quite a change getting used to sharing the bath across the hall with all the occupants of a dorm wing, waiting her turn for a shower or to brush her teeth. And she probably would never have enough time at a lavatory to put on her makeup. She would have to do that at this mirror above the chest, so another lamp was going to become a necessity.

She saturated the cotton ball again and gave special attention to the fine lines at the corners of her eyes. Laugh lines, they were often referred to by the makeup ads in magazines. But her lines could more correctly be attributed to crying and she was sure there were deeper creases there now than a few months ago. She studied her reflection intently. Large green eyes, set wide apart. High cheek bones that gave her face an almost gaunt appearance since she had lost weight. A full mouth that did not smile of late without a conscious effort.

She picked up her hairbrush, gently coaxed her wheat-colored hair into the casual style she wore, noting the lighter colored streaks she used to pay dearly for and which nature now provided for free. Perhaps she would let her hair grow longer and arrange it in a French twist when she dressed up. *If* she dressed up. So far she had been unable to imagine any sort of social life other than a luncheon date with a female friend. She'd had nothing more in Tuscumbia since Quent had left.

It really was true, what she had read about a couple's friends deserting the ex-wife. Besides, she would have felt so odd at a gathering of wives with their husbands, so noticeable. She didn't want charity. Or pity. No, what she wanted was her husband back and her life to be the way it used to be. She had been defined by her role as Quentin Howard's wife so long that when he took that away she didn't know who she was. For a while she had hoped that she would wake up and realize it had all been a nightmare, but finally she had faced the fact that the nightmare was her new reality.

The shrill ringing of the phone startled Paula so that she almost dropped the brush. She crossed the room quickly and picked up the receiver as the second ring ended.

"Hello?"

"Paula?"

She drew her breath in sharply. "Yes?"

"It's Quent."

"I know." Did he think after thirty years of marriage she would forget the sound of his voice? "Is something wrong?"

"No. No, nothing's wrong. I . . . I just wanted to know if you got settled in okay."

"Yes," she answered quickly.

"Good." After an awkward pause he asked, "Were you able to take everything you'll need in the car?"

"Yes. Everything." This time she broke the too-long silence. "I didn't bring very much. Just a few summer clothes and sheets and towels. I didn't know how sparsely dorm rooms are furnished until I got here, so I had to go out this afternoon and buy some things."

She stopped to get her breath and before she could continue, Quent asked, "Do you need money?"

"Oh no. That's not why I told you—"

"I know it isn't," he cut in impatiently. "But just the same I think you should allow me—"

This time she interrupted, "To pay my way to college? Would that ease your conscience, if I took your severance pay?" Her voice was rising and she seemed unable to control it. "I've already told you I don't want your money. Haven't you ever heard that old adage, 'The gift without the giver is bare'? I think it applies to this situation." She stopped, breathless, tears stinging her eyes.

"Dammit, Paula, I was just trying to help. I know you don't have much cash at the moment. And I wanted you to know I'd be glad to help if—"

Suddenly ashamed of her outburst, she

didn't wait for him to finish. "I know, Quent, I know. And thanks for offering, but I really don't need money right now." That wasn't exactly true but pride would not let her accept anything from her ex-husband.

"Well, it shouldn't be too long till we can settle the problem of the house. You have everything out now?"

"Yes. It's all in storage, except for Amy's things. Next time she comes home she wants to sort through and take some stuff to Chris's place."

"I know. She called me."

"I . . . I think it would be good if you could go there with her. It will be hard for her to see the house for sale, and everything looking so bare."

"I offered, but she said Chris would go with her."

"Oh. Well, I guess that would be best."

"Look, Paula, are you sure you want to sell the furniture, too?"

"Yes. Unless you want it?"

"No, nothing but my big chair from the den. And I'll wait till the house sells to take that."

Paula thought of the house with its antique brick walls and wrought iron fence covered by ivy. Their house. Built with love to raise a family. And now for sale. A pain wrenched her heart and she bit her lip to keep from crying out.

"Paula?"

Did he feel her pain through the miles that separated them? Was he going to ask her to reconsider . . . "Yes?" she asked hopefully.

"Have you, uh, heard from Jeff lately?"

Her voice was flat with disappointment when she answered. "I had a postcard a couple of weeks ago."

"I haven't heard from him since I moved out of the house."

She was silent, waiting. When Quent didn't speak, she made excuses for their son even though she knew how angry he was with his father. "Well, you know how he is about writing. And he must be busy. I wouldn't worry." What she was thinking but couldn't say had to do with time. Given enough time she hoped the anger would dissipate and Jeff would forgive and accept and understand. Actually those were the things she wanted for herself, weren't they? And if she hadn't found them, how could she expect their son, half a world away, to do so?

"I guess I'd better say goodbye now, Paula. You have my phone number, don't you?"

"Yes." So this was all. In a moment he would

hang up and the connection between them would be broken.

"You'll call if you need anything?"

"Yes." *I need something now, I need you. I want to come home, to our house, and have you there to meet me. I want to be your wife and—*

"Goodbye, Paula. Take care."

"Goodbye, Quent." For a long moment she stood holding the phone, listening to the hum of the wire, feeling somehow still attached to the man who had already severed the connection at the other end.

Unable to bear the light, she switched it off and went to stand at the window. From the eighth floor she could see across the commons with its eerie shadows cast by street lamps shining through the trees. And beyond were giant silhouettes of the buildings where her classes would begin tomorrow. What am I doing here, she asked herself again.

Quent's voice a moment ago had taken her back to the past. To something she wanted but could no longer have. The tears she had held back now spilled out of her eyes and flowed down her cheeks. She had thought her tears, like her past, were all behind her. But it had taken only this to prove her wrong, to reveal her weakness.

Why had Quent called? To find out if all

her things were out of the house? He could have driven by and checked for himself. To ask if she had heard from their son? Surely it bothered him that Jeff refused to answer his letters. To learn if she was okay? And if he cared about her welfare, didn't that mean he still loved her? Maybe if she had waited a little longer before . . .

The carillon in the commons chimed the hour and Paula turned in that direction. Brushing the wetness from her cheeks with the sleeve of her satin sleep shirt, she stood a little taller. The past was gone. And here at the university lay the future. Tomorrow she would begin a new day.

Two

Paula stepped off the crowded elevator and found herself in an early morning traffic rush unlike any she had ever experienced. Bodies hurled pell-mell through the lobby, zigzagging expertly to avoid collision, but Paula, with no prior practice, found herself being jostled and saying "Excuse me" to retreating backs that seemed not to have noticed. Moving with the flow that appeared to be headed in the general direction of the front entrance, she saw a wide, open door on her right and impulsively stepped inside.

The room beyond was enormous, with tall windows draped in soft blue damask to match the walls. From the high ceiling hung a heavy crystal chandelier which caught the sunlight, reflecting a prism of colors. Traditional sofas and chairs, upholstered in deeper blue and rose, were placed in intimate groupings with polished mahogany tables between. An open baby grand piano sat at one side of a white marble fireplace with an ornate gilt-framed portrait above it. Paula stepped closer, mesmerized by the life-sized woman who wore a blue gown which left her graceful neck and shoulders bare except for a single strand of creamy pearls. She had hair almost the color of Paula's, arranged in much the same casual style. Her smile was wistful and her wide eyes reflected the same cerulean shade as her dress. Paula read the inscription on the nameplate. "Mrs. Rachel Winthrope—1990." The person for whom Winthrope Hall was named.

"Paula?" She turned to see Sharon in the doorway. "Did you get bumped in here by the crowd or are you playing hooky on the first day of school?"

"I got bumped, sort of. And then I saw this beautiful portrait. I was wondering if the date on it was when she died or maybe when the building was dedicated?"

"Beats me. Are you going to the cafeteria?"

"Yes, that's where I'd started."

"Then we'd better head over that way. I've got an eight o'clock class."

"Me, too." Paula followed Sharon into the lobby and out the front entrance where the

heat and unpleasant odor hit her simultaneously. "What *is* that smell?"

Sharon met her astonished look with amusement. "You may as well become accustomed to
it because it's an early morning fact of life here
at the university. What you smell is the Winthrope Paper Mill."

"You mean it smells this way every morning?"

"You've got it. The university is on the river
downwind from the mill."

"But can't something be done about a company that pollutes the air this way?"

"I understand the mill provides jobs for a
lot of people. It, along with the university,
pretty well supports the town," Sharon shrugged,
"so who would complain?"

"You have a point, but . . ." Paula suddenly
stopped in the middle of the sidewalk, forcing
the student closest behind to veer sharply to
avoid bumping into her. "Did you say Winthrope Paper Mill? As in Winthrope Hall?"

"The very same."

"Well, I guess building a hall for the university is the least someone could do who is
responsible for ruining the air a whole town
breathes."

"I'm sure it helped a lot of people tolerate
the smell better," Sharon smiled, "especially

35

the university directors and faculty. But that's not the Winthropes' only conciliatory gesture toward the town. The office complex at the mill is like an art museum, complete with oriental gardens. It's open to the public after office hours and on weekends."

"Have you seen it?"

Sharon shook her head. "No, I don't have a car, and it's about five miles upriver from campus."

"If you'd like to go, we could drive there this weekend."

"I'd love it."

They had reached the steps to Gaither Hall and conversation stopped as they maneuvered around students hurrying down.

"I feel like a salmon swimming upstream," Paula said as they reached the lobby and the aroma of brewing coffee and frying bacon replaced the peculiar outdoor scent of paper pulp.

Paula walked alone across the commons toward Oldham Hall. The tall oaks and magnolias looked different in the morning sun than when they were draped in darkness. A squirrel, apparently accustomed to the human species who shared his domain, darted in front of her and stopped for a moment poised on hind legs, studying her as though asking for a handout. When it saw that she had nothing to offer, it scampered away.

Oldham Hall was surely one of the most antiquated buildings on campus. Its exterior brick walls were a faded terra cotta color with six massive white marble columns flanking circular stone steps. Its name, etched in stone over the entrance, was followed by the date 1890. For a moment Paula felt a sense of awe at how many students before her had walked these steps in the many years that they had existed.

The carillon behind her chimed the hour and she hurried inside. Her schedule listed Introduction to Learning Disabilities as meeting on the third floor. At the end of the long hall she saw a stairway and quickened her pace toward it, realizing she was going to be late for her first class.

Breathless from running up two flights of stairs, Paula opened the door to Room 301 and was greeted by the icy stare of a short, stocky man with steel-gray hair and oversized black-framed glasses. He stopped talking and waited with poorly concealed impatience as she made her way to the vacant front row chair, directly in front of the lectern which almost dwarfed the man. Dr. Colbert. Paula looked up and met his disapproving gaze.

He cleared his throat. "As I was saying, class begins promptly at eight. One point will be deducted from your grade for every time you are tardy." Paula lowered her eyes and felt the color rise in her face as he continued: "If you have problems getting to class on time, I suggest you set your clock and leave earlier."

Paula stole a glance at the students on either side of her. All were very young.

"You will be seeing a lot of each other this summer. I am assuming, of course, that you are in the proper class." His eyes came to rest on Paula as if to confirm a legitimate reason for her presence before he went on. "As you must surely know, this department has one of the finest summer programs for exceptional children in the country." Dr. Colbert took off his heavy glasses and polished them with his handkerchief. "We earned our reputation by being a team who gives whatever it takes to help these students. We are all team players. I will tolerate no self-aggrandizement, no clock-watching," another glance at Paula, "and no frivolous attitudes." He put his glasses on and opened a black notebook that rested on the lectern and began calling roll. "Averill. Blockly. Collins. Crenshaw. Elkhart. Farmer. Howard."

Paula met the professor's eyes as the other students before her, repeated "Here," and he gave a slight nod. Now she understood why the only vacant chair had been on the front row.

Dr. Colbert was nearing the end of the roll now. "Tucker. Valcourt. Vogel."

The masculine voice that answered sounded familiar and Paula glanced back but was unable to see the person on the back row who had spoken. Vogel? It could be the man she had collided with yesterday in the cafeteria. Dr. Colbert began his lecture and Paula quietly opened her notebook and began writing as rapidly as she could.

With only ten minutes between classes, the room emptied quickly after the professor's precisely timed dismissal. When Paula had gathered her belongings and turned to leave the back rows were vacant except for Ruth, who waited for her by the door.

Paula smiled at her. "I didn't realize we would have classes together, though I knew you were in special education."

"There are many areas within the field. But

I applied for a grant to specialize in learning disabilities," Ruth shrugged. "So here I am."

"I got a grant for the summer program, too," Paula told her. "It was the only way I could have come unless I borrowed tuition money."

Ruth raised her eyebrows. "No alimony?"

Paula shook her head, then seeing Ruth's clouded expression, explained. "My husband offered, but I said no. And he wants to help out until our house sells, but . . ."

"Too much pride? Don't be foolish, honey. Grab what you can get before some sweet young thing takes him for all he's worth."

Paula smiled. "You're talking like an American divorcee."

Ruth looked momentarily disconcerted, then shook her head vehemently. "No, I'm talking like a woman who understands men. I've seen it happen too many times."

The two women were so engrossed in conversation as they walked down to the second floor that neither saw the man standing beside the stairs until he spoke in a low voice. "Would you like me to direct you to Room 214 so you won't be late again?" He looked at Paula and grinned.

"Why, hello." It was the man from the cafeteria. "I suppose I could use a little help. I seem to be losing points instead of making them."

"I found Dr. Colbert's sarcasm really unnecessary," Ruth said. "Whatever happened to Southern gentility?"

"He did seem to come down on you pretty hard," he said, still looking at Paula, ". . . for a first time offender. But rumor has it Colbert runs a tight ship." He stopped at a door numbered 214. "By the way, since we're going to be team mates, I'm Derek Vogel."

"I'm Paula Howard." She had not noticed yesterday how blue his eyes were. But she had been too embarrassed even to look at him then.

"Ruth Valcourt."

Derek looked at Ruth. "I guess we'll be seated on the back row again. I'm sure the same rules apply to all three classes."

"How did you know where to sit last hour?" Paula queried as they entered the room.

"Same as here." Derek nodded toward the chalkboard at the front of the room. "Instructions were on the board but Dr. Colbert erased them before you came in."

"Oh." Paula left her companions and found her seat, thankful she would not have to face what promised to be a rigorous internship all alone. She would have Ruth Valcourt and

Derek Vogel who were at least in her own generation.

Promptly at ten minutes past nine a tall thin brunette entered the room carrying a huge black briefcase. She strode toward the desk, deposited herself and her baggage on top of it and began. "Good morning. Welcome to Diagnosis and Remediation of Learning Disabilities. I'm Faye Browne—that's with a silent 'e' on both—and I'm Dr. Colbert's assistant. Since you're all here it won't be necessary to call roll. So," she smiled and crossed one shapely leg over the other, "let's get started."

Well, Paula mused, for someone who runs a tight ship, Dr. Colbert seems to have one rope with a little play in it.

"Oh, one other thing. There will be a get-acquainted party at my apartment this evening at seven. It is BYOB. And there will be printed directions on the desk of how to find me." She smiled coyly and gave a good imitation of a Scarlett O'Hara voice. "Y'all come, heah?" Then suddenly businesslike, she began a barrage of questions which she called on students by name to answer. Paula, fortunately, was not one of those favored but she noticed that Derek Vogel was called on twice.

* * *

The hour passed quickly and after a ten minute break Paula found herself once more in the presence of the formidable Dr. Colbert. After a cursory glance to ascertain that he had lost no one in the interim, he spent the remainder of the hour outlining the term paper he expected from each of them on the Theories of Learning Disabilities. Then she found herself on the sidewalk in the sweltering noonday sun. Her beige silk blouse clung damply to her breasts and the pleats of her white linen skirt were rumpled from three hours of sitting in wooden desk chairs.

"A glass of iced tea would taste good right now. I'm glad it's time for lunch," Paula sighed. "I'd forgotten how much work school is."

"Yeah," Ruth agreed. "It's like childbirth. They say you tend to remember only the good things, or there would never be a second time. I'm going to pass on lunch and head for the library. I want to check out some of those resource materials before someone else grabs them."

"But won't you need to eat something?" Paula asked with concern.

Ruth patted her shapely hips. "I can live on the fat of the land for a few hours. I'll get a

Coke at the machine in the library annex, not to worry. Bye-bye."

Paula waved and turned toward the commons. The heat made wavy lines appear to be rising from the brick-paved street as she crossed and the shade from the low-hanging oak limbs was a welcome relief.

"Mind if I walk along with you?" Derek Vogel asked as he fell in step beside her.

"Of course not." She hadn't realized how tall he was until now.

"Are you going to the cafeteria?" When Paula nodded, he went on. "Maybe we ought to have lunch together. That way we'd stand a better chance of avoiding another collision." Paula laughed. "By the way, did the stains come out of your blouse?"

"Oh, dear. I put it in water to soak and forgot all about it until just this minute. And I'm soaking your handkerchief, too, though I wasn't sure I would ever see you again to return it."

"And now it looks like you'll be spending every day with me."

"I'm beginning to wonder what I've gotten myself into."

"I'm harmless enough. No ulterior—"

"No, I didn't mean that. I meant the LD program. I haven't gone to school in thirty years and now I've probably jumped in over my head, but—"

"Thirty years? Since grade school?"

"College graduation."

"You're kidding. Unless you were a child prodigy who was graduated at twelve?"

"Thank you." Paula's cheeks felt even warmer than before. "You're very kind."

"No, honest." As they reached Gaither Hall he looked at her with keen interest. "So what brings you back to college now?"

"I . . . I plan to get a job. I haven't worked in a long time and I needed to specialize in something. I thought I'd like to work with exceptional children."

"Your kids left home? They call it the empty nest syndrome, don't they?"

"Yes. And yes, they do." On an impulse she added, "And my husband left home, too. So the nest is truly empty, isn't it?" She hurried up the steps, not waiting for his reply.

Derek caught up with her at the top step. "Sorry. I didn't mean to give you the third degree. It's none of my business why you came back to school. You should have told me so." He dodged a broad-chested jock coming out of the lobby and held the door for Paula.

"It's okay." At his look of consternation she continued, "Really. I just got divorced and I'm

45

not used to talking about it yet. I lived in a small town so there was no need before I came here."

"Well, just for the record, I'm divorced, too. And I don't like to talk about it either, so we'll call a moratorium on the subject, okay?" Paula nodded as they reached the line. "And during lunch we can discuss something safe like how to make a passing grade in the internship program. That is, if you still want to share a table with me?"

"Of course I do." Paula smiled at him reassuringly before turning her attention to the salads behind the glass partition. He seemed like a nice man and she would have to learn to deal with her marital status without getting upset every time she talked about it.

Paula was blow drying her hair when she became aware of someone knocking at the door. Opening it quickly, she faced a startled Ruth Valcourt with a hand upraised to knock again.

"Hi. I hope you haven't been waiting long."

"I was beginning to think you weren't here," Ruth lowered her hand and stepped inside, "and I started to panic. I wanted to ask if I could go with you to Miss Browne's party this evening. To be a no-show would probably be grade point suicide."

"I'd planned to ask you but I've just gotten back from the library and decided I'd shower and shampoo my hair while the bathroom wasn't crowded."

"Good idea. I'm on my way there soon as I confirm I have transportation and what time you're leaving."

"About six-thirty. The map looked fairly complicated, so I wanted to allow time to get lost."

"Isn't it a custom to be late to cocktail parties?"

"I'm not sure. And after this morning I'm taking no chances on that."

Ruth laughed, then asked, "What are you taking to drink?"

"A bottle of white wine. And I'll have to stop someplace for that. You'll need to stop, too, won't you?"

"No, Louise and I have a case of Jamaican rum in our room." She smiled. "We decided we could spare a bottle for a good cause." Ruth had reached the hallway when she stopped and turned back. "Are you wearing something formal?"

"A silk jumpsuit is the best I can do."

"I have a long white skirt, linen so it isn't

especially dressy. I guess I'll wear that with some flat sandals and a low-cut blouse." She struck a cover girl pose.

"You wouldn't want to steal the show from your hostess, would you?"

"No way. That wouldn't be a smart thing to do. But," Ruth's eyes sparkled, "there's no harm in looking nice for Dr. Colbert, is there?"

"Do you think he'd notice?"

"We shall see, won't we? I'm betting Dr. Hatchetface will turn out to be the life of the party."

Both women laughed at the thought as Ruth waved and headed down the hall. Paula stood for a moment, looking after her. It was comforting to know she would not have to face Faye Browne's cocktail party alone.

After a stop at the shopping center where they had gone yesterday and a couple of wrong turns, Paula and Ruth entered the Oakwood Apartments complex exactly at seven.

"Nice," Ruth observed as they got out of the car. "Oh, there goes Derek Vogel. If we're committing a faux pas, so is he."

"I recognize another student there on the

steps in front of him," Paula said, "so I suppose we'll just follow the leader."

When they reached the door it was still open, with Faye Browne busy greeting Derek, so they hesitated a moment. But when she took his package, slipped her arm through his, and escorted him toward the room divider that served as a bar, the two women exchanged questioning looks, shrugged, and stepped inside.

"Here, let me take those for you." A young student in a red miniskirt took their bottles. "I'm Janet. Just wander around and get to know everyone. And there's food on the table over near the bar." She was gone before they could tell her who they were.

Paula looked around the already-crowded room. The lighting was dim, there was jazz music and laughter and everyone seemed to be engaged in conversation. "I suppose we had better separate and circulate," Paula said.

"By all means." Ruth gave her a bright smile. "Good luck." She turned and joined a group of three young people. Paula stood for a moment, watching her. The white linen skirt topped with a magenta blouse, looked fantastic on her. Long gold hoop earrings and wide bracelets made a striking contrast with her dark skin tones in the shadowed room.

Paula was still trying to decide where she might fit in when Faye Browne crossed the room toward her. She had accentuated her thinness by wearing a black bodysuit and a white sequined tee over it. She was taller than Paula to begin with and now, in her stiletto-heeled pumps, she seemed much more so.

"Well, hello. You're looking a little lost. I'm sorry we've neglected you."

"I'm fine. I just got here a minute ago," Paula returned the woman's smile, "and I was trying to decide which way to begin."

"Why not begin right here." She tapped a long red fingernail on a young man's shoulder and continued, "Mark Bradley, say hello to Paula Howard. She's from Tuscumbia." To Paula she added, "Mark's uncle owns a recording studio in Muscle Shoals. I'm sure you two can find something to talk about."

"How interesting," Paula said with as much sincerity as she could manage. "My husband plays music. And he's done some recording there." She had forgotten to say former husband.

"Rock?" Mark asked hopefully.

"I'm afraid not. He plays country-western."

"Oh."

Paula watched Faye Browne's lithe figure retreating toward the bar, stopping now and then for a quick word along the way. Her eyes swept the room in quiet desperation, then she turned back to her commandeered conversation partner and smiled. "Tell me which rock musicians you listen to. My son has introduced me to a few of their tapes." It was going to be a long evening and she asked herself again, *What am I doing here?*

Paula finally worked her way to the bar.

"May I serve you something, Miss Howard—or is it Mrs.?"

It was Dr. Colbert who stood behind the bar addressing her, and Paula became even more flustered about answering the question.

"It's Mrs.," she said, then added quickly, "but I'm divorced."

"Then it's Miz, I suppose." He looked at her intently. "I don't like that term very much. Do you?"

"Well, I . . . I've never used it," she answered.

"Then don't," he said flatly. "It's a stupid word. It sounds short for miserable." He gave her a sly wink. "And most of you ex-married women are pretty happy, aren't you?"

"I can't speak for most women," Paula answered softly.

"But you can speak for yourself?" He leered at her openly now and Paula realized he must have had too much to drink.

"May I have a glass of wine, please?" She indicated the bottle of California Chardonnay she had brought.

"Certainly, Miss—Mrs. Howard." He opened the bottle and poured a glass so full a little sloshed onto the counter top. "Sorry," he said as he handed it to her. "It's these dim lights— can't see my hand in front of me."

"Thank you." Paula took the glass and turned toward the buffet table, studying the assortment of food.

"I'd recommend the cucumber sandwiches," a familiar voice spoke close to her ear and she turned to find Derek beside her.

"Hello." She smiled with genuine pleasure at his presence. "Thank you, I'll try one."

"Hello, yourself. You look great in that out-fit. I've been admiring you ever since we got here."

Paula felt her face flush with pleasure. "Thank you." She had done her best with her limited wardrobe and she had obviously succeeded. She wore a wide beige braided belt with her coffee-colored silk jumpsuit, and long beige and gold pendant earrings swung with her loose shining hair.

When Derek continued to look at her, making no effort to engage her in conversation, Paula spoke again. "It's a nice party, isn't it?"

He met her eyes before he answered, "It is now."

Paula quickly looked away before he could see how his words affected her. She wasn't used to such intensity in a man's gaze. Moving a little farther from the table, she whispered, "I think the bartender has been sampling a few too many of his offerings."

"Oh? Did he make a pass at you?"

"No, but we had a very important discussion on the proper title for a formerly married woman."

"And what did you conclude?"

"We didn't. That was when things got silly and he called me Miss-hyphen-Mrs. Howard and spilled some of the wine he was pouring."

"He's drunk all right," Derek said in an undertone. "We'll have, the devil to pay in class tomorrow. So don't be late even if you have to sleep on the steps of Oldham Hall."

"I wouldn't dare."

"What? Be late or sleep on the steps?"

"Either one." She bit into the dainty cucumber sandwich. "This is good."

"I never recommend anything that isn't to a friend," he told her solemnly.

"Derek." Faye Browne touched the shoulder nearly even with her own, her hand lingering intimately for a moment. "Could I please ask a big ole favor?" Derek reluctantly pulled his gaze from Paula and focused on his hostess, waiting for her request. "Benny is ready to drop with exhaustion from tending bar. Could you please, pretty please, spell him for a while?"

"Certainly." As he took a step to follow her, Derek glanced back at Paula and grinned. "Benny?" he mouthed silently.

Paula suppressed a giggle with effort. So the ferocious Dr. Benjamin Colbert was Benny to his glamorous assistant. Maybe Ruth Valcourt's assessment had been on target after all.

"Well, that wasn't so bad," Ruth's yawn turned into a groan. "But oh how I'll hate to get up in the morning."

"It *is* almost midnight." Paula signaled for a left turn onto University Boulevard, noting that the car close behind her was the only one in sight.

"I'm glad Derek Vogel insisted on escorting us back to the dorm." When Paula didn't answer, she went on. "He's a nice guy. And really good looking, don't you think?"

"I guess so." Paula concentrated on the street, picking up speed as she leveled out of her turn.

"You guess so?" Ruth's voice was slightly incredulous. "Come on now. No one could miss those gorgeous Paul Newman eyes, and that terrific tan. He's just come back from the South Pacific, you know."

"I wasn't aware of that. What was he doing *there*?"

"He was stationed there, as a Naval Aviation officer, and he's just retired."

"And starting a new career like me, I suppose," Paula mused.

"Yes, you two have a lot in common." After a brief thoughtful silence, she went on, "I wonder if he's married?"

"No, he's divorced," Paula said quickly.

"I see. Another point in common. For someone who hasn't noticed how handsome the guy is you sure are well informed on the minor details," Ruth teased.

"Divorce is not such a minor detail," Paula answered quietly. Then as she slowed for a turn into the parking lot behind Winthrope Hall, she returned Derek's parting blink of lights and spoke again. "And as long as you were learning all about his career I'm surprised you didn't ask if he had a wife and kids and a dog."

Ruth laughed. "Look, I don't operate that fast. Besides, we'll be sitting together all summer so there's no hurry. I'll find out about the kids and dog tomorrow."

"Please, Ruth, don't ask him."

"Well, if you really don't want to know . . . ?"

"He'll tell us what he wants us to know. We can be friends without learning his life history."

"Of course we can," Ruth agreed as they got out of the car and started for the front of the building.

"Ouch, my feet hurt," Paula said. "I'm going to go barefoot."

"Wait," Ruth stopped, "I just remembered something. Let's try the side door by the stairs in our wing."

"But they lock every door except the front at six."

"Sure they do, but some of the girls prop the side doors back open later so they can get in without going to the front."

"And I felt so safe, all locked in every night."

"It doesn't pay to feel too secure anywhere."

No, not even in a thirty-year-old marriage, Paula thought sadly as she limped along behind Ruth toward the side door which was held open by a crushed empty cola can. She had trusted other people to abide by the rules and once again she had been fooled. I must be very gullible, she concluded, or very stupid. Maybe the terms are synonymous.

Three

Derek Vogel was right in his prediction about Dr. Colbert's mood following the party. He was morose and caustic in his first class and even Faye Browne in second period had not shown the intellectual tenacity she had exhibited the day before. By the last class of the morning Paula was rather exhausted herself but she was hoping Dr. Colbert would be feeling better as the day advanced and his hangover lessened.

When the bell rang, an immediate hush fell over the room. Dr. Colbert, already standing behind the lectern, cleared his throat and began. "Today we will continue our discussion of your term papers. We will begin with format. The paper is to be written according to the APA guidelines." He paused. "I assume you are familiar with the APA style?"

Paula was vaguely aware of the fact that term papers followed certain rules, but it had been a long time since she had needed this kind of information.

"Very well," Dr. Colbert continued. "Now, *Miss* Howard, please refresh our memories on where your references are to be placed."

Paula took a deep breath, trying not to panic. She didn't have the faintest idea what the answer was and she knew it would be futile to hedge. "I don't know."

"You don't know." He looked at her intently. "There are only two probable answers, Miss Howard. At the bottom of each page or at the conclusion of the paper." His voice sounded playful but his stoic expression did not change. "So let me repeat the question. Where do you place your references?"

Paula knew she had a fifty-fifty chance of getting the right answer but she also knew if she guessed wrong, she would face more of Dr. Colbert's biting sarcasm. "I'm sorry," she said in a barely audible voice, "I don't know."

Dr. Colbert took off his glasses and slowly polished them while the students waited in expectant silence. *"Miss* Howard," Paula met his eyes, "this is your first experience at our university, is it not?"

She took a shallow breath, tried to steady her voice. "Yes, sir."

"Then perhaps I should make something clear to you. This is *not* a happy hunting ground."

Paula dropped her eyes, cheeks aflame. Beside her, Janet giggled nervously. "Now," Dr. Colbert put on his glasses again, "we will leave our first question unanswered so that Miss Howard may discover the APA rules for herself after class."

Dr. Colbert's voice droned on. Paula mechanically took notes while her mind protested what had just happened. Why had he singled her out for humiliation? Was it because she was an older student? Derek had been right. "Benny" had taken his hangover out on someone today, and unfortunately that someone had been her.

Class finally ended and Derek and Ruth were waiting for her at the door. Shooting smoldering looks in Dr. Colbert's direction, which he—absorbed in putting his notes in his briefcase—did not see, they closed ranks around her and left the classroom.

"I have never known anyone to be so insulting as that horrid man," Ruth spluttered. "You had done nothing to deserve that remark."

"Except sit there looking beautiful and vulnerable," Derek added.

"I think he resents me because I'm an older student," said Paula.

"Then he should pick on all of us," Derek told her. "We all fit that category."

"But I'm a minority race," Ruth reminded him, "and you are male, and ex-military at that, so he wouldn't dare bother us."

"I guess you're right," Derek said slowly. "What you said makes sense in a perverted sort of way."

"And I'm divorced," Paula said, "so I have two strikes against me. But I don't understand why he thinks I'm looking for a husband."

"Neither do I," Ruth answered. "But there was no doubt that he does."

"Anyone going to the cafeteria?" Derek asked as they reached the outside of the building.

"Sure," Ruth said. "The troops need reinforcements to face a long afternoon in the library. And just think, next week when tutoring begins we'll have to spend all of our evenings in the library." She touched the palm of her hand to her forehead and voiced Paula's familiar refrain. "What am I doing here?"

"Hunting a husband?" Paula asked softly.

Ruth laughed. "Not on your life, honey, but I certainly do miss the one I have. I'm not so sure leaving him for a whole summer was a good idea. This is the first time we have spent apart since we married."

If I had a husband, I would not have left him, Paula thought sadly. I never really wanted a career. Maybe Dr. Colbert senses that. But he's dead wrong about my motives if he thinks I'm trying to replace the husband I've lost. Nothing could be further from my mind.

"Paula, stop daydreaming and come back to the real world, will you?" Ruth put a hand on her arm, interrupting her reverie. "I've asked you the same question twice already."

"Sorry," Paula said, "I guess three hours of classes have exhausted my short attention span." Her answer was only half in jest. It was hard to listen attentively and take notes, but she would learn to do what she had to do. It would get easier.

The time passed quickly and it was late afternoon when Paula emerged from the library. A quiet had descended on the commons at this hour and she slowed her steps, savoring the sweet fragrance of the jacaranda trees whose lavender blossoms littered the sidewalk.

Hearing someone behind her, she turned and saw Derek Vogel striding in her direction.

"*Miss* Howard," he called in imitation of Dr. Colbert's voice "Have you learned all you need to know about APA style today?"

Paula laughed. "Probably not, sir. But I know more than I did this morning."

Derek fell in step beside her. "It is boring stuff, isn't it? I almost dozed off a few times while I was copying rules and regs. Reminded me of military paperwork. I never liked that either."

"I would have expected an officer to have a secretary who attended to that."

"Who told you I was an officer?" Derek looked at her with a puzzled expression.

Paula hesitated, embarrassed to let him know he had been discussed, then told the truth. "Ruth said you were a retired Naval officer, just back from the South Pacific."

"Well, so I am." He gave a mock salute. "Rear Admiral Derek Vogel of US Naval Aviation at your service, ma'am."

"I'm impressed," Paula responded sincerely. "How long did you serve?"

"Twenty-five years. What about you?"

"Oh, I wasn't in . . ." Paula began, then realized the implication of his question. She answered quietly, "Almost thirty years."

"It seems a shame to end a marriage after that long, doesn't it?"

"I guess time doesn't count."

"I guess it doesn't," Derek said quietly. "Shall we compare scars?"

He motioned to a nearby bench shaded by a tall live oak and they made their way toward it. When they were seated Derek took her books and placed them with his in the space between them. After a little time lapsed he said, "I'll go first." He was silent so long that Paula thought she had misunderstood him, then he spoke again. "I joined the Navy when I was a nineteen-year-old kid just graduated from junior college. Finished my degree piecemeal through the years and worked my way up the ladder with a little effort and a few lucky breaks and ended up nearer the top than I ever expected to."

"I'm sure it was more hard work than luck," Paula told him. So he would be about forty-five, she calculated quickly. Seven years younger than she.

"I was married before I was old enough to vote, and it lasted twenty years." Paula did another rapid calculation. He would have been divorced five years. "And I have a son who is twenty-three. Todd is carrying on the family tradition as a Navy pilot now." Something in his tone caught Paula's attention but he did not elaborate. "Your turn now."

"Okay." Paula took a deep breath and began. "My husband Quent—Quentin—had spent thirty years as an engineer, so he decided to retire from his job last winter on his fifty-fifth birthday. And . . ." she paused, forced herself to go on, "he also decided he didn't want to be married anymore. There was no else involved. Maybe I could understand it better if there had been." She clasped her hands tightly together. "He said he just needed time to figure out who he was and what he really wanted from life."

"Ah, the mid-life crisis," said Derek.

"It created a crisis for the whole family. We have a son who is twenty-one—Jeff—who is a Peace Corps volunteer in India. Can you imagine how it must feel to be on the other side of the world when you suddenly find out your parents are divorcing?"

"Is he your only child?"

"No, we have a daughter who is twenty-six. Amy is a flight attendant engaged to a pilot. They plan to be married this summer. She's devastated at having her parents divorce before the wedding."

Derek looked at her intently. "So much for your children. Now what about you?"

"Well, I . . ." Paula faltered, at a loss for

words to express her own feelings, "I have to make a new life. And coming here is the first step."

"Do you have plans for after the summer?"

"Not definitely. I have a tentative job offer in our local elementary school if the extra position gets approved." Paula shrugged hopelessly. "If not . . ."

"Where would you like to live, Paula?"

"I don't really care."

"It doesn't actually matter since you can't go home again?"

Paula nodded, too stricken to speak. Derek covered her clenched hands with his own and she felt immeasurably comforted by the touch of his warm, firm flesh.

They were silent for a time, then Derek shook his head. "How did we get started on this? And after we'd called a moratorium on the subject."

"You said we should—"

"Compare scars? I don't know why I said that—I never discuss personal issues with anyone. But I'm glad we did."

"Me, too," Paula agreed. She suddenly became aware that Derek still held her hands and gently withdrew them.

Derek grinned at Paula. "Say, why don't we

o out for dinner and drown our troubles in a bottle of wine?"

Paula shook her head reluctantly. "I really shouldn't. I have so much studying to—"

"I've heard of a great place downtown for Chinese. What do you say?"

"You tempt me. I love Chinese food." She reached for her books and stood up. "But I really do have to study."

Derek took the remaining books and also stood. "I promise to have you back at Winthrope Hall by eight."

She smiled at him. "Deal."

After they took different directions toward their respective dorms, Paula thought about their conversation. She had bared her soul to Derek Vogel and she hoped she wouldn't be sorry. It had felt good to talk about her life. She supposed that was why people went to counselors when things like this happened. She'd thought of doing that but there was no one to talk with in Tuscumbia except her doctor, who besides being too busy to listen, was Quent's cousin. And their minister, but she'd stopped going to church after Quent left home. It had been too embarrassing to face the church members alone, knowing they knew. She was pretty sure the minister would have told her to pray about it, which she had, but God seemed to have deserted her, too. There was an old saying by Ben Franklin that her mother used to quote. "God helps those who help themselves." She was trying to do her part and she hoped God would meet her halfway.

As for Derek, she *was* surprised that he had talked about himself. She supposed their similar situations and age proximity had been a factor for he had admitted he was not a man who told his troubles to anyone. He'd suggested comparing scars but she didn't feel that she had really seen his. He had kept more hidden than he had shown. Still, it was a beginning.

Paula stood at the brightly lit bathroom mirror applying eye shadow.

"You're looking mighty pretty for a night with homework," Ruth observed as she stepped from a shower stall, wrapped in a large terry towel.

"Ummm." Paula studied her eyes and smoothed the subtle color toward the outer corners of her lids.

"Come on, girl. 'Fess up," Ruth chided her.

"She's got a date," Sharon volunteered

from a nearby lavatory where she was brushing her teeth.

"Do tell." Ruth surveyed her with a sly smile as other students nearby looked interested. "And would I happen to know the lucky man? Like maybe does he have Paul Newman eyes and a golden tan and—"

"Right you are," Sharon interrupted her

"Where are you going?" Louise asked as she stepped from another shower stall.

"Some Chinese restaurant downtown," Paula told them as she stroked mascara on her eyelashes.

"That would be the Inn of the Paper Moon," Sharon said. "I hear it's a wonderful place."

"Lucky girl," said Louise.

"Yeah, in more ways than one," Ruth added thoughtfully.

Paula dressed carefully in a paisley skirt and peach silk blouse, added a matching leather belt with a gold buckle and gold hoop earrings. She sprayed Obsession on her throat and wrists and studied her image in the mirror above the chest of drawers. She had taken as much care with her appearance as if she really was going out on a date instead of just having dinner with a classmate.

She wasn't interested in Derek Vogel in a romantic sense any more than he was interested in her, no matter what Ruth Valcourt tried to make out of it. So why did she feel this faint surge of excitement? And why did she keep remembering how nice it felt having Derek hold her hands in his?

Derek Vogel was an attractive man but he had been divorced for five years. If he were looking for another woman he could have found dozens by now. She supposed he had made the most of his bachelor status, and who could blame him? But wait a minute. Why was she jumping to the conclusion that he was blameless for his divorce? Maybe he had walked out on a loving wife and a good marriage just like Quent had.

Another thought struck her like a blow. Maybe the women Quent met would come to the same conclusion about him that she had about Derek. He was, after all, a very attractive man also. And though he said there was no one else and she had no reason to doubt him, how long could things remain that way? Especially with the divorce final and the house being sold and her away at the university.

Oh, Quent, why? she asked silently. *Why us? Why now, after all those good years?* But had they been as good for him as they had been for her? In retrospect she supposed not, or else he would not be searching for something now.

It would help if she knew what he wanted. If she had been able to figure that out they might still be together.

Stop it, Paula, she told herself. *It is over. Done. And all your wishing won't bring it back. So get on with your life. Go down to the lobby and meet the nice man who is probably waiting now to take you to dinner.*

Derek *was* waiting in the lobby when she stepped off the elevator. It was obvious he had also dressed with care for the occasion. He had exchanged jeans for tan slacks and a navy poplin jacket over a striped shirt and navy tie.

"Hey, don't you look gorgeous," he said in a low voice as he took Paula's arm and guided her through the crowd of milling students and down the steps toward his car.

Paula smiled at him. "I could say the same."

"Thanks, but I was buying dinner anyway."

"A compliment wasted," said Paula, going along with his lighthearted banter.

Derek pulled into the traffic and headed downtown. He drove his late-model Firebird with the ease of a man who felt confident of his skill and Paula was sure he did everything well, even making love. Now why did that thought pop into her head, she wondered.

"It feels good to get away from Gaither Hall for a meal."

Derek's words startled Paula from her reverie and she blushed as though he had read her thoughts. "Like we're playing hooky from school," she answered, "but I really don't mind the cafeteria food. Anything I don't have to cook tastes fine to me."

"Same here. After Navy chow, eating at Gaither Hall is right up there with four-star dining."

The Inn of the Paper Moon was dark except for colorful Chinese lanterns that hung from the ceiling. Derek took Paula's hand again as they followed the slim hostess in a black silk cheongsam to a table in one corner of the crowded room. Soon an attractive waitress came to take their order and Paula couldn't help but notice how she smiled at Derek.

Over their egg rolls, Derek returned to the topic of their earlier conversation. "So when have you seen your son?"

"Not for almost a year. But he's due home at the end of summer."

"For a visit or to stay?"

"I'm not sure. His tour of duty is up. But I think he might sign up for another two years."

"Was this his first stint?"

Paula shook her head. "He joined when he was eighteen."

The waitress brought steaming bowls of duck soup with wonton and when she left, Derek said, "My son will be taking leave sometime this summer and I've invited him to come to the university. If he does, I would like you to meet him."

"I'd like that, too," Paula assured him. "My daughter may also be coming to the campus soon. We have a lot of plans to make for the wedding and . . . I really don't want to go back to Tuscumbia just now."

"There are ghosts yet to be exorcised?" Derek looked at her intently, waiting for her reply.

She did not meet his eyes as she answered. "Maybe. I'm not sure."

"And you don't want to risk the fragile shell you've grown." Derek made it seem more like a statement than a question so she left it at that.

Derek ordered green pepper steak and he ate with obvious pleasure. "I haven't had anything like this since I was in the Orient."

"Have you enjoyed your world travels?"

Derek looked thoughtful. "Yes. I wouldn't have missed the experience for any stateside job I can think of."

"Why did you decide to become a teacher

now? Won't that seem very dull by comparison?"

"That's two questions." Derek smiled. "I think seeing so much of the world and the conditions under which the majority of people live has left me with a desire to do something about it in some small way." Paula nodded. "And no, I won't find it boring. People are the most fascinating creatures on earth. Especially young people, who haven't yet learned to cover up their true feelings and responses."

"I never thought of it quite that way," Paula mused.

"I've done a lot of thinking about what I want to do when summer is over. I don't want to sound sanctimonious and I'm not sure of the place yet but I am certain it will be some place where what I do will really count for something." He stopped, self-consciously, as the waitress once again approached their table, this time bearing a small tray with two fortune cookies. "You choose first."

She took the nearest cookie, opened it, silently read the message inside and smiled sadly.

"Well?" Derek asked expectantly.

"It says 'You will find true love and happiness.' I think it must have been meant for someone else."

"Not necessarily," Derek answered softly, then opened his own fortune and read it aloud. "You will soon take a long journey." He grinned. "Seems a little late on this prediction, too."

In the car driving back, Derek glanced at his watch. "We still have half an hour to spare. Do you want to stop by the river and watch the sun set?"

"Yes, I'd like that," Paula answered.

The tranquil river meandered along between huge live oaks draped in Spanish moss that cast grotesque shadows in the dusk. They sat in silence for a time, admiring the changing colors of the clouds reflected on the still, dark water beneath.

Finally Derek asked quietly, "What are you thinking?"

"How beautiful it is."

"I was thinking how beautiful you are. And how much I like being with you," Derek said softly. He gently cupped her chin and looked into her eyes, his nearness and his touch making her tremble. Slowly he bent to brush her lips with his and his arms went around her and the kiss became more compelling. For a moment Paula responded then she pulled away.

"Derek, please, no."

"Why not, Paula?" His words were husky against her ear, his warm breath sending another shiver coursing through her body.

"I'm sorry," she said. "I'm just not ready for this."

"I didn't mean to rush you. It's just that you're so damned desirable I got carried away."

"Me?"

"Don't you know?"

Paula shook her head slowly, whispered, "I don't feel desirable."

"You'd probably be the last person to judge that rightly, so just trust me on this. And if you'll allow me, I'll show you what effect you have on me."

Paula was silent a moment, weighing Derek's words, then she answered, "I need a friend—not a lover."

"All right, Paula." Derek sighed. "So friend it is."

Back in the dorm, Paula had difficulty concentrating on her notes from class. Derek's words kept inserting themselves between the lines. Was he just being kind because he knew the pain of being rejected himself? His kiss had seemed more than charitable. Was she being gullible? Easy prey for an experienced worldly man on the make? Derek didn't seem like a tomcat but what did she, sheltered housewife from a small town, know about that?

And what must Derek be thinking of her right now? That she had behaved like a simpering Victorian maiden? Well, he would just have to think whatever he would because she wasn't going to jump from one man's bed to another, no matter how attractive he might be. Still she had to admit Derek Vogel was the most attractive man she had met in a long time. Ruth was right about those Paul Newman eyes. She could just imagine them gazing off toward a distant horizon from the cockpit of a plane. Or gazing down at a woman he was making love to. A woman he found very desirable. Paula shivered, remembering Derek's words.

But if she were a desirable woman why would her husband of thirty years walk out on her? And not for another woman but for nothing at all? The clock in the commons struck twelve and Paula closed her notebook and turned out the light. She would have to keep her mind on studying or Dr. Colbert really would have grounds for his assumption that she was husband hunting.

As Paula lay in that semiconscious state between waking and sleep, the shrill ring of her phone broke the stillness. Groping for it in the dark, she was instantly awake.

"Hello?"

"Mom?"

"Amy, what's wrong?"

"Nothing, Mom. Why do you ask?"

"Because it's after midnight, and I thought—"

"Oh no, I'm in Denver and I forgot about the time there. I'm sorry I—"

"It's okay, honey. I'm glad you called, but I just thought you—"

"I know. I called earlier from St. Louis and you didn't answer."

"I went out to dinner."

"Oh." Her daughter's voice sounded small and forlorn.

"With a classmate. We had Chinese."

"Oh." This time the voice was unmistakably brighter. "How is my mom, the student?"

"Okay, so far. It isn't going to be easy, but then I didn't expect it to be."

"You'll do fine."

Wasn't this conversation reversed? Shouldn't a mother be offering these encouraging words to a daughter? "Thanks for the vote of confidence. I need it."

"What I called about is I'm off weekend after next and I wondered if I could come down and we could talk about the wedding. If you won't be too busy?"

"Of course not. That was my answer to the second question. And you can come down any time you want. I have an extra bed in my room here and you can eat with me in the cafeteria. And there's a huge pool, and tennis, and—"

"I'll just be there a couple of days, Mom. But don't worry, I'll entertain myself while you're studying. And maybe we could shop for your dress while I'm there."

"That sounds like a good idea."

"You're sure I won't be in the way?"

"Amy, of course you won't," Paula assured her. "I'll have plenty of time to help you plan the wedding." She would manage, no matter what else she had to leave undone.

"I've gotta go, Mom. Time for boarding. Could you meet me if I fly in there about nine on Friday evening?"

"Sure, honey. I'll be waiting. And it's so nice to hear your voice. I've missed you."

"Me, too, Mom. Love you."

"And I love you."

The line went dead and Paula fumbled to replace the receiver. Why hadn't she told Amy the truth about having dinner with Derek? Was it the sound of Amy's voice—somewhere between disappointment and resentment? Or was it her own guilt because a man who was not Amy's father had kissed her in a dark car and she had enjoyed it? Going to college and dating when she was a middle-aged mother was going to be more difficult than she had imagined.

Sleep did not come easy for Paula a second time.

Four

The highway paralleled each gentle curve of the river as it led northeast away from town and Paula's Grand Am kept a steady pace in the procession of cars that crept along the black asphalt. It was only midmorning but already the road's tar surface was glistening from the heat.

"I thought Saturday would never come." Sharon sighed. "What a long week this has been."

"Not for me." Paula shook her head. "I can't believe I've been in school five days already."

"How do you feel about it now that you're a real student?"

"Well," Paula thought for a moment, "it's not at all what I expected. The classes are hard, and the program is more demanding than I could have imagined. But getting used to campus has been easier than I thought it would be." She glanced at Sharon and smiled. "Because you and Ruth and Louise have helped me so much." She thought of Derek Vogel who had also befriended her but resisted adding his name aloud. Looking back at the road, she added, "I see a sign ahead. Do you suppose that's where we turn?"

"Yes, this is it." Sharon read the sign aloud as they approached it. "Winthrope Paper Mill, Inc. Visitors welcome."

Paula slowed, turned into the wide drive leading to a large parking area. Ahead they could see the low redwood buildings that blended so unobtrusively with the lush landscape as to be almost invisible.

"I'm impressed already," said Paula as they walked toward the entrance flanked by natural stones interspersed with a panoply of brilliant blooms.

Inside, a smiling young woman greeted them. "Welcome to Winthrope Paper Mill. We're just about to begin our next tour, if you would care to join us." She indicated the half dozen or so people moving about the wide hallway. Raising her voice she continued, "We will start with our office complex, which is to your left and through the door." She turned and walked in that direction. "Okay, everyone please follow me now."

Paula and Sharon looked at each other, nodded and joined the group. The office complex was a spacious area with desks and other office accessories arranged at widely spaced intervals. On the inside wall that ran the length of the room hung paintings that would have been at home in any art gallery. The desks faced the opposite wall which was almost entirely of floor to ceiling glass panels that showed an enclosed courtyard beyond.

"Wow," Sharon whispered, "can you imagine working in a place like this all day?"

"I think we chose the wrong profession," Paula whispered back. "This makes me wish I were a business major."

The color scheme encompassed shades from bone-white to taupe, accented by highly polished wood furniture. Deep plush carpeting and elegantly upholstered chairs gave an unmistakable message of understated opulence.

"This is our main office area," the guide told them. "Here you see the first display of paintings collected by the Winthrope family over the years. And beyond this area," she took a step toward the nearest window, "is part of our outer courtyard which contains hundreds of species of rare plants." A man was kneeling in the soil outside the window and he glanced up as the guide spoke, caught her eye and threw up a dirt-streaked hand in acknowledgement of her friendly wave. "You may visit the garden later at the end of our tour, or return to any part of the building that interests you, so we'll move along rather quickly now."

Next the guide led them through executive offices with one open side that shared a common middle wall. Folding doors could be closed for privacy and here desks faced a glass wall and inner courtyard. The desk tops were decorated with family pictures and other mementos that reflected their occupants' personal lives.

"That looks like a very expensive paperweight." Sharon pointed to a gem-encrusted object on a nearby desk. "Wouldn't you think it might be risky to leave it lying around with so many people walking through?"

Paula studied the paperweight. "It does look valuable. And yes, I think it could be easily taken by someone."

They moved across the entrance into the opposite wing to a series of conference areas, from cozily intimate to accommodations for a group as large as a football team, all adorned with objects d'art.

The guide paused, then announced, "And this is our Board Room." She opened double doors to reveal a magnificent polished mahogany table surrounded by plush armchairs in a deep shade of gold. At the head of the table were three portraits, the center one a life-sized likeness of a man in a riding habit whose gold jacket and cap matched the chairs' fabric so completely there could be no doubt the effect had been intentional. Behind the man, a black stallion stood, as aristocratic in bearing as the man himself.

"This," said the guide in reference to the portrait that dominated the room and already held the crowd's attention, "is Gregory Winthrope IV, Chairman of the Board of Winthrope Paper Mill." She made it sound like an introduction and Paula half expected the man to step down and say hello. "And to his right is Gregory Winthrope III, Chairman Emeritus, and on the other side is Mrs. Gregory Winthrope III."

"I wonder how Rachel Winthrope fits into the picture?" Paula whispered to Sharon.

Sharon smiled. "Nice pun."

They filed around for a look into the Winthropes' private offices, then returned to the central hallway, and followed the guide down a wide staircase to the lower level where sculptures and displays of various collectors' items such as pottery and other ancient artifacts were housed.

"As you have probably noticed, the Winthropes' interest in preserving Indian culture is evident in their entire collection. But what you may not know is that the Winthropes trace their own ancestry to the Cherokee tribe that formerly inhabited this region." A sound of surprise escaped the crowd as the guide spoke again. "This concludes our official tour. There are rest rooms to your right and an employee kitchen and dining area with vending machines to your left if you would care for a snack. Both courtyards and the formal gardens can be reached through the doors at the back," her gracious smile included each member of the group, "so take your time and enjoy our habitat as long as you like. And thank you for coming to see us. It would be our pleasure to have you visit us again soon."

"Very good PR," Paula mumbled under her breath to Sharon as the group dispersed.

"And good reason for it," Sharon added. By unspoken agreement they headed toward the inner courtyard.

After wandering about enjoying the sights

and scents of their lavish surroundings, Sharon glanced at her watch. "It's almost noon already. I think I've had enough of the great outdoors in this heat, and I'd like to take another look at that collection of Indian jewelry—if we have time?"

"We've got all day." Paula assured her. "I want to see the outer courtyard and formal gardens, so I'll wait for you there."

Walking slowly, Paula could almost imagine that she was in her own backyard with its brick walk leading to the marble fountain encircled with flowers that bloomed alternately with the seasons. As her children had grown older she became less involved in their activities and had spent more time gardening, joining the local garden club and exhibiting her roses in shows from time to time.

On a day like this, she would have been digging and planting and pruning while Quent played golf with his regular foursome. Later they might have had friends over for barbecued steaks on the patio. Her life had been as predictable as the seasons.

Having explored the entire courtyard but reluctant to leave its mesmerizing serenity, she sat down on a stone bench in the shade of a mimosa. In the nearby fountain, a bronze cherub spouted water into a shallow lily pond.

Paula smiled to herself imagining what might happen if she surrendered to her sudden urge to take off her shoes and go wading among the lily pads.

At that moment the gardener whom she had glimpsed early on the tour rose up from behind a trellis of bougainvillea. Startled, she gave a small gasp that caught his attention. He nodded slightly and went on clipping and gently removing the dried blooms from their stems.

Paula silently watched him for a time. He looked inexplicably cool in his dark cotton coveralls and deep-billed cap, completely absorbed in his task. She imagined him to be a man who had worked these beds from inception to fruition, and she wanted him to know what pleasure his labors had brought.

"The flowers are lovely," she said, and for a moment she thought he had not heard her voice above the cascading stream of water.

Then he straightened and looked at her briefly. "Thank you."

"I'm sure you must put a lot of effort into all this," she indicated the entire courtyard. "I garden on a small scale myself and I have some idea what it requires."

"I can't take the credit," he answered quietly. "I have a lot of good help."

Of course, Paula thought, today was Saturday. On weekdays there were probably a dozen gardeners working here. He remained still, shears in hand, waiting for her to terminate the conversation.

She smiled. "I'm so glad I found this place and I'll be coming back as often as possible to escape the real world."

He asked, smiling slightly but not looking at her, "And where is the real world?"

"The university." On an impulse she added, "Downwind from the obnoxious paper mill that generates the cash to provide all of this, I suppose."

Looking in the direction of the university, the man asked softly, "Is it so bad?"

"It's almost nauseating, especially early in the mornings." Paula took a deep breath. "I can't understand why anyone would locate a paper mill so close to a beautiful town."

"The mill was here first," came his quiet answer. "The town grew around it."

"Well, surely with all the new methods of air quality control something could be done about that horrible stench."

He looked at her solemnly. "Like what?"

"I don't know," Paula said in exasperation, "but I should think people as rich as the Winthropes could find someone who does. How can people who are descended from the Cherokees pollute the sacred land of their forefathers?" He opened his mouth to speak but she went on, "And no amount of university buildings or museums and gardens can make up for that." She stopped, flustered at the intensity of his gaze. Belatedly she remembered that this man was an employee of the Winthropes. She should have realized he would not understand what she felt. "I'm sorry."

"There's no need to be," he said, laying his shears aside, removing his cap, and standing up. There was something vaguely familiar in his stance, she thought briefly, as she also stood. "People should never apologize for having the courage of their convictions. Although I'm afraid in this instance I can't agree with you." He glanced at her ringless hand, "Miss . . . ?"

"Paula. Paula Howard."

"Miss Howard," he finished, then extended his hand. "I'm Greg Winthrope."

Paula's breath seemed to stop as she instinctively took a step backward. "Oh . . . I am sorry, Mr. Winthrope. How stupid of me." The words rushed out. "But I thought—the way you are working here like this . . ."

He touched her arm in a conciliatory gesture. "It is I who should apologize. I'm sorry if I misled you, Paula. It wasn't intentional. There just didn't seem to be an appropriate—I always spend Saturdays—"

Now it was he who tried to explain and she who interrupted. "Please. It wasn't your fault that I was babbling like an idiot."

"Quite the contrary. You presented some very legitimate concerns. But solving the problems you mentioned is more complex than you imagine." He stopped, clearing his throat. "I'd like to discuss this with you over dinner—tonight, if you're free?"

"I . . ." Paula stopped, took a deep breath. He was obviously just trying to put her at ease, and she would not impose her gauche behavior on him further. "No, thank you so much. It's very kind of you but I really mustn't let you do this."

"Why not?" He asked sincerely. "Your honesty intrigues me, Paula Howard." He looked thoughtful. "It is something I seldom encounter in anyone, much less a woman."

"Well . . ."

"So if you are free?"

"Yes, I'm free."

"Then I'll pick you up at seven. Where will you be?"

"The reception room of—Winthrope Hall."

A slight smile touched the corner of his mouth before he started to speak, only to be interrupted by Sharon's voice at the courtyard entrance.

"There you are, Paula. I've been looking for you in the gardens. I must have misunderstood." She joined them as she spoke.

"I sat down for a moment, and I never got that far," Paula explained absently as she debated whether to introduce her friend to the man who stood there or just say goodbye and beat a hasty exit. Her good manners won. "Sharon, may I present Gregory Winthrope. Sharon Swafford."

Sharon stood, mouth agape, speechless for a long moment. Then she turned puzzled eyes toward Paula. "Is this a joke?"

Paula shook her head. "No, Mr. Winthrope works in his gardens on Saturdays."

Sharon's gaze returned to Gregory Winthrope, recognition dawning as she studied his handsome features. "How do you do . . ." Tentatively she extended her hand.

"Greg." He took her hand. "I'm very pleased to meet you, Sharon." He released her hand and asked courteously, "Have you enjoyed your visit?"

"Oh, yes. It's all very beautiful. I could

spend hours here and not learn all I want to know about some of the exhibits."

"Then you must come again, anytime." He turned to Paula. "Goodbye for now. I'll see you this evening."

As they walked toward the gate, Sharon asked softly, "What did he mean by that? Are you coming back here tonight?"

"No." Paula hesitated, then realized the truth would come out sooner or later so it might as well be now. "He's taking me to dinner."

Sharon stopped dead still and repeated her earlier question, "Is this a joke?"

Paula nudged her through the gate. "No, I'm completely serious. Come on and get in the car and I'll tell you about it."

As they walked toward the white car, gleaming in the noonday sun, Sharon looked at the attractive woman beside her with admiration. "Well, all I can say is that you are one lucky lady. I can't wait to hear the details."

The reception room in Winthrope Hall was crowded with young people when Paula entered a little before seven. Talking and laughing among themselves, they did not notice her as she crossed the room to a wing-backed chair beside the fireplace and sat down. She was wearing the coffee-colored silk jumpsuit she had worn to Faye Browne's and for the second time Paula wished that she had brought her best summer dresses with her.

She wondered if it had been a mistake to accept the invitation to have dinner with Gregory Winthrope. In spite of Sharon Swafford's prediction that she would have a fabulous time, just saying his name filled her with apprehension.

Why had a man like him asked her to dinner anyway? She was younger than he but surely a man of his social background wouldn't lack for dinner companions of whatever age he chose. Paula smoothed the fabric of her jumpsuit with nervous fingers. What would she, small town housewife, find to talk about with a wealthy businessman? She didn't imagine the issue of pollution from the paper mill could be stretched to fill a whole evening. She felt a sudden urge to go back to her room and forget about dinner. With butterflies in her stomach she didn't feel like eating anyway.

But promptly at seven Gregory Winthrope arrived and his piercing eyes searched the room until they came to rest on the woman seated under the portrait of Rachel Winthrope. Paula did not know what a striking resemblance she bore to the lady in blue, but Greg Winthrope stood watching her pensively until she turned and saw him across the room and went to meet him.

"Good evening, Paula. Have you been waiting long?"

"Only a few minutes." She hesitated at the doorway, suddenly shy with this handsome stranger who was looking at her with such intensity.

"You look lovely," he said softly, and took her arm. "We'd better go. I'm parked at the front entrance in a no parking zone."

"I should think you could," Paula's gesture encompassed the building, "in consideration of all this."

He laughed. "Not a chance."

Paula was aware of a few heads turning as they walked through the lobby. Perhaps some of the students recognized him, she thought.

As they went outside Paula saw the dull gold Jaguar at the curb and felt a shiver of anticipation knowing that she would be riding in it to dinner.

"What a nice car," she said.

"Thank you, Paula." Greg opened the passenger door and waited for her to get in.

The powerful engine hummed quietly as Greg expertly maneuvered through the busy university traffic. On the main highway he turned to her and spoke. "I made reservations at Magnolia Manor. I'm always hungry after a day of real work and they have excellent food. Have you been there?"

Paula shook her head. "I've mostly been to the cafeteria at Gaither Hall so far."

Greg laughed softly. "Then a nice dinner is long overdue."

Magnolia Manor appeared at first sight to be an antebellum mansion. Located a few miles out of town, it would not have been visible from the road except for its brightly lighted portico. Greg drove the Jaguar slowly up the winding driveway overlaid with the shadows and scent of magnolia trees that lined each side.

Paula breathed deeply. "This is magnificent. I'm glad you brought me here."

"Are you really?" Greg showed his pleasure in her approval.

"It looks like a replica of Tara. Was it once a plantation?"

"Yes, and like Tara it predated the Civil War. But when the last of the family died, a local restaurateur bought and renovated it."

The valet who parked their car called Gregory Winthrope by name as did the maître d' who showed them to a table by a tall window overlooking a lighted gazebo.

"Shall I order for us, Paula?"

"Yes, please," Paula answered, feeling too intimidated by the room's opulence to concentrate on the menu. The crystal prisms of the gigantic chandelier that swung from the high ceiling caught the light from the candles that burned on the tables below and Paula was unaware that the sparkle was reflected in her eyes when she looked at Greg. Soft music came from the baby grand piano across the hallway in what Paula imagined to have been the library before the house was converted into a restaurant.

Greg ordered dinner and what Paula knew to be a very expensive California red wine which the waiter brought immediately. After the ritual tasting and approval, the waiter poured two glasses, and they were left alone.

Greg touched his glass to hers. "To a happy evening and getting acquainted."

Paula smiled as she drank to Greg's toast, already feeling happier than she had in a long while.

Greg lost no time in following through on his intentions. "What brings you to the university, Paula?"

"I'm working on a degree in special education."

"An interesting field, I imagine."

"Yes, I think so."

"Ben Colbert is known throughout the state for his work in that field. Is he one of your instructors?"

"Yes, I'm doing an internship in learning disabilities. Dr. Colbert teaches two of my classes and supervises my tutorial work."

"And what did you do before summer?"

Paula took a sip of wine before answering. How much about herself did she want to tell this gently probing man? "I . . . was a housewife . . . in Tuscumbia." She looked down at the bare third finger on her left hand. Something more in the way of an explanation would be necessary. "I am . . . recently divorced so I decided to return to school and get recertified to teach."

"I see," Greg said softly. "I apologize for my question."

"There's no need for that," Paula answered quickly. "I'm becoming accustomed to explaining my situation."

"My turn now," Greg said quietly. "I have also been married. My wife, Rachel, died three years ago."

So Rachel of Winthrope Hall had been his wife. "She was very beautiful."

He studied her a moment. "You look a great deal like her."

"Oh?" Paula blushed, not knowing quite how to respond, finally saying a faint, "Thank you."

"I've become something of a boring recluse since she died. My mother is always scolding me about my lack of a social life." He smiled to himself. "Can you imagine a man of sixty-two being scolded by his mother?"

"I would never believe that you are sixty-two."

"You're very kind to an old man," he said with mock seriousness, then asked, "Are you a mother, Paula?"

"Yes. I have a son and a daughter."

"How nice. Rachel and I had hoped for a large family but we . . . couldn't have children. I'm alone now except for aging parents. After my wife died it seemed foolish to maintain a house that had always been too large even for the two of us so I disposed of it and moved back into the family home. Well," he looked toward the approaching waiter, "here comes our salad. We can postpone our autobiographies until later."

Paula had not realized how hungry she was

until the Caesar salad was set before her. As she picked up her salad fork she glanced around the candlelit room and felt as though she must be dreaming. This was not what she had expected summer to be like at all.

Greg had ordered a hearty fare for them— prime rib, baked potato, string beans, and dark rye bread. As they ate, he told her about the mill, finishing with, "And so you see, it has always been a part of this town and a part of my family so that we are inexorably joined together. And because the air pollution is a necessary part of paper production until someone can find a solution, we have tried to create something beautiful to compensate."

"And you certainly have succeeded," Paula said. "I'm sorry I sounded so critical today."

"I was glad that you spoke your mind. Too many people don't, especially to me. I sometimes feel as if I get only positive feedback from everyone even though I encourage honest expression."

"Then to be honest, I would never have said what I did if I'd known I was talking with the Chairman of the Board instead of a gardener."

His eyes surveyed her with amusement. "I'm beginning to see more than one advantage to my Saturday gardening. It is probably a very good way to learn the truth, at least from the public. Now, shall we have coffee and a dessert?"

After they had finished generous slices of French silk pie and a silver pot of rich dark coffee, Greg looked at Paula and smiled hesitantly. "Would you like to go out on the veranda and dance?"

"Why, yes, I would love to."

As he led the way past the grand piano, Greg spoke to the man sitting at the keyboard. They continued out the French doors onto a wide, dimly lit terrace where several couples were already dancing.

Greg waited for a moment, listening to the music. The song changed and she recognized "Some Enchanted Evening." Then Greg held out his arms and she went into his embrace and began moving as he led. He was a good dancer and he held her at just the right distance for proper dance floor etiquette. There was no need for conversation and they made none. Paula surrendered herself to the night and the music and the scent of magnolias that enveloped her. She felt young again, like a girl attending her first prom.

She wondered if Greg had requested this song as they passed the piano. Perhaps it had been his and Rachel's song and he was lost in dreams of her right now, pretending the woman he held was his wife. Paula thought briefly of Quent. She had memories, too, but not of moonlit dances on the terrace of Magnolia Manor. This was a whole new world for her. And back in her familiar world Quent was living and breathing and doing all the things he had always done—only now without her.

"Penny for your thoughts."

"Oh," she took a deep breath, "I was thinking what a different world I'm in now." At least that much was true.

As they left the dance floor, they paused to allow another couple to pass.

"Well, hello, Ben."

Paula turned quickly and matched Dr. Colbert's startled look.

"Hello, Greg," he answered, still staring at Paula. "Miss Howard."

"Paula," Greg touched her arm, "you already know Ben Colbert. And this is his wife, Shirlene."

"Hello." Paula smiled at the petite silver-haired woman who surveyed her gravely and nodded.

As they walked on, Paula felt a chill of apprehension. Dr. Colbert would be certain she was husband hunting now, and his wife would probably concur. With the age difference between her and her escort they would both think the worst. She straightened her shoulders, held her head high. What did it matter? She hadn't done anything wrong so they could just think whatever they wanted.

Later when Greg escorted Paula to the lobby of Winthrope Hall, he took her hand and looked at her solemnly. "Thank you for having dinner with me, Paula. May I see you again?"

His question caught her off guard. "Why . . . yes. And I had a lovely time tonight. Thank you."

He gave her hand a slight squeeze, then released it. "Good night, Paula. I'll be in touch."

Paula stood watching him as he walked away. He was really quite handsome. Much to her surprise, she had enjoyed this evening, dining and dancing in a fine restaurant escorted by a charming, wealthy man. It had been a new experience having a courtly gentleman order dinner for her, though it was an old-fashioned southern custom.

Greg Winthrope was a man she would like to go out with again. He made her feel attractive and womanly and her bruised ego needed that right now. But she wanted nothing more. Emotional involvement led to getting hurt and she never intended to leave herself open to that again. Besides, maybe Quent would come to his senses, and . . .

Paula turned toward the elevator. She would not let herself fantasize about Quent anymore. He had walked out of her life and he was not coming back. Her mind knew that, had accepted it, but her heart was still hoping it was not true.

As the elevator rose to the eighth floor, Paula thought about the past week. In only six days at the university she had learned her way around the campus, developed note taking skill and study habits, made a few new friends, and gone out to dinner with two attractive men. That was really quite an accomplishment for a small town housewife turned coed and she felt justifiably proud just thinking about it. Nobody ever said it would be easy, but maybe, just maybe, she was going to get her life together again after all.

Five

"You've scarcely touched your lunch, Paula." Ruth's face mirrored her concern.

"I'm just not hungry. I'm really nervous about this afternoon."

"That makes two of us," Derek said, pushing his own half-empty plate aside. "I haven't been so apprehensive since I flew night raids in Nam."

"There's nothing to be afraid of," Ruth assured her table mates. "They are just kids. Not problem kids, but kids with problems."

"That's part of what scares me," Paula told her. "I don't feel competent to work with these students."

"Me either," Derek added. "I don't even know what *I'm* doing so how in hell am I going to teach them anything?"

"By faking it at first if you have to. These

kids need firm guidance and if they sense your fear they'll move in like hyenas on a wounded rabbit."

"You make them sound vicious," Paula said.

"No, just human. They're frustrated and they lash out at whoever gets near them." Ruth stood up. "And if we don't get back to Oldham Hall by one we are going to be in heap big trouble."

Derek also stood and picked up his tray. "Here, put yours on top," he told Paula. "We can't run the risk of a collision today." She placed her tray on his and gave him a quick smile. "And don't sweat the small stuff. We're older than these kids, and bigger, and we know more, so what is there to be scared of?"

"That sounds convincing," Paula said.

"Yeah, I just hope I can remember that when we get back to Oldham Hall."

"Courage, troops, courage," Ruth told them as they left the cafeteria.

The above-ground basement of Oldham Hall designated for the tutorial program was a dim, cavernous place with ceiling fans and makeshift partitions low enough not to impede air flow to the numerous alcoves furnished with tables and chairs. Instructional materials were kept in a central pod to be distributed daily under the watchful eye of Faye Browne.

The area was buzzing with a cacophony of sounds as the three arrived, winded from a hasty trek across the commons. Small clusters of tutors and their soon-to-be-assigned students apprehensively surveyed each other as they waited for their arbitrary pairing. Dr. Colbert had been talking to Faye Browne and he looked up as they entered, frowned and pointedly checked his watch.

"Made it by the skin of our teeth," Derek said in a low voice.

"Thank goodness," Paula whispered back.

Dr. Colbert rapped on a nearby cabinet with a metal ruler and a sudden hush descended on the room. "Good afternoon, students. Welcome to the university. For those of you who don't know, I'm Dr. Colbert and this is Miss Browne." He nodded in the direction of his assistant and she acknowledged the recognition with a bright smile and quick wave. "We are all here for one purpose," his eyes rested briefly on Paula, "and one purpose only. We . . . are . . . here . . . to . . . learn. Each of you will be assigned to someone who will work with you every day. That person, with the help of Miss Browne and myself, will also plan and carry out your individual study program. No grades will be given here but you will be tested again at the end of summer to see how much progress you have made. So you will be expected to put forth your very best efforts. Now," he paused and looked around the room, "are there any questions before we divide up?"

"Yeah, man, when can I go home?" came a *sotto voce* from somewhere in the group. It was followed by muted snickering. If Dr. Colbert heard he chose to ignore it. "Now, Miss Browne will call the names of each student and tutor assigned to work together and tell you where to go."

"I'd like to tell you where to go, man," the same person spoke in an undertone close behind Paula and out of the corner of her eye she saw that the voice belonged to a tall boy who looked almost old enough to be a university student. Someone is going to have a real challenge handling that one, she thought. After several names had been called, Faye said "Miss Howard, Kurt Yearwood."

Paula and a small, wiry boy opposite her stepped forward at the same time. Facing him up close, she noticed that the top of his head barely reached her chin. She smiled at him, "Hello, Kurt."

He remained silent, not meeting her eyes nor returning her smile.

"Complete this survey and return it to me, please." Faye thrust a stack of materials at her. "You have the last room on the right."

"Come on, Kurt." Paula led the way to the assigned space and sat down, motioning the solemn boy to take the other chair. "I'll have to ask you a few questions. This shouldn't take long." The boy still hadn't looked at her and she was getting more nervous by the minute but she made an effort to appear nonchalant as she opened a folder and picked up a pencil. "Is Kurt your real name or a nickname?" The boy nodded. I set myself up for that by asking two questions at once, Paula chided herself, then tried again. "Your real name?" Another barely perceptible nod followed.

"And your age is . . . ?"

For the first time she heard his voice when he mumbled "Twelve."

She tried not to look surprised but the truth was she would never have guessed him to be more than ten.

"What grade have you just completed?"

"Fourth," came the almost inaudible answer.

Paul did a quick calculation. He should be going into seventh grade so that meant he had failed twice. Poor kid. "Where are you from, Kurt?" she asked more gently.

"Kentucky." So he had come a long way to be part of this program. His parents must have wanted help very badly for him. And what if he didn't find it here, all because of her? Paula felt the weight of responsibility settle on her at that moment as surely as if someone had placed a heavy coat around her shoulders.

She continued asking questions and getting one-word answers as she filled in the blanks on two more pages. "Here is the last question, Kurt. What are your hobbies?"

The boy had a habit of brushing back a pale lock of hair that fell over one eye and he did this again before he answered. "Nothing."

Thinking perhaps he had misunderstood the question, Paula coached him. "Do you like to ride your bike, or collect baseball cards, or go fishing, or . . ."

"No."

"Then tell me what *you* like to do."

"Nothing."

Paula shrugged, wrote "none" in the blank and set the questionnaire aside. "Well, I guess you're glad that is over?" She smiled at him. "So am I." Kurt Yearwood's impassive expression never changed. "Okay, I'd like to have you read a few sentences now." She pointed

110

to the middle of the page and pushed the booklet closer to him but he made no attempt to touch it, simply leaning slightly toward it and knitting his brows. After a long pause, she said, "You may begin now." Still no response. "Suddenly," she said the first word expectantly.

"Suddenly the . . ."

"Rain."

"Rain blew the . . ."

"No, rain began to . . ."

"Rain began to find . . ."

"Fall."

Belatedly she realized she had chosen a level too high for the boy who sat there struggling with simple words a third grader should know. She had started two levels below his grade just like the book said, but apparently Kurt's case didn't fit the book. Now what?

Faye Browne rang a small bell and raised her voice. "Tutors, if you have finished your survey, you may give your students a short break while you turn it in."

Thank you, Miss Browne. Thank you, Lord.

As Paula came out of her cubicle she glimpsed Derek next door and saw that the student with him was the one who had earlier made the smart-aleck remarks. At that moment the boy rushed past, bumping her in passing without a word of apology.

"Hey, just a minute," Derek called from right behind him but the retreating student did not look back. "I'm sorry, Paula," Derek told her. "I'd like to chase him down and haul him back by the scruff of his neck to apologize for his rude behavior, but I guess I need to check on the discipline policy around here first."

"No harm done." She watched the tall boy's head bob through the milling group and disappear. "I wonder what his big hurry is?"

"Time for a cigarette, I'd say. That's another thing I need to check out. I don't guess it's much of a problem with most of the students they get here."

"How old is this one?"

"Twelve."

"I would have guessed him to be older. But then I thought my student was about nine or ten and he's twelve, too."

"You're kidding? That little guy?"

"Yes, and he's only going into fifth grade."

"So is Irvin Pendergrass. But it has to be worse for him because he's so mature. I figure he developed that smart-ass attitude to compensate."

"Well, at least he talks."

"Comparing notes already?" Ruth joined them as they continued toward the center pod where Faye Browne was taking survey sheets and answering questions.

"Oh, Ruth, I'm glad to see you," Paula said. "I've already made a horrible blunder. I started my student reading at a level way over his head and I didn't know what to do. Fortunately Miss Browne rang the bell and gave me a reprieve. How can I get out of this without embarrassing him any worse than he already is?"

"Just tell him to begin on something new when you go back after the break. And make sure to start at a really low level."

"But won't he resent reading such simple stuff?"

"Not if he can call the words, honey. But don't worry, those stories may have easy words but they were written to interest older students who can't read well."

"I'm glad we've got an old classroom pro to rely on for help," Derek said.

"If that's meant to be a compliment, I'd like it better without the reference to my age," Ruth commented dryly, then added, "I noticed they paired you with Mister Smart Mouth. Have you got him squared away yet?"

"Hardly. I don't know how far I'm allowed

to go in straightening him up but as far as I'm concerned he's pretty bent out of shape."

"And I've got his female counterpart. Norma Oakley is eleven going on twenty, two grades behind, and has all the symptoms in the book."

"At least you got one of the few girls in the program," Paula told her.

"Well, considering what she's like, that's not much consolation."

"How is it going, Derek?" Faye smiled at him as she took the survey pages.

"I haven't punched the punk yet," Derek said in a low tone, "but I have been tempted to. Seriously, what are the limits on discipline?"

"We're not allowed to use physical force, except to restrain a student from hurting himself or someone else. For all other misbehavior, we lecture or isolate the student or withhold privileges."

"Such as?"

"Break time. Refreshments, when we have them. Or a group activity." She turned to Paula. "And how did you get along with Kurt, Miss Howard?"

"Oh . . . fine." There was no point in revealing her inadequacies to this woman when Ruth had already counseled her on what to do. Thank goodness for a friend who had worked with children in special education already.

"Miss Howard?"

"Yes, Miss Browne?" Paula faced the counter again, half expecting that her mistake with Kurt had been discovered after all.

"Please see me in my office after the session is over today." Now she was sure of it. "I need to discuss some information about your student."

"All right."

Derek was waiting for her by the door that led outside. "What was that all about?"

"I have no idea, but I think I may already be in trouble."

"What for? Beginning at the wrong reading level? No way." He nodded toward a cluster of students in the shade of a nearby oak. "Look at that. Irvin is passing out cigarettes and I forgot to ask about the rules. So I guess I'd better ignore it until I know for sure." He sighed. "Right now I could use one myself, and I quit smoking four years ago."

Paula smiled. "I wouldn't mind a puff either. And I've never smoked at all."

"A drag. Only amateurs puff." He shook his head. "If this tutoring can drive us to take up such bad habits as smoking after only one short session, God only knows what will be next. It's going to be a long summer."

As Paula left Oldham Hall after her meeting with Faye Browne, she was surprised to find Derek sitting on the steps.

"Well, hello."

He stood up and reached for her armload of books. "Here, let me carry those. It has been a long time since I've carried a pretty girl's books."

"Thanks for waiting."

"What are friends for?"

"I need a friend right now."

"That bad, huh?"

"I'm afraid so." Paula slowed her steps unconsciously and Derek matched her pace. "Kurt Yearwood has some serious problems. His parents are divorced and both are remarried."

"That doesn't sound too bad. Probably fits half the kids in the program."

"But neither parent wants him. They had a court battle to see who *had* to take him."

"Damn, what a rotten thing to do to a kid."

"And that's not all. The judge gave custody to both parents, his mother during the school year and his father in summer. And he's run away from each during the past year."

"Who could blame him?"

"There's more. He . . . tried to kill himself just before summer."

"Christ," Derek swore softly. "How?"

"He swallowed pills but they found him and pumped his stomach."

"And then they sent him here?" Derek's voice was incredulous.

"His psychologist thinks if he can learn to read better it will help him overcome his feelings of failure and rejection."

"Well, maybe I don't understand what we are supposed to be doing here, but this sounds like a very disturbed guy to me."

"I said the same thing to Miss Browne. I don't feel qualified to help him."

"And what did Miss Browne say to that?"

"She said they chose me for his tutor because I'm a mother and divorced so they felt I would be able to empathize with his problems."

"I hate to admit it but they're probably right. Though I don't like having you get all this mess dumped on you."

"I don't mind about that, but what if I can't help him? What will happen to Kurt then?"

"Hey, it's only the first day. Give yourself a

chance before you chalk it up a loss." He picked up speed. "We had better move along or they'll close the cafeteria line before we get there."

"You could have eaten an hour ago if you hadn't waited for me," Paula said apologetically. "But I'm glad you did."

Derek grinned at her. "It was self-preservation. You most likely would have rushed in here late and knocked me down."

"You aren't going to let me forget that, are you?"

"Nope. That was quite a way to meet. You sure got my attention. Did you do that on purpose?"

Paula smiled, feeling better in spite of everything. "You'll never know, will you?"

Paula was sitting at her desk, absorbed in writing lesson plans for the week, when the phone rang. Maybe Quent . . . She moved a stack of papers off it and picked up the receiver as it rang a second time. "Hello?"

"Paula, is that you?"

"Yes, Mother." Paula unconsciously sat a little straighter. "What a nice surprise. How are you?"

"I'm fine, dear." After a brief pause she

went on. "I got your letter." The pause was longer this time but Paula waited silently. "So . . . the divorce is final?"

"Yes, Mother. It is." She braced herself for the inevitable.

"Well . . . I had hoped that you and Quent would be able to work things out."

"So had I, Mother."

"It would have been so much better for Jeff and Amy."

Paula made a concerted effort to keep her voice neutral. "It would have been better for all of us."

"Do you think if you had stayed in Tuscumbia instead of going off to school . . ."

"Mother, the divorce was final before I thought about coming to the university. It was only after I realized I would have to support myself that I decided to teach again."

"Well, I just thought maybe if you had stayed there in your home Quentin would have realized after a while that he . . . It's just that I hate to see your family break up, and I've always thought so much of Quentin. He has really been like a son to me."

"I know, Mother. And Quent is very fond of you, too. But my staying in Tuscumbia wasn't going to change anything. We had a trial separation." Despite her intentions, her voice was becoming defensive.

"You were such a wonderful wife and mother and homemaker, Paula. I don't see how Quentin could turn his back on his home and family and everything he has worked for all these years." Her mother's statements sounded more like questions.

"I don't understand it either. But he has and it *is* final, Mother."

"Oh, dear. Isn't there something else you could try? What about a minister? Or a marriage counselor?"

Paula took a deep breath. "Quentin refused to see anyone. He said they would just talk him out of what he knew was the right thing for him."

"You see, that shows he is uncertain in his own mind—"

"No, Mother. It shows he is a good person who could be convinced to change his mind about what he wants if someone lays a guilt trip on him." What was she saying? Why was she defending the man who had walked out on her without any consideration for what she wanted?

"Paula, I didn't mean to upset you."

"I'm *not* upset, Mother." She gripped the receiver more tightly.

"I know you have done everything possible to keep your marriage from failing. It's just that I can't bear to think of you having to start over at your age . . ."

"I'm not that old, Mother. You married Roger when you were about my age."

"But that was different. I had been alone for years, so I knew how to take care of myself."

"And I'm *learning,* so don't worry about me." Seizing the opportunity, she changed the subject. "How is Roger?"

"Not very well, I'm afraid. He's having some digestive problems."

"Has he seen a doctor?"

"Yes. And the doctor has scheduled tests." She paused for a moment, talking with someone in the room. "But he says to tell you he's fine and the doctor and I are making a mountain out of a molehill."

Paula was very fond of the gentle man who was her mother's husband. "Tell him to mind the doctor and you or he will have to answer to me."

"We had a postcard from Jeff yesterday. He had been to the Taj Mahal and he sent a picture of it."

"Yes, he sent me one, too."

"How is he taking the . . . divorce?"

So here it came again. "Not very well," she said honestly. "I wish he were here so Quent and I could sit down and talk with him as we did with Amy."

"Well, she seems to be taking it all right. She called from the airport last week when she was flying through, all bubbly about her engagement and the wedding plans. Her parents' divorce obviously hasn't discouraged her from marriage."

"I guess she doesn't believe in the old saying 'Like mother, like daughter.' "

Jeanette Driskell's voice became falsely cheerful. "And how are your classes going?"

"I'm having to work very hard. But I've settled in and made a few friends."

"It must be very difficult to go back to school after such a long time. But I'm sure you'll do well, dear."

"I hope so, Mother."

"So take care of yourself and let us hear from you when you have time and keep us posted on the wedding. We'll have to make travel plans, you know, and booking a flight farther ahead is more economical."

Paula grouped her answers to all of her mother's admonitions into one affirmative response. "Yes, Mother. And I'm glad you called. Give my best to Roger."

"Will do. And best love to you, dear. Good night."

"Good night." Paula slowly replaced the receiver feeling there was something more she should have added. Hadn't her mother's probing questions implied that she was at fault? She had expected Quent's mother to blame her but she resented her own mother reaching the same unfair conclusion. The tears came then, tears of guilt and regret and anger. Hot, scalding tears that dripped onto her carefully-prepared lesson plans. How on earth can I help Kurt Yearwood when I have so many problems of my own, she asked silently.

It seemed that every time she took a step forward, something happened and she slipped back two or three. After a little while she blew her nose determinedly and gave herself a pep talk. She had come to the university and managed to find her way around a campus teeming with thousands of students. She had adjusted to living in a dorm and sharing a communal bath and going to a cafeteria for meals, and so far she was keeping her head above the water in a very hard academic program.

But would she be able to help Kurt Yearwood? What she needed was access to a good child psychologist but she might as well wish for the moon. She supposed she could always check some psychology books out of the library. Wait. Louise Montgomery was a counselor. She must have had many courses on human behavior.

Paula picked up the phone, dialed three numbers. "Ruth?"

"Hi, Paula. How did your meeting go with Miss Browne?"

"That is what I'm calling about. I need a counselor. Does Louise offer room service?"

"I'll ask her." Paula could hear faint voices, then Ruth spoke into the phone again. "She'll be right over. See you tomorrow. Good luck."

"Okay. Thanks, Ruth."

Paula had just hung up the phone when she heard a soft knock on the door.

"My, that was fast service," she told Louise as she stepped aside for her to enter.

"I strive to please," Louise answered. "But a night call will cost extra, you know."

"Would a cup of coffee and some cookies be acceptable down payment?"

"Fair enough. If the coffee is decaf and the cookies low calorie."

"Yes on the decaf." Paula measured coffee and plugged in the pot. "No on the cookies."

"Okay. Fifty percent isn't bad. I'll take it."

Louise sat down and tucked her feet up. "Now what can I do for you?"

Paula repeated everything Faye Browne had told her about Kurt Yearwood then finished with, "And I'm afraid he needs a lot more help than I know how to give. Just working on his reading problem is a big challenge for me, and coping with his emotional problem is overwhelming."

"Well, you've got one thing going for you already. You are concerned. And he will sense that." Louise was silent while Paula poured coffee in styrofoam cups and put oatmeal cookies on a paper plate which she set between them on the bed. "This boy is feeling totally rejected, and right or wrong, he probably feels that his parents don't want him because of his learning disability."

"But that still leaves the worst part."

"Yes. And without knowing Kurt, it would be impossible to speculate on why he did that." She paused, took a sip of coffee. "In any case, the boy needs a lot of acceptance and sincere attention. Anything you can do to strengthen his self image will be helpful, but I think I should tell you that kids who try suicide once often try it again."

"Oh, no. I didn't need to hear that," Paula wailed.

"Now, Paula, you are not responsible for this boy's life. It was messed up long before today so it's not going to help for you to become obsessed with his problems." She looked at Paula intently. "Or cry your eyes out over him."

"I wasn't crying about Kurt." Paula stopped, embarrassed, then said quietly, "My tears were for the mess I've made of my own life."

"I'm sorry I mentioned it then," Louise said, "but as long as I have, the counselor's ear is still open if you want to talk about it."

"Oh, it was nothing, really."

"Nobody cries tears for nothing." Louise bit into another cookie, chewed slowly.

"My mother called me from Florida. She's having a hard time accepting my divorce, and I feel she somehow blames me for breaking up my marriage. There was a subtle message that I should have tried harder to keep things together."

"And it hit a raw nerve?"

"Yes, I suppose so. Sometimes I feel that way, too. But I did everything I could to persuade my husband to stay. Even though it hurt my pride to grovel."

Louise patted her hand. "Any man would be a fool not to stay married to you, Paula. He has the problem, whatever it is—not you."

"Thanks for saying that, Louise, but Quent is a nice guy."

"Maybe. But he's a nice guy with a problem, is all I can say." She stood up. "Thanks for the snack."

"Thank you, Louise." Paula walked with her to the door. "I feel better on both counts now."

"Any time I can help, on either count, let me know."

Paula absently nibbled at the remaining cookie crumbs on the plate. She would do her best with Kurt. Just as she had with her marriage. That was all she could do, even though sometimes her best just wasn't good enough.

Six

Bone tired and hungry, Paula stepped off the elevator of Winthrope Hall and met Sharon on her way out.

"Hi, Paula. I was wondering where you were."

"Slaving away in the library," Paula answered.

"Didn't you make it to the cafeteria?"

"Not a chance. But I've got food in my room." An idea came to Paula and she asked, "Do you have to study tonight?"

"Not necessarily. I've got all weekend."

"Then how would you like to go with me out to the airport to meet my daughter?"

"Well, I . . ." Sharon smiled. "Why not? I'd love to."

"Okay, we'll need to leave about eight. I'll give you a ring when I'm ready."

Putting her books aside, she rinsed her face in cold water and looked at herself in the mirror. She had lost a couple of pounds, which made her cheekbones more prominent, and there were faint blue smudges under both eyes. She wanted to be rested and unhurried for Amy's visit but she knew that was impossible. She only hoped she wouldn't be late for her arrival.

After eating some fruit and a muffin, Paula had a long, hot shower and she was blow drying her hair when the phone rang.

"Hello?"

"Paula, this is Derek."

Standing in her bra and panties, she felt a moment of panic as though he could actually see what she was wearing. "Why, hello."

"Are you about ready to leave for the airport?"

"Yes, soon. I'm allowing an hour just in case the plane is early or I make a wrong turn."

"That's why I called. I'd like to take you to meet your daughter."

"Thanks, Derek, but that really won't be necessary."

"I made a few inquiries and the route to the airport goes through a rough part of town and then a fairly isolated road. It isn't a safe place for a woman alone at night."

"I won't be alone. Sharon Swafford is going with me."

"I don't feel that area is safe at night for even two women alone, Paula."

She hesitated. Derek might think she didn't want him to meet Amy if she refused his offer. "Okay, thanks. Shall I pick you up at Rhodes Hall or do you want to meet me here?"

"I'll drive. I'll be there a little before eight."

"We'll be out front by eight. See you then," she replied.

Paula dressed carefully in white slacks and a navy knit top. Perhaps Quent would ask about her when Amy saw him next and she wanted him to know that she was doing quite well without him. Of course, if he thought she was having a very difficult time making it on her own he might have pity on her and . . . damn his pity! She didn't need it or want it. Well, Paula Howard, she told herself. You are certainly defensive tonight. She supposed it had something to do with seeing Amy again and feeling strange about being here at the university instead of at home with Quent.

Sharon met her in the hallway and she explained about Derek as they rode the elevator. "I could just stay here since you'll have someone with you," Sharon said.

"No, I don't want you to. Besides, if I showed

up alone with a man Amy would probably think he was my date."

"Well, you have been out with him."

"Yes, but we're just friends."

"Okay, but you are divorced, so I should think you're free to date anyone you want to."

"Technically, that's true, but it would be hard for Amy to see me this soon with anyone except her father."

They left the elevator and walked through the main lobby. As they came out the doors Paula said, "There's Derek, double-parked over there. We'd better hurry."

Sharon climbed in back past the bucket seats. As she fastened her seat belt, Paula made the introductions.

"Hi, Sharon. Glad you could come along." Derek's sincere smile put her instantly at ease.

"Hello. Nice to meet you, sir."

"Hey, I'm old enough to be your father but just address me as one of your peers, okay, or I'll begin to feel my age."

"Oh, I'm sorry. I didn't mean to—"

"No problem. It's this military officer persona. Why, some of the guys in my dorm stand at attention and salute me when I get out of the shower."

Paula laughed. "You're kidding."

"No, but they do it as a joke because they know I'm an ex-Navy man."

Paula smiled to herself as she imagined Derek with a towel wrapped around his middle stepping briskly past a row of saluting students in various stages of nudity. Suddenly she wondered if he was tanned all over, and blushed.

They drove through dimly lighted streets filled with warehouses and boarded buildings which made Paula glad Derek had insisted on accompanying them. Next came a dark stretch of woodlands that gave even more evidence of the wisdom of not being alone.

As they approached the bright lights of the airport Derek said, "I'm going to let you two out at the terminal and then find a parking place. I'll join you in the waiting room." He pulled to the curb behind a yellow cab and the two women got out.

Inside the busy terminal, people were rushing back and forth while loudspeakers announced the arrivals and departures of various airlines. "Your daughter must lead an exciting life." Sharon indicated the bright lights, the noise, the crowds that surrounded them. "Imagine being a part of all this."

"Yes, she certainly does, although flying the friendly skies is not exactly a mother's idea of a safe job for her only daughter." Paula looked at her watch. "She should be here soon. Let's check the board."

By the time Derek joined them, the loudspeaker was announcing Amy's flight and they walked nearer to the arrival gate.

"There she is." Paula caught her daughter's eye as Amy emerged from the wind tunnel and they waved to each other. She felt a surge of love and pride at the sight of the beautiful girl with blond hair swept back in a ponytail, in her dark uniform and crisp white blouse, flight bag slung over one shoulder. She rushed forward to envelop her in a joyful embrace. "Oh, it's so good to see you, honey," she whispered.

"You, too, Mom. Have you been waiting long?"

"Not at all. We just got here."

"We?"

"Yes," Paula turned to include the other two who had stepped closer. "Derek, Sharon, this is my daughter, Amy."

They exchanged greetings and after an interval of silence, Derek asked, "Anyone hungry besides me? Have you eaten, Amy?"

"No, actually, I was too busy serving the passengers."

"You're not fooling me. You airline people don't eat that stuff you pass off as food."

Amy laughed. "That is probably true on the *other* airlines, but we're different."

"I'll file that for future travel," said Derek. "Sharon?"

"I'd like some pie and coffee."

"Paula?"

"I'm famished. I've only had a snack since lunch."

"No wonder you've lost weight since I last saw you, Mom." Amy looked at her mother with concern.

"Do you have more luggage, Amy?" Derek asked.

"No, I travel light."

"Okay, then. Away we go, and where we'll end up is anybody's guess."

When they reached the sandwich shop, Paula and Sharon were the first to be seated in the booth. After an awkward moment, Derek sat down beside Sharon, leaving the place by Paula for her daughter.

After they had given their orders, Sharon said, "Amy, I think your job must be so exciting. I'll bet you've been all over the world."

"Well, no, but I have been in all the major U.S. cities."

"Have you ever had any close calls, like losing an engine or anything?"

Paula put her hands over her ears. "I don't think I want to hear the answer to that."

Amy put her arm around her mother. "Relax, Mom, the answer is no. Only a skid on an icy runway once."

"Flying is safer than driving a car," Derek said.

"Spoken like a true pilot," Paula chided.

"Pilot?" Amy asked, looking at Derek with new interest.

"Naval Aviation, retired."

"How long?"

"Let's see, three weeks, two days, ten hours . . ."

"My fiancé is a pilot. Chris was in the Air Force for four years, then became a commercial pilot. Did you consider that?"

"Oh, for about five minutes." Derek grinned at her. "But after twenty-five years I was ready to hang it up and try a new approach—no pun intended."

The waitress brought their food and the conversation turned to comments on the merits of rye versus wheat bread and whether chicken salad, which Paula and Amy ordered, had less cholesterol than the ham and cheese Derek was eating.

"Anyone else want dessert?" the waitress asked as she returned with the check and a refill on coffee. Paula and Amy declined but Derek ordered apple pie à la mode while surreptitiously folding the check under the edge of his saucer.

Paula reached for the ticket. "This has to be my treat."

Derek playfully slapped her hand. "Leave me to my pleasure. How often does a man like me get to escort three beautiful women at the same time?"

"You can enjoy our company without having to pay for it," Paula answered.

"In fact, we'll treat you," Amy added as she reached for the check, too.

"No fair. I can't fight mother *and* daughter. So I'll just put this out of sight for safekeeping." He tucked the ticket into his shirt pocket as the waitress brought his pie, then grinned at Sharon. "I'm glad to have one agreeable female companion."

"With my tight budget I never look a gift horse in the mouth," she told him.

"I'm not sure I like your analogy, but I agree with your philosophy," Derek laughed as the foursome stood to go home.

* * *

"I'm so glad I met you," Amy told Derek as they got out in front of Winthrope Hall. "Thanks for the food and the fun. It was really nice of you and Sharon to come with Mom to meet me."

"My pleasure, Amy. When will you be leaving?"

"Same flight on Sunday evening."

"Then count on me for the trip back out. Meanwhile, enjoy your visit."

She stood waving as he drove away, then said to Sharon, "What a nice guy. I really like him."

"Me, too," Sharon agreed.

Paula and Amy said good night to Sharon in the hallway and Paula unlocked her door. "Well, here it is."

"Oh, Mom, it is *so* cozy," Amy exclaimed with genuine surprise.

"Do you like it—really?"

"I love it."

"You can have the bed by the window. And there are towels in the chest. We all use the communal bath across the hall."

"No problem, Mom. If you can do it, so can I."

"Well, it wasn't easy at first, but I've learned to live with it," said Paula with more conviction than she felt.

Amy began unpacking her flight bag.

"Mom, are Derek and Sharon serious abou each other?"

"What? Heavens, no. They don't even date.'

"Oh? Then why did he come to meet my plane? I thought they . . ."

"Derek and I have classes together, and he heard me talking about my daughter's visit so he offered to drive me out to meet you. I had already asked Sharon and we decided to accept his offer."

"I'm glad you did, Mom—I enjoyed meeting him. Is he divorced?"

"Yes, for about five years, he said. So I guess he likes being a bachelor."

"It seems strange, you being in college and having friends my age. I guess you're like a mom to them, too." She studied Paula for a minute. "There is something different about you, though."

Paula shook her head. "I'm the same old me, honey."

"No, you're not," Amy told her softly. "But I love you just the same."

After Amy had showered and put on her mother's terrycloth robe, she sat tailor fashion on the bed and looked very serious. "Now, Mom, let's talk about my wedding."

"Okay, honey." Paula sat down beside her and waited expectantly.

"I want a garden wedding. In *our* garden."

"But honey, the house may—"

"Be sold? But Chris says you always have thirty days to vacate and I want to be married the first Saturday in July."

Paula felt instant panic. "Amy, that is only *three weeks* from now. We can't possibly get a wedding together by then. I thought you were going to marry at the end of summer. I don't think the house will be sold by then, but if it is, like Chris said, there will be at least thirty days to . . ." Paula stopped to get her breath.

"We won't need to send formal invitations, just an announcement in the newspaper. Almost all of the guests live in Tuscumbia anyway and we can call the few who don't. We'll have cake and champagne on the patio—catered. I've already checked with Mrs. Thompson about that. So there really isn't anything for you to worry about, Mom."

"It does sound as though you have put a lot of thought into it," Paula conceded. "But what about music?"

"Chris has a friend who plays classical guitar. We're asking him."

"And the wedding pictures?"

"No problem. The photo shop has a new

139

photographer who will be available that week-end."

"What about flowers?"

"We won't need anything except for the wedding party, and we'll order roses to blend in with the garden flowers. It's going to be so romantic. Roses and candlelight and guitar music and the fountain sparkling and . . ." she stopped, held her hands to her temples, "Oh no—I forgot the candelabra."

"We could borrow those from church. And folding chairs, too. Have you spoken to the minister?"

"He wasn't available, so we've asked an Air Force chaplain Chris knows. I'm asking three girls I work with to be bridesmaids and Chris has an equal number of ushers."

"Have you chosen a dress yet?"

"Yes. It's ivory satin with a lace overlay."

It seemed useless to try and persuade her daughter to change her mind when the plans had already progressed this far, so Paula resigned herself to acceptance. "Well, I suppose that you have thought of everything, Amy, but my mind is still reeling. I think I need to sleep on it."

Amy yawned. "Me, too, Mom. Jet lag is beginning to catch up with me." She slipped out of the robe and pulled back the spread. "Nitey-nite."

The childish phrase and the way her long blond hair fanned out across the pillow touched Paula as she bent to kiss her daughter's cheek. "I can't believe you're all grown up and getting married so soon," she said with a catch in her voice.

"Mom," Amy protested sleepily, "if I'd waited any longer, I would have been an old maid."

Long after Amy slept, Paula lay awake thinking about this new and unexpected turn of events. She had always imagined that she and Amy together would plan the details of Amy's wedding, but now she had been informed about it after the fact. Would things have been different if she had been home instead of here at the university? If only they hadn't put the house on the market, Amy surely would have kept her plans for a late August wedding. So here was one more thing to feel guilty about, as if she didn't have enough already.

The cafeteria was less crowded on Saturday mornings than usual as students took advantage of no classes and slept in. Paula and Amy were lingering over second cups of coffee and conversation with Ruth and Louise.

"I can't believe how much your daughter looks like you, Paula."

"Thank you, Ruth. That's a very nice compliment for me."

"For me, too, Mom." Amy looked fondly at her mother.

"You look more like sisters than mother and daughter," Louise observed.

"I agree with you, Louise," Amy told her. "My mom could pass for a regular student here."

"Instead of a creeping coed?" Ruth asked wryly.

"None of you are in that category," Amy assured her.

"So what do you have planned for the day?" Louise asked Paula.

"We're going shopping later on, and I haven't mentioned this yet, but I was thinking of taking Amy to see the Winthrope Paper Mill."

"Paper mill?" Amy looked a bit skeptical.

"It's really a museum and gardens."

"They say it is lovely," Louise assured her.

"You haven't been?" Amy asked.

"Not yet."

Amy met her mother's eyes and with her unspoken approval issued an invitation.

"Then why don't you and Ruth come with us?"

Ruth looked hesitant. "That sounds great," she said, "but wouldn't you two rather spend the day by yourselves? We can always go another time."

"We'd love to have you," Amy assured her.

"Well, if you are sure . . ." Louise began.

"We're sure," Paula said. "So let's get started as soon as we can before the heat becomes unbearable."

"Mom, I'm so glad you brought me here. This is fantastic," Amy said as the guide concluded her remarks and left them on their own.

"I'm ready for a Coke," Ruth said and headed for the soft drink machines.

"I'll join you in a minute," Louise told her.

Paula looked at Amy. "Would you like to see the gardens?"

"Sure, Mom. I don't want to miss a thing."

As Paula led the way into the courtyard she saw Greg Winthrope pruning a jasmine vine that spilled over the courtyard fence a few feet ahead of them.

"Good morning," she said as they came nearer.

Greg turned at the sound of her voice and smiled with evident pleasure. "Why, good morning. I hadn't expected you today."

"I wanted my daughter to take the tour and see all this for herself," Paula answered.

"I'm very impressed with everything," Amy said. "I've never seen another business quite like it."

"Amy," Paula put an arm around her, "I'd like you to meet Mr. Gregory Winthrope." To Greg she added, "This is my daughter, Amy."

Greg smiled warmly. "How do you do?"

Amy gave her mother a quick look of surprise before she responded. "Hello, Mr. Winthrope."

"Are you enjoying your visit to the university?" Greg asked.

"Why . . . yes. But how did you—?"

"I told him." Paula said quickly. "I've told everyone that my daughter was coming to the campus this weekend.

"Now that I see you, Amy, I can understand why," said Greg.

"Thank you," Amy answered with as much grace as she could muster. Unspoken questions were plain in her eyes.

Greg pushed up the sleeve of his coverall and looked at his watch. "It's later than I thought. Would you two care to join me for lunch?"

"Oh no, thank you. We had a very late breakfast," Paula explained.

"And we have two other people with us," Amy added.

"Which reminds me, we really should be going." Paula looked apologetically at Greg, and he nodded.

"I enjoyed meeting you, Mr. Winthrope," Amy said, "and taking the tour."

"Thank you, Amy." To Paula he added, "Enjoy your daughter's visit and take care."

"Goodbye." She turned with relief and walked quickly toward the area where they had left Louise and Ruth. Why had she ever thought it would be a good idea for Amy and Greg to meet? She surely didn't want Amy to know she had been out with him.

"When did you meet that man Mom?"

"Oh, the first time I came here with Sharon."

"He must be very wealthy."

"I'm sure he is. His family built Winthrope Hall in memory of his late wife."

"I didn't make the connection. Is he married now?"

"No." Paula opened the door, waved toward

two figures at the far end of the dining area. "Want a Coke before we go?"

"I'd rather have some pistachio ice cream."

"Pistachio? You hate that flavor."

"Not anymore."

"Want to come downtown shopping?" Amy asked Sharon when they got back to the university. "We've got to find Mom a dress for my wedding and we may need a second opinion."

"I don't know—I was headed for the library. Oh what the hey, I'll do that tonight," she said, and they headed for the car to ride downtown.

As they approached the bridal shoppe of the first large department store, Paula turned to Amy. "I forgot to ask you last night, have you decided on your colors yet?"

"I'm wearing ivory, and the bridesmaids dresses will be pale green."

"Then I should be able to find something in cof—"

"And Chris's mom is wearing beige lace."

"But the bride's mother always chooses first and I would like—" Paula stopped, then forced herself to start again. She would not make an issue over protocol. She would not get off to a bad start as a mother-in-law. "Then I'll look for a pale peach. It's my second-best color."

"That will look nice with your hair," Sharon said.

"May I help you, ladies?" asked a smartly dressed salesperson.

"Yes," Paula told the saleslady. "I'm looking for a dress to wear to my daughter's wedding."

The woman smiled graciously. "We have a large selection. Did you have a particular color in mind?"

"Well, I—"

"Something in a beige tone would look well with your coloring. Anything from eggshell to taupe."

"Actually, I was thinking of a pale peach."

"Over this way." She indicated a rack of various shades from light pink to deep salmon.

"Are these my size?" Paula asked doubtfully when the clerk held a dress before her."

"Oh, these are not for sale. They are samples. We order your selection in the size you need."

"Order? How long does it take?"

"Six to eight weeks. And since this is the busiest month for weddings, you had better allow eight."

"But my wedding is in three weeks," Amy said.

The saleslady gave her a disapproving frown. "I'm afraid I can't help you, then."

"But couldn't she buy one of these if we can find her size?" Amy persisted.

"Definitely not," the woman told her in an offended tone. "These are *samples.*"

"Never mind, honey. We'll look in the dinner dresses." Paula put an arm around her daughter and guided her out of the bridal department. This was supposed to be a happy occasion and she was not going to let this incident make it otherwise.

When they had exhausted all of the department stores they began a door-to-door search of the small dress shops. Just as Paula had begun considering the possibility of a draped bed sheet, they found a pale champagne lace that was acceptable in every way except price. Paula was shocked when she realized it cost more than she had in her checking account.

"I . . . I'd like to put a deposit on this and have you hold it for me," Paula told the clerk.

"We accept all charge cards and personal checks."

"I would rather you held it, just for a week or two," Paula insisted.

"Mom, if you're a little short, I'll pay for it," Amy said softly.

"Absolutely not." Paula's voice was sharper than she had intended, but it was embarrassing not to have access to instant credit, although it had been her own idea to give it up. She turned to the clerk. "How much do you need on deposit today?"

"Let me find out. We rarely do this anymore."

"I really would like to buy the dress for you, Mom."

"Your dad will pay for the wedding," Paula said. "All of it. So I'll just get a check from him this week to take care of the dress." It is the least he can do, she added silently.

"Okay, Mom. Dad can pay for the dress and you can reimburse me. But I'm going to buy it now so we can take it with us and you can try it on again tonight and let me help you with the hem." Amy's voice was firm. "And I won't take no for an answer."

Paula knew it really would be helpful if Amy pinned up the hem while she was here. She would just have to swallow her pride and accept her daughter's offer.

After the ordeal of the dress was over, they stopped for some ice cream.

"Would you like to swim when we get back?"

Sharon asked Amy. "There should be time before the cafeteria opens."

"A dip sounds heavenly." Amy smiled as she imagined it. "I didn't pack my suit, but I could use another one anyway, and they were on sale in the first department store we shopped."

"How about you, Paula?"

"I didn't bring one either, Sharon." Paula thought of the huge pool she had seen. It would be nice to spend some free time there— if she ever had any. Well, she had tomorrow. "Let's shop for swimsuits," she said. She could surely spare that much from her meager checking account.

Arms loaded with suits, Amy and Paula made their way to the fitting rooms. "All full. Wait, there's one at the back. Amy, can we share?" Paula asked.

"Sure, Mom, if it's a big one."

Amy turned her back in the cluttered cubicle. "Fasten me, please."

Paula fumbled with the tightly stretched clasp. "What size is this, Amy?"

"My usual."

"Well, they are making them smaller or else you're getting bigger," Paula teased her as she secured the fastener.

Amy studied herself in the mirror and Paula surveyed her, feeling a sense of uneasiness she would not acknowledge, she made a subtle suggestion. "Honey, I'd like to see you in that black maillot. It should make you look inches taller."

"Okay, Mom, if you'll try the wild one with the sea grape design."

Amy bought the black suit and Paula chose a white one-piece. When they left the fitting room, they found Sharon browsing among large beach towels with bright designs.

"Aren't these darling?" She indicated the rack of towels.

Amy reached for one with white shells on black. "You need this one, Mom."

"No, I'll just use a white bath towel I already have."

"I like this one." Sharon indicated a floral pattern on a background of teal blue. "My suit is that exact shade."

"Are you going to buy it?" Amy asked as she selected one for herself.

"Not today. Maybe when they mark them down."

Amy chose a bold abstract print with black accents and turned to her mother. "Mom, why don't you and Sharon get the car while I pay for our stuff." When Paula started to protest, she said, "You can pay me back later. It will save time we could spend at the pool."

Paula looked at Sharon who nodded her agreement. Together they headed for the escalator.

Seven

The drive back to campus was mercifully brief. When they reached Paula's room, Sharon said, "I'll meet you in ten minutes by the elevator."

"Wait," Amy told her. "You may want to bring this." She reached in the large bag she carried and gave Sharon the blue towel.

"Oh, I couldn't . . ."

"It's a present from me."

"But I can't let you buy—"

"When is your birthday?"

"In August, but—"

"Happy birthday, Sharon. From Mom and me."

"Well, I—"

"Please take it, Sharon," Paula urged, "Amy loves to give presents."

"Thank you." Sharon took the towel. "See you in a minute."

Paula turned to Amy when she had unlocked the door. "What a sweet thing to do."

"And here's yours, Mom. You sure made my shopping easier, selecting your own suit."

"Not the suit, too."

"Mom, I wouldn't give you just a beach towel for such a special occasion."

"I don't want you to spend all your money on me, Amy."

"Okay, Mom. We'll call it a birthday and Christmas present."

"But Christmas is six months away."

Amy shrugged. "So I like to shop early."

After a refreshing swim, Paula lay in a lounge chair beside the pool, half-listening to the conversation of Amy and Sharon beside her. The afternoon sun felt good on her pale skin and after slathering on a generous amount of Sharon's sunscreen she knew she was in no danger of burning. She had not been near a pool in ages. Not since she and Quent had chaperoned teen socials at the community clubhouse when Amy and Jeff were in high school. Theirs had been a typical small town existence but now, looking back, it seemed mundane. They had drifted through the best part of their lives without ever knowing the excitement of new places and people, but she had been totally content, insulated in her predictable life. Hadn't she? She was the product of a small town who had scaled her dreams and ambitions to fit the parameters of her small world. Until now. Maybe Amy was right. Maybe she was different from the person she used to be.

"Mom? Mom, are you asleep?"

"Ummm, no. Just relaxing."

"Then I hate to interrupt, but Sharon says the cafeteria is open and I'm starved. We missed lunch, you know."

Paula sat up and wrapped her new beach towel around her. "Never let it be said that I deprived my starving daughter of a decent meal."

Louise and Ruth joined them in the cafeteria and they consumed hearty helpings of fried chicken and vegetables, finishing with bowls of rice pudding topped with swirls of whipped cream.

"So we missed both shopping and a pool party all in the name of education first, fun last," Ruth said to Louise.

"I can swim in my backyard at home,"

Louise answered. "But shopping . . . Why did I listen to my head instead of my heart?"

"We can go again another Saturday," Paula promised.

"Then maybe I won't die of envy." Louise turned to Amy. "Have you enjoyed the day?"

"Yes, it's been great. And I am really glad I've gotten to know Mom's friends."

"It has been nice for us, too," Ruth told her. "I feel that we know two Paulas now."

As they left their table Amy suddenly stopped. "There's Derek, over by the window. See, he's waving to us. I'm going over to say hello. I'll catch up with you in the commons."

Paula watched her daughter as she headed toward Derek's table. She certainly had developed an instant rapport with him. Of course, Derek was easy to know and he had been charming to Amy, and their common interest in flying was undoubtedly a factor, too. She suddenly wondered what Amy would think if she knew her mother had been passionately kissed by this man.

Amy sat on an unmade bed, slowly brushing her hair while Paula modeled her new dress. She had put on high heeled shoes and swept her hair up in a French twist.

"What do you think, Amy? Will these bone slippers do or will I need shoes dyed to match?"

"Those are okay. They barely show anyway, even with the hem shortened."

"Good. I already have a small bag to match them so that will solve two problems. Now, what about my hairdo?"

"I like it. It makes you look very elegant. And I like your dress, too, Mom."

Paula turned to look at herself in the mirror above the chest. "I wish I could have ordered something really special. I just had no idea you would decide to marry so soon."

"Neither did I."

"Amy, if it is because of the house, we could always specify that—"

"No, Mom, it has nothing to do with the house, really." Paula turned back to the mirror and began taking pins from her hair. "Mom, I . . . there is something I need to tell you."

Paula felt her knees grow suddenly weak and she crossed the room and sat down on the bed beside her daughter. "Okay."

"I . . . Chris and I . . . are going to have a baby."

Paula took a deep breath while a gamut of emotions surged through her—surprise, disappointment, anger, dread, guilt, pain. "Oh, Amy," she said softly.

"So when we knew for sure, we decided to get married as soon as possible."

"When . . . did you know . . . for sure?"

"I missed my period the first of May. So I'm about two months now." Amy reached out to touch her mother's hand. "Mom, please don't be upset. We wanted children right away. It happened a little sooner than we expected but we *are* happy about it, and I hope you will be, too."

"I just . . . never dreamed this would happen. I had hoped that . . ."

"That you would be looking at wedding pictures before sonograms? Mom, Chris and I love each other so much, and we knew we would get married anyway. So it just happened."

"Have you told your dad?"

"No, Mom. We haven't told anyone. And we hadn't planned to until after the wedding."

"But now I know."

"That doesn't count."

"Thanks, I think."

"Mom?"

"Yes, Amy?"

Amy's voice was tremulous as she said, "I'm sorry if I've disappointed you."

Paula reached to enfold her daughter and hugged her hard. "Amy, it's not that. I just wanted things to be perfect for you." Paula stroked her daughter's silky hair and held her close to her breast, rocking her gently as though she were a baby herself.

"Thanks, Mom. I wanted so much to tell you and I'm glad I did."

After a late breakfast Paula and Amy attended a chapel service on campus and now lay sunning at the pool. Sharon and Amy were engrossed in a discussion Paula only intermittently followed.

"Mind if I join you?" A male voice broke into her reverie.

"Hello, Derek." She suddenly felt very exposed in her white swimsuit.

"Derek, you came," Amy said, smiling. "I was hoping you would."

"Yours was the best invitation I got," he told her as he spread a towel and stretched out on the chaise beside Paula. She could not help but notice that his lean muscular body was evenly tanned to the edge of his black trunks. She imagined a white beach and blue water and hula skirts swaying in the warm breeze.

"You're getting a nice tan. It looks good with your white suit, Paula."

"What? Oh, thank you," Paula answered, feeling awkward and suddenly shy.

"Ummm. It feels good to relax after all those hours squinting at microfilm."

"Did the report take that long? I was hoping to do mine tonight after we get back from the airport," Paula said.

"You won't have to. I got what you needed."

"Derek, I can't allow you—"

"It's already done, so you can't refuse." He grinned. "Now you owe me."

"Anytime, and thank you."

Derek and Amy swapped flying experiences for a while, then Sharon stood, put on her glasses, and said, "I really have to go. I've postponed my library assignment as long as possible."

"Hey—I was just about to suggest we go to the Inn of the Paper Moon before we head out to the airport. Can you come with us?" Derek asked.

"I'd really like to, but I expect to be at the library for hours."

"What a shame," Amy said sincerely. "You people work like slaves."

"Exactly. That's just what I told Paula, uh, your mom last week." Sharon picked up her towel. "Thanks again for my birthday gift,

Amy. And I hope all the wedding plans go smoothly."

Amy impulsively embraced the shy girl standing beside her. "Goodbye, Sharon. I hope I'll see you again."

Amy walked with her new friend to the gate and Paula watched her wistfully.

"You seem subdued today, Paula," Derek said.

How could he sense her moods so well? Was she that transparent? "I just wish Amy . . . could stay a little longer," she replied.

"How is your backstroke, Derek?" Amy asked as she rejoined them.

"Rather rusty, I'm afraid."

"Good. Then I challenge you to a race to the end of the pool and back."

"You're on."

"Loser buys dinner."

"That depends," Derek hedged.

"Don't think I'd lose deliberately in order to pay. I've got a very healthy competitive spirit."

"In that case, I'll take your bet."

Paula watched them move toward one end of the pool.

It was hard to believe she was going to be a grandmother.

* * *

Amy fastened her hair into a neat ponytail. "I hope you haven't neglected your work this weekend because of me. Everyone but you seemed to be spending an awful lot of time on class assignments."

"Let's just say I planned ahead," Paula answered.

"Speaking of planning ahead, should we go down to meet Derek yet?"

Paula looked at her watch as she fastened it onto her arm. "In a few minutes."

"I wish Sharon could have come with us," Amy said. "She's missing a great opportunity to be with Derek."

"I don't think she's interested in Derek," Paula said mildly.

"Well, she should be. He's is a great guy."

"But he's old enough to be her father, honey."

"Well, Dad is dating someone that young."

Paula drew her breath in sharply. "He is?"

"Oh—I thought you knew. Haven't your friends—?"

"I'm not in touch with anyone back home," Paula said quietly. She sat down on the closest bed, feeling as though she had just received a blow to her solar plexus. "Do you know who she is?"

"No, I don't know her name, and I don't

think she's from around Tuscumbia. I'm sure he met her through the band."

"Band? What band?"

"Haven't you talked with Dad lately? The country-western band he plays guitar for."

"I didn't know about that, either."

"Well, neither did I until I went home to get my things. As Dad was driving by our house he saw Chris's car, so he stopped to talk with us." She shook her head. "He looked so . . . different."

"How do you mean?" Paula asked, dreading the answer.

"He was wearing faded Levi's, and a tee shirt with the band's logo, and gold chains. His hair is a lot longer now and he's grown a beard."

"I see." And she could—she could see it all in her mind's eye. Quent changed into a man she didn't know, a hip musician who moved in a world that was totally alien to the life they had shared together. "And the girl?"

"She was sitting in his convertible, and the top was down so we saw her clearly, but we didn't meet her."

What did she look like? Was she pretty? "Convertible?"

"Yes, a red BMW. Dad just said she was a singer in the band. He seemed sort of embarrassed about it."

"Then maybe they're not—"

"Oh, yes, they are. I asked a friend who dates a guy in the band. And she said Bootsie was about my age and she had seen her out with Dad."

"Bootsie?"

"That's her stage name, because her trademark is all the different boots she wears. I don't know her real name."

"I see."

Amy crossed the room and put her arms around her mother. "Don't look so shocked, Mom. Chris says it's just a stage Dad is going through. He said he wouldn't be surprised if Dad came back to you when he gets it all out of his system."

"That isn't going to happen, Amy."

"I'm really sorry if I upset you, Mom. I thought you already knew."

"I didn't. But it's okay." Paula made an effort to sound more cheerful. "I'm glad I heard this from you instead of someone else."

"Oh Mom," Amy's voice was tearful, "I wish everything could be the way it was before . . ."

"Me, too, honey." Paula hugged her daughter closer. "But it can't be. So we have to make the best of the way things are."

"I know. And I'm proud of you for what you're doing. You have some really nice friends and you are different, too, but not in the silly way Dad is. I could never imagine you going out with a younger man."

Amy's words reminded Paula of Derek. "We should have been downstairs by now. Derek is probably double parked and wondering where in the world we are."

Amy picked up her flight bag. "All set, Mom. Let's go."

The Inn of the Paper Moon was more crowded than when Derek had brought Paula there on a Wednesday evening. Paula started to say so, then realized she would rather Amy not know about that. By coincidence they were seated at the same table as before but neither she nor Derek commented on the fact.

After they had placed their orders, Derek grinned at Amy. "So, are the plans all made for the big event?"

"Yes, we have everything worked out. I'm going to have a garden wedding at our house— at least it was our house before—I mean . . ." she stopped and looked toward her mother for help.

"Our house is for sale now," Paula said, "but we plan to have the ceremony and reception on the patio."

"Beside a fountain surrounded by my mom's roses. With classical guitar in the background."

"Sounds nice," Derek told her. "Reminds me of my wedding. It was in a courtyard gazebo of a famous old hotel."

"How romantic," said Amy.

Derek cleared his throat. "Yes. Well, where are you off to now?"

"This flight terminates in Chicago. I'll have a one night layover and then head back South."

"Do you ever fly with your fiancé—Chris, isn't it?"

"That was how we met. And sometimes our paths do cross."

"Flight paths, you mean?" Derek asked and they both laughed.

"Paula, you're very pensive tonight." Derek looked at her with concern. "Too much sun and fun this weekend?"

Paula forced herself to smile. "Oh no. I've had a wonderful time with Amy. I'm just sad to see her go."

"She always gets tearful when I leave, no matter how many times I've done it." Amy put her arm around her mother. "Moms are like that, I guess."

"Not all moms," Derek said quietly and his

166

eyes met Paula's and she knew he was thinking of Kurt Yearwood, too.

The waitress brought their orders then and Paula's mood lifted as they ate the delicious food. After sharing their fortunes, Derek reached for the check.

"I'm afraid this is getting to be a habit," Paula said.

"I always pay my debts. That daughter of yours has a mean backstroke."

"She should. She was on her school swim team for two years."

He scowled at Amy. "Hey, you didn't tell me that. I had no idea I was competing with a pro."

"You didn't ask." Amy laughed. "All is fair in love and contests."

"Love and *war*," Derek corrected her. "But never mind, let's get moving. You have a plane to catch."

At the flight gate, Amy turned to Derek and held out her hand. "Thanks for dinner, and chauffeuring, and everything."

Derek took her hand. "It was my pleasure. Have a good flight, and a wonderful wedding, and a happy life."

"Thank you, Derek. Good luck with school and a new career. And I really appreciate all the kindness you've shown to Mom."

"Again, my pleasure."

"Bye, Mom. I'll call soon. Don't worry about the wedding or . . . anything."

Paula gave Amy one last fierce hug. "Goodbye, honey. Take good care. I love you."

"I love you, too, Mom. Don't study too hard. And thanks for a really super weekend."

Paula stood watching her daughter as she hurried to board the plane that would take her miles away. When Amy's blond ponytail disappeared from sight, Derek touched her arm lightly. "I could do with a cup of coffee. How about you?"

"It's getting late and I really should try and get some studying done."

"Indulge me." He grinned at her. "I might fall asleep driving back to the campus."

"If you insist," she relented.

Derek guided her along the concourse, weaving around baggage-laden passengers, to a small dimly lit coffee shop. When they had ordered he said, "I like Amy."

"She likes you, too."

"I feel that I know a younger version of you now."

Paula winced inwardly, remembering Amy's words about being a mother image for her university friends.

Derek was silent as the steaming cups of

coffee were placed on the table, then he looked at her and asked quietly, "So what is the matter?"

She felt tears sting her eyes and fought to contain them. "It's . . . nothing, really."

"Your face tells me differently, Paula." Derek's eyes locked with hers and held. "Would you like to talk about it?"

"I can't," Paula whispered.

Derek took a sip of coffee as he appeared to struggle with some decision, then he said softly, "She is not the first girl to be pregnant before marriage, nor will she be the last."

Paula gasped. "How did you know—did Amy tell—?"

"Just a hunch, based on observation."

"I suppose *I* should have been more observant. I don't know how to deal with this. I keep wondering what I did wrong. I've tried to teach my children to be responsible people."

"I'm sure they are."

"And Amy was knowledgeable about birth control."

"So she and her fiancé obviously want a child."

"Yes, she told me that. But why couldn't they have waited a little longer?"

"It doesn't matter, Paula. What matters is that they love each other."

"It was all going to be so perfect, the garden wedding and reception. And now this hurry-up ceremony before she outgrows her dress."

"She will be a beautiful bride nevertheless. And a happy one, too, unless I'm badly mistaken."

"Yes, to both. But it seems such a travesty to have a big wedding and go through the ritual of joining two people together who are already about to be parents."

"Times have changed, Paula. Even having a child before marriage or with no marriage is commonplace. You know that."

"Yes, but those people are not my children."

Derek gently probed further. "Paula, how old were you when you married?"

"Almost twenty-one."

"And how long had you known your husband?"

"About six months."

Derek raised his eyebrows at her revelation but stayed on track. "And Amy has dated Chris for how long?"

"Since soon after he began working for the airlines. Over three years."

"So Amy is twenty-six, and she has been dating this guy for over three years and they are engaged to be married. Tell me, Paula, if that were you, would you have remained a virgin?"

"I guess I never really admitted to myself that Amy probably wasn't. But being pregnant is a different matter."

"You mean it's okay to sleep around if you don't get caught?"

"My daughter was not sleeping around," Paula said indignantly. "She simply expressed her love fully with the man she plans to marry."

"Exactly." Derek looked pleased. "I think you have this in the proper perspective now."

Paula thought about it for a moment. "Perhaps. But telling my husband still won't be easy."

"Paula, you don't have a husband." Derek's voice was compassionate as he went on. "I sense that you have always been the go-between in your family but you no longer have that role. Let Amy tell him. Or Chris. It is not your problem."

Paula sipped her coffee, weighing Derek's words. He was right, of course. She always had explained the children to Quent and vice versa. Was it a mistake to have done that? Didn't all mothers fulfill the roll of go-between? Now who would go between? Certainly not Quent's new girlfriend.

"Just when I thought we had solved all your problems and you could smile now, you look ready to cry again. What is it, Paula?"

"Some news Amy brought." She felt the corners of her mouth quiver and smiled brightly to cover it. "Quent has grown a beard and let his hair grow long. He has joined a band and . . . he's dating the band's twenty-five-year-old singer."

"Oh, Christ."

She felt tears in her eyes and fought to control her voice as she went on. "So I guess he has found what he was looking for. A new career and a new image and . . . a new love."

"Paula, he is a classic case of mid-life crisis, don't you see that? This has nothing to do with you. He's probably just belatedly sowing a few wild oats."

"Well, he could have sowed them with me instead of a girl young enough to be his daughter."

"No, he couldn't, Paula." He shook his head. "I never thought I would be presenting a case for the guy, but no. You were part of the status quo, the establishment. And he was craving change." His eyes studied her with a curious intensity. "But he was a fool to look for anything else when he had you."

Derek's kind words were Paula's undoing.

Her tears spilled down her cheeks unchecked as she made a futile effort to stop them. Derek grabbed her hand. "Come on, let's get out of here."

When they were inside the car, he made no move to leave the parking area. "Okay," he said quietly. "Let it go." He enfolded her and the warmth of his touch and the compassion in his voice allowed Paula to vent her pent-up emotions at last. She cried for Amy and a hurry-up wedding. She cried for a husband who had not been satisfied with a good life and a family who loved him. She cried for Jeff who was so far away. And she cried for herself who was left to pick up the pieces and go on living.

"It . . . it's just that nothing has turned out right," she whispered brokenly. "Why did it all go wrong?"

"It hasn't all gone wrong," Derek told her gently. "You are at a crossroads, and taking a different direction is always difficult. But it will get better, I promise. I'm living proof of that." He stroked her hair, much as she had comforted Amy, and she experienced for one of the few times in her life being the receiver instead of the giver of consolation. Then he kissed her softly on the forehead and said in a husky whisper as he released her, "I had better get you back to the dorm. You've had quite a weekend and you have a hard week ahead."

"Thank you, Derek," she whispered. "For everything."

"You are welcome, Paula. For everything."

Eight

"I hate Mondays," Ruth mumbled as she stood at the lavatory sink brushing her teeth.

"I can see that. You're foaming at the mouth just thinking about them." Louise, standing at the next lavatory, splashed cold water on her face.

"Good morning." Sharon stuck her head inside the door as two students rushed out. "Anyone ready for breakfast?"

"Bah, humbug," Ruth said.

"You go ahead and save us a table," Louise said. "We'll be over in about ten minutes."

"Don't count on me," said Ruth. "I think I'm going back to bed."

Louise laughed and waved her hand. "Just a bad case of Monday morning blahs. Pay her no mind."

"Hello, everyone," sang Paula as she appeared in the doorway and headed toward a shower stall.

"Not another cheerful morning person," Ruth groaned.

"Good morning, Paula." Louise blotted her face with a small hand towel. "Are you skipping first period class today?"

"No, but I slept through my alarm so I'm going to skip breakfast."

"She wouldn't dare miss Dr. Ben's class," Ruth shook her head, "or even dare to be late. He would think for sure she had been out partying all weekend." She raised her voice over the sound of running water. "See you in class, honey."

"Okay." Paula let the warm water pour over her as she lathered, then switched to almost cold for a wake-up shock effect. Wrapping a thick towel around her, she hurriedly dried her hair. No time for a curling iron this morning. She had not realized how exhausted she was until now. It had been a very emotional weekend, planning and shopping for Amy's wedding, learning that she was pregnant, and hearing the devastating news about Quent's metamorphosis.

Sleep had been slow to come after Derek brought her home. Her mind conjured up images of Quent in gold chains and jeans with long hair and a beard. Quent playing guitar for a country-western band and driving a red BMW. Quent dating a young singer named Bootsie. Paula fumbled with her skirt fastener, unusually awkward in her haste and rage. She didn't know the person her husband had become. Correction—her ex-husband—as Derek had reminded her last night. What a spectacle he must be making of himself. And what a field day all the town gossips must be having. How could she face them at Amy's wedding?

And that reminded her of another problem. She would have to ask Quent for money to pay for her dress and prepare him for the other wedding expenses. She was sure he would have no idea how much it would cost. Well, damn the cost. If he could buy a new convertible and no telling what for some young bimbo, then he could very well afford to foot the bill to see his daughter married in style. His pregnant daughter—but if he knew that he would probably say she didn't deserve a wedding. Of course, the new Quent might take the news much better than she imagined. But somehow she didn't think Bootsie's guitar picking hot-rodder would take too kindly to the idea of becoming a grandfather.

* * *

"Hey, wait up, Paula."

Hearing a deep voice from somewhere behind her, Paula stopped and turned to see Derek and Ruth approaching from the direction of Gaither Hall.

"You were sprinting like an Olympic athlete," Ruth said, panting as they caught up. "What is the hurry? We still have ten minutes." She thrust a muffin at Paula. "Since you couldn't come to breakfast, we brought breakfast to you."

"Here is my contribution." Derek held out a styrofoam cup of steaming black coffee. "Why don't we take five and sit over there on the steps?"

"This is really very thoughtful of you both," Paula told them as she sat down and took the cup from Derek.

He grinned at her. "We didn't want you to pass out from hunger and lack of caffeine and have to haul you from class to class all morning, so we decided to feed you."

Ruth looked at her watch. "Five minutes and counting. Oh, how I hate Mondays."

"I'm finished." Paula swallowed a large bite and washed it down with coffee.

Derek picked up her books. "Come on, then, lady. The good doctor waits for no one." As she stood up, he looked at her with concern in his startling blue eyes and asked in a low tone, "Bad night?"

She started to deny it but his eyes caught and held hers, demanding an honest answer. "Yes, it was," she admitted.

The morning dragged interminably as Paula forced her mind to focus on taking notes while visions of Quent and his new love hovered on the periphery. His behavior was an insult to her and their children and she was probably an object of pity among most of the people who had known them as a couple. Of course, some might think if she had been a good wife Quent wouldn't have done this, but nothing could be further from the truth, she thought indignantly. She had been a supportive, loving partner, all any man should have wanted.

It wasn't enough that Quent had rejected her and walked out on her. Now he was flaunting some nightclub singer for everyone to see. Just like he had traded in his serviceable Buick for a red BMW, so had he exchanged his loyal wife for a flashy girlfriend. What had happened to the Quent she knew? Paula looked at her notepad and realized she had been scribbling words that were unreadable and muttered something unprintable under her breath. Mercifully, the bell rang and for the time being she was spared any more effort.

* * *

Fortified with food and the fellowship of her two friends, Paula made her way back across the commons for the afternoon session. The noonday heat was stifling and an almost tangible lethargy had settled over the campus.

"This place is hotter than the tropics," Ruth said as they approached Oldham Hall. "At least there we have a constant breeze from the ocean."

"This place is probably hotter than hell," Derek countered, ". . . though I have no desire to prove it."

"It does take some getting used to, I guess," Paula told them, "but to me it's just another typical summer."

"Spoken like the true native that you are," Derek said as they entered the cavernous ground floor. The area was not air-conditioned and the ceiling fans pulled a warm breeze through the room.

Paula walked ahead of Derek and Ruth to where Kurt Yearwood was waiting a little aside from the others. "Hello, Kurt," she said. She forced her voice to be cheerful. "Did you have a nice weekend?"

The thin boy neither looked at her nor answered her question but instead spat on the floor directly in front of her sandal-clad feet. Her first impulse was to scold him for such rudeness but she checked her response. He wants to make a scene, she told herself. Don't let him do it. She reached into her purse, took out a tissue and held it out. "Here," she said quietly.

Surprised by her reaction, Kurt quickly looked at her and encountered her level gaze. This was a moment that would establish which of them was in control of the situation and both knew it. *I am letting you off the hook. Don't challenge my authority,* her eyes told him. He read her message and wavered for a moment, then took the tissue and bent to swipe at the small glob of moisture that glistened on the dark tile floor.

"Nice going," Derek said softly as he and his charge passed her on the way to the alcove where they worked.

Paula followed Kurt to their table and opened a workbook. "Today we will begin with a review of the short vowel sounds. Give me a word that has a short 'a' sound, please."

Kurt hesitated, pushed back a lock of hair, and said "Apple." With a sigh of relief Paula knew the crisis had passed.

The hum of voices in the hot room droned on with an almost hypnotic rhythm which was

181

finally interrupted by the ringing of Faye Browne's bell.

"Whew—what a long afternoon," Derek said as he and Paula watched the students rush past them to get outside. "I could do with some fresh air myself."

"Me, too. I almost fell asleep doing those monotonous phonics drills."

"How is it going?" Ruth asked as she joined them near the doorway.

"Very slowly." Derek held the door and Ruth and Paula stepped outside.

"Say, isn't that a cigarette I see in Irvin's hand?" Ruth motioned to a small cluster of students under a live oak tree.

"So it is," Derek said. "I'm clear on the no smoking rule now so I guess I'll just have to take care of this."

As he walked toward the group, Norma Oakley saw him coming and nudged Irvin Pendergrass, who thrust his cigarette into Kurt Yearwood's hand.

"Here, man, take a draw," Irvin urged the younger boy.

Kurt, whose back was to the approaching tutor, looked shocked, then pleased. He put the cigarette in his mouth just as Derek spoke.

"Okay, Irvin, put out the cigarette and come with me."

Irvin turned with a look of innocent surprise. "What you talking about, man? I ain't got no cigarette."

And to his chagrin, Derek saw that it was so. He looked at Kurt, stopped in mid-draw by his words. "So I see," he said dryly. "But I guess it won't take but a word from Kurt here to prove that you did have, up until a minute ago." His eyes were locked with the unsuspecting culprit who had gone pale but still held the offending cigarette to his lips. "What about it, Kurt?" he asked kindly. "Who was really smoking that cigarette?"

Kurt lowered the cigarette, glanced quickly at Irvin, and looked defiantly back at Derek. "Me."

"Ah, come on, Kurt, stop covering for Irvin. He isn't doing you any favors." Derek waited expectantly for a retraction but none came. With a long sigh, he motioned toward the building. "Okay, whoever was smoking, come inside with me."

Kurt Yearwood dropped the cigarette on the ground and stamped it out with his shoe, then followed Derek inside.

"Irvin Pendergrass, you ought to be ashamed of yourself, letting Kurt take the punishment for what you were doing," Ruth told the tall boy who stood watching the retreating figures.

"I didn't do nothing," came the hostile denial. Norma snickered and rolled her eyes.

"Breaking the rules is bad enough, but denying what you did is worse." Ruth scowled at him and shook her head. "And as for you, Norma," she turned her accusing eyes on the girl who stood close beside Irvin, "I saw you warn Irvin that Mr. Vogel was coming, so you are also guilty in this little episode."

"I didn't do nothing either," the girl answered belligerently as the bell announcing the next session sounded from the doorway.

A chastised Kurt was sitting at the table when Paula walked into the alcove they shared. "Kurt," she said softly, "I hope you told the truth about what happened. It is good to be loyal to your friends but when someone tries to make you the fall guy—the one who has to pay for someone else's mistake—then it is better to defend yourself." The boy did not look up or make any reply. Paula resumed the phonics drill that had occupied them before the break.

"What a day," Derek said as he joined Ruth and Paula.

"It is still Monday, you know." Ruth grimaced. "Tuesday will have to be an improvement."

"Oh, Derek," Faye called after them as the three headed toward the door.

"Yes?"

"I'd like you to come up to my office so we can discuss this afternoon's incident."

"Now?"

"Yes, please." Her voice was all honeyed charm.

Derek looked at his two classmates and shrugged. "See you later."

"Oh, and would you help me carry this material?" She indicated a stack of workbooks on the counter. "I have to check all of these before I go home today. Poor me."

Derek picked up the stack of books and followed Faye toward the door to the back hallway while Paula and Ruth stood watching.

"It simply amazes me how that woman can turn into a helpless southern belle at the drop of a hat," Ruth said.

"Or in the presence of an attractive man," Paula observed tartly.

Ruth smiled. "I didn't think you had noticed."

"I'm not blind."

"Well, let us hope Derek Vogel isn't either. Otherwise that Lady Lothario will seduce him in her office before he knows what's happening to him."

"She wouldn't dare. A teacher and student? It just isn't ethical," Paula said indignantly.

"A graduate assistant, not a teacher—and it happens all the time, ethics or not." She shook her head sadly. "Believe me, our friend Derek is fair game for Miss Scarlett O'Hara II. And you have seen that computer-like mind in action when she's playing her professional role, so don't underestimate her tactics when she goes after a man. But it won't do any good to stand here watching the lioness haul her prey to her lair. Let's drag our weary bodies over to Gaither Hall."

"I'll second that motion." Paula cast one last look in the direction where Faye and Derek had disappeared and followed Ruth outside.

The cafeteria was already crowded when Paula and Ruth joined the line. Paula's spirits lifted somewhat as she smelled the aroma of coffee and steaming food. This was one part of campus life that she appreciated to the fullest. She was a good cook but the monotony of preparing three meals a day was a chore she did not miss at all.

"How about two helpings of dessert?" Ruth asked her. "A jolt of sugar will give you a boost of energy."

"Okay. I'll take a piece of this cherry pie and put ice cream on it."

"I'd count that one, honey," Ruth said. "Oh, there are Louise and Sharon, over by the window." She waved. "We're coming. We're coming."

When they had finished dessert and coffee, Louise stood up. "I'm going to the library and work until it closes. Anyone want to come along?"

"Not me." Sharon also stood. "I've got test papers to grade. I'm heading to the dorm."

"And I've got lesson plans," Ruth added. "So I'll go with you, Sharon."

"Paula?" Louise spoke again.

"I . . . I think I'll have another cup of coffee before I leave." Paula glanced once again toward the door which she had chosen to face while she ate.

Ruth, who had observed her expectantly watching for Derek, said in a low voice, "You may as well come with us, honey. He won't get here before they stop serving."

"Who?" Sharon asked.

"Our friend Derek who has been detained due to business."

"Monkey business," Paula muttered.

Ruth smiled with satisfaction. "A very astute observation. I'm glad you're coming around to my point of view."

"What are you two talking about?" Sharon asked with a puzzled frown.

"Nothing to trouble yourself about, child." Ruth told her, then added, "Come on, let's get going."

Paula watched her friends leave the cafeteria, then returned to the coffee urns and refilled her cup. She knew it was foolish to wait for Derek but he had waited for her after she and Faye Browne had talked about Kurt. Maybe he would need to talk today. But wasn't that what Faye was doing right now? She hoped that was all Dr. Colbert's sexy assistant was doing. Derek Vogel was too nice a man to have some scheming siren take advantage of him. Wait a minute. She was sounding like a mother. No wonder Amy had suggested that she was probably a mother figure to her new friends. She supposed Derek was savvy enough not to be taken in by Faye's faux helplessness. It was easy to see that she was about as helpless as a barracuda.

Paula slowly sipped her coffee as the crowd of students dwindled. She waited a few minutes longer after the line closed, then, with a sigh, drained her cup and returned to Winthrope Hall.

As she unlocked her door, Paula heard her phone ringing. Maybe Derek . . . she raced across the room. "Hello?"

"Paula? This is Greg Winthrope."

"Why, hello," she said.

"I hope I'm not interrupting anything?"

"No, I just got in—from the cafeteria."

"And that is my cue to ask you out to dinner Saturday night. If you don't have plans?"

"No, I don't have plans. And yes, I will be happy to have dinner with you."

"Good. I missed being with you last weekend, but you have a lovely daughter."

"Thank you."

"Did Amy enjoy her visit to the university?"

"Oh, yes, she had a wonderful time. All of my classmates made her feel so welcome." An image of Derek and Amy racing at the pool came to Paula's mind.

"I'm glad. When she comes again I'd like to take you both to dinner."

"Amy's getting married in three weeks, so I don't really expect her back."

"I'm looking forward to hearing more

about this when we have dinner. Shall I pick you up at seven? Same place as before?"

"Fine. I'll be there."

"Good night then, Paula."

"Good night, Greg. And thank you."

Paula held the phone a moment longer before she hung up. Greg Winthrope had asked her out again and she knew he would take her someplace nice for dinner. She would welcome the break in her routine and she enjoyed the way he made her feel so special. Then why was she disappointed that the call had not been Derek Vogel telling her about his meeting with Faye Browne? With a sigh, Paula sat down at her desk and opened her notebook. Normally she would have taken a hot shower before she studied but in case the phone rang again she didn't want to miss it.

"That will be all for today." Paula closed the book and smiled. "Goodbye, Kurt. Have a nice weekend."

Without replying, Kurt Yearwood bolted from the room. Paula sighed. All of her efforts to reach him so far had failed.

"Ready, Paula?" Ruth stuck her head through the opening in the partition that separated their space.

"As soon as I gather up this material."

"You're looking rather deflated. Has Kurt been acting out again?"

"No, and I almost wish he would. He just doesn't respond at all."

"Is he still having trouble with phonics?"

"Phonics. Sight words. Comprehension. You name it and Kurt has a problem with it."

"Poor kid."

Derek was just turning away from the counter as they arrived with their materials. "Thank God it's Friday," he mumbled.

"Right," Ruth answered. "Care to join us at Gaither Hall for happy hour?"

"I'd like nothing better," he looked regretful, "but I've got a meeting with Faye—Miss Browne—to discuss Irvin."

"He hasn't been smoking again, has he?" Paula asked.

"No. At least, not where anyone could see him. But Faye—we are working on some behavior goals that may help."

"I'm ready to go up to my office now, Derek," Faye trilled in her sugar-coated southern drawl.

"I'm coming." Derek smiled at Paula. "See you at the pool in the morning?" She nodded before he turned to follow Faye.

As they walked toward the cafeteria, Ruth shook her head sadly. "The *invincible* Miss

191

Browne seems to be stalking our friend with single-minded purpose, doesn't she?"

"Yes, it looks as though *her* behavior goals don't need any work. I've watched her play up to Derek all week."

"This is one time I wish my intuition had been wrong. Derek is such a nice guy. Too bad he has poor taste in women."

"Faye Browne is intelligent and attractive and—"

"What about kind and warm and caring? She is none of those things and he should be able to see through her facade."

"Well, I doubt if any man would. My husband—ex, I mean—is dating a girl young enough to be his daughter and I thought he had normal intelligence."

"He doesn't if he left you, honey—I already had that figured out. And you should have heeded Mama Ruth's advice on the alimony. Now he will be spending what rightfully belongs to you on that sweet young thing."

"Speaking of spending, I have to call him and discuss the cost of Amy's wedding. I've been putting it off all week, but I promised myself I would do it tonight."

"Lots of luck."

"Ruth, Paula—wait for me," Sharon called from behind them.

"I thought you said at breakfast you were going to skip supper for some research at the library," Ruth said as Sharon joined them on the cafeteria steps. "Did you finish early?"

"No, I decided to wait until tomorrow because I didn't want to come back to the dorm alone after dark."

"Why not?" Ruth asked as they joined the line inside.

"You haven't heard? A student was attacked outside the library last night."

"Oh no. Was she hurt?" Paula asked.

"Yes. They said she fought her attacker and she's in the hospital. Some say she was raped, others say she was robbed and beaten up. No one knows what really happened except the university officials, and they aren't talking. I can't believe you two didn't hear anything about it all day."

"You can believe it," Ruth told her. "We live in our own little world at Oldham Hall. Campus news wouldn't dare intrude into Dr. Colbert's program."

"Where is Louise?" Paula asked with concern. "She often stays late at the library."

"She's meeting us here," Sharon said. "She knows about what happened and she's not going to take any chances from now on."

"Good." Ruth picked up a tray and cutlery.

"We'll figure out a buddy system at dinner tonight. Then none of us will be at risk."

Paula slowly dialed the unfamiliar number and took deep breaths to steady her voice while it rang. One, two, three. Maybe he was not—

"Hello?"

"Quent? This is Paula."

"I know." A too long pause.

"I need to talk with you—about the wedding. Amy's wedding." Why was this so awkward? She had been married to this man for thirty years. He was the father of the bride-to-be. It was his responsibility to pay for his daughter's wedding, divorced or not.

"What about it?"

"We need to talk about the cost."

"Okay."

Why was Quent making this so hard for her? She took another deep breath and plunged in. "Amy plans to have a garden wedding—at our house."

"What if the house sells before then?"

"In two weeks. The first weekend in July."

"That soon?"

So he had no idea she was pregnant. "And there will be a reception, of course. She's not

194

sending invitations so that won't be an expense. And the roses will be in bloom which means much less decorating to do."

"Get to the point, Paula. I have to be at the club to play at nine. What will I be paying for?"

His brusqueness made Paula aware that she had been hedging. "Okay. There is the caterer, and a cake, some flowers, and a musician. The minister, the photographer, your tux rental, and of course, Amy's dress." She hesitated, then added, ". . . and mine."

"How much are you talking about, cost-wise?"

"Well, I don't exactly know. But I'd say about four thousand dollars."

"Four thousand dollars? My God, Paula, that would make a down payment on a house."

"But they aren't buying a house. And a girl only has one wedding, or at least, that's all she expects to have."

"I think that much money could be better spent for something else."

"Like a BMW?"

"Now wait a minute. How I spend the money I've earned is my own—"

"You wait a minute. I had a part in the accumulation of what we have, and I—"

"I offered to give you whatever you felt was fair, so—"

"Nothing is fair. You took my life away. You couldn't compensate me for that!"

"I didn't take your life. I simply asked for mine."

"Why? So you could date some hot little number in sexy boots who is young enough to call you Daddy? Sugar daddy, that is."

"Who told you—never mind." There was a silence on the line while he obviously got in control of himself. "Okay, I'll pay for the wedding, whatever it costs. Tell Amy to have all the bills sent to me. And Paula, we *are* divorced, so I *am* free to go out with anyone I choose. And I'm not the one who went off to college. You did. Don't forget that."

"I only left because I have to prepare to support myself again. I only came after you moved out and we were going to sell the house, and—"

"Okay. Let's drop it, shall we?"

"All right." It was as near an apology as either of them would be able to make. "But one thing more."

"Yes?"

"I'll need a check for my dress. Right away."

"Okay. How much?"

"Three hundred."

"I'll put it in the mail tomorrow."

"Thank you." She swallowed hard. "So I guess that's all for now. Goodbye."

"Paula?"

"Yes?" Her pulse quickened in anticipation.

"Is school going okay?"

"Yes." Her voice was flat with disappointment. "My classes are hard, but I'm making it."

"That's good. Take care."

After they said goodbye, Paula held the phone for a long moment, imagining a different conversation, a different ending. Why had she said those awful things to Quent? She had never meant to mention the convertible or the girl. And why had he made that strange remark about her going off to college? Surely he understood that she had to prepare herself for re-entering the job market.

Was it possible they could have gotten back together if she had stayed? Did Quent have an image of her as a carefree coed, partying with some campus jock? If Dr. Colbert could imagine that, why not her husband? Ex-husband. Wasn't she ever going to stop thinking of Quent as still married to her?

She stood up and crossed to the window. She had to get a handle on this. There was nothing she could have done to save her marriage. It had been Quent's choice to end it and she was making the best of things as they were. This was her life, and for now it was interesting and challenging and even fun. She looked out over the shadowed commons and thought about the danger lurking there.

And sometimes frightening, she added.

Paula lay beside the nearly-empty pool relaxing in the morning sun. She glanced again at the clock over the dressing room door. Derek should have been here by now if he was coming. She had studied late last night and her eyelids grew heavy and she napped, turning intermittently to avoid burning.

"Paula?" She floated back to consciousness and saw Derek standing beside her. "Paula?"

"Ummm? Hi." She smiled groggily.

"Want to go for a swim?"

"Sure." She sat up. "Maybe that's what I need to wake me up." She followed him to the edge of the pool, aware of the admiring glances being directed at his tanned torso by the other female sunbathers.

Sliding into the cool water, she swam three lengths of the pool, following a little behind Derek whose powerful strokes cut the surface with practiced ease. Then she turned and floated on her back as he treaded water nearby.

"Sorry I was late."

"I thought maybe you slept in. I didn't see you in the cafeteria."

"No, actually I was at Oldham Hall. Faye is helping me devise a behavior modification chart for Irvin." He did not meet her eyes.

"So you missed breakfast?" She sounded like a suspicious wife, cross-examining a husband.

"Yes, I . . . well, Faye brought some home-made raisin bread and we had coffee."

"Oh? I somehow can't imagine her making bread." Why had she said that? She was sounding like a shrew.

"It was really quite good." Derek's voice had a slightly defensive tone. "I thought Sharon would be here. Has she already left?"

"No. She went to the library instead. She was afraid to go last night after what happened."

"I heard about that. Faye said they believe the attacker was someone on campus, so he will probably strike again. You will be careful, won't you?"

"Yes," Paula told him solemnly. "Ruth and Louise, Sharon and I have formed a buddy system for after dark."

"Good. I'll escort you whenever I can but there will be times I'm not around. Now, about this evening. I wish Sharon were here because I was going to ask you both to go for pizza. I've heard of a great place out by the Interstate."

So Amy had been right. Derek would be interested in a girl of Sharon's age to date. "I don't know what Sharon has planned but I'm going to dinner with Greg Winthrope." Paula watched Derek's expression change to surprise.

"Of Winthrope Paper Mill?"

"Yes." She forced herself to remain nonchalant.

After a moment, he asked, "Have you known this . . . Greg very long?"

"Oh, a couple of weeks," she said airily as though dating one of the city's most prominent men was nothing unusual.

"We could go for pizza Sunday night," Derek said hopefully.

"Why don't you ask Sharon to go with you tonight? Amy thought you two should get together."

Derek looked further surprised. "She did, did she?" He shook his head. "I don't rob cradles."

Neither do I, Paula added silently before

she said aloud, "Then why don't you ask Faye Browne?"

Derek looked thoughtful. "Maybe I will."

Now whatever had made her suggest a thing like that? She was annoyed with Derek for being late and not realizing what Faye Browne was up to, but she had turned down his invitation to dinner and let him know she had other interests. She smiled at him. "I'll race you to the other end of the pool—and I've never been on a swim team so I'm not accepting any bets."

"What is a race without stakes?"

"Just fun," she answered as she turned over and swam away.

Nine

"Ruth?" Paula knocked lightly on the half-closed door.

"Hi, Paula," Ruth looked up from her typewriter, "Come in. Did you have a good time at the pool?"

"Yes, it was lovely."

"You're getting so dark. Are you trying to compete with me?"

"No, but my tan made me think I might look nice in your magenta blouse so I came to ask if I could borrow it for tonight."

"I'd be happy for you to wear it. I'm flattered that you liked it so much. Have you got a big date?"

"Sort of. I'm going out to dinner."

Ruth smiled. "Well, around here that qualifies as a big date. So where are you and Derek going?"

"I'm not going with Derek."

"But I thought—"

"Greg Winthrope is taking me to dinner."

"No wonder you're getting dressed up." Ruth went to the closet. "This may be a little loose on you, then again, maybe not. It fits me pretty snugly but my husband likes me to have a little bosom showing." She closed her eyes and sighed. "Ah, me, I do miss that man. It seems like forever since it's mattered whether my bosom shows or not."

Paula laughed. "Three weeks gone and counting."

Ruth took the blouse from the closet and gave it to Paula. "I'd lend you my long skirt to go with this but it would fall off your hips."

"I'll wear my short white linen. We're just going out to dinner, nothing formal. Thank you so much. I'll return the favor any time."

"Don't mention it. That's what friends are for."

As Paula applied her makeup she was interrupted by a knock at the door.

"It's me, Ruth."

"Come on in."

"Wow. You look stunning, especially your hair."

"Thank you. I decided it was long enough for a French twist now."

Ruth held out her hand. "I brought this scarf and flower that match the blouse to see if you could use either of them. And now that I see your hairdo, I opt for the flower."

"Yes, it would be nice." Paula turned away from her. "Would you fasten it in for me?"

"Sure thing, and let me tuck this wisp of hair up, too. Do you have an extra hairpin?" Ruth surveyed the results. "Perfect." She walked to the door, hesitated, looking serious. "Paula, they say fools rush in where angels fear to tread, so just call me a fool, but are you sure going out with Gregory Winthrope is what you really want to do?" Paula looked puzzled and Ruth went on quickly. "I mean, what about Derek? I thought you and he . . . until Faye Browne started batting her false eyelashes at him . . ."

"Derek and I are friends, just like us, Ruth. So Faye Browne has a perfect right to chase him if she wants. And catch him if she can."

Ruth groaned. "Don't wish that slinky siren with the computer brain on Derek. She's not his type at all."

"I'm sure Derek is capable of deciding who his type is without our help." She looked at her watch. "I have to go—Greg is probably waiting in the lobby already." She grabbed a small clutch bag from the bed. "Thanks again for the flower and the blouse."

"You're welcome." Ruth stood in the hallway watching Paula rush toward the elevator, a knowing look on her face. "Well, pardon me for butting in," she said softly, ". . . but I know what I see."

Gregory Winthrope was waiting by the lobby desk when Paula stepped out of the elevator. She had almost forgotten how handsome and distinguished he looked when he was dressed to go out. Any woman would be proud to have him for an escort, she thought.

Greg was speaking with the student at the lobby desk as he looked up and saw Paula. He came toward her, both hands held out to take hers. "Paula, how beautiful you are," he said.

She felt color rise in her cheeks. "Thank you."

"You've done something new to your hair and it is very becoming." Still holding one of her hands he led her outside to his car. "I was lucky enough to get a legitimate parking space this time." He helped her in and closed the door. "I've got a surprise for you, Paula. I hope you'll be pleased."

"I'm sure I will be."

"We're having dinner on our town's famous

riverboat. They have excellent seafood and entertainment."

"How nice," she told him sincerely, thinking that it really was fun to go out with Greg Winthrope.

The *River Queen* was already crowded with passengers when Greg and Paula boarded, but the maître d' led them to a secluded table near an open window. "You specified a view in your reservation, Mr. Winthrope," the man said as he seated Paula. "I hope you are pleased, sir?"

"Very nice, thank you." Greg gave the man a folded bill.

"The steward will be with you soon to take your order for drinks."

Paula looked across the water which was already darkened by evening shadows as the boat rocked gently in its mooring, lulling her with a sense of tranquility. She felt Greg's dark eyes bathing her in approval and a part of her reveled in his open admiration. She needed this to make her feel more alive, more womanly, and it was something that had been lacking in her life for too long. When had Quent last looked at her this way? Was romance something you sacrificed after thirty years together?

The steward appeared beside their table and Greg ordered a white wine she had never heard of but which she knew would be expensive. Then a horn sounded three short blasts and they got underway. As the boat headed into the deep channel of the river they silently watched the dots of light that were beginning to blink in the semidarkness on the receding shore.

Greg touched his wine glass to Paula's. "To many evenings together." He smiled at her and they drank in unison. From the deck a band began to play as Greg spoke again. "Now tell me about your lovely daughter."

Paula was pleased that he had remembered to ask. "Well," she began slowly, "Amy is engaged to a pilot. They plan to be married in two weeks."

"How nice. And where will the wedding be?"

"In Tuscumbia. At our house—former home. Amy wants a garden wedding."

Greg's eyes registered keen interest. "A garden wedding?"

"Yes, we have a flower garden in the backyard. There are brick walks and a fountain and roses. And tulips and hyacinths and shasta daisies, and . . . I could go on and on. There are flowers in bloom every season except for a few weeks in midwinter. After the children were gone, I spent a lot of time planting and pruning that garden."

"I would like to see your garden, Paula."

A sudden inspiration struck Paula and without further thought she acted on the impulse. "Then come to the wedding."

Looking chagrined, Greg made a feeble protest. "I really wasn't hinting."

"We live in a small town and I imagine almost everyone will be there, so one more person can make very little difference. Do come, if you would like to."

"I would be happy to come if my schedule will allow. You said two weeks from today? I'll check my calendar Monday morning and let you know." He beckoned a waiter who had been unobtrusively standing by and asked, "May I order for us again tonight?" When Paula nodded, he ordered shrimp cocktails and lobster with baked potato and a salad. "Now I want to know how your program has been going these past two weeks. Has Ben Colbert kept you busy?"

Paula smiled wryly. "Every moment. By the time I attend three morning classes, tutor a student all afternoon, then prepare lesson plans and do library work, I scarcely have time to eat and sleep."

"Speaking of the library, Ben told me about the attack on a student leaving there one evening recently. I hope you're taking proper precautions."

"My friends and I are watching out for each other."

"Good. The University Board will address the matter of more security at our meeting next week, but no amount of security can protect everyone all the time."

"And no one can protect the careless against themselves. Except for the front entrance our dorm is supposed to be locked every evening by dark, but most of the time someone props a back door open for easier access from the parking lot."

"I would hope they have discontinued that now."

"No, I'm afraid not. At least, one door was left unlocked last night. I discovered it when I went out this morning."

"I'll bring this up at the Board meeting. Perhaps we can get a new rule added to the dormitory Thou Shalt Nots."

"We've already been warned in our regular dorm meetings but some of the students choose to ignore it."

Greg looked at her with concern. "I will

worry about your safety now. And I'll do whatever I can to assure it."

When they had finished their lobster and been served a refreshing lime sherbet, Greg asked, "Would you like to go up on deck and dance? The River City Band plays nothing but golden oldies."

"That's my kind of music," said Paula with a carefree laugh.

He led Paula up the narrow stairs and onto the crowded deck. The only lights were from the makeshift stage on the bow where middle-aged musicians in white tux made music from a variety of instruments. Resting one arm lightly on her back, Greg expertly led Paula to the outer edge of the crowd. Here in the semi-darkness they danced to the languid rhythm of "Slow Boat To China."

A cool breeze blew off the water and overhead the black sky was dotted with stars. Paula felt as though she were in a make-believe world where happy endings were once again possible.

"You dance well, Paula," Greg said close to her ear. "I love dancing with you."

"I'm only following a good leader."

"Then we dance well together," he whispered.

The music became "Bridge Over Troubled

Waters," and they continued skirting the edge of the dance floor. Paula closed her eyes, shutting out everything but the music.

"Well, well. Hello." Paula's eyes flew open at the unmistakable sound of Dr. Colbert's voice.

"Ben. How are you?" They stopped and stood facing the couple.

"Miss Howard."

"Hello, Dr. Colbert, Mrs. Colbert."

The woman beside him gave a disapproving nod as he spoke again. "This is a fine evenin' for dancing. We've been twirlin' aroun' the deck, too. Do you mind if I take a turn with Miss Howard?"

Greg glanced at Paula and read the reluctant acceptance in her eyes. "Of course not," he said graciously, and stepping to one side, asked, "And may I dance with your wife?"

"She's all yours, my frien'."

Ben Colbert clamped a heavy hand on Paula's back and led her away. His steps were awkward and uncoordinated and with his face close to hers, Paula was almost overpowered by the strong smell of liquor. His hand slid lower to rest on her hip and he pulled her closer so that their bodies were touching from shoulder to knee. She resisted the impulse to jerk away, knowing he was almost drunk and

211

any resistance on her part could create an embarrassing scene.

"It's a nice night for romance, don't you think, Miss Howard?" She nodded and he went on. "May I call you Paula?" She nodded again. "A boat ride on the river, dance music, starlight, and a beau'ful woman." Paula remained silent. "You are a beau'ful woman, Paula." He leered at her, eyes not quite focused. "But you know that, don't you?"

She made no response to his question as she tried to think how to extricate herself from a situation that was becoming more unbearable by the minute. If only Greg would rescue her, but Dr. Colbert had led her to the center of the crowd and she had completely lost sight of her escort.

The band began playing "Harbor Lights" and Ben Colbert pushed his face closer and asked, "How about a li'l kiss, Paula?"

Her body stiffened in his embrace and she missed a step. "Please excuse me, Dr. Colbert but I really don't feel like dancing anymore."

He did not loosen his grip on her as she tried to figure out some polite way to escape his unwelcome attention.

"Excuse me, Ben. I believe this dance is mine." Greg's friendly but authoritative voice has an instant effect on Ben Colbert's behavior. Pushing her a polite distance away, he removed his hand and gave her a lopsided smile. "Thank you for the dance, Miss Howard. Have a good evenin'." To Greg he added, "Le's get t'gether soon for drinks at the club."

"I'll try."

Paula went gratefully into Greg's arms and he led her back to the deck rail and stopped. "Somehow I feel that you are no longer in the mood for dancing. The magic has gone out of the moment, hasn't it?"

"I'm afraid so."

"Don't let Ben upset you. He gets a little obnoxious when he drinks, but he has a great deal of pressure in his work and that seems to be his only way to unwind."

"It's just that he has such a . . . a Jekyll and Hyde personality."

Greg laughed. "Yes, I guess he does at that. He works hard and he plays hard. There seems to be no moderation for a man like him."

"How do you manage so well?" Paula asked. "You have a great deal of responsibility, too."

Greg smiled at her. "I dig in the dirt every Saturday. I find it excellent therapy for pressure. By the way, Ben has asked me to arrange a tour for the students in your program. Do you know about that?"

"No, when will it be?"

"Next Wednesday."

"I'll be looking forward to Wednesday, then," she said, and her mood brightened. A field trip would mean a brief reprieve from the daily lessons and perhaps even Kurt Yearwood might enjoy the experience.

Paula leaned her arms against the rail and watched the huge paddle wheel churning the water to create swirls of white spray that caught the deck lights in a prism of colors. "Isn't it lovely?" she asked softly.

"Not as lovely as you," Greg answered.

A sudden breeze from the direction of the wheels covered them with a fine mist and Paula shivered.

"You're cold." Greg put an arm around her and drew her against him. He rested his head against hers and they silently watched the mesmerizing motion of the boat plowing through murky water. What was Greg thinking, Paula wondered. Was he remembering a night like this with Rachel? Surely a man had different kinds of memories when death separated him from the woman he loved. At least he didn't have to wonder why Rachel left him. Or feel that if he had been a different kind of man she might still be with him. And he did not have to imagine her with a boy young enough to be their son.

"Oh, I almost forgot something important," Greg's voice broke the silence. "I am to invite you to my mother's champagne brunch tomorrow. Will you come?"

"Well, I . . ."

"She would like very much to meet you."

"Of course. What time?"

"Brunch is at eleven, promptly. I'll pick you up about ten-thirty in the lobby?"

"I'll be there," she smiled. "Promptly."

Greg chuckled and pulled her closer and Paula didn't resist. She liked feeling the warmth of his muscular body. It gave her a sense of security that she missed terribly.

They stayed on deck until the *River Queen* had docked; they were among the last to go ashore. As they stepped on the gangplank a very inebriated Ben Colbert swayed precariously just ahead of them while his wife tried to hold him steady. Greg moved quickly to her aid.

"Here, Shirlene, let me help," he offered gallantly.

"Well, hello agin, my frien'."

"Steady, Ben. Watch your step now. Okay, you're on dry land." Greg released his hold and the man wavered, then recovered himself. "Can you make it to your car, Shirlene?"

"Yes, thank you, Greg. We're parked just over there."

" 'Nite, my frien'. 'Nite, young lady."

With a sinking feeling, Paula watched the Colberts weave toward the street. She was certain he was even more convinced that she was trying to find a husband—preferably a wealthy one. How could he know that she had met Greg Winthrope by accident? And would he remember by Monday morning that he had asked her for a little kiss tonight?

Paula was removing her makeup at the lavatory mirror when Louise came into the bathroom. "Why, it's Cinderella home from the ball."

"And home early, so my coach wouldn't turn into a pumpkin."

"Do come and tell your stepsisters all about it. But wait until I go potty because I don't want to miss a word." Louise disappeared into a private cubicle as she spoke.

A few minutes later, Paula sat in her terry-cloth robe on the foot of Ruth's bed, completing her retelling of the evening. She had told about Dr. Colbert asking her to dance but not about him asking for a kiss. She ended with a question of her own. "What does one wear to a champagne brunch?"

"I think a pretty skirt and blouse would be fine," Louise said.

"I'd vote for that silk jumpsuit you have," Ruth added.

"But I wore that on my first date with Greg only two weeks ago."

"He probably won't even remember it," Louise told her. "Men are like that."

"The way she looked in that suit, he would remember," Ruth said. "But I have a jumpsuit. It's emerald green, which would match your eyes. I've been saving it for another party or something special."

"Then I couldn't possibly wear it," Paula protested.

"Yes, you could. At the rate my social life is going I won't need it, and we have to make sure you put your best foot forward when you meet Mama and Papa Winthrope."

"First impressions are so important, you know," Louise reminded her.

"Well, I do want to look my best," Paula said, "so I accept your offer."

"I've got a perfect pair of white earrings," Louise said. "I'll rummage through my drawers and try to find them."

"Then she shouldn't wear the gold belt," Ruth said to Louise. "I think the matching scarf I tie in my hair would go around her waist and loop." She, too, began searching drawers.

"I'm beginning to feel like a store window mannequin. Are you two going to dress me in the morning?" Paula giggled.

"No, honey, we'll be sleeping in, so you are on your own. And speaking of sleep, you need to run along. We can't have you waking up with dark circles under your eyes." Ruth gave Paula the suit and scarf and practically pushed her toward the door.

"Wait," Louise called. "I've found the other earring I was looking for." She placed them in Paula's hand. "Have fun."

"Yeah, have fun," Ruth called without much enthusiasm as Paula walked toward her room, then shook her head sadly. "I still don't feel right about this. I wonder if we did her any favors."

"What do you mean?" Louise looked puzzled.

"I just don't know about this Gregory Winthrope. Sure, he's handsome and sophisticated and he has a lot of money, but he is so much older than Paula."

"But he's real down-to-earth," Louise giggled. "Literally. I think any big executive who digs in his own flower beds has a good sense of values."

"Spare me the counselor talk, honey. I didn't mean to imply there is anything wrong with *him*. I just don't think he is right for *her.*"

"Well, she deserves something better than the guy who walked out on her for no reason."

"I agree, and I've got just the man for her."

"You mean Derek Vogel?"

"Sure thing. I've seen the way he looks at her with those gorgeous blue eyes when he doesn't know I'm watching. But Paula says they're just good friends. And of course, that's all they will ever be if Faye Browne sinks her talons into that sweet guy."

"I take it you don't approve of that at all."

"You've got that right. I think I know a good match when I see one and those two would be as mismatched as one brown and one purple sock."

"Well, Miss Matchmaker, you can lose sleep over this if you want to, but I'm hitting the sack."

"Me too," Ruth closed and locked the door. "But if I can see it, why can't they?"

"Love is blind," Louise mumbled sleepily as she crawled into bed.

"That is *not* what the expression means, but

you may be right. I'll think about it tomorrow. Good night." Ruth yawned and turned out the light.

Greg Winthrope drove the sleek Jaguar slowly through the wide tree-lined streets of the city's finest old neighborhood. Antebellum mansions with tall pillared porticos sat far back on either side, partially obscured by a panoply of ivy, boxwood, magnolias, and Spanish moss.

Paula forced herself to take deep, even breaths to dispel her nervousness. *There is nothing to be nervous about,* she told herself again. *I have been invited to breakfast by the parents of a man I have casually dated a couple of times. It is not imperative that I make a good impression.*

Greg, seemingly sensing her apprehension, made small talk, pointing out houses whose occupants had played a part in Alabama's history. Then he slowed the gold car and turned into a winding drive that led to a magnificent old red brick structure which Paula was sure had belonged to the Winthrope family since it was built.

As Greg opened Paula's door he looked at

her with admiration. "You look adorable, Paula. Everyone will love you."

A uniformed maid opened the massive front door as they went up the steps. "Morning, Mistah Gregory. I was watching for you. Morning, Miss." Her eyes swept over Paula with friendly interest.

"Mellie, this is Paula Howard." To Paula he added, "Mellie has been with us since I was a child. In fact, her son was my first playmate."

"Hello." Paula exchanged smiles with the large dark woman who was staring at her with open approval.

"Everybody is in the dining room, Mistah Gregory, so take Miss Paula on in there and show her off."

"That I will, Mellie." He took Paula's arm and led her across the hallway with its graceful winding staircase, to double doors that opened into a spacious room where several people stood talking.

A regal white-haired matron looked up as they entered and a flicker of something Paula could not determine crossed her features before she smiled and came forward with outstretched hands.

"Good morning, Mother." Greg took one of the slender blue-veined hands and kissed the cheek she inclined slightly toward him. "May I present Paula Howard. My mother, Lillian Winthrope."

"How do you do?" Paula took the other hand, laden with clustered diamonds.

"I'm so pleased to meet you." Her smile did not quite reach her eyes. Her voice was cool and smooth.

A quick survey of the room's guests told Paula all of the women were dressed in skirts and she rued her borrowed emerald jumpsuit.

"As soon as you have met my husband and our other guests I will have Mellie serve the buffet," Mrs. Winthrope added.

"Then I'll make quick work of the introductions," Greg said as he put an arm affectionately around his mother. "I'm famished. Has Mellie made her fabulous raspberry tarts?"

Mr. Winthrope was engrossed in conversation with another elderly couple but he stopped in mid-sentence as they approached.

"Father, may I present Paula Howard."

Paula quickly extended her hand which the older Mr. Winthrope took and held as he studied her benignly.

"I'm delighted to meet you, Miss Howard."

"Please call me Paula," she said impulsively, feeling an immediate rapport with this older version of Greg.

"And this is Mr. and Mrs. Gaither, my parents' next-door neighbors and lifelong friends." Paula smiled and exchanged proper pleasantries with the elderly couple whom she knew to be somehow connected with the university's Gaither Hall.

She was also introduced to a Mr. and Mrs. Oldham, a Mrs. Rhodes, and other people whose names were the same as those she had encountered on campus. Just as she was beginning to feel totally out of place among the city's scions, Dr. Benjamin Colbert's haggard face appeared in the doorway.

"Benny. I had given up on you." Mrs. Winthrope went forward to meet the Colberts, embracing them both. "Shirlene, how sweet you look."

Sweet was not an adjective Paula would ever apply to the dour-faced Mrs. Colbert, but she reasoned any woman married to the unpredictable Dr. Colbert had little to smile about.

The finishing touches had been added to the buffet; the guests gathered around the table to fill their plates.

"It looks lovely as always, Mrs. Winthrope," Shirlene Colbert remarked as she took a generous serving of grits.

"Thank you, dear. And Mellie has made your favorite butter pecan coffee cake."

"Oh, you spoil me, Mellie." Shirlene's face dimpled with delight and Paula caught a glimpse of how she must have looked in younger days.

"Here you are, Miss Shirlene. I saved a corner piece just for you." Mellie placed a large portion on a plate and gave it to her, then looked at Paula. "Miss Paula, would you care for some of my coffee cake?"

"Yes, I'd like a small piece, please. I want to save room for your special raspberry tarts, too."

Mellie beamed proudly. "I've been making that recipe for Mistah Gregory since he was a little boy."

"And every batch is better than the time before," Greg spoke from behind her.

"Ah, go on, Mistah Gregory. Don't be telling lies on the sabbath."

"Honest, Mellie." Greg took three tarts from the tray and put one on Paula's plate.

To her dismay, Paula found herself seated between Greg and Ben Colbert. "Good morning, Dr. Colbert," Paula said as she arranged her large linen napkin in her lap.

He nodded, then looked at her intently. "Fancy seeing you again so soon, Miss Howard."

She smiled to acknowledge his facetious remark but remained silent.

"For a stranger to this town, you seem to have made friends rather quickly and with all the right people."

Paula glanced toward Greg but he was engaged in conversation with someone across the table and had not heard Ben Colbert's words. Hoping to avert any further insinuations, she asked, "Have you always lived here, Dr. Colbert?"

"No. Just since university days."

"Coffee, Mistah Ben?"

"Yes." He took the steaming cup Mellie offered and drank it immediately. Then he picked up the champagne goblet beside his plate and downed its contents with one gulp.

"But I believe your wife is a native," Paula continued in an effort to keep the conversation on a safe topic.

"Yes," he answered, "my wife was to the manor born while I, like you, Miss Howard, had to charm my way into the sacred environs of the University Club."

Paula felt color rise in her cheeks as she imagined that all the people sitting nearby must have heard Ben Colbert's pointed remark. But when she glanced around her, no one seemed to be paying the slightest attention to them. She concentrated on eating her raspberry tart as Dr. Colbert morosely drank his coffee.

Greg turned to her with a smile and said in a low voice, "This isn't so bad, is it?"

Paula returned his smile and shook her head, grateful that he was unaware of Dr. Colbert's insulting remarks. After lingering over more champagne and coffee interspersed with quiet conversation, the guests finally began to take their leave. Greg and Paula were among the first to say their goodbyes.

At the door, Paula extended her hand to Greg's father. "I enjoyed meeting you, Mr. Winthrope."

He placed an arm around her shoulder. "You must come back to see us, Paula, so that we can get to know you better."

Paula spoke more formally to Greg's mother but no less sincerely. "I had a lovely time, Mrs. Winthrope. Thank you for inviting me."

The woman's dark eyes swept over her again in appraisal and something else she could not quite name. "I'm glad you enjoyed it. I'm afraid we are rather boring to anyone who doesn't know us very well." She turned to Greg, dismissing Paula. "Will you be back for dinner, Greggie? It's leg of lamb and your favorite peach cobbler."

Greg kissed her wrinkled cheek. "I wouldn't miss it."

In the car Paula asked, "Have you always known Mrs. Colbert?"

"Shirlene? Yes, since grade school when she was Shirlene Marie Oldham. The Oldhams you met today are her aunt and uncle. Her parents died in a plane crash several years ago."

Paula was quiet, thinking about Dr. Colbert's remarks. So he had married a wealthy woman who belonged to the elite social strata that controlled the university. By his own admission he had charmed his way in, but she wondered if Shirlene or anyone else found him very charming now.

At Winthrope Hall Greg said, "I hope to see you again soon, Paula. It has been a wonderful weekend for me."

"I've enjoyed it, too," she told him, and realized she really meant it.

On her way upstairs Paula smiled to herself. Attending a champagne breakfast with the town's University Club members was pretty heady stuff. And the people there had accepted her graciously even though she wasn't one of them. At least, everyone except Dr. Colbert and Greg's mother, who had been carefully polite but very cool. Mrs. Gregory Winthrope III must have thought she was a serious threat to her darling Greggie, a scheming divorcee bent on catching a rich husband. She and Ben Colbert had probably compared notes on her after she left and if they had, she was certain they had been in complete agreement. Neither of them would ever believe the last thing she wanted was a new husband. Or that the thing she wanted most in all the world was to have her ex-husband back.

Ten

Paula placed the borrowed jumpsuit on a hanger. She was grateful to Ruth for sharing her wardrobe and there was no need to tell her or Louise that she had been the only one at breakfast who wasn't wearing a skirt. Had younger women been there, many would no doubt have been dressed as informally as she. But Shirlene Colbert, who was at least sixty, had been the most youthful woman there, and Mrs. Winthrope's generation always wore hose and heels and girdles and pearls.

The phone's sharp ring abruptly ended her reverie. "Hello?"

"Paula? Where in hell have you been?"

She recognized Derek's voice instantly although the tone—somewhere between a bark and a growl—was new to her. "AWOL, apparently, sir, from your behavior," she said in an offended voice and added a question of her own. "Do you plan to arrest me?"

After a moment of silence on the line, a contrite Derek responded. "I'm sorry I spoke to you like that, Paula. It's this damned military persona I can't seem to discard. But I saw Sharon at breakfast and she had no idea where you were. I was ready to form a search party if you hadn't answered just now."

She felt obliged to offer some explanation since he was obviously concerned about her. "I went out to brunch." She refrained from saying where or with whom.

"Well, next time, please let someone know. I thought you had a buddy system over there."

"We do, and Ruth and Louise knew where I was."

"Oh. I didn't see them this morning. I guess they slept in."

"Yes, they did, and Sharon was asleep last night when I announced my plans. I hadn't expected anyone to worry."

"Well, I did but now that I know you're safe, I'll get on with the other reason I called. Guess who is here on campus?"

"I—I really don't have any idea."

"My son Todd. He flew in and surprised me late last night, because today is Father's Day."

"I hadn't realized that." She was struck with a sudden feeling of guilt. Had Amy and Jeff remembered Quent today? She had always been a part of the celebration, too, buying gifts and planning a special dinner. Had someone made dinner for Quent this year? She doubted that Bootsie would help Quent celebrate being the father of two children as old as she was. And thinking of Quent and his young songbird made her so angry she didn't care whether he even had dinner, much less a special one.

"We're going over to the state park, maybe take a boat ride on the lake and do a little sightseeing. Todd has never been in this part of the country before. Sharon is coming with us and I want you to come, too."

"Well, it sounds like fun, but—"

"Will you come then?" She hesitated only a moment before agreeing. "Great. We want to leave in about half an hour and have a picnic in the park."

"What can I bring?"

"Nothing, except your swimsuit in case we decide to go in the water at the lake. Sharon said she would meet us in the parking lot at one. Can you be ready that soon?"

"Yes, of course."

"Great," Derek repeated. "See you then."

It was evident he was excited about Todd's visit and the day's activities. She knew she ought to study but Derek had been so nice to Amy and she was pleased that he wanted to include her in their plans. Of course it was probably because he needed another female along since Sharon would be with Todd.

Paula had already changed into yellow crinkled-cotton slacks and a yellow and white striped tee shirt. She brushed her French twist into a ponytail, fastened it with a white scarf, then put her swimsuit and beach towel into a white canvas bag and went to knock on Sharon's door.

"Hi, Paula. Where have you been?"

"Greg Winthrope invited me to a champagne brunch at his parents' house."

"Wow. Was it fun?"

"Not really." She found she didn't really want to discuss it.

Noting Paula's beach bag, Sharon said, "I see Derek finally reached you. He was getting frantic about where you were. And I'm glad you are going with us. I had breakfast with Derek and Todd and they planned the whole day while we ate."

"I'm looking forward to meeting Todd."

"He's really nice. Cute, too. He has his daddy's eyes."

"Are you ready to go?"

"Soon as I put a few things in my bag."

"Then I'll meet you at the elevator. I want to return Ruth's jumpsuit and tell her where we're going. No more disappearing acts for me today."

"Who is it?" Ruth called in answer to Paula's knock.

"Me, Paula."

"Well, don't stand out there wasting time," she opened the door. "Come in and tell us how it went."

"I don't have time now." Paula gave her the hanger. "Derek's son is on campus and they asked Sharon and me to go on a picnic with them to the state park. We're leaving in a few minutes."

"How nice." Ruth smiled broadly. "The details on brunch can wait." She gave Paula a speculative look. "My, you do get around. Maybe Dr. Colbert had you figured right."

"Don't you start that, too. Derek just needed a female chaperon for his son's date today."

"He could have asked me," Louise said, from across the room where she sat at her desk, drinking coffee. "Counselors make excellent chaperons."

"Or me, or Faye Browne, but the fact is he

asked you. So run along and have fun, and we'll hear about brunch later."

"Okay, but you'll never guess who was there."

"Don't keep us in suspense," said Louise.

"Benny."

"Not him again?" Ruth shook her head. "What was *he* doing there? Now the suspense is worse than ever."

"Tell you about it later," Paula called back over her shoulder as she hurried to meet Sharon.

The blue Firebird pulled into the parking lot, Derek at the wheel. When they approached, Todd got out of the car, smiling at Sharon. "I see you found her." He looked at Paula. "Hello, I'm Todd."

"Hello, Todd." She held out her hand and he took it briefly, then helped Sharon into the backseat and got in with her. Paula sat beside Derek and he reached across her to close the door, brushing her lightly with his bare arm. Their eyes met quickly as he said "Sorry." She wondered if he had felt the same tingling as she had when they touched.

Derek spoke. "First stop is an ice machine so we can cool down the beer."

"There's a large supermarket in the shopping center a few blocks from here on University Drive," Paula remembered.

"Now I know why we brought you along." Derek grinned at her. "And maybe later you can put some sandwiches together. We bought a lot of stuff and dumped it in the cooler but it needs a woman's touch."

"Chauvinist. I didn't know this would be a working holiday," Paula answered.

"Don't let him kid you," Todd said, "Dad has lived by himself so long he's become a real gourmet cook."

"Keep a civil tongue in your head, boy. You're ruining my image as a bumbling bachelor who needs a lot of TLC."

"Take it from me, Dad, women don't like to cook these days."

"I do," Sharon said.

"You do?" Todd seemed surprised. "I thought you were a career girl."

"There's no reason a girl can't have a career and also be a good cook."

"I'm glad you feel that way." Todd smiled at her.

"My generation didn't," Paula spoke up. "We thought you could be one or the other—but never both."

"And you are going after it—belatedly?" he asked her.

"Actually, no," she answered quietly. "I'm still doing one at a time. I'm not a homemaker anymore."

"Here we are," Derek said. "Cross your fingers and make a wish that this machine will give us ice or we may spend the day driving all over town looking for some."

"Need any help, Dad?" Todd offered.

"Nope, stay put. I can handle it."

Derek fed the machine a handful of quarters in exchange for two bags of ice which he emptied into a metal chest in the Firebird's trunk. Getting back into the car, he grinned at Paula. "A hot day, a cold beer, and a shady tree. What more could a person ask for?"

What indeed, she thought as they joined the stream of cars leaving town. Who needs pearls and protocol and champagne brunch?

The state park covered several hundred wooded acres bordered on opposite sides by a man-made lake and a river with a dam and hydroelectric power station at the point where they converged.

"Would you like to swim before we eat?"

Derek asked as they meandered through the winding shady trails.

"I vote yes," Todd said. "After that big cafeteria breakfast I need to work up an appetite."

"All-you-can-eat situations are hazardous to my son's health," Derek said in an undertone to Paula. "He will never learn to 'just say no.' "

"Especially to French toast and pancakes and donuts," Todd added.

"How do you stay so trim?" Paula asked.

"Slim genes, I guess. Mom and Dad are both tall and skinny."

"That always helps." So Mrs. Vogel was tall and thin, Paula mused. She had pictured the woman as about her own average height, and voluptuous.

"Say, Dad, I forgot to tell you. Mom and Mac have taken up biking."

Derek looked surprised. "Motorcycles? Have they joined Hell's Angels?"

"Nah, I mean bicycles, like you pedal. But they did join a biking club, and they ride all up and down the coast on weekends."

"Sounds like fun."

"Yeah, if Mac doesn't kill himself. He is kinda outa shape, you know."

"That's what a cushy desk job will do for you, son," Derek said lightly. He pulled into a parking lot near the water. "This looks like a good place to leave the car. There's a bath-house over there where we can change."

"I was hoping we were going skinny dipping since it's so hot," Todd kidded.

"Wash your mouth out with soap, boy. This is not the West Coast where anything goes, including nude swimming. You are in the South now where people act civilized. So out with you. Last one in the water has to prepare lunch."

A sandy beach sloped gradually into the placid lake and they swam leisurely, laughing and shouting back and forth. Finally Paula called, "Enough—I'm going ashore to dry off in the sun a while."

"Enough for me, too," Derek said. "We'll leave these young'uns to their fun. They have more energy than we old folks do."

"Ah, come on, Dad. You're Joe College now."

"Anyone over forty here is called a creeping coed," Paula called as she stepped out of the water.

"My dad is over forty? You could have fooled me."

"He doesn't look it, does he?" Sharon said.

"That's what all those military calisthenics will do for you," Todd told her.

Paula spread her beach towel and lay down, letting the hot sun dry her skin. "I like your son," she said.

Derek eased himself down on a towel beside her. "He's a good kid. Sure surprised me showing up here last night."

"You two seem to have a very special relationship."

"Like fathers and sons should. Or mothers and daughters, I guess."

"Yes, I feel Amy and I are close. But Jeff . . ."

"Doesn't have a close relationship with his dad?"

"Not really. They have been at cross purposes ever since Jeff started making his own decisions."

"Because they are not the choices his dad would have made for him?"

"Exactly. And I'm not saying Jeff always chose the right thing."

"Maybe there isn't any one right thing. Just whatever feels right for the person involved."

They were silent for a moment, each lost in their own thoughts.

"My husband tried to force our son to go to college."

"There are worse things."

"Not for Jeff, I guess. He went to the other side of the world to avoid it."

"Maybe not altogether. Most young guys have a sense of adventure, a touch of wanderlust. I've enjoyed roaming the world myself. The experience will probably make a better person of him, make him a more considerate and self-reliant man."

"I hope you're right."

"Trust me. The voice of experience has spoken."

Paula sat up and reached into her beach bag for sunscreen and began applying it to her body. When she had finished, Derek reached out his hand.

"Here," he said and she gave him the bottle. "I'll do your back."

Derek's strong hands gently massaging her back sent a shiver of excitement surging through her. She had forgotten what a man's touch on her bare body could do to her and fought the desire to turn and wrap her arms around him. She asked herself silently if she was so starved for love that she would offer herself to any man who touched her intimately.

"Turn over," Derek said. He took one of her feet between his hands and stroked it. "The soles burn, too." He administered the soothing balm to the other foot and surveyed it clinically. "You have a well-turned ankle," he declared finally.

Paula laughed. "The voice of experience speaking again, I presume."

"Absolutely."

"Then I thank you for your evaluation."

They lay in companionable silence, dozing and waking again as the noise from the swimmers grew louder from time to time. But Paula's body was still acutely aware of the sensations caused by Derek's touch and she wondered what might have happened if they had been here at the lake alone.

"Hey, Dad, how about some chow? We're starved."

"Huh? What time is it?"

"Nearly two."

Derek stood and pulled Paula up beside him. "Come on, lady. Help me make something presentable from the mish-mash of food I've brought."

Paula made sandwiches while Sharon got plastic plates, cutlery, and napkins out of a paper bag and set them on the picnic table that Todd had spread with a clean, white sheet.

"Anything else I can do to help?" Todd asked.

"Yes, give me a hand with these jars, please." Paula indicated pickles, mayonnaise, and mustard.

"I'll open the chips and cookies," Sharon said.

"Everyone want a beer?" Derek took a can from the cooler and set it on the table.

"I'd better not." Sharon said shyly. "Do you have any soda?"

"Sure. There is Coke and 7-Up and Dr Pepper and—"

"Coke, please."

"Me, too," Paula said.

"Todd?"

"I'll have a beer, Dad."

Paula set a plate piled high with sandwiches in the middle of the table. "Okay, listen carefully. There's ham and Swiss cheese on rye bread, chicken salad on oatmeal bread, turkey, cheddar, and tomato on wheat bread. Add your own condiments."

"I'll have one of each," Todd said.

"A boy after my own heart," Derek looked at Paula and grinned.

They traded jars around the table until each had seasoned to their satisfaction, then ate hungrily. When they had finished the sand-

242

wiches and chips and sampled all the cookies, Derek stood up. "Okay, ladies, we'll clear the table while you dress, then we'll change and head for the boat docks."

"I don't know, Dad, do you think it's safe after all we ate?"

"If we start to sink, we'll throw the ladies overboard."

"That wouldn't help," Sharon told him. "You and Todd are the ones who ate three sandwiches each."

"No fair counting," Todd answered.

As they walked toward the bathhouse, Sharon said softly, "I really like Todd. He's so much like his dad, only younger."

"Yes, even the same blue eyes and sandy hair."

"I wish I knew if he is serious about anyone."

"Why don't you ask him?"

"Oh, I couldn't do that. But I wish you would ask Derek."

"Derek may not know."

"I think he would. So will you ask him?"

"If you really want me to, but I still think you should just ask Todd." Paula had almost forgotten the games people played when they were young and dating. She had often heard it said, "The more things change, the more they stay the same." And she supposed the mating game was a given.

Paula sat in the back of the boat, feet braced on the seat in front of her, Derek across the narrow aisle. Todd was at the wheel with Sharon beside him.

"Which way to the dam, Dad?"

"Take a right and go under the bridge."

"Maybe we can take her through the lock."

"Sure—if we get there when something is going up."

Paula had watched boats navigate the locks on a dam before but she had never actually done it. And from high above the water, the various small craft had always looked terribly vulnerable.

Derek reached across and covered her hand with his. "It's perfectly safe."

How did he always know what she was thinking? She smiled at him and nodded with more assurance than she felt.

As luck would have it, a large vessel was preparing to enter the lock, and several small boats went along for the ride. Paula looked up at the gigantic steel structure, saw the walkway where people who looked no larger than toy soldiers were watching, and shivered.

Derek looked at her with concern. "Cold?" he asked.

"A little." The sides of the steel locks rose so high above them that the boat was in deep shadow. It was cooler here, and a fine mist from the spillway blew against their faces.

"Come on over here beside me and I'll keep you warm." Still holding her hand, he drew her gently toward him. Pressed against him, with his arm tight around her, Paula felt warmth seeping through her, and with it came an unbidden fantasy of Derek holding her—skin to skin, kissing her, making love to her.

Derek Vogel was a very attractive man. And he was virile and sexy and she was sure he would be a wonderful lover. Only she wasn't looking for a lover. They had settled the matter between them the first night he took her to dinner. He had done nothing to indicate he wanted to renegotiate the settlement. So why did she have these fantasies? She hadn't changed her mind. She did not want an affair with anyone.

Through the lock, they traveled downriver for several miles, then circled back to the dam where they tied up at a dockside restaurant.

"Whew, the sunny South is hotter than Hades," Todd complained as he helped Sharon out of the boat. "I feel like I'm in a sauna with my clothes on."

Derek laughed. "You get used to it."

Inside, the restaurant was dim and cool. Only a few tables were occupied at this hour so they chose a place overlooking the water. A waitress set glasses of water on the yellow oil-cloth tabletop. "Do y'all need menus?"

Derek looked at the others, then shook his head. "Just draft beer for me."

"I'll have the same," Todd said, and looked at Sharon. "Want a beer?"

"I'd better not. I've never even tasted beer," she admitted.

"Paula?"

Her throat felt parched from the sun. "I'll have one."

"Well, if Paula is going to have a beer, I guess I'll try one," Sharon said.

"Here you are, hon. Enjoy." The waitress set a frosty mug in front of Derek first and gave him a flirtatious smile. She deposited the remainder of their order with less enthusiasm, Paula observed.

Sharon gingerly lifted the foaming mug and took a tentative sip.

Todd watched her, waiting. "Well?"

"It's pretty good," she said with a note of surprise.

"Welcome to the grown-up world." Todd grinned at her and lifted his own mug and drank.

The jukebox in the corner blared out an old country-western hit, the sound reverberating to make the salt and pepper shakers tremble on the tabletop.

"That one is too good to waste," Todd said as he looked at Sharon. "Want to dance?"

When she nodded, he took another long draw from his mug and stood up, pulling her toward the tiny dance floor near the jukebox.

"Want to join them?" Derek asked Paula. She shook her head, suddenly overcome with a wave of sadness that threatened to make her cry. Quent made this kind of music, and in a club somewhere, a woman called Bootsie sang the love songs he played.

Derek took her hand. "Let the ghosts go and come dance with me."

This time Paula allowed herself to be led to the other side of the room. Derek pulled her into his arms and began moving to the music. He held her possessively close, not socially correct as Greg had done, and she could feel the hardness of his lean body as the music pulsated between them. He danced well as she had known he would, leading her effortlessly so that they moved as one. It felt good to be

247

held in a man's arms this way. He wasn't her husband, but Quent was gone and he wasn't coming back to her. And she needed some-thing—someone—to fill that void.

Derek was here. She was physically attracted to him, and she was sure the attraction was mutual. He was single and available and she was tempted to soothe her wounded pride and take whatever solace he could offer. But in her heart she knew it would not be enough.

The song ended and another began. Todd and Sharon moved slowly by, arms around each other, Sharon's head resting on Todd's shoulder. It made her heart ache to see them. Young love, raging hormones calling out to each other, fragile dreams.

"The bubble bursts too soon, doesn't it?" Derek whispered near her ear.

She nodded, tears stinging her eyes.

"I wouldn't trade places with them for the world. Not unless I could do some things a hell of a lot differently."

"Me either," Paula whispered.

"You're my kind of lady," Derek said and brought her hand to his cheek, then brushed her palm with his lips sending a wave of long-ing coursing through her veins.

No, I'm not, Paula told him silently. *You are*

248

*footloose and fancy free and likely to stay that way.
And I'm just a wife without a husband.*

As the music ended, Derek waved to Todd
and Sharon. "We should be getting back to
the boat. We need to navigate the locks before
dark."

While Todd took care of the check, Derek
readied the boat. This time he took the wheel
and Paula sat in front with him. When she
glanced toward the rear seats, Todd and
Sharon were sitting in one seat as she and
Derek had, looking at each other as if they
were the only people in the world.

Even though she had not arranged their
meeting, Paula felt somehow responsible for
the shy girl who had befriended her from the
moment she arrived at Winthrope Hall. And
she had a feeling Sharon was as naive about
love as she had been about drinking beer, so
she only hoped Todd's intentions were serious. *Like father, like son?* she asked herself and
was reminded of Sharon's request to find out
from Derek if Todd was serious about anyone
else.

"Derek," she leaned closer to him and spoke
in a low voice, "those two certainly seem to have
hit if off well. Does Todd charm all the girls
this easily?"

"I don't think so. He's actually somewhat

249

of a loner. I've never seen him quite as out-going as he has been today."

"Does he date anyone in particular back in California?"

"Not as far as I know," he grinned at her, "so you can relax your vigil. I believe my son's intentions are honorable."

"I didn't mean—"

"It's okay, Paula. You are simply acting like a mother because you are one."

Paula felt color rise in her face as she re-membered again Amy's words about being a mother figure. She supposed Derek thought of her as a safe person to take out because she wouldn't expect him to be serious about her. Date an older woman, she is always so grateful, went the popular male joke. Was she a joke to Derek?

They made it to the locks just before dark, pausing near the spillway to marvel at the tons of white spray caught in a thunderous display of lights that changed colors against the dark sky.

"This reminds me of Fourth of July fire-works," Derek said against Paula's ear. His warm breath caressing her earlobe sent shivers down her spine but she smiled and nodded just as though his action had not sent her own emotions careening like a skyrocket gone out of control.

Waiting inside the lock, with the massive steel walls surrounding them, they began their slow descent to the lower river level. Derek touched Paula's shoulder and pointed high above them where a wafer thin moon was just visible in the black sky. "Make a wish," he told her.

"I wouldn't know where to begin," she protested helplessly, thinking of Amy and her wedding and Jeff in a faraway land and Quent who had become a foreigner at home and herself at the university.

From the darkness, Derek's husky voice wrapped her in warmth. "Then I'll wish for both of us."

After they navigated the lock, they made good time returning upriver to the park. When they were driving back toward the university, Todd announced, "Sharon and I are going to stop somewhere for a snack and then go to a movie. You guys will come, too, won't you?"

"I'm sorry, Todd, but I have library work to do for tomorrow."

"I'll keep you company, then," Derek said, "unless you have another escort?"

"No, I don't. I'd planned to use the library

this afternoon so I didn't make any arrangements with anyone."

"Then just drop us here," Derek told his son as they reached the campus, then as an afterthought, asked, "unless you would like to eat with Todd and Sharon somewhere while we still have access to wheels?"

"No, thanks. I couldn't eat another bite," Paula answered.

Derek helped Paula from the backseat and they said goodbyes.

"Will I see you again, Paula?"

"I don't know, Todd. When are you leaving?"

"Tuesday morning."

"You'll see her tomorrow night if she accepts my invitation to go out for pizza," Derek told him.

"How could I refuse? He's giving me a second chance on it." As they turned toward the library, she asked, "Didn't you have pizza last night?"

"No, we—I decided not to go."

Now what did that mean? Paula wondered as they walked in silence. He *had* said "we" before he caught himself. And according to his earlier statement Todd had not arrived until very late. But she had no right to question what Derek had meant or with whom he had been. After all, he had asked her to go out with him for pizza and she had gone for a starlight cruise with Greg Winthrope instead. So if he had acted on her suggestion and taken Faye Browne to dinner, she had no one to blame except herself.

Eleven

"All right, listen up." Derek's no-nonsense tone brought an immediate hush to the group of students clustered just outside Oldham Hall.

"Thank you, Mister Vogel." Faye Browne gave Derek a brilliant smile, then turned to face the group. "I'm going to call roll now, students, and assign you to cars for the ride out to the paper mill." She took a step forward, snapped open a small black notebook. "Clyde Benton."

"Here." A tousled-haired boy with freckles waved his hand.

Faye read three more names and indicated a tutor who would drive. When nearly all the assignments had been made, she assessed the remaining students with a quick glance, then said, "Kurt Yearwood." Kurt listlessly raised one hand without speaking. "You go with Miss Howard. Norma Oakley."

"He-ah." She made it a two-syllable word, then whispered something to Irvin Pendergrass who stood beside her.

"You are assigned to Miss Howard also." Faye looked at Ruth. "You, too, Mrs. Valcourt."

"What about me?" Irvin demanded. "Am I gonna hafta walk?"

"No, Irvin. You may ride with Mister Vogel."

"Aw." Irvin groaned dramatically. "Why cain't I go with *them?*" He nodded toward Paula and her group who were now walking toward the line of cars parked on the street in front of Oldham Hall.

Faye hesitated a moment, then made a mark in her notebook. "All right, Irvin."

"Is that wise?" Derek spoke in a low voice to Faye.

"Why not?" She shrugged and turned to Derek. "I'll just ride with you since there are only three students left."

"Hey, wait for me," Irvin yelled as he loped awkwardly after Paula and caught up in time to squeeze into the backseat beside Norma.

"Well, look who's here," Ruth said without enthusiasm, and added in an undertone as

255

Paula started the car and turned on the air-conditioner, "Thank you, Miss Browne."

"You got a tape player, Miss Howard?" Irvin asked as Paula pulled away from the curb.

"I'm afraid not, Irvin."

"Don't matter none," Norma said softly. "She won't have no good tapes anyway."

"You got a radio, don't ya?" Irvin persisted.

"Sure." Paula looked at Ruth. "Why don't you find some music for them?"

As Ruth scanned the dial, Irvin yelled from the back, "Hey, right there. Stop!" Then began making jerking motions with his head and upper body, keeping time with the raucous sounds.

"*That* is music?" Ruth looked at Paula, grimaced. "Sounds more like someone being tortured."

"Cool, man. Turn it up some more." Irvin slapped his hand on the back of Ruth's headrest. "Go, baby, go."

"Irvin, settle down." Ruth turned to look sternly at him. "The *music* is loud enough already, and if you don't stop bouncing around back there, you'll cause Miss Howard to wreck the car."

Paula turned to smile at her. "Reminds me of car pool days with Jeff and Amy."

"You got kids, Miss Howard?" Norma asked.

MORE PASSION AND ADVENTURE AWAIT... YOUR TRIP TO A BIG ADVENTUROUS WORLD BEGINS WHEN YOU ACCEPT YOUR FIRST 4 NOVELS ABSOLUTELY *FREE*
(AN $18.00 VALUE)

Accept your Free gift and start to experience more of the passion and adventure you like in a historical romance novel. Each Zebra novel is filled with proud men, spirited women and tempetuous love that you'll remember long after you turn the last page

Zebra Historical Romances are the finest novels of their kind. They are written by authors who really know how to weave tales of romance and adventure in the historical settings you love. You'll feel like you've actually gone back in time with the thrilling stories that each Zebra novel offers.

GET YOUR FREE GIFT WITH THE START OF YOUR HOME SUBSCRIPTION

Our readers tell us that these books sell out very fast in book stores and often they miss the newest titles. So Zebra has made arrangements for you to receive the four newest novels published each month.

You'll be guaranteed that you'll never miss a title, and home delivery is so convenient. And to show you just how easy it is to get Zebra Historical Romances, we'll send you your first 4 books absolutely FREE! Our gift to you just for trying our home subscription service.

BIG SAVINGS AND FREE HOME DELIVERY

Each month, you'll receive the four newest titles as soon as they are published. You'll probably receive them even before the bookstores do. What's more, you may preview these exciting novels free for 10 days. If you like them as much as we think you will, just pay the low preferred subscriber's price of just $3.75 each. *You'll save $3.00 each month off the publisher's price.* AND, your savings are even greater because there are never any shipping, handling or other hidden charges—FREE Home Delivery. Of course you can return any shipment within 10 days for full credit, no questions asked. There is no minimum number of books you must buy.

4 FREE BOOKS

TO GET YOUR 4 FREE BOOKS WORTH $18.00 — MAIL IN THE FREE BOOK CERTIFICATE T O D A Y

Fill in the Free Book Certificate below, and we'll send your FREE BOOKS to you as soon as we receive it.

If the certificate is missing below, write to: Zebra Home Subscription Service, Inc., P.O. Box 5214, 120 Brighton Road, Clifton, New Jersey 07015-5214.

FREE BOOK CERTIFICATE

4 FREE BOOKS
ZEBRA HOME SUBSCRIPTION SERVICE, INC.

YES! Please start my subscription to Zebra Historical Romances and send me my first 4 books absolutely FREE. I understand that each month I may preview four new Zebra Historical Romances free for 10 days. If I'm not satisfied with them, I may return the four books within 10 days and owe nothing. Otherwise, I will pay the low preferred subscriber's price of just $3.75 each; a total of $15.00, *a savings off the publisher's price of $3.00.* I may return any shipment and I may cancel this subscription at any time. There is no obligation to buy any shipment and there are no shipping, handling or other hidden charges. Regardless of what I decide, the four free books are mine to keep.

NAME

ADDRESS _____ APT

CITY _____ STATE ____ ZIP

TELEPHONE ( )

SIGNATURE _____ (if under 18, parent or guardian must sign)

Terms, offer and prices subject to change without notice. Subscription subject to acceptance by Zebra Books. Zebra Books reserves the right to reject any order or cancel any subscription.

ZB0194

GET
FOUR
FREE
BOOKS
(AN $18.00 VALUE)

ZEBRA HOME SUBSCRIPTION
SERVICE, INC.
120 BRIGHTON ROAD
P.O. Box 5214
CLIFTON, NEW JERSEY 07015-5214

"Yes, I do. They're grown-up now."

"Oh." Norma turned her attention back to Irvin. "You like Ice-T?"

"Yeah, man. He's the greatest."

"He?" Ruth looked puzzled. "Isn't that a drink?"

"Oh, Miz Valcourt. Stop kiddin' us," Norma said with an exasperated sigh.

"I'm kidding?" Ruth rolled her eyes at Paula and shrugged helplessly.

The music changed and Irvin and Norma began to clap their hands and grunt along with the lyrics. "Uh-huh. Uh. Uh. Uh."

Paula glanced in the rear view mirror and saw that Kurt was pressed against the window, seemingly unaware of the music or the lively pair beside him.

Ruth leaned toward Paula and said in a low voice, "Don't look now, but guess who is behind us." Without waiting for an answer she went on. "Paul Number Two with Miss Scarlett riding shotgun."

Paula nodded gravely. No wonder they'd gotten stuck with Irvin. She adjusted the rear view mirror and saw the Firebird following close behind them. Was it only her imagination or did Faye Browne appear to be sitting on the console instead of the passenger's bucket seat?

She unconsciously slowed the Grand Am for a better look and Irvin advised loudly, "Put the pedal to the metal, Miss Howard. That bluebird is gainin' on us."

Startled, she obeyed his directions without thinking, and Ruth observed her with a knowing smile.

As the caravan of cars neared the mill, Irvin was the first to see the sign. "There it is, man. See? Win hope paper mill and ink."

"That's Win-thrope," Ruth told him, "and the i-n-c stands for incorporated."

"Whatever," Irvin mumbled.

"What's incorporated, Miz Valcourt?" Norma asked.

"Well, it means people being legally joined together under the law."

"You mean like getting married?"

Ruth's eyes met Paula's amused glance. "Sort of."

Paula pulled into a parking space as Derek's Firebird stopped beside her. The passenger door opened and Faye Browne emerged, showing a lot of leg under her tailored black skirt. Paula's mind conjured up an image of those long shapely gams pressed against the dashboard only inches away from Derek's hand on the gear shift. As she got out of the car, she slammed the door with more force than necessary, then belatedly realized Kurt Yearwood was still inside and opened it again.

The students and tutors, awaiting further instructions, formed a circle around Faye. Even in the sweltering heat and humidity she managed to look cool in her crisp red linen jacket that covered a black and white polka-dotted shell.

"Students, remain with the people you rode out with."

"All *right*," Irvin said aloud and Norma giggled.

Faye ignored the interruption and continued. "Each group will be assigned a guide when we enter the building. Remember, *no* loud talking. *No* running. And do touch *anything*."

Irvin groaned. "Are we 'llowed to breathe?"

Amid the laughter that followed, Faye focused her disapproving gaze on the questioner and said without smiling, "Only if you can do it quietly." She turned and started toward the main redwood building and the group followed single file along the flagstone walk.

Inside the cool lobby, Ben Colbert and Greg Winthrope were waiting. After Greg's brief welcome the staff who would serve as guides appeared and the tour began.

As their guide pointed out the paintings displayed along the wall Irvin and Norma trailed behind her with rapt attention. But Kurt crossed the room and stood staring into the garden. When the group moved toward the next room and he did not follow, Paula said his name. He didn't respond so she spoke again. "Kurt. Time to go."

Reluctantly, he followed, but inside the executive offices he immediately went to look at the lush courtyard displayed beyond the wide expanse of glass. Paula had never seen him show this much attention to anything before and she continued to watch his behavior with interest until she heard Ruth gasp.

"Put that down, Norma. Remember what Miss Browne told us?"

Norma slowly replaced the gem-encrusted paperweight Paula and Sharon had admired on an earlier visit. "I didn't hurt nothing." She looked sullen. "I just wanted to look at it."

"Holy cow!" Irvin, who was already in the hallway beyond, suddenly rattled the life-sized suit of armor that confronted him. "Is he for real?"

The guide, Ruth, and Paula all rushed toward the site of the clanging noise.

"Irvin, stop that," Ruth scolded. "Remember the rules? *No* touching."

Irvin, fascinated with the metal figure before him, continued to test each bendable part with avid determination.

"Irvin." Ruth stepped in front of the iron man. "Listen to me. Look, but don't touch."

"Aw, gimme a break. This dude is super cool, man."

Ruth looked at the woman with them. "I'm sorry, I guess he just got carried away."

She gave Ruth a forced smile. "No harm done."

Paula suddenly remembered Kurt and turned back. He still stood mesmerized at the window.

"Kurt." She walked closer, touched his shoulder. "We have to move along now but we can go out in the courtyard and gardens at the end of the tour if you like."

Kurt visibly brightened at her words and his lagging footsteps unconsciously speeded up.

At the door to the Board Room Irvin was overcome with another burst of enthusiasm. "Man, oh man. Will you get a load of that?" He rushed toward the life-sized portrait of Gregory Winthrope and his horse, stopping inches from it to gaze up in awed silence.

"That is Mr. Gregory Winthrope IV, whom we saw in person at the beginning of the tour."

Irvin, hearing part of what she said, turned

to her with a puzzled expression. "Huh? Where? I didn't see no horse."

"Oh, I thought you meant . . ." she stopped, looked helplessly at Ruth and Paula who were trying hard not to smile.

"I rode a horse like that," Kurt said suddenly as he moved closer to Irvin for a better view.

"You lying, man." Irvin shot him a dark look and returned his attention to the black stallion.

"I am not," Kurt said defiantly.

"Where? Where you ride a horse like that?" Irvin demanded.

"On my grandpa's farm."

"Liar."

"Irvin." Paula stepped between him and Kurt. "That's enough. If Kurt says he rode a horse, you have no proof he didn't."

The guide motioned the group to follow. "Now we're going downstairs to the real museum."

"Let's go, man." Irvin spun around, bumping into a chair whose casters sent it careering into the long mahogany table.

"Irvin, control yourself," Ruth cautioned and rolled her eyes back at Paula. "If I live through this day . . ."

"Come on, let's go," Paula said to Norma

and Kurt as she hurried toward the door. Kurt cast another long look at the black horse and joined her. "Norma?"

"Just a minute." Norma was adjusting the money belt that sagged at her waist. She gave the purple pouch another hard tug. "I'm coming."

Touring the lower floor required the constant vigilance of both tutors as Irvin and Norma ignored repeated admonitions not to raise their voices and not to touch the objects. Kurt, however, had withdrawn into his usual behavior and slouched along with an air of complete disinterest. The excitement level of the other two peaked about midway through the exhibits when the guide showed them the Indian headdress displays. Irvin impulsively stuck his head under the most elegant artifact which, along with several others, was suspended from the ceiling for easy viewing.

"Wa hoo," he said loud enough to get the immediate attention of all who were nearby.

"Irvin Pendergrass!" Ruth's voice rose menacingly. "Get yourself out of that headdress immediately!"

Irvin shrank back as though afraid Ruth would strike him but his face remained framed by the sparkling clusters of stones and long white feathers that hid his usually prominent ears. "I cain't," he said in a strange high voice. "I'm stuck."

Somehow he had managed to entangle himself in the suspension wires and was now a captive impersonator of some ancient Indian warrior.

"Then don't move," Ruth warned him. "Don't even breathe." She stepped forward at the same time their guide regained her composure enough to speak.

"Oh, my. Do you think we should call—"

"We can take care of it," Paula assured her with a confidence she did not feel. It was important not to create a scene which would lead Dr. Colbert and Miss Browne to conclude she and Ruth could not handle three students between them.

"Hold still, Irvin. You'll have to back out of this *slowly* while we pull the wires apart," Ruth told him.

"This thing is heavy," he complained as Norma giggled nervously and the guide wrung her hands.

Damn Faye Browne, Paula thought as the sharp wires cut into her fingers. If Irvin Pendergrass had come out with his own tutor, Derek would be here now and this probably wouldn't have happened.

Once extricated, a more subdued Irvin completed the tour without further mishap, to the great relief of the three adults. It was difficult to tell who was most grateful as they approached the dining area where other students were milling about—their guide, who said goodbye and returned to her desk, or Ruth who sank down on the nearest bench and sighed heavily.

Paula did a quick survey of the room and saw Derek speaking with Faye Browne. She glanced in their direction then clapped her hands for attention.

"Okay, students. Have you enjoyed the tour?" Amid affirmative responses, she held up her hand for silence. "You may take a rest room break as soon as I finish speaking. Mr. Vogel and Mrs. Valcourt, will you station yourselves by the doors, please? Students, you may also look at the courtyard and gardens but *only* accompanied by a tutor. And in a few minutes you should find a table and be seated for refreshments."

Miss Browne clapped her hands sharply and spoke again. "Sit with the group you were assigned to. *No* switching places with anyone." She nodded to Janet and Mark. "Miss Farmer, Mr. Bradley. Will you please come to the kitchen with me?"

Paula felt a hand on her arm. "Can we go outside now?"

"Sure, Kurt. Just let me see if Norma or Irvin want to come, too." She glimpsed Irvin's back as he bolted for the door marked "Men" and saw that Norma was waiting her turn beside the door where Ruth stood guard. "I guess they don't. Okay, let's go."

Kurt headed through the double doors and straight for the lily pond. Paula felt a moment of panic and hurried after him. She'd had quite enough disasters for one afternoon without her charge jumping into that cool, inviting water, and Kurt was so unpredictable anything was possible.

But he turned to her, his face alive with discovery. "There's fish in this pond," he said and pointed to a large white fish with black fins. "What kind is that one?"

"I'm afraid I don't know," Paula answered.

He leaned over for a better view. "And there's a gold one with dots all over it."

Paula had never heard Kurt speak so many words at one time. "Do you like fish, Kurt?"

"Yeah. My grandpa had a pond with fish in it." He shook his head in awe. "But not like these."

"Your grandpa—do you see him often?"

He was silent so long she was about to repeat the question when he said in a flat voice, "Naw. He died."

"Oh. I'm sorry." After a moment she went on. "Your grandpa must have been very special to you."

"Yeah." He watched the fish intently.

Paula could not let this opportunity to reach Kurt slip away. "What other animals did your grandpa have on his farm?"

He shrugged. "Chickens, pigs, cows, stuff like that."

"And the horse you used to ride?"

"Yeah." His thin shoulders drooped dejectedly.

"Did you visit your grandpa's farm often, Kurt?"

He turned to her as though surprised by her question, and brushed back a lock of his hair before he answered. "I lived there . . . till my mom got married."

"Oh." Paula wondered why this significant fact was missing from Kurt's detailed background information. Reluctantly she said, "I guess we ought to go back inside, Kurt. They'll be having refreshments now." Paula gestured toward a table where Ruth sat with Norma and Irvin. "Sit over there by the far wall, Kurt. I'll stop by the kitchen and get our refreshments."

As she passed the table where Derek sat across from Faye, he looked up and smiled. "How is it going?" he asked softly.

"Just great." She would not for one moment let him see that Irvin Pendergrass had kept her in a state of anxiety all afternoon while he enjoyed a relaxed tour of the mill in the scintillating company of the glamorous Miss Browne.

As the students sat quietly talking and finishing their Cokes and cookies, Ben Colbert and Greg Winthrope joined them. Dr. Colbert rapped on a nearby table with an empty can.

"Students, before we go I'm sure you want to show Mr. Winthrope your appreciation." He clapped his hands and the people in the room joined him. Even Kurt applauded, Paula was pleased to note.

As Dr. Colbert continued to speak, the guide for Paula's group rushed into the room and whispered something to Faye Browne, whose face registered surprise.

Dr. Colbert, seeing her expression, left his sentence unfinished and stepped closer to her table. "Miss Browne, do you have something to say?"

"No—I—yes." The normally controlled Miss Browne appeared flustered and Dr. Colbert looked at her with annoyance as she stood and spoke softly to him, shielding her mouth with her hand. His face paled, then flushed and he took off his glasses and polished them furiously before he spoke again.

"Students," he paused as his eyes swept the room, "it has come to my attention that we have a problem here. It seems," he glanced apologetically toward Greg Winthrope, "that a very valuable paperweight has disappeared during our tour. Now," he took a deep breath, "since no other visitors were in the building this afternoon we must assume that someone here has taken it." After a long silence while his words sank in, he spoke again. "We will not leave this room until the matter is settled so I trust whoever has this property will give it to their tutor while we finish our refreshments." He turned toward Greg, said something to him, and they walked out into the courtyard.

Paula looked toward Faye Browne's table and met Derek's quizzical look. He thinks Irvin took it, she thought. And perhaps he did. No, wait. He was already in the hallway doing battle with the suit of armor before Norma put it down, and they had been the last group to go through the office complex. So that left only Norma and Kurt. Kurt? He had been the last to leave the room.

Paula unconsciously turned to look at the boy who sat beside her. "I saw who did it." His words were barely audible but Norma's quick denial came from across the table before he could call her name.

"Liar," she hissed.

It was the second time in one afternoon he had been accused of lying and Kurt half stood from the table as he spit out the words. "I am not. You stole it. I saw you."

"Kurt, sit down." Paula automatically pushed him back down on the bench and her eyes went to the bulging money belt fastened at Norma's waist, as she remembered the girl's earlier preoccupation with adjusting it.

Ruth's eyes followed Paula's and she surveyed the pouch for a moment, then spoke quietly. "Norma, I think we had better go to the rest room and have a little talk."

"No." Norma sat, hands gripping the edge of the table, seemingly unable to move beyond denial of her guilt.

"Norma, I would prefer to do this in private," Ruth pleaded softly. "Please come with me." She stood up.

"No," Norma stubbornly repeated.

Ruth sat down again. "Okay, you leave me no choice. Let me have your money belt."

"No!" Norma's voice rose angrily. "It belongs to me."

"But what you've got in it doesn't," Ruth said flatly. "So give it to me."

After a long silence, Norma fumbled blindly with the fastener, reached inside the purple pouch and pulled out the paperweight. She dropped it on the table with a thud that caused both Paula and Ruth to cringe. "There." Tears were coursing down her cheeks now and her voice was choked with rage. "Take it."

"Why?" Ruth looked at her sadly. "Why, Norma?"

"They got so much stuff here nobody needed it anyway."

"That's not a reason to take another person's property."

"And I ain't never had nothing purty in my whole life."

"You have shamed black people here today, Norma."

"Whadda you know about black people?" Norma looked at her scornfully. "You don't know nothing about being poor and wantin' nice things and having kids call you bad names."

"Oh yes I do, young lady. I wanted pretty things as badly as you do, but I went to school and studied hard, and then I worked for what I wanted."

271

"Well, it ain't the same in this country as where you come from. Blacks ain't got a chance to get nothing here," Norma insisted.

"I'm talking about this country! I was born in Georgia and that's where I grew up so don't try to tell me I don't know about being black and poor and wanting things you don't have." Tears were spilling from Ruth's eyes now but she seemed not to notice. "You can be somebody if you really want to, Norma Oakley, and don't let anyone convince you that you can't." Ruth suddenly stopped, aware of the silence that surrounded them. "Well, listen to me." She shrugged self-consciously, then straightened her shoulders. "I guess I'll just climb down off my soapbox now. Excuse me." She stood up and headed for the rest room.

Faye Browne also stood and spoke quickly. "All right, tutors, we need to return to the parking lot and get underway as soon as possible. Students, please stay with your proper group." She crossed the room and matter-of-factly picked up the paperweight and gave it to the guide who was hovering anxiously beside the door.

Paula sat waiting until the others had left the room, then stood. "Stay here," she told the students at the table, though none of them had made any effort to leave. She would have to check on Ruth and she felt apprehensive about what she should say.

As Paula approached the rest room door, Ruth walked out. Not meeting her eyes, she asked, "Ready?"

"Ready."

The five of them were silent as they walked toward the car. Paula fumbled with the keys and finally got the door unlocked.

"Miz Valcourt." Norma's voice was hesitant. "Would you . . . like to sit in back . . . with me?"

Ruth looked startled for a moment. "Sure," she answered, and climbed into the small backseat. Norma followed her.

"I'll sit in front," Kurt volunteered and Irvin got in beside Norma without a word.

"Tell me 'bout how you grew up, Miz Valcourt," Norma said softly as Paula turned onto the highway and set the cold air control to full force.

"Another time," Ruth answered tiredly.

"You won't forget?"

"No." Ruth sighed. "I won't forget."

Paula was studying when she heard a light knock at her door. When she opened it, Ruth stood there, looking contrite.

"May I come in?"

273

"Sure." Paula motioned to the bed. "Come sit down. Want some coffee?"

"No, thanks. I just came to eat crow."

"There's no need for that, Ruth." Paula sat down on the bed facing her.

"I think there is." Ruth twisted her hands, looking embarrassed. "There I was scolding Norma Oakley for shaming our people and I had done something much worse than taking a paperweight. I turned my back on my whole family." Paula was silent and in a minute she went on. "I felt like Norma did growing up and I vowed I would do something to change things. When I first heard Helen Keller's story she became my idol. I kept thinking if she could overcome all the obstacles in her life why, I could rise above my problems. So I went to college and when I finished I got a job teaching in the American Schools in Jamaica."

"There's nothing wrong with that."

"No. But when I married my husband I took his culture as well as his name for my own—like the biblical Ruth, his people became my people. It was easy to pretend I was a native of the island. Especially after he finished medical school and we settled in Kingston."

"Then Louise doesn't know?"

"Yes, Louise was the only person I ever told after we moved there. But my son," she dropped her voice almost to a whisper, "thinks I have no family, even though he is studying at Emory not fifty miles from his grandparents."

"Then you don't ever see them?" Paula asked softly.

"Not since I was married. I've called once in a while, and sent photos of my family." She shrugged. "I've got lots of brothers and sisters and I guess I've always felt nobody needed me so I would just do whatever made me happy."

"Well, are you?"

After a moment, Ruth spoke. "I thought so—until this afternoon." She stood up. "Anyway, I just wanted to say I'm sorry for the way I've misled you. I know you've got enough problems without having a friend who isn't what you think her to be."

Paula stood, too. "Ruth, you are exactly what I think you are—kind and generous and funny and concerned about other people. And where you were born makes no difference at all to me."

"Then we're still friends?" Ruth asked shyly.

"Of course we are." Paula hugged her impulsively.

Paula struggled to focus her attention back on the assigned textbook material after Ruth left and she was reading the same page for the second time when the phone rang.

"Paula? Greg here. I hope I'm not interrupting anything?"

"No, Greg. I'm just reading tomorrow's class assignments."

"Then I *am* interrupting, so I won't take a lot of your time. I just wanted to say I'm sorry I didn't have an opportunity to talk with you this afternoon."

"That's all right," Paula assured him. "I was really too busy supervising the students in my group to talk anyway."

"Did they enjoy themselves?"

"Very much, and it was so nice of you to give them a tour during office hours."

"I've been doing this for Ben every summer for years now. He has come to expect it and my staff enjoys participating."

"I hope what happened today won't jeopardize future tours."

"Certainly not, Paula. It was unfortunate, but if the object taken had not been recovered, it would have been replaceable. I hope the young lady involved is all right."

"She seemed fine," Paula told him. "And something positive came out of the tour for the student I tutor."

"Really?"

"Kurt Yearwood has been very withdrawn and nothing I've done so far had helped, but he showed an interest in the gardens today and especially the fish in the lily pond."

"I'm glad to hear that."

"And he was quite taken with the horse in your Board Room portrait. Said he had ridden a horse, too."

"Is that so?"

"Anyway, I plan to follow up on this by finding stories about farms and animals. And maybe a book on different kinds of fish so he can identify some of those he saw today."

"That sounds like a good idea, Paula. Say, I'll be cleaning the lily pond next Saturday. I wonder if your student—Kurt—would like to help?"

"I'm sure he would, but how—"

"I'll speak to Ben about it and let you know. Would you be able to bring the boy out if Ben approves?"

"Why, yes, of course."

"I'm going to say good night now and let you get back to those books, Paula."

"Good night, Greg. And thanks."

Paula thought about Greg's offer. She felt sure Kurt would be excited. But what would Dr. Colbert think of the idea? Probably that she had devised another scheme to spend time with Greg Winthrope. He might even say no to the plan because of his unfounded suspicions.

And what would Dr. Colbert think if he knew she had asked Greg to attend her daughter's wedding and he had accepted? For that matter, what would Quent think when he saw her distinguished escort? She smiled to herself. He would be surprised to say the least. And so would a lot of other people. Now thoughts of the wedding—only ten days away—crowded out all else from Paula's mind and she resigned herself to the fact that she would get no studying done tonight.

Twelve

By Friday things were back to normal at Gaither Hall. The episode at the paper mill was all but forgotten by everyone except those directly involved.

Paula had searched the library and university book store for farm-related stories and had found very little so far that Kurt could read except juvenile material suitable for early elementary students. So, at Ruth's helpful suggestion, she had begun working with Kurt to create some experience stories based on his own farm memories.

"Now Kurt, you were telling me yesterday that tobacco was the main crop on your grandpa's farm. Do you remember how to spell tobacco?"

"T-a-b-b-"

"No, let's go back to the first letter and—"

"Miss Howard?" Faye Browne appeared in the doorway. "Would you mind if Irvin sits in your class for a while?"

"Why, no, of course not." Where was Derek? Her noncommittal expression gave no indication of the reason for her odd request.

"He can just observe whatever you are doing until Mister Vogel returns."

Irvin appeared behind her, carrying his folding chair and Paula moved her own chair farther toward the wall to make room for one more in the cramped space. After he was seated she explained, "Kurt and I are writing a story about his grandpa's farm."

"He growed tobacco," Kurt said.

Paula's first impulse was to correct Kurt's grammar but she resisted. That could come later. It was enough now that he was talking, never mind talking properly.

"Cool, man." Irvin looked impressed. "Did you roll your own?"

"Yeah," Kurt answered in a low voice, "after it was cured."

"Cured? How come it sick?" Irvin laughed.

"You have to fire it," Kurt said.

"Fire it? What for, gettin' sick?"

"No, stupid, you smoke it in the barn."

"Who you calling stupid, man?" Irvin grabbed the front of Kurt's tee shirt.

"Irvin! Take your hands off Kurt." She took a deep breath. "We have some words here that are confusing you, Irvin. So please let Kurt explain them and then we'll get on with putting our story together."

Perhaps because of the relationship of the subject to the cigarettes Irvin smoked, he showed a certain amount of interest in hearing how tobacco was grown and prepared for market. Paula surreptitiously glanced at her watch from time to time, wondering what was keeping Derek, but the period ended and he hadn't returned. She debated whether in Irvin's presence to remind Kurt about tomorrow, but before she could decide what to do Kurt spoke.

"I'll be in front of Oldham Hall at nine o'clock, Miss Howard."

Irvin gave him a puzzled look. "What for, man? They ain't no school tomorrow."

"I know that. I'm going to the paper mill."

"Paper mill?" Irvin turned accusing eyes on Paula. "How come he gets to go there?"

"Kurt is working on a special project, Irvin."

"What kind of special project? How come I ain't going?" Irvin demanded.

"It has to do with the stories we're writing," Paula explained as she stood up.

Irvin gave Kurt a smoldering look. "How come I ain't writin' stories?"

"Because . . ." she faltered, searching for an honest answer without offending Kurt.

"Because you ain't never lived on a farm," Kurt said importantly.

"Who cares?" Irvin got up so quickly he almost overturned his chair and bolted through the door before Paula could say anything more.

As Paula and Kurt followed, Ruth waited for them to pass, then said, "Are my eyes playing tricks on me or did both those guys just leave your palatial quarters?"

"They aren't and they did," Paula smiled. "In that order."

"Where's Derek?"

"Beats me. Faye Browne just popped in after the break and asked me to take Irvin until Mister Vogel got back, only he never did."

"Strange." Ruth lowered her voice as they approached the central pod. "And Miss Browne is still here so he evidently didn't elope with her."

Paula looked worried. "He didn't say a thing at the break about leaving." She gave her material to Faye.

"Did you have any problems with your visitor, Miss Howard?"

Paula shook her head. "No, everything went

fine." Except for a fight I barely averted, she added silently. "But I thought Mister Vogel was coming back?"

"Well, obviously he didn't make it." Faye looked beyond Paula to Ruth and took her materials. "Any problem with your student, Mrs. Valcourt?"

"None at all," Ruth answered sincerely.

Outside, Paula returned to her earlier concern. "This just doesn't seem like something Derek would do."

"True. But if anything were wrong, Faye Browne would surely know."

"That doesn't mean she would necessarily tell us," Paula retorted.

Ruth looked solemn. "True again."

Derek had not been in the cafeteria, Paula was sure of that. Now back at the dorm, she considered her options. She could call his room on some pretext or other or she could do nothing and wait for tomorrow. Derek was a mature man who had simply left Oldham Hall early today and not returned and she hadn't heard from him since. But why should he report his every move to her?

Paula sat down at her desk and opened her notebook. After staring at her notes for several

283

minutes, she picked up the phone and dialed Derek's number.

He answered before the first ring had stopped and his voice confirmed her intuition that something had happened.

"Derek? It's Paula."

"Paula?" His mind seemed to be making some adjustment at the sound of her voice.

"I didn't see you at the cafeteria tonight. And you left early this afternoon so I thought—is anything the matter?"

He waited a long time before he answered. "I had a call from Todd's flight commander. Todd is . . . missing."

"Missing?" She couldn't comprehend his words.

"His plane is missing. His squadron was flying maneuvers—war games. And Todd didn't come back. That's all they know."

"Oh, Derek," she tried to steady her voice, "when did it happen?"

"They notified me at two." He cleared his throat. "And it happened last night. Look, I'd better hang up now. I could get another call any time."

"I'm sorry. I didn't think of that."

"Thanks for calling, Paula."

"Goodbye, Derek."

Paula stood holding the receiver in her

hand. She hadn't asked if there was anything she could do. What an awful thing to hear over the phone. And to face the waiting, alone. She put the receiver down and moved to the window where she could see the lights from Rhodes Hall.

She thought a minute. She was almost certain he had not eaten since noon and it was nine now. She would drive to the nearest fast-food place and get something and that would be her excuse to go to Rhodes Hall.

Paula had already showered and dressed for bed and she quickly removed her sleep shirt and pulled on a pair of slacks and a knit top. She thought of telling Sharon what had happened but decided morning would be soon enough. She scribbled a note and taped it to the outside of her own door in case anyone looked for her before she returned.

"With Derek at Rhodes Hall."

That ought to set tongues wagging, she thought wryly, but she would explain it all later.

The parking lot was deserted and she hesitated, looking in every direction before walking rapidly to her car. Once inside, she locked the doors again and drove toward University Boulevard.

Paula parked across the street from Rhodes Hall and headed for the well-lighted front entrance. The night air was heavy and her clothing felt damp against her skin as she made her way past the students who lounged on the wide stone steps.

Inside, she met the interested glances of two young men, one behind the desk, the other standing beside it. She knew Derek's room number would be the same as his phone minus the first two digits so she was saved the embarrassment of asking.

Noting her Hardee's bag, one of the students remarked loud enough for her to hear, "Special delivery."

"Uh-huh." Paula pushed the elevator button and waited with her back to the pair. "She could deliver room service to me any time."

When the elevator finally came, she stepped inside and as the silent cage rose to the fifth floor she was suddenly struck with a horrible thought. Faye Browne had known about Derek's call, and perhaps even knew what the message had been. What if she were with him now?

The elevator stopped and Paula forced herself to put one foot in front of the other and make her way to Derek's room. "507. 505. 503. 501," She counted softly. The end of the hall. She looked at the door, slowly raised her hand, hesitated. What if . . . ? Never mind what if! Derek needed a friend. She knocked softly. No answer. She knocked again. Then the door opened and Derek was standing there looking so worried she knew she had been right to come.

"Paula." His voice was flat, tired.

"Have you heard anything since we talked?"

He shook his head. "No."

She held out the bag. "Here, I've brought you a sandwich. You haven't eaten, have you?"

He seemed uncertain for a minute, then shook his head again but did not take the food.

"May I come in?" He stepped aside for her to enter, then closed the door.

"You shouldn't come out this time of the night alone, Paula."

"I was careful." She crossed to the desk, took out the sandwich and a carton of milk. "It's ham on rye." She looked at him expectantly.

"Thanks." He sat down at the desk, unwrapped the sandwich, stopped, realizing she was still standing. "Here. Take the chair." He began to get up but she motioned him to stay seated.

"I'll just sit here." She sat on a corner of the bed which was neatly made with white sheets and a navy blue blanket. A quick look around the room told her that Derek had added only the basic necessities, creating a barracks atmosphere.

"I didn't tell Sharon about the call, but I'm wondering if I should have."

"I don't think so." He took a bite, chewed slowly. "There's nothing anyone can do but wait."

"And time passes faster when you aren't alone, so do you mind if I wait with you?"

"If you like."

Paula tried to make small talk but it was obvious that her efforts were meeting with no success. "Do you want to tell me about it, Derek?" she asked quietly.

He pushed the remainder of his food away and sat for a moment, then shook his head as if to clear his mind. "I've thought about it sometimes," he said slowly, "when something happened. Wondered how it would feel if it were . . . my son." He was silent for several minutes but Paula didn't speak. "And when I got the call today . . . there are no words to . . . it just seems so unreal . . ." he looked at her with stricken features. "Christ, he was here only three days ago. *Three* days. Sleeping in this room. Visiting his old man at college, meeting Sharon. There were three planes flying reconnaissance. The only other thing I know is that two came back but . . . Todd's didn't. They lost radio contact and it went off the radar screen. They've sent search planes, of course, and destroyers and patrol boats," he shrugged helplessly "but the Pacific is a big expanse of water—by night or day."

"There is a very good chance that he's all right, Derek. You have to believe that."

"It's been at least twenty-four hours with no contact and no sign of the plane. They should have heard or seen something by now, unless . . ."

"Have they told his mother?"

"Yes. I guess she knew before I did, with Mac right there in the middle of things."

"Have you considered flying out?"

"No." His tone was harsh. "They don't need me. Marsha has Mac, and her father. And I can get there in a few hours if . . . I need to."

"Yes, I suppose you can." So the woman Derek had been married to was named Marsha. He had never used her name before.

"It may be days, or even weeks before they

tell us . . . anything certain." He stood up, walked to the window, stood staring into the darkness. "And it's this damned waiting that is so hard. You want to know but you're afraid of knowing."

Paula went to stand beside him, touched his arm, and he turned toward her. Without conscious thought, she reached up to touch his face in a gesture of comfort and he closed his hands over hers. He brushed her fingertips with his lips, then wrapped his arms around her and held her hard against him. A wave of desire washed over her and she trembled but he held her away and said softly, "I should take you back to your dorm."

"No, I want to stay," she answered firmly. "Why don't you try and get some rest? Here, lie down near the phone." She turned back the sheet, rearranged the pillow. "And I'll just curl up over there," she indicated the bed on the opposite side of the room, "and get some sleep, too."

He sat down on the side of the narrow bed and leaned back against the wall. "I could never sleep now."

"Then I'll sit here with you." Paula sat beside him, arranged the pillow at her back, and tucked her feet up. "Tell me about growing up on that farm in Iowa."

As Derek talked, the tenseness seemed to drain from his taut muscles. The pauses grew longer and he nodded, then dosed fitfully and finally fell into an exhausted sleep, his body slumping toward Paula. She leaned against him, felt the steady rhythm of his beating heart and his warm breath on her forehead.

Dear God, let Todd be safe, she prayed. She reached out to turn off the desk light and closed her eyes. Soon she drifted into a dreamless sleep and did not awaken until dawn lit up the room.

For a moment Paula didn't remember where she was. Then the awful news about Todd returned to her thoughts. During the night she had shifted to a reclining position and Derek lay beside her, one arm across her shoulder. As she eased from beneath his hand, he stirred and opened his eyes.

"Paula . . . ? What—" he sat up. "Oh, I must have fallen asleep."

"We both did." She stood up stiffly, feeling the movement in every joint in her body, and looked at her watch. "I'd better go back to Winthrope Hall now."

Derek flexed his shoulders. "I could make you a cup of coffee."

"Thanks, but I really can't wait. I'm taking Kurt Yearwood to the paper mill at nine."

"I'd forgotten about that."

"Would you like me to bring you something to eat before I leave?"

"No thanks. I just want a cup of coffee," he passed a hand over the stubble on his jaw, looking haggard and drawn, "and a shave and shower."

Paula picked up her purse and walked to the door. "I'll come back as soon as I can."

He followed her, stood with his hand on the doorknob. "Thanks, Paula, for helping me make it through last night. I owe you." He gently touched her cheek with his hand.

"That's what friends are for, Derek. I hope you hear some good news before I get back."

As Derek's door closed behind her, she was grateful to see the hallway was deserted. She was alone on the elevator, too, and a different student was stationed behind the desk now. He eyed her curiously, and said, "Good morning."

Blushing, she returned his greeting. It was clear what he must be thinking as he observed her rumpled appearance. Well, some things were not the way they looked on the surface, she thought grimly, straightening her shoulders as she walked toward the front entrance.

* * *

After Paula dressed, she hesitated a moment, considering whether to wake Sharon and tell her about Todd before she left. Then she knocked on her door. "Sharon?" She knocked again.

"Who is it?" came a muffled reply.

"It's Paula. I need to talk with you."

In a moment a sleepy Sharon, wearing a loose knee-length tee shirt, opened the door.

Paula stepped inside. "Sharon, I'm sorry to wake you but I have to leave campus in a few minutes and there's something I think you should know." Sharon looked more alert. "It's about Todd. He was on flying maneuvers with his squadron," Sharon nodded, "and there's been a problem."

Sharon swallowed, whispered, "What kind of problem?"

Paula wished she didn't have to say the words. "His plane has not come back yet."

"You mean it crashed?"

"They don't know. It was over the ocean and," she finished lamely, "they just don't know."

"Is Derek in Coronado?"

Paula shook her head. "No, he's staying by the phone at Rhodes Hall." She led the stunned

293

girl to her bed, sat beside her and told her everything she knew about what had happened. When she finished, Sharon buried her face in her hands and cried softly.

"I really believe that he is okay," Paula told her gently.

Sharon stood up, reached for her jeans lying on a nearby chair. "I'll go and wait with Derek. I want to be there if he hears anything."

"That's a good idea. I'll give you some fruit and muffins to take along."

Paula returned with a generously filled bag as Sharon finished dressing. "I wish I didn't have to leave, but I promised to be with Kurt Yearwood this morning at the mill and he's looking forward to it so much."

"Don't worry, Paula. I'll stay with Derek until we know something."

Remembering Derek's words about the uncertainty of hearing anything, Paula was not hopeful the day would bring any news but she kept the thought to herself as they walked toward the elevator together.

Paula sat on the stone bench, shaded from the sweltering noonday heat by the mimosa's luxuriant foliage. This was her favorite spot in the courtyard and today the beauty and tranquility of the surroundings were a welcome balm to her turbulent emotions. Her mind kept returning to Todd. If his plane had gone down and he had managed to get out alive, what were his chances of survival in the ocean until he was found? She thought of sharks and shuddered. And what of Derek? Would he stay on at the university or go back to the West coast? The thought that he might leave before the end of summer was so painful it surprised her. Summer was almost half over already and when it was gone she would see him no more anyway, so what could a few weeks matter?

A sound from the nearby lily pond caught Paula's attention and she looked up. It was the first time she had ever heard Kurt laugh and she felt rewarded for bringing him out here when she wanted to stay with Derek. She supposed Greg to be about the age of Kurt's grandfather, and felt grateful that fate had placed Greg in the boy's path at this point in time.

Greg straightened, waved to her. "We're all finished here," he said. Coming closer he asked, "How would you and Kurt like to drive over to my house for lunch? Mellie is making raspberry tarts. And we could go to the stables and show Kurt the horses afterward."

"I really would like to," Paula regretted the words that would wipe the happy look of anticipation off Kurt's face, "but someone back at the university is waiting for word on a family member in a presumed plane crash. I need to give my moral support."

Greg looked genuinely disappointed but he said, "We'll do it another day." He smiled at Kurt, shook his wet, soiled hand. "And that is a promise, Kurt." The boy nodded solemnly. "Thank you for helping today. I'll be calling on you again."

Kurt turned to Paula. "Could I?"

"I don't see any reason why not," she assured him, then added, ". . . but we really must be going now."

As a consolation for turning down Greg's invitation, Paula stopped at McDonald's on the way back and bought a carry-out lunch. Finishing two Big Macs, a large order of fries, and a chocolate shake kept Kurt too busy to talk during most of the ride to the university. Paula wondered why such an enormous appetite hadn't contributed to a bit more growth to the boy's small stature.

After she let Kurt out in front of Oldham Hall, she resisted the urge to stop at Derek's dorm and drove toward her own. She felt hot and sticky from the morning's sun and wanted to freshen up before she went back to Rhodes Hall.

As Paula got out of her car, Derek's Firebird pulled into the parking lot. If he had left the phone that meant he'd heard something. A quick glance told her that he was alone and she strained to see the expression on his face. The car stopped and he was out, striding quickly toward her, a mixture of emotions playing on his features.

"Paula!" He closed the distance between them. "They found him. He's alive!"

"Oh, Derek!" He grabbed her in a ferocious bear hug. "Is he all right?"

He took a deep breath, hugged her harder, laughed and held her away from him. "Can you believe it? In all that gigantic body of water they found him floating in his life jacket and picked him up by helicopter? And he's okay, except for a few bruises and dehydration. Christ, I still can't believe it."

"That's wonderful, Derek." Paula brushed tears from her eyes.

Derek looked sober. "They got off course and ran out of fuel. The plane was going down and they tried to eject, but—there was a malfunction. The other kid . . . went down with it." He looked at Paula, his eyes pained. "It could have been my son. And I'm so thankful it wasn't, but how can I be glad it was someone else instead of Todd?"

Now she understood why she had been unable to read his emotions as he had walked toward her. "You don't need to feel guilty, Derek. Things happen. You had no control over how this turned out."

"I've talked to Todd already. He's at Balboa Naval Hospital in San Diego." He stopped, grinning happily at her. "That's where I'm headed right now. And Sharon's going, too. She came on over to pack after we got the word. I had her leave a note for you, but I'm glad you got back in time so I could tell you in person." He looked at his watch. "We've only got a few minutes to spare. I wonder what's keeping her?"

"I'll go check." Paula smiled at him. "Have a good trip, and give my best to Todd."

"Paula." Derek held onto her hand, pulled her back to face him. "Thanks for being there for me last night."

"You're welcome, Derek," she answered simply.

He cupped her face in his hand. "We'll be back late tomorrow night so I'll see you Monday." He bent and kissed her lightly. "Goodbye."

Paula turned away quickly without meeting

his eyes. It was only a friendly kiss and she did not want him to see that it had affected her much more than that. She smiled and waved to Derek, then breathed a deep sigh of relief. "Thank you, God," she said softly.

Thirteen

Paula stood at the window and looked down. The campus lights were beginning to blink on in the gathering darkness and students hurried back and forth across the commons. The carillon chimed the hour and she was filled with a sense of how right it was for her to be here in this place at this time. In a month so many things had changed and she dreaded the thought of returning to Tuscumbia next weekend for the wedding.

The shrill ringing of the phone broke the stillness and in the shadows she reached for it and said hello.

"Paula, this is Mother. I'm afraid I have bad news."

Her mother had never been one to beat around the bush, Paula thought, even as she braced herself for whatever was coming. "What is it, Mother?"

"It's Roger. They've found out what his problem is, and he's checking into the hospital Wednesday for surgery."

"What *kind* of surgery?"

"Gallbladder. The surgery is scheduled for Thursday afternoon so there is no way we can get to the wedding."

"Of course not, Mother."

"Roger is insisting that I come but I am *not* going to leave my husband to be taken care of by strangers so soon after a serious operation."

"Of course not, Mother," Paula repeated.

"He wanted to postpone going into the hospital until next week but the doctor said it must be done now." Jeanette Driskell sighed dramatically. "So we have no choice but miss the wedding. I called Amy's apartment a few minutes ago but no one answered."

"She's probably on duty, Mother." *Or at Chris's place,* she added silently.

"Well, if I don't reach her before the wedding, give her my best love."

"I will."

"Do you have all the plans made, Paula?"

She thought about letting the misconception stand, but told the truth instead. "I believe so. Amy has seen to all of it."

"What a pity you aren't in Tuscumbia now so you could be sure everything is perfect for her big day." Paula was silent with effort. "I guess people don't put as much store in tradition nowadays, but I'm sure it will be a lovely wedding in spite of . . . everything."

After they said goodbye, Paula realized that she was actually relieved that her mother wasn't coming. She had been having some misgivings about how Jeanette Driskell would react to her bringing Greg Winthrope. But her mother was right, of course. She should be in Tuscumbia attending to last minute details of the wedding.

What was she doing here? *Now wait a minute,* she told herself sternly. *Roger had a gallstone before you came to the university. Jeff joined the Peace Corps while you were still married to his father and a stay-at-home mother. And Amy got pregnant before you became a coed, too. So how are you to blame for any of this? Don't flatter yourself that what you are doing or not doing could have affected anything. God—not you—is still in charge of the world and random happenings.*

The relentless heat of the Alabama summer permeated the campus. Not a leaf stirred in the still air and the desultory movement across the commons appeared to be in slow motion as Paula and Ruth made their way toward Winthrope Hall.

"I'm really grateful to you for the idea of doing experience stories with Kurt," Paula said. "I can't believe how much more responsive he is now."

"That's half the battle. If he's receptive, he can learn."

"If I can teach him," Paula added ruefully.

"Never fear," Ruth assured her. "You've got what it takes to be a wonderful teacher. I'd place empathy and caring at the top of the list and you are those qualities personified, honey." When Paula looked unconvinced, she continued. "Spending time with your student on Saturdays is above and beyond the call of duty, you know. Only a dedicated teacher would do that and I hope Doctor Ben has duly noted this fact."

"He probably thinks I contrived the whole thing to spend more time with Greg."

"Well, didn't you?" Ruth asked innocently. "There is nothing that says you can't kill two birds with one stone. By the way, who will take Kurt out this Saturday while you're in Tuscumbia?"

"No one—and he was pretty disappointed

303

when I told him there would be no trip this weekend."

"I could go with him but I have no way to get out there. Do you suppose Derek—"

"No. Greg won't be at the mill either. He's . . . going to be in Tuscumbia, too."

Ruth looked surprised then interested. "So you've invited Mr. Money to attend. That ought to impress a lot of people."

"But I didn't invite him to impress—not really."

"I wasn't criticizing you for it. In fact, I'm pleased as punch you asked someone. Only are you sure Greg is the one you should have asked? Why not Derek?"

"Because I *date* Greg. Derek and I are friends."

"Whatever you say." Ruth shrugged. "By the way, where is *friend* Derek?"

"He's taking Faye Browne's Monday test. Since he hadn't had a chance to study because of going to see Todd, she offered to let him wait and do it after hours today."

"How very generous," Ruth said dryly. "Good excuse for another little tête-à-tête in her quiet, cozy office."

A vivid image of Derek and Faye in a steamy embrace flashed through Paula's mind and she forced it away and deliberately changed the subject as they neared the dorm.

* * *

Paula stepped from the shower stall wrapped only in a large terry towel held together by a tuck at one side just above her bosom. She took another student's place at the crowded lavatories and began brushing her teeth. Catching sight of her wet hair in the mirror above the basin, she smiled wryly at her image. This Paula was tanned, tousled, and not so timid as the woman who had looked back at her from this mirror less than four weeks ago. This Paula was a college coed and coping. And doing pretty well at it, she might add.

As she opened the door to her room, the phone was ringing and she ran to pick it up. "Hello?"

"Mom? Thank goodness you're there."

"Amy, what is it?" Her heart beat faster as she waited for the daughter's reply.

"It's Dad."

"What happened?" Fear gripped her, and she felt her knees grow weak and sank into the chair beside the desk. "Is he—"

"You won't believe what he plans to do," Amy wailed.

Relief flooded over Paula. If Quent were going to *do* something, he must be all right. "Tell me."

305

"He is going to bring Bootsie to the wedding."

Paula's response was tempered by her knowledge that Gregory Winthrope would be attending, too. "A lot of people will be there, honey. I'm sure she won't even be noticed."

"Sitting beside him? How could anyone miss her?"

"Amy, everyone will be looking at the beautiful bride. And the groom."

Amy seemed not to have heard. "And there's more. Dad plans to bring *her* to the rehearsal dinner. That's how I found out about this whole thing. The Rylands needed to know exactly how many reservations to make for dinner at the Coach House Inn. So I called Dad to see if Grandmother Howard would be coming and he said yes, and . . . Bootsie, too."

"Well, I suppose the Rylands won't mind one extra person for dinner," Paula said.

"But Mom, that isn't the problem," Amy hesitated for a moment, "Chris and I haven't told them that you and Dad are . . . not together anymore."

"Oh," Paula said while visions of herself on Greg Winthrope's arm danced through her head.

"Now everything's ruined. I'm going to just

306

call the whole thing off and Chris and I will elope. We're flying to Hawaii for our honeymoon anyway, so we'll just leave Friday and have the ceremony over there at one of those little wedding chapels."

"You will do no such thing!" Paula took a deep breath. "Now calm yourself and let's start from the beginning. First of all, I want to know why somebody hasn't told Chris's parents about your dad and me?"

"It just never came up. I only saw them once and you and Dad were still married then. And after, well, Chris didn't want to tell them without me."

"They have to know now. They'll be staying at our house, so it would be impossible not to tell them."

"Not if you and Dad—"

"Don't even think about it. And why all the secrecy anyway? Divorce is not a disgrace."

"I know, Mom, but Chris's mother is very religious and she doesn't believe in divorce."

"Good. Then she shouldn't get one. But I'm afraid she will have to accept mine."

"Mom, could we just wait and tell them after they meet you and Dad, and see what nice people you are?"

Paula thought for a moment, then said, "I can't promise anything, but I will talk to your dad about it. However, we will only go through with this charade until after the rehearsal dinner. Then you *must* tell them before the wedding." Amy was silent, as though still considering her options. "And furthermore, everything has been finalized. The cake, the flowers, the photographer, announcement in the paper. All brides get last-minute jitters, but they *don't elope.*"

After a moment of silence, Amy said, "I guess it was a silly idea, Mom."

Amy sounded calmer so Paula pushed her advantage. "And I'm afraid you'll just have to accept your dad's . . . friend . . . at the wedding. You need to remember that he *is* paying for everything, except the rehearsal dinner, which is why I have a little leverage there." Paula stopped for breath. "So that should entitle him to invite whomever he wants—don't you think?"

A contrite Amy answered. "I'm sorry, Mom. I guess you're right. I just wish it didn't have to be this way."

"Me, too, honey. Poor timing on Dad's part, wasn't it? So we'll just have to make the best of it."

"But will you check with Dad about the rehearsal dinner?"

"Yes, I'll do it right now. And then I'll call you back."

Paula replaced the receiver and laid her head on her folded arms. If only Quent had postponed his mid-life crisis until after Amy was married.

Paula thought about the Rylands. She had never met them but it was obvious they were pretty straitlaced. Surely Chris and Amy had not expected to have his parents come to Tuscumbia for a weekend and not learn the truth. But for the sake of a gracious rehearsal dinner she would try to persuade Quent to leave his Bootsie home.

Of course, the wedding was another matter.

She turned on the desk light and found Quent's number. As she dialed she glanced at her watch. Maybe he had already left for the club and she would have a reprieve until tomorrow.

"Hello?"

"Quent, this is Paula."

After a brief surprised silence, he said politely, "How are you?"

"I'm fine, but there is a problem we need to discuss."

"Okay."

He wasn't going to make this easy for her so she took a deep breath and plunged in.

"Amy called me a little while ago. It seems she and Chris have failed to tell his parents about . . . us."

"What about us?" An impatient edge crept into his voice.

Why was he making this harder than it had to be? "About our divorce," she said flatly.

"Then I guess they'll just have to tell them."

"Yes, and they will, but there isn't going to be enough time before the rehearsal. Chris will be driving them from the airport in Huntsville just in time for that." She hesitated, then added, ". . . and then we have to go to the rehearsal dinner. So if we could not call attention to the fact that we are not . . . together until Chris and Amy have a chance to tell them later Friday evening—"

"You mean act like we're still married?"

"Not exactly, but just act like Amy's parents, and not bring anyone else to the dinner."

"Oh." He was silent a moment. "That might be okay, except I've already asked somebody."

"Quent, please—just for the rehearsal dinner. For Amy. This is so important to her," she insisted. "And you can bring anyone you want to the wedding." *And won't you be surprised when I do too,* she added silently.

"I sure as hell will. I'm not paying for all this and be told who I can invite."

"Of course not. But you will let Amy have just family at the dinner, won't you?" It was more a statement than a question.

"All right." His tone was grudging but it was as much as she had hoped for.

"Thank you, Quent. I'll see you Friday." She hung up before he could change his mind.

Paula sat staring into space, trying to imagine spending a whole evening with Quent, her ex-husband, pretending to be friends so the Rylands could see what nice people they were, to quote Amy. And she and Quent *were* nice people, but they just happened to also be divorced and the sooner the Rylands knew that, the better.

Late that evening, disaster struck again.

Paula rushed to answer the phone, expecting her mother with a report on Roger Driskell's surgery.

"Paula, Greg here."

"Oh, Greg, hello."

"I apologize for calling so late, but I'm afraid I have bad news and I wanted to let you know as soon as possible. Something urgent has come up at the mill and we're having a meeting of the Board of Directors on Saturday." He took a deep breath, "So that means I won't be able to attend the wedding. I'm sorry, Paula. I'd been looking forward to it."

Paula absorbed his words slowly. "I understand, Greg, and I'm sorry, too."

"I would try to drive up afterward but with a problem of this magnitude, the Board meeting will probably last for hours. So I hope Amy has a beautiful wedding and that all goes well."

"Thank you, Greg."

"I'll be in touch when you get back to campus next week. Have a safe trip. I'll be thinking of you. Good night, Paula."

"Good night." Paula placed the receiver carefully in its cradle, her eyes stinging with unshed tears. What a disappointment to have Greg cancel at this late date. Now she would be alone at the wedding while Quent showed off his young singer. Maybe Derek . . . No, she couldn't ask him at the last minute. He'd know he was only a substitute for Greg.

Needing someone to commiserate with her over this unexpected turn of events she put on her robe and went to Ruth's and Louise's room, knowing one or the other would surely be up and willing to listen to her tale of woe.

At her knock, Ruth opened the door. "Well, Paula, what brings you out, my dear?"

"I have a need for tea and sympathy. Is there a counselor in the house?"

"Over here." Louise looked up from her book. "Come in and tell Mrs. Freud your concerns."

"That will cover sympathy," Ruth closed the door, "and I'll see to a cup of tea."

"So," Louise patted the bed next to her desk, "pretend it's a couch and let's hear what is bothering the mother-of-the-soon-to-be-bride."

Paula got right to the point. "Greg can't come to the wedding." She explained why.

Louise looked thoughtful. "Is it too late to ask someone else? Derek?"

"I really couldn't. Not after asking Greg first."

"He doesn't have to know," Louise said.

"Yeah, what he doesn't know won't hurt him." Ruth poured boiling water over the tea bag, then asked, "Rum?" and held up a nearly full bottle.

"No, thanks," Paula shook her head and took the cup, looking anguished. "I know it'll just kill me to see Quent with another woman, and half the town will be watching to see how I handle it."

"And you *will* rise above it, I'm certain,"

Louise told her warmly, "with all the grace you normally show."

"I just remembered that my mother will be calling to report on my step-father's surgery. She's probably been trying and getting no answer." Paula stood up. "Thanks for everything. I do feel better."

Ruth closed the door. "What a pity. Having an escort for the wedding would have shown that dumb husband of hers a thing or two."

"Ex," Louise reminded her, "and yes, it would have been a real coup for Paula."

"I'm not so sure she won't give him something to fret about yet."

"What are you thinking?"

"That Derek Vogel could fit the bill nicely."

"But Paula said she couldn't ask him on such short notice."

"Right." Ruth gave her a conspiratorial smile. *"She* can't. But there is nothing that says *I* can't."

The heat from the sidewalk rose to meet them as they reached the bottom steps of Oldham Hall. Ruth turned in the opposite direction from the cafeteria. "I'll see you two this afternoon."

Paula looked surprised. "But aren't you going to—"

"Gotta check on something in the library." She waved and walked away.

Derek cleared his throat. "That wasn't very subtle, but it was the best she could do on such short notice." Paula looked at him with a puzzled frown. "She thought I'd rather say this without her present, I suppose. I, uh, don't ordinarily invite myself to private functions, but it has come to my attention that you need an escort to your daughter's wedding. And I'd like to offer my services."

"How did you—oh, Ruth." Derek nodded. "But I couldn't ask you to—"

"You're not asking me, Paula. I'm asking you. Will you allow me to escort you to Amy's wedding?"

"I'd be happy for you to go, of course, but I—"

"Then it's settled." He smiled at her. "Now, where shall I make a reservation for a room for the night?"

Paula smiled back. "The Coach House Inn. It's the only decent place in town."

"Good enough. And what time shall I show up for the ceremony?"

"It begins at eight," she told him. "I'll give you directions to find the house before I leave tomorrow." Suddenly feeling less bereft, she added sincerely, "Thank you, Derek. It's so nice of you to do this."

"Not at all," he assured her. "I'm very fond of Amy, and that's what friends are for. I'm just disappointed you didn't call on me for help yourself."

"Well, I didn't want you to feel—"

"That you'd asked someone else and I was just a stand-in?"

"Yes, I guess so."

"I have no problem with that. It's your right to ask anyone you choose." His voice took on a different tone. "I've learned to accept that I'm not every woman's first choice."

Paula nodded her head. "Nor I every man's."

The noonday sun pressed down with a vengeance as they walked on toward Gaither Hall in silence, each lost in their own thoughts.

Fourteen

Paula was driving over the speed limit, something she rarely did. But this was not an ordinary day and the wheels were turning faster in her mind than on the Grand Am she drove along the two-lane highway toward Tuscumbia. Derek Vogel had offered to take Kurt Yearwood for the afternoon and Faye Browne had surprisingly agreed to the arrangement, perhaps because she had imposed Irvin Pendergrass on Paula just the week before.

Freed from the afternoon tutoring session, she had left the university at one and was almost home—except home was a word that seemed not to fit her destination. Tuscumbia and the house on Northwoods Drive were part of a world she no longer inhabited. Winthrope Hall was where she lived and her classes and tutoring were reality now. She glanced at her watch—almost three. And there were boxes to retrieve from storage, clothes to be pressed, the house to check over, and all the last minute details of the wedding to help with although Amy had assured her everything was taken care of.

The Tuscumbia city limits sign came into view and Paula slowed the car, feeling an overwhelming sense of sadness at the sight of the familiar tree-lined streets. This was the town where she grew up, married, raised a family, and finally got divorced. Blinking away tears, Paula turned onto Main Street and headed toward the mini-storage unit which now held all the tangible possessions that remained of her life in this town.

Paula had not imagined how much it would hurt to see the house again. A black wrought iron fence covered by trailing ivy vines partially obscured it from the street. Surrounded by magnolias and pines that she had watched grow taller as her children grew, its antique brick front exuded a quiet dignity. She was glad Quent had given in to her insistence that no "For Sale" sign be placed in the yard.

She drove toward the garage, then remembered that she no longer had a remote control to operate the door, so she pulled into the boxwood-lined circular drive that led to the front entrance. Parking behind two unfamiliar cars, Paula sat gripping the wheel, overcome by a sense of unreality. Before she could bring herself to leave the car, the front door opened and Amy rushed down the steps.

"Mom, you're here!" she cried.

When she saw her daughter, Paula's strange inertia vanished and she quickly got out of the car and embraced her.

"I thought I heard a car." Amy looked puzzled. "Why were you sitting out here?"

"I—well, I just got here, honey. And I've been rushing all day so I was taking a minute to catch my breath."

Amy laughed. "I know what you mean. Things have been pretty crazy around here, too. I'm beginning to feel like air control in Atlanta with all the takeoffs and landings that have been going on."

Paula opened the trunk of her car. "Then we'd better get this cargo unloaded before the next flight comes in." She gave her daughter a small bag. "Here, this one is lightweight."

Amy reached for the second bag. "I'll get that one, too, so you can bring one of those boxes."

Paula reached for the largest storage box.

"You just missed seeing Chris," Amy said as they walked up the steps. "He left about five minutes ago for Huntsville to meet his parents. And Stephen Hall—he's the chaplain—rode along with him."

The cool dim interior of the house contrasted sharply with the bright heat outside and Paula hesitated for a moment, temporarily blinded, then followed Amy who continued talking.

"Nell—she came with me last night—took my car to the mall to shop for a few things. And Kaye, who came this morning with Denise, has gone to Ivy Green for the tour with Wesley—he's one of the groomsmen. Denise is upstairs now doing her hair. Chris picked up Alan and Joel—they're groomsmen, too—at the airport at noon and they are sacked out at the motel. Nobody has heard from Marty Ford—the guy who plays guitar, you know? But except for Marty everyone is accounted for."

"My goodness, it sounds complicated." Paula looked worried. "Have you had time to get the house—"

"My first priority, Mom." Amy set the two bags on the floor just inside the guest bedroom. "The girls all pitched in this morning and it looks great. You couldn't have done it better yourself."

A wave of guilt swept over Paula as she put down the box. She *should* have been here. If only she . . . but Amy was not finished and she temporarily pushed aside her regret to focus on her daughter's words.

"Everyone should be here by the time Chris gets back so you have a couple of hours to rest and get unpacked and dressed."

"Which reminds me, I'd better get my dress out of the car before its plastic bag melts from the heat." Paula put an arm around Amy as they walked back through the house. "You're right, honey. The house looks wonderful, but I'm sorry I wasn't here to help."

"It's okay, Mom." She took her mother's hand and squeezed it. "You're here now and that's what matters."

When they returned from the car, Amy hung the dress in the closet, then turned to look at Paula solemnly. "Mom, thanks for going along with what I asked you—about you and Dad. Chris and I really appreciate it."

Paula nodded, then asked, "But you plan to tell Chris's parents later tonight?"

"Cross my heart," Amy looked anxious, ". . . but I hope it doesn't spoil—"

"Spoil or not, it *must* be done. Remember,

your dad will be bringing his . . . friend . . . to the wedding tomorrow. And I," Paula hesitated, "have invited someone, too."

Amy's apprehension was visible before she consciously controlled it. "Who?"

"Derek Vogel."

"Derek?" Amy's face instantly brightened. "Oooh, neat. When is he coming?"

"Not until tomorrow afternoon. He has a reservation at the Coach House Inn."

"Then maybe Chris can meet him when he checks in. I've told him a lot about Derek and how nice he was to me."

"Then you don't mind? His coming to the wedding, I mean?"

"Mind? I'm thrilled. I would have asked him myself but I thought *you* would mind." She hugged her mother. "You have some really nice friends, Mom, but then, you're pretty nice yourself."

Paula hugged her back. "And so are you. Now, why don't you take a break while I get unpacked? You must be exhausted after all the cleaning and coordinating and everything."

"I'm fine, but I do have to make a few phone calls so I'll leave you to your bags and boxes."

Paula closed the door and sank down on the bed. Here she was staying in the guest bedroom of her own home. The saddest part was that she felt like one.

Paula applied light brown mascara to her long lashes, making a conscious effort to steady her trembling hand. In a few minutes she would be seeing Quent for the first time since their divorce, and facing her ex-husband again overshadowed the importance of meeting her daughter's future in-laws.

She had taken her best summer clothes out of storage and now wore a freshly ironed cut-work embroidery dress. Its long overblouse and softly gathered slit skirt accented her slender figure and the pale ivory color showed off her deep tan. Looking at herself as she passed the full length mirror that hung in the hallway, she knew she didn't look twenty-five, but maybe forty. She would settle for that.

"Here comes my mom now." Amy crossed the living room to embrace her. "Don't you look pretty."

Paula smiled. "You stole my line, Amy. So do you."

Amy turned to the others and said proudly, "Here she is, the mother of the bride. And this is Nell. And Denise. Over there is Alan and Joel. Kaye and Wesley are still dressing, so you'll meet them later." Paula acknowledged each person in turn before Amy continued. "Nell and I were just going to serve drinks on the patio. It should be completely shaded by now."

"Some of us Yankees would just as soon sip our mint juleps in here," Alan grumbled good-naturedly as he held the door for Paula.

"I suppose our summer heat is rather oppressing if you aren't used to . . ." her voice trailed off as she looked at her beloved garden. How she had missed all this.

Taking a glass of chilled fruit juice she wandered away from the lively talk and laughter. Slowly she made her way across the garden, pausing to admire the colorful floribundas and miniature roses that lined the walkway. As she neared the fountain she saw that between the Pascali and Tiffany her newest acquisition, the "Christopher Columbus," was blooming and she hurried to examine it. She had prepared the bed last October, never dreaming what the winter would bring. And in March, with heart as chilled as her fingers she had planted the bush, uncertain of what would happen to her. Now she had returned and found this vibrant bloom, a talisman of the future.

Absorbed in the cup-shaped beauty of its

pepper red petals, she didn't hear steps approaching.

"Mom," Amy said softly. "Here's Dad."

Paula turned, met Quent's unreadable gray eyes and managed a tentative smile, taking in how different he looked with longer hair and a beard.

"Hello, Paula." His neutral voice held no clue to what he was feeling.

"Hello, Quent," she answered quietly. He was more trim, too, or perhaps his close-fitting black dress jeans and black silk shirt only made him seem so.

"Well," Amy took a deep breath, looked from one to the other of them and smiled hopefully, "I guess you two have some catching up to do. I'll be inside watching for Chris."

Glancing around her as Amy walked away, Paula said, "The garden looks lovely."

"Yes. The real estate people have someone taking care of it."

"Oh."

"How have you been?" Quent asked politely.

"Okay." *Do you really care, Quent?* she thought. *How would you react if I told the truth, said I'd been lonely?*

"How is school?"

He was making an effort to be congenial

and she would meet him halfway. "It's still not easy but almost half the summer is behind me now." She smiled ruefully. "I think I'll make it." Grasping for something to fill the awkward silence that followed, she asked, "Are you enjoying retirement now?"

He shrugged. "It's better than working nine to five." Abruptly scowling, he added, "Just for the record, I don't approve of this."

Taken aback by his remark and not following his train of thought, Paula asked, "What?"

"This pretense of being still married."

Paula nodded. At least they had found one thing they agreed upon. "Neither do I. But Amy promised she and Chris will tell the Rylands after dinner tonight and I think we should try and make the best of it until then."

"Well, all the same—"

"Look, Amy's waving to us from the patio. The Rylands are here." Paula took a step toward the house, stopped and turned back to face Quentin. "Quent, let's do this one last thing together—for Amy."

Chris met them on the walk as they approached the patio. He kissed Paula's cheek and shook hands with Quentin. "I'd like you to meet my folks." He put an arm around the tall, thin woman who stood surveying them speculatively. "My mother, Teresa."

"How do you do." Her clipped voice matched her erect posture.

Putting his other arm on the shoulder of the man beside her, Chris continued. "And my father, Lawrence."

"Glad to meet you." The silver-haired man in a pinstriped suit cordially gripped Quentin's hand, then Paula's.

"How was your trip?" Paula asked.

"Very turbulent." Teresa Ryland looked pained. "We flew through thunderstorms most of the way from Boise," she glanced meaningfully toward the dark cumulus clouds gathering above them. "I wouldn't be surprised if it rains out the garden wedding tomorrow."

"Oh, no!" Now it was Amy who looked distressed. "I've been so busy all day I forgot to check the weather report."

"Don't worry," Chris put his arm around her, drew her close, "I've ordered a nice day for tomorrow."

"Have you brought in your bags yet?" Quentin asked Lawrence.

"Yes, we have," Lawrence said, "But we feel that we are imposing, taking your bedroom."

"No, we . . . want you to have it," Paula finished lamely.

"And it certainly wasn't necessary to remove

all of your things from the drawers and closets," Teresa added.

"Teresa, would you and Lawrence like some refreshments before the rehearsal begins?" Amy asked quickly.

"I'm not sure my stomach has settled enough for food, dear, but I guess I could drink something," Teresa Ryland answered.

As Amy led them toward the patio's built-in bar, she spoke over her shoulder. "Chris, will you see that my parents are introduced to Kaye and Wesley and Stephen?"

"Sure." He looked around, beckoned to a young man standing with Alan and Joel. "I'll begin with the guy who has agreed to tie the knot."

As Paula was being introduced to the remaining two members of the wedding party, she became aware of Quent's mother standing nearby, watching her intently.

"Why, hello Edith. How are you?"

After a brief hesitation, Edith Howard said, "Fine, Paula." Her bird-like eyes swept from Paula's toes to the top of her head. "You're looking well."

"I *feel* well." Paula smiled brightly.

Edith glanced at her son, who was engaged in another conversation nearby. "Quentin looks tired, don't you think?"

"I hadn't noticed." And if he does, it's probably from trying to keep up with a twenty-five-year-old.

"I'm sure he isn't eating well, though I do try to have him over for a home-cooked meal as often as I can." Edith's voice had become unmistakably accusatory. "But his schedule is so unpredictable since he joined the band. Poor man, I guess he needed something to keep him from being lonely."

"No doubt," Paula agreed wryly. Something called Bootsie.

Having made her point, Quentin's mother changed the subject. "Amy said your mother wouldn't be here."

"No, unfortunately not." Why did she feel a need to apologize for that?

"And Jeff will miss the wedding, too."

"Yes, Edith," Paula said aloud, and added silently *I'm not to blame for that, either.*

"Paula, why are you calling me Edith?"

"Would you prefer that I call you Mrs. Howard?"

"No, but you have always called me *Mother* Howard before."

"We aren't related now," Paula said emphatically. "Not since your son divorced me."

"Well, he must have had a reason. It's clear

to everyone that *you* went off to school and *he* is still here."

Paula felt her anger rising and she made a conscious effort to keep her voice low. "Is it also clear to everyone that he moved out of the house first, joined a band, and got a girlfriend?" Suddenly inspired, she suggested, "Maybe Quent's little songbird would like to call you Mother. Or Grandmother, since he is old enough to be her father."

"Okay, folks," Stephen Hall said before an open-mouthed Edith could reply, "let's gather round and go through the whole ceremony. If you do it right the first time, no extra practice."

Stephen approached Paula and asked quietly, "Do you want someone to escort you to your seat tomorrow, Mrs. Howard?"

"No, Stephen, I have an escort." She thought of Derek and how glad she was that she would not be alone to face the town's whispers as Quent flaunted a younger woman at their daughter's wedding. But for this evening she could pretend that everything was as it used to be when she was still Quent's wife.

At a quarter of seven, Stephen Hall gave his final instructions and the group dispersed.

"Mom, will you please drive the bridesmaids to the Coach House?" Amy called.

"Stephen is taking the guys, Grandmother Howard is riding with Dad, and Chris and I will take his parents."

"Sure, honey." How thoughtful of Amy to arrange it so that she didn't have to share a ride in Quent's new BMW, but she imagined Edith Howard would repeat their earlier conversation to Quent on the drive to the restaurant, and that could have disastrous results. She didn't know what had come over her. She had always been polite to Quent's mother and the relationship between them had been cordial, if not close. Then it suddenly occurred to her that she had never crossed Edith Howard before. Perhaps it was long overdue.

When Paula and the girls entered the Coach House Inn, Quentin and his mother were already there, talking with Quent's sister and her husband. After a brief hesitation, Paula joined them.

After an awkward moment she fell in step beside Quentin who seemed taller in the black western boots he wore. They followed the others into the private dining room which looked elegant by candlelight. Starched white tablecloths were accented with pale blue napkins and flowers that reflected the blue patterned wallpaper. Greenery spilled from the mirrored mantle of a white brick fireplace near the head of the U-shaped table. Candlelight enhanced the gleaming silverware and sparkling crystal and illuminated Amy's animated face. Paula thought she had never seen her daughter look so happy as she did that night, basking in the obvious admiration of Chris and surrounded by her family and friends.

A waiter appeared to fill their wine glasses and toasts were made to the bridal couple with echoes of good wishes reverberating around the table. Paula glanced at Quentin who sat beside her and their eyes met in mutual pride. Were his eyes misty like her own, or was it only the reflected candlelight? She was close enough to breathe the scent of his familiar cologne and feel the warmth from his body. A wave of longing swept over her so that she clasped her hands tightly together to restrain herself from touching him.

"What a charming place," Teresa Ryland remarked from across the table. "So quaint."

"Yes, it is," Paula agreed. "It was built more than a hundred years ago."

"It's very well preserved." Lawrence Ryland looked around the room appreciatively. "They don't build them like this anymore."

The waitress brought dishes of chilled consommé and Teresa sampled hers before she spoke again. "This is the first time Lawrence and I have ever been to Alabama."

"Fine state," said Lawrence politely.

"Except for the dreadful heat and humidity. My hair feels like cotton candy." Teresa touched her short brunette curls to emphasize her point.

Lawrence cleared his throat. "Have you two always lived here?"

"Yes, always," Paula told him.

When the consommé cups had been replaced by salad plates Teresa Ryland spoke to Quentin. "Amy tells us you have retired." Her tone sounded almost accusing.

"Well, sort of." Quentin paused. "I play guitar with a band now. In a local club."

"A nightclub?" Teresa asked.

"Yes. As a matter of fact, I'm performing tonight. Would you like to come out later?"

"I'm afraid not," Lawrence said regretfully. "We've had a long day."

"Besides," Teresa added loftily, "we don't patronize places that sell hard liquor." She looked at Paula. "But don't let us keep you from going."

"I wasn't going." Paula refrained from adding, I wasn't asked, said instead, "I've had a long day, too."

They concentrated on the salad until the waitress brought the main course, Rock Cornish game hens with rice pilaf stuffing, snow peas, and yeast rolls.

"What, no grits?" Quentin asked in an undertone and Paula almost laughed when she met his eyes. For a moment it felt like things used to be. Was Quent feeling that, too?

After coffee and baked Alaska, they rose to leave the table and Paula and Quent expressed their thanks to the Rylands for hosting the dinner.

"I'm just sorry our other children couldn't be here tonight," Lawrence said. "There are three older and three younger than Chris, you know."

"Yes, he told us," Quentin answered.

"But the younger ones are away in school and the older ones have small children, so it wasn't possible for any of them to come on such *short* notice," Teresa explained.

"We understand," Paula assured her. "Amy's brother is in India and we wish he could be here, too." At the thought of Jeff so far away she suddenly felt like crying. Quent, seeming to sense this, took her arm and guided her toward the front door. The light touch of his hand felt familiar and right and for a moment she forgot they were no longer married.

"Mrs. Howard," Kaye called after them and Paula stopped. "Would you mind taking us by the Cabana Club? We want to hear Mr. Howard's band. All the guys are going, too."

"Sure, Kaye, I'll be glad to drop you girls off."

As he opened the door, Quent asked, "Would you like to come, too, Paula?" She looked at him quickly but could not tell from either his voice or face if he really wanted her to.

"Thanks, but I guess I should go back to the house, and make sure the Rylands are comfortable."

"Okay." Did he sound disappointed? "See you tomorrow."

"Good night, Quent."

The neon sign blazed across the dark sky like a comet, alternating letters to spell "Cabana Club" as Paula pulled up to the entrance.

Before the passenger door closed, Paula caught a glimpse of the large poster beside the club entrance. There was a picture, too, but it was only a blur from where she sat and she would not get out of the car to look at it. Each time people went in she could hear through the open car window the sound of music and laughter. Why not park the car and go inside for just a little while? Quent would be surprised, and maybe pleased, to see her.

A car behind her honked and she shifted gears and drove on. No, she would not let her curiosity get the better of her. And she would not humiliate herself by running after him. No, damn him, she would just drive away as though her heart were not breaking all over again. And she would not look back. There, she'd made it. The car was headed for Northwoods Drive and her pride was still intact.

Paula let herself in the front door and walked quietly toward the kitchen. She felt the beginning of a tension headache and she thought a cup of tea might help her to relax. An earlier peek in the cupboards had confirmed they were well-stocked for the weekend. Bless Amy's heart, she'd thought of everything.

She heard voices coming from the den and stopped, unwilling to intrude.

"Son, how *could* you deceive us this way? We thought Amy's parents were such nice people."

"They are nice people, Mother," Chris said patiently. "They just happen to no longer live together."

"They are *divorced*." Teresa Ryland made it

sound like a contagious disease. "And we have never had a divorce in our family."

"Please don't be upset," Amy pleaded. "Chris and I will never get a divorce."

"I wish we could be sure of that. But you've had a bad example set by—"

"Teresa," Lawrence interrupted firmly, "I think we should say good night now and let this thing rest."

"That's a good idea, Dad," Chris said softly.

Teresa Ryland walked into the hall, saw Paula moving slowly toward the kitchen. Both women stopped.

Tight-lipped, Teresa spoke first. "Chris and Amy just told us about you and Amy's father. Needless to say we are shocked."

"I'm sorry they didn't tell you sooner," Paula said sincerely.

"So am I. It would have made all the difference."

"In what?" Paula asked quietly. "In how you feel about us? Or how you feel about Amy?"

"Why, I . . ." Teresa stopped, flustered, at a loss for words.

"Amy is the same person she was before you learned of this. And in case you don't know, her father and I were divorced only this spring. Amy grew up in a happy home loved by two parents, and I expect she will pattern her own marriage and parenting behavior after that."

"Well, I didn't mean—I'm sorry if—"

"No apology necessary, Teresa. It's been a long day for all of us."

"Yes," Lawrence took his wife's arm. "We'll say good night now and go upstairs."

Paula stood watching the couple make their way up the steps. Tears blurred her eyes, and her head throbbed painfully.

"Mom, I'm so sorry you had to hear this." Amy gently put her arms around her mother.

"Me, too, Paula," Chris added as he embraced them both. "My mother is really a nice person but she has very strong moral convictions."

"They seem to have worked well for you," Paula smiled crookedly, willing her tears back. "I just hope she can accept the news about . . ." she stopped, looked doubtfully at Amy.

"It's okay, Mom. Chris knows I told you."

"About the baby? Oh, she'll be fine with that. My oldest sister was pregnant before she got married, too."

Thank goodness for small favors, Paula said to herself, although how Teresa Ryland could disapprove of divorce and approve premarital sex seemed a contradiction in values to her.

"Well, if you two will excuse me, I'll make myself a cup of hot tea and go to bed."

"Sure, Mom. Chris and I thought we'd go over to the club a little while and listen to the band."

"Just have her home before midnight, Chris. It's bad luck to see the bride before the ceremony on her wedding day."

"Oh, Mom, that's just an old wives' tale."

"And I'm an old wife." Ex-wife, she corrected silently, as they kissed her good night.

Paula changed into a terrycloth robe and scuffs and took her tea out onto the patio. In the heavy magnolia and rose-scented night air insects punctuated the stillness and from a branch in the tall pines came a hoot owl's lonesome call.

A ferris wheel of emotions spun in Paula's mind as scenes from the past few hours exploded like carnival fireworks. Superimposed over it all was Quent himself. A Quent who was vaguely familiar yet so very different. A bearded Quent with longer hair, wearing tight-fitting country-western stage clothes. And although she would have preferred that he dress more conventionally for the occasion, she had to admit that she liked his new image.

She should have told him so. But she had taken special care to look *her* best and he had not even seemed to notice. And why should he when he was dating some cute young singer and she was just a middle-aged ex-wife? Well, tomorrow was another day. And she would see how well he managed to maintain that inscrutable posture when Derek Vogel arrived on the scene.

Thinking about Derek made her feel warm and happy. It had been so good of him to offer to come, especially after she'd asked Greg Winthrope first. An invitation she had to admit was prompted mainly by a desire to show Quent and the whole town that a man of refinement and wealth found her attractive even if her ex-husband didn't.

Sitting there on the dark patio of the house she knew so well, Paula's life at the university took on a dreamlike quality. Derek, Greg, Sharon, Ruth, Louise, all seemed unreal. Yet she knew she didn't belong here either. Who was she now? Where did she belong?

Still too restless to sleep, Paula put down her cup and wandered into the garden. She paused to touch the Christopher Columbus, bent to breathe the heady fragrance of its petals that now appeared to be black velvet. Like its namesake, she also had begun a voyage into the unknown. Would she discover a new world, too?

A low rumble of thunder gave an ominous hint of tomorrow's weather. That's all we need, Paula thought. Already we have a pregnant bride, an impossible mother of the groom, a missing guitar player, and a bimbo accompanying the bride's father.

Paula reached the fountain and stopped, lost in thoughts of tomorrow. Here, beneath the arbor laden with climbing Peace roses, her daughter would take the vows of marriage, promising to love one man until death parted them. Tears gathered in her eyes.

Please, God, for Amy let it be forever.

Fifteen

The sound of the door chimes awakened Paula and she sat up quickly, forgetting for a minute why she was there. On the bedside table a digital clock flashed 8:23 and she remembered and moaned softly. I should have set the alarm, she chided herself, but I was so sure I'd wake early.

After a hasty shower, she put on white cotton slacks and a navy sweater and went to the kitchen. The aroma of freshly made coffee told her someone had already been there and she gratefully poured the steaming amber liquid into a ceramic mug and tilted it to her lips. "Ouch," she said aloud, feeling the pain on her tongue as the coffee moved like hot lava down her throat.

The chimes rang again as she reached for a cinnamon roll and while she considered answering the door she heard footsteps hurrying down the stairs.

"Good morning, Mom." Amy came in carrying a large florist's box.

"Good morning, honey." Paula kissed her daughter as she set the box on the counter. "I'm sorry I overslept. I'm sure there are things I could be doing to help."

"It's all under control, I think. The girls are experimenting with hairstyles. Chris and the guys have gone to the church for chairs, and his parents walked over to Ivy Green." As she spoke she was opening the box and removing tissue paper. "Oh no. They've sent *orange* roses. I ordered Carmella like you said."

Paula took a boutonniere, studied it. "They've substituted something else. As soon as I finish my coffee I'll drive over and exchange these for a more subtle color—maybe Brandy if they have that."

Amy made a silly face. "I could use some of that right now."

"Oh no." Paula touched her daughter's abdomen lightly. "Bad for my grandchild." Suddenly aware that her remark was probably in poor taste on Amy's wedding day, she added quickly, "Don't worry, I'm sure the Blossom Shoppe will have something lovely, and if not, why, we'll just pick some posies from the garden." She carefully lifted out the bridal bouquet, an exquisite arrangement of Jardins de Bagattes and baby's-breath. "At least they got this one right." She gave the flowers to Amy. "Better keep them cool."

As Amy opened the refrigerator door, she suddenly turned to Paula. "I almost forgot to tell you, a case of Dom Perignon arrived a little while ago, from Mr. Winthrope."

"Well, what a nice surprise."

"I had the deliveryman put it in the fridge on the patio. We planned to serve only fruit punch at the reception since Chris's mom has this thing about alcohol, but I suppose it will be okay."

"There was wine at dinner last night," Paula reminded her.

"She had no problem with that. It was for the traditional bridal toasts."

"Then we'll just toast some more," said Paula emphatically. *They will need all the good wishes they can get with Teresa in the wings,* she thought to herself. Thank God Boise was a long way from Atlanta. "Has the guitar player arrived yet?"

"No, but Chris talked to Marty's booking agent last night and found out the group is doing a gig in Vancouver. They were supposed to fly back to Atlanta yesterday but fog had the airport socked in."

"Do you think—"

"Who knows? There's one morning flight that could get him back in time today. The agent is supposed to call us as soon as he has any word." As if on cue, the phone rang. "I'll get it, Mom—could be him now."

Still standing, Paula finished her roll and coffee before Amy returned from the hallway. One look at her face and no questions were necessary.

"That was Marty. He hadn't called before because he thought he'd make it and he didn't want us to worry." She sank into a chair, put her elbows on the table, hands propping her chin. "Marty and Chris flew together in the Air Force and he feels terrible about letting him down."

"Chris will understand."

"Sure he will," Amy nodded, looking anguished, "but what will we *do* without music?"

"Well," Paula groped for some reassuring answer, "you plan to use a recorded wedding march, don't you?" Amy nodded. "So why not use some other tapes, too?"

"We already have some tapes for dancing afterward, but we wanted live music during the ceremony and reception."

"You can still have your live music. Your dad plays guitar."

"Oh, Mom. Not country-western for my wedding."

"Your dad knows lots of other songs," Paula persisted. "Why, he could play for hours without a hint at the type of music he's playing now."

"But I don't think . . ."

"Ask him, honey. If he plays I promise everyone will love it."

"Well, if you really think so . . ." Amy still looked doubtful.

"Talk it over with Chris when he comes back. I'm sure he'll agree, then call your dad." Paula bent to kiss her daughter's cheek and picked up the florist's box. "I'll be back soon. Don't look so forlorn, everything's going to be fine."

A blast of hot air hit Paula when she opened the door and she appraised the sky as she walked toward her car. Dark clouds scudded overhead, intermittently blocking the sun. There was a distinct possibility that it *would* rain on the garden wedding according to Teresa Ryland's dire prediction.

It had taken the Blossom Shoppe quite a while to locate the right color and rewire the flowers, and by the time Paula pulled into the driveway a downpour seemed inevitable. She heard the sound of a lawnmower from the back and fervently hoped the job was almost done. Inside all was quiet and as she refrigerated the florist's box, she called out, "Anyone home?"

"Out here, Mom."

She found Amy and Chris on the patio. "Sorry I took so long, but these are perfect so it was worth the time."

"Thanks, Mom. We were waiting to see if you'd like to have lunch at the Coach House with us. The girls have gone already."

"It's sweet of you to ask but I think I'll just stay here. Is there anything I can be doing?" She looked at the folding chairs stacked against the patio wall.

Chris followed her glance. "We're leaving the chairs and candelabra under cover as long as we can, just in case it rains before tonight."

"And what if it rains *tonight?*"

"I guess we could postpone the ceremony for a little while if we had to. Our plane doesn't leave till 10:05."

"Chris," Paula said patiently. "Sometimes a summer rainstorm lasts for several hours. We need to think about what to do in case that happens today." Thunder rumbled as if to accentuate her words. *Thank you, Lord, for helping prove my point,* she said silently. "What about the church?"

Amy shook her head. "They're having a statewide youth retreat there this weekend. That's why the minister wasn't available."

"Then I guess that leaves the house." She went into the hallway, followed by Chris and Amy, stopped beside the front door. "We could push the furniture against the walls, set up the chairs in the living and dining rooms, maybe a few for family out here. Amy, you could come down the steps, Chris from the back hall, and stop here next to the stairway for the ceremony."

"It might work." Chris looked doubtful.

"There will be fewer showing up if it rains, and we could still serve refreshments on the covered part of the patio." Amy was beginning to smile hopefully. "And while the guests are being served the chairs can be folded up and voila," she gestured expansively, "the dance floor is ready. Now, go along and enjoy your lunch. And when you get back we'll decide on an absolute maximum time for switching to Plan B in case of rain."

Paula closed the door behind them and took a deep breath. She tried to estimate how long it would take to carry out the plan she had so blithely devised but her mind refused to co-operate. Getting her shears from the small garden workroom off the patio, she went to cut apricot miniatures for the refreshment table. In case of rain she would cut some of the floribundas too, and place them in baskets on the stairs and in the hall. Her head began to throb again and she never got headaches. She would make a cup of tea and have some fruit and cheese as soon as she finished arranging the roses in the cut-glass bowl she had gotten from storage.

While her tea steeped, the phone rang and she hurried to answer it. "Hello?"

"Paula? It's Derek."

"Why hello." Her pleasure in hearing his voice was obvious, then she became apprehensive. "Where are you?"

"Here. At the Coach House. I've just talked with Amy and met Chris. I approve of him, incidentally. And they said you were alone so I thought I'd call."

"I'm so glad you did," she told him sincerely. "Have you had lunch?"

"No, just a late breakfast. Is everything going well?"

Paula sighed. "Don't ask."

Derek chuckled. "Well, Amy and Chris looked

very relaxed for people about to take such a big step."

"I've decided it's just a facade, instilled in them by the airlines. Always wear a happy face, don't alarm the passengers, even if the plane is going down."

"Is it? Going down, I mean?"

"Probably, if it storms."

"Oh. Anything I can do to help?"

"Light candles. Say prayers. Chant incantations. Do an anti-rain dance."

"Sounds like you could use a little rest before the crowd returns. So what time shall I show up?"

"Make it seven. And if it rains you can help move furniture and set up chairs."

"Fair enough. And Paula?"

"Yes?"

"Everything is going to be fine."

It was interesting, she thought as she sliced an apple and cut a small piece of cheese, just talking to Derek had lifted her mood and left her calmer. She really was looking forward to seeing him. It seemed much longer than twenty-four hours since she had told him goodbye.

The door chimes sounded and with a sigh she left the kitchen again.

"My, we're glad someone is here. We'd hate

to get caught in a thunderstorm." Teresa and Lawrence Ryland stepped inside and Paula closed the door against a strong gust of wind.

"I thought you two were at the Coach House."

"No, we've just now torn ourselves away from Ivy Green. It is absolutely fascinating."

"I was just having a snack. Would you all like something?"

"Sounds good to me." Lawrence nodded. "I've *walked* up an appetite."

"I'll have something light," Teresa added.

As Paula led the way back to the kitchen, the phone rang again and she retraced her steps to take the call. Maybe Derek again? "Hello?"

"Amy, is that you?"

"No, this is Amy's mother."

"Paula? I didn't expect you. This is Irene Thompson."

"You don't sound like yourself, Irene." Alarm bells sounded in Paula's head at the sound of the caterer's voice.

"I don't sound like myself because I've got summer flu. Coughing my head off, and fever." A fit of coughing followed which emphasized her words.

"Then you won't be able to—"

"No way could I drag myself out of bed right now."

"But why didn't you let us know sooner, so we—"

"I kept thinking I'd be able to make it. Right up till this minute I was sure I was gonna beat this bug but, anyway, I think I've got it figured out how to manage every-thing."

"Tell me." Paula gripped the receiver, hop-ing the woman wasn't delirious or drunk. She was the best caterer in town but rumor had it she finished off the leftover spiked punch af-ter every job.

"Well, the cake is ready and I've got every-thing else here to make the canapes and the punch. So I thought I'd send Elmer Findley over with it if you could manage to put it to-gether." Elmer was Irene's live-in companion who drove her van on deliveries when he wasn't fishing or coon hunting.

"Yes," Paula said quickly. "As soon as pos-sible, Irene. I'll be waiting right here."

Teresa looked up as Paula came into the kitchen and leaned against the counter. "Is anything wrong?"

"Wrong?" Paula asked weakly. "Not unless you consider spending the afternoon making dozens of canapes and mixing gallons of punch a problem."

"Why, no problem at all."

"Teresa always does the wedding receptions for our church families," Lawrence explained.

Paula repeated Irene's conversation and finished with, "You're a lifesaver. Amy will be so grateful when she learns that you have saved the day."

"Well, I'm just glad she didn't take the call. In her condition she doesn't need to get upset about . . ." Teresa stopped, embarrassed.

"How did you—" Paula also stopped.

Teresa shrugged. "Mother's intuition, I suppose."

"And you're not . . ."

"We've got nine grandchildren already," she smiled wryly. "So who's counting?"

Paula wasn't sure if Teresa meant counting babies or months until this baby was born, but she didn't press it.

Elmer Findley arrived moments later and Lawrence helped him unload the van. On an impulse Paula sent one of the bottles of Greg Winthrope's expensive champagne to Irene to help cure her cough. Then as she watched Teresa Ryland roll up her silk blouse sleeves and take charge of the kitchen, she thought that having this woman in the family might not be so bad after all.

They had just put the last tray of canapes in the crowded refrigerator when the storm hit. Great gusts of wind, jagged lightning, and loud peals of thunder accompanied the deluge of water that poured from the dark clouds.

Teresa looked at Paula. "Oh dear, what else can go wrong?"

She shrugged helplessly. "What is there left?"

"Don't tempt fate." Teresa shook her head. "I think I'll go and lie down for a while before I dress."

As they went into the hall Amy rushed down the steps. "Mom, it's raining," she wailed piteously.

Teresa Ryland paused, then at Paula's nod continued on upstairs. Paula hugged her daughter reassuringly. "Now, Amy, summer storms don't usually last long."

"But what if—" the door chimes sounded, barely audible against the noise of the rain. "Who could be out in this . . ." she opened the door and Chris almost fell inside.

"That's some storm out there." His clothes

were soaked and water dripped from the plastic bag he held in one hand. "I brought Dad's tux, and mine, too. I'll dress here after we set up the chairs."

"Oh Chris, our garden wedding is ruined." Amy's voice quivered as she fought back tears.

Chris gave the bag to Paula and enfolded his bride-to-be. "Please don't cry, darling. You might get my shirt wet." She managed a tremulous smile. "Thanks to your mom we've got a plan to fall back on if the storm doesn't let up by six," he glanced at Paula for confirmation, ". . . or thereabouts. So meanwhile, I could use a cup of hot coffee, couldn't you?" He led Amy toward the kitchen and Paula headed toward the guest bedroom. It was time she made her own preparations for the wedding. She wouldn't want to look as frazzled as she felt when she faced the wedding guests— especially Derek. Another thought struck her: and when she met Bootsie.

The storm moved on and a late afternoon sun helped to dry what moisture the summer-parched earth had not absorbed.

"Happy is the bride the sun shines upon," Teresa Ryland proclaimed, though the bride was nowhere in sight.

"Or sets on, as the case may be," Lawrence added before he joined Chris and the men setting up chairs on the close-cropped lawn facing the fountain.

Teresa was supervising the bridesmaids as they added apricot festoons to the serving table. She was already wearing her beige lace gown. Paula observed that the color did not become her at all and wished again she could have had first choice, as was her prerogative.

Quent's sister Holly had agreed to serve refreshments in the absence of Irene Thompson and Pete had been assigned the important job of operating the tape recorder on cue. Paula could not think of anything that had been overlooked as she returned to her room to change.

She had already arranged her hair and she carefully lowered her lace dress over her head then realized, as the material wrinkled at the floor, that she should have put on her slippers first. She had forgotten to unpack them so she crossed to the closet and pulled out her largest bag. She rummaged through it twice before she accepted the fact that her bone-colored pumps were not there.

"Damn. Now what do I do?" she said aloud.

Paula dragged a storage box out of the closet and studied its contents, finally lifting out a pair of beige satin mules with matching boa trim, a long-ago gift from Quent she had seldom worn. Ripping off the feathery edging, she slipped them on and was relieved that only her toes could be seen.

She fastened a pearl comb in her hair, sprayed a touch of Obsession on her wrists and earlobes, then pinned on her corsage.

Paula stepped into the hallway just as the chimes rang. It was too early for Derek so it must be the photographer, she thought, hurrying to open the front door.

"Hello, Paula. I'm afraid I'm early." Derek stood before her, splendid in a navy suit and matching figured tie. "I didn't realize how little time it would take to get here from the motel."

Paula finally found her voice. "Hello, Derek." She resisted the sudden urge to walk into his arms and willed herself to take a step backward instead. She had never seen Derek dressed in suit and tie before and he was so handsome he took her breath away.

"You're beautiful." His voice was only a husky whisper but in the quiet Paula imagined it echoed to every room.

"You look smashing, too." She felt a warmth begin deep inside her and spread to suffuse her high cheekbones. "I'm glad you're here."

"So am I." His eyes continued to bore into

hers and she held her breath as he bent his head toward her lips.

"The door isn't closed all the way so I guess we can just go on—well, hello Paula. Why are you standing here in the dark?" asked Holly. She stopped, then looked from Paula to Derek, who had taken a quick step away from her.

"Hello, Holly." Paula tried to compose herself. "I had just opened the door for Derek Vogel. Derek, this is my . . . Quent's sister Holly, her husband Pete Arnold and their daughters Kathleen and Elizabeth."

Pete stepped forward to shake hands as Holly found the light switch and returned her avid gaze to Derek. "A friend of the bride or groom?"

"I'm—" Derek began but Paula said quickly, "Derek attends classes at the university."

"Oh?" Holly looked from him to Paula. "I see."

"Aunt Paula, where are we supposed to sit?" Kathleen asked.

"Over there." Paula gestured toward the credenza. "You'll find the book and pens there, too."

"What about our corsages, Aunt Paula?" This time it was Elizabeth who spoke.

"Still in the fridge." She turned to Derek. "Will you excuse me?"

"Of course. Is there anything I can do?"

"Thank you, but everything is taken care of, I think."

"I could use a few pointers on getting the best sound out of that fancy tape player of Jeff's." Pete looked at Derek. "Want to take a look at it?"

"Sure." Derek met Paula's eyes. "You'll know where to find me."

Holly followed Paula to the kitchen. "Well, he's some hunk. Does Quent know about this?"

Paula stuck her head in the refrigerator. "There's nothing to know." She removed the florist's box and gave two corsages to Holly. "Here, for the girls." She took out two more. "Yours and Edith's. I hope you can manage without me for a little while. I have to help Amy dress now." Without waiting for Holly's answer, she took the box and went upstairs.

Paula fastened the veil securely in Amy's pale gold hair. "I love you," she whispered then kissed both her cheeks and stepped back to look at her. While the bridesmaids expressed their admiration the camera of the photographer who had joined them earlier kept on unobtrusively recording these special moments.

"I'm going downstairs now, honey," Paula told her daughter softly. Amy, looking at her image in the full-length mirror, seemed not to have heard.

"Don't worry, Mrs. Howard, we'll bring her down on time," Nell assured Paula as she turned to go.

When she reached the stairs Paula saw Quent standing below and her heart gave a sudden lurch as she realized a woman—a very *young* woman was with him. Her knees turned to rubber and she reached out to grip the banister as she closed the distance between them.

Quent looked very distinguished in his dinner jacket—until she noticed that he wore his black cowboy boots. *Well, I'm wearing bedroom slippers,* she remembered as she tried not to look at the girl standing close beside him.

"Hello, Paula."

"Hello," a voice answered but it didn't sound like hers.

"Paula, this is Bootsie."

"Hi." She had a throaty voice and Paula looked at her now, saw her thick dark auburn hair, brown soulful eyes.

"Hello." It was that stranger speaking for her again. The girl wore royal blue, a short, flared skirt and sequined satin shirt with matching fringed boots. Paula's cursory glance confirmed all her imagined fears. The girl had the firm legs of a Dallas Cowboys' cheerleader and her tight bodice showed off her voluptuous breasts.

Quent looked at his watch. "Almost time." He looked at the girl. "Better take a seat."

She gave him a wide smile. "Okay."

Paula watched Bootsie's shapely behind as she moved toward the patio, thankful that the girl would not be standing there when Amy came down, then turned to Quentin who did not meet her eyes. "She's very pretty." She couldn't help the sharp edge that her words carried.

He did not acknowledge her comment but Paula saw the familiar flush that gave away his discomfort creep up his neck. Well, damn him. He deserved to be uncomfortable.

A sound at the top of the steps caught their attention and they looked up to see Amy, radiant in her ivory lace gown, coming slowly down the stairs. Paula heard Quentin's sharp intake of breath, saw him brush at the corner of his eye. And for a moment, standing there together, they became simply the parents of the most beautiful bride either had ever seen.

Paula led the way toward the patio where Derek waited beside the door.

"Derek, you came!" Amy held out her hand to him and he kissed it in an affectionate gesture.

"You are a beautiful bride, Amy Howard."

"I'd like you to meet my dad," she turned to a scowling Quentin. "This is Derek Vogel. He's a friend of Mom's from the university."

Derek offered his hand and Quentin reluctantly shook it as each of them surreptitiously took the measure of the other.

The music began and Paula turned to Amy and said softly, "Be happy, honey." Then she took Derek's arm and they made their way slowly down the brick walk between the beds of roses to the front row of chairs.

The candlelight flickered on the raindrop-laden roses, creating a thousand sparkling diamonds as the bridesmaids in filmy pale green organza gowns walked single file toward the fountain to take their places beside the waiting groomsmen. And then only Chris was left, standing straight and tall as a dark green pine, waiting for his bride who came to him with shining certainty on the arm of her father.

"Who gives this woman to be wed?" Stephen's voice carried all the authority of his official role.

"Her mother and I do." Quentin took his daughter's hand and placed it on the arm of her soon-to-be husband, then turned toward the row of chairs where Paula sat. For a moment she thought he would sit beside her. It seemed so right perhaps he almost did. Moments later she heard soft guitar music and knew he was sitting somewhere in the back, filling in for Marty Ford.

As the familiar words were repeated a kaleidoscope of memories flooded Paula's mind. "I, Amy, take thee, Chris" . . . *I, Paula, take thee, Quentin* . . . "to love, honor, and cherish" . . . *even if he walks out?* . . . "in sickness" . . . *does midlife crisis count?* . . . "for better" . . . *is Bootsie better?* . . . "till death" . . . *what about divorce?*

"I now pronounce you husband and wife."

The Howards and Rylands joined the members of the wedding party for photographs beside the rose arbor.

"Just a little closer, put your hand on her waist, Mr. Howard, there, now smile . . ." Paula could feel the outline of Quent's familiar body warm against her back and she trembled when his hand touched her. "Okay, one more now and you can cut the cake."

Chris and Amy had chosen not to have a formal reception line so Paula was able to join Derek at the refreshment table.

"Champagne?" he asked and when she nodded he served her then touched the rim of his glass to hers. "To weddings," she said. "To happy endings," he answered. Did she detect a cynical note in his voice? "Ummm. Great champagne."

"Thank you." There was no need to tell him Gregory Winthrope had sent it as an apology for not coming.

"He plays well." Derek nodded toward Quentin who sat beside the fountain strumming his guitar. She saw that Bootsie had joined him but what did it matter? Anyone could see that Paula Howard was not a heart-broken humiliated wife tonight.

People that Paula had not seen since her divorce stopped to talk and be introduced to Derek. She could just imagine what they'd be saying about the two of them tomorrow. Let Quent deal with that for a while.

"Paula, how are you?"

"Fine, Cynthia. Derek, Cynthia Gill. She's the school principal who helped me get the summer grant."

They exchanged greetings, then Cynthia said, "Do you still want the job we talked about if it gets funded?"

Paula hesitated briefly while Derek looked at her. "I . . . think so."

"The chances are looking good. And you're

my first choice. By the way, I see you have the new 'Christopher Columbus.'"

"You're a rosarian?"

"Sort of—it's a new hobby for me. And I'm envious. Mine hasn't bloomed yet but I'm watching it closely."

"You know what they say about watched pots."

Cynthia laughed. "Right. Maybe I ought to give it a rest. Anyway, I'll let you know as soon as I hear anything on funding."

"So you want to come back?" Derek asked quietly as he brought them more champagne.

Paula shrugged. "I don't have anything else."

Derek tilted his glass and drank before he asked. "Have you looked for anything else?"

Before she could answer, Amy's arms encircled her from behind. "Oh Mom, everything is perfect. I couldn't be happier."

"I'm so glad, honey."

"Derek, aren't you going to dance with me before I leave?" Amy asked. "I'd like to see if your footwork is as good as your backstroke."

"Is this another trick, young lady? Have you danced on Broadway?"

"Judge for yourself, and no bets this time." Amy led him away and Paula finished her champagne and refilled her glass before she continued greeting the other guests.

"He's really a nice guy, Paula." Pete Arnold nodded toward the table where Amy, Chris, and Derek now stood talking.

"Yes, I think he'll make Amy very happy."

"I meant the other one. Derek."

"Oh."

"Nice going, kiddo. I'm glad for you." Pete gave her a friendly wink and walked away before she could explain.

Amy and Chris said their goodbyes, then she flung her bridal bouquet directly toward the place where Kaye stood beside Wesley.

"Good catch," Alan called from across the patio.

"Yes, isn't he?" Amy answered as the bridal couple disappeared inside amidst a wave of laughter and last good wishes.

Paula realized she had eaten scarcely anything all day and she selected a canape and got another drink. How many glasses did this make? Three? Four?

Someone called out, "Sing for us, Bootsie" and several voices joined in. The girl needed no urging but stood beneath the arbor and sang "The Rose." Her mellow voice caressed the syllables before she let them go. *What did you expect*, Paula asked herself crossly. Singers have good voices. Bootsie held the last low note, then suddenly the garden was quiet. And as the guests applauded Quentin put down his guitar, broke off a full-blown rose and offered it to her.

In slow motion Paula saw red as the flower passed from Quentin to Bootsie, not the red of the Christopher Columbus but the red of a flag waved in front of a raging bull. How dare he? Now he had gone too far. She started toward the fountain—her heels wobbled and she had trouble walking on the brick path— then someone put a cassette in the tape player and Robert Goulet's voice filled the silence. Quent was saying something to Bootsie and she laughed—a melodious sound that matched her singing. Paula's drink was sloshing out of the glass and she tried to lift it high enough to throw—

"Come dance with me, Paula." Derek took her wrist, turned her around, spilling the rest of the champagne on his sleeve.

"No, I—"

"We haven't danced all night." His other arm was firmly around her waist, leading her back toward the patio.

"But I have to—"

They were on the patio now and he held

her close, making her forget for a moment what it was she wanted to do—*had* to do.

"There's too many people here," he whispered close to her ear. "Let's take a drive."

"Now?" She missed a step and he held her more tightly. Her head was spinning and she couldn't seem to focus her eyes.

"Yes, love. Now."

Keeping a gentle grip on her, he guided her to the door, through the hallway. Once outside the house, he gathered her up and carried her to his car, opening the door with one hand and gently placing her inside.

Derek drove slowly, letting the wind from the open windows cool them. Finally he stopped the car and Paula, who had been experiencing the weightlessness of a ride in space, asked dreamily, "Where are we?"

"Coach House Inn," Derek said quietly. "You're invited for coffee."

Walking on air, Paula allowed herself to be led through the deserted lobby and up the ancient elevator to Derek's room. A hurricane lamp glowed from a table beside the mahogany four-poster bed, casting soft shadows on the floral wallpaper.

Paula turned to face Derek, making a concerted effort to focus her eyes. "How *dare* he do that?"

"What?" Derek asked, obviously taken aback at Paula's sudden vehemence.

"Give *her* Christopher Columbus?"

"Who?" He looked even more bewildered, then understanding dawned on his face. "You mean the rose."

"It isn't fair. She's young and pretty and talented and she's got great legs."

"If you want a woman who looks like an ice skater. Some of us don't."

"And big breasts."

"Too big."

Paula glared at him. "Quent *likes* big breasts." She dropped her arms to her sides, thrust out her chest. "And look at me."

"You're perfect."

"So why did my husband leave me?"

"Beats hell out of me, lady."

"So he could have a sexy young singer like *her.*" Paula swallowed a sob in her throat and hiccupped.

"Paula," Derek took her shoulders gently. "Come sit down and I'll call room service for coffee."

"No!" she pulled back and the walls started spinning so that she reached for Derek as he reached to steady her. And then she was in his arms and he was kissing her. Gently at first, then with a passion that left them both breathless.

"You're all any man could want," he whispered, cradling her head against his chest.

"But I'm," she hiccupped again, "not young anymore, and she—"

He tilted her chin up and silenced her words with his lips, teasing the corners of her mouth with his tongue. After a moment he shuddered and drew away abruptly.

"What is it?" she asked and tried again to focus on his face but he was still too near and his features ran together like a Dali painting.

"Better come sit down," he told her brusquely and took her arm but she jerked free.

"You don't want me either."

He looked at her gravely. "Lady, you don't know how wrong you are."

Paula took an unsteady step toward him. "Then make love to me."

Derek stepped backward. "No." He took a deep breath. "It's not you asking. It's the champagne and the hurt and—"

"Please, Derek." She took another step and brushed against him and with an agonized groan he reached for her, crushing the ribboned rose she wore, leaving its heavy scent between them.

His mouth covered hers and her lips parted

to receive his tongue of fire. Sensuously caressing every curve, his hands moved down the sides of her body, finally pressing her hard against his arousal.

"Now tell me I don't want you, Paula." He gripped her shoulders, held her away from him. "But I'm damned if I do—or don't."

Her eyes wide with wonder and want, she whispered brokenly, "Then do, Derek. Please do."

His eyes locked with hers, he slowly unfastened the zipper of her lace dress, removed it from her shoulders and arms and let it fall to the floor.

Wearing only her lace bra and bikini panties, she held her breath as his eyes traveled the length of her and back.

"You're beautiful." He took her face in his hands. His lips, soft as a butterfly's wing, brushed one eyelid, then the other. Pulling her back against him, his mouth sought hers in another fiery kiss she thought would never end.

The room whirled and dipped and she was lying on the four-poster bed with Derek trailing hot kisses down her throat and between her breasts as he removed the fastener of her bra. He reverently kissed each delicate mound, suckled each sensitive point as she gasped with pleasure.

He took off her slippers and pantyhose, kissing the arch of each slender foot as he did and then deftly removed the final lace barrier from between them and caressed the center of her mounting desire. "I am going to regret doing this to you," he mumbled hoarsely.

"You are not doing this to me," she protested breathlessly. "We are doing this together."

Her words were the impetus he needed to be freed from his self-imposed restraint. Throwing off his own clothes, he pulled his wallet from his jacket before he tossed it aside and removed the condom from its wrapper. With a joyous surrender he entered her and they were spinning, falling, spinning, falling, careening. Even in her champagne haze Paula was acutely aware that Derek was an expert lover—kissing, touching, tasting until he set the night aflame. Again and again they rose to the pinnacle of their passion, then a thousand fire sparks lit up the night.

"Paula, Paula." Her name was a love word on his tongue calling her back to reality and they lay burning in each other's arms, completely spent and sated. "Now do you feel desired, my love?" Derek whispered as he held her against his fiercely beating heart. Not waiting for her answer, he spoke again. "No twenty-five-year-old could make love the way you did tonight. If you have ever loved a man this way before he was a fool to leave you."

She tried to think about Derek's words. Her husband had taught her how to please him and she had unconsciously responded to Derek in all the ways that had become second nature to her lovemaking, but had she ever loved Quent with the passion she had felt with Derek this night? Her thoughts blurred as his words, his nearness, his touch drifted in and out of her mind until she slept.

Sixteen

In the silence just before dawn Paula awakened with a strange sensation of heaviness. It was a moment before she became aware that the weight of a man's arm held her captive, and moments more before she realized that her captor was Derek Vogel and that she lay naked in his bed at the Coach House Inn.

"Oh . . . my . . . God," she whispered, lying perfectly still so as not to wake him while she tried to think what to do. She might be able to find her clothes and slip out of his room without his knowledge but then what? She had not driven herself here last night, so she would have to call a cab. Someone might recognize her and then word would spread all over town that Amy Howard's mother had slept with a strange man at the Coach House Inn the night of her daughter's wedding. Not a pretty story. She didn't dare risk it. She could try walking home. Two miles in the dark in a pair of high-heeled bedroom slippers? Hardly. So the only other alternative was to wake Derek and ask him to take her home. And soon, before it got light. But first she would get out of his bed and make herself a bit more decent. She winced at the word that had come unbidden to her mind and revised it to "get dressed."

Gingerly she moved out from under Derek's arm and the comforter that covered them. He groaned softly but his deep even breathing resumed and on hands and knees she groped about the floor until she found her bra and panties and hose. Nearer the door she finally located her dress. When she stood up her head began to throb and she resisted the urge to lie down again. On tiptoe she felt her way along the wall to the bathroom. Closing the door, she flicked on the light switch and bright sparklers exploded in her head. When she could focus she looked at her tousled image in the mirror and repeated "Oh . . . my . . . God."

Repairing her hair as best she could and wearing her wrinkled dress, Paula crept back to the bedroom and stood a few feet from the four-poster. "Derek," she said softly, then repeated more loudly, "Derek, please wake up."

He sat bolt upright in bed and turned on the bedroom light. "Christ."

"Derek . . . I . . . I'm sorry to wake you but I need to go home, now, and I—"

"I'm not dreaming? You're really here, Paula?" He grinned wryly.

"Yes." She felt her face getting warm. "But I need to get back before daylight, and—"

"I'll dress as fast as I can." He glanced at her again and she turned away quickly and felt herself grow warm all over as she visualized his nakedness as he threw back the cover. She heard the bathroom door close, water running, and then he was back, stuffing his shirt in his trousers as he walked.

As she stood waiting for him to open the door, Derek said softly, "Paula?" She turned but did not meet his eyes. "If you have any regrets—I'll say I'm sorry."

"I . . . I don't know," she whispered.

"Okay." His hand brushed her arm as he opened the door and she was startled at the response she felt. "Apology on hold—for now."

They were silent as they drove through the dark deserted streets but when he turned the

Firebird onto Northwoods Drive, Derek said, "You have no door key."

"The patio doors will be unlocked."

"Shall I walk around back with you?"

"Oh no. Thank you."

He pulled to the curb in front of the house, reached across her to open the door, brushing her sensitive breasts with his sleeve. She drew her breath in sharply and waited a moment before she felt steady enough to get out of the car.

"Thank you," she said again.

"Anytime." Was there a double meaning in his tone? Did he think she was thanking him for last night? Was he offering a repeat performance?

Paula let herself in quietly and took off her shoes. She would make a pot of coffee and while it dripped she'd take a hot shower and look presentable by the time her houseguests awakened. She had made it just in time, already the sky had brightened so she didn't need a kitchen light to see what she was doing.

She measured coffee, added water, plugged in the cord. Turning she found herself staring into Quent's inscrutable face. "Why, good morning. I was just—"

"Getting home?"

Aware of her wrinkled dress, wilted corsage,

face devoid of makeup, she knew denial would be useless. Guilt fueled her counterattack. "What are you doing here?" she demanded.

"I slept here." At her look of surprise, he went on. "Not in the guest room, though I could have used the empty bed and gotten a damned sight more sleep than on the den sofa."

She flushed, and felt her anger rising. What right had he to question her behavior? "Why didn't you go home? Too much to drink? Wouldn't your boots-and-bosoms-bimbo drive you?"

"I'll pretend you didn't say that. And in case you've forgotten, this is my house, too. Now to answer your first question, I'm taking the Rylands to Huntsville to catch a 6:17 flight to Boise and I had to sleep here to satisfy that nutty woman that I wasn't going to *over*sleep and cause them to miss the plane."

"Oh." Suddenly realizing that she couldn't face the Rylands looking the way she did, Paula took a step toward the door. "Quent, I—I'm sorry for what I said."

"Me, too." His look was more contrite than she had any reason to expect.

"It's just that I—"

"You'd better go now. I hear voices on the steps." His mask was firmly back in place and what she had been about to say was lost in the need for haste. He turned away and reached for a cup and she wanted to go to him and put her arms around his hunched shoulders but went instead to take a shower, wondering what might have happened last night if she *had* slept in the guest bed with Quent in the next room. Had he actually stayed because he thought she would be there? No, more likely he had stayed for the reason he gave or else to check up on when she came in.

Paula put away the sweeper and took the last load of clothes from the dryer. Arms piled high with warm folded sheets and towels, she went upstairs. There were still beds to make and packing to do before she left.

As she tucked the pale blue fitted sheet under the corners of the king-sized mattress she tried to keep her thoughts firmly fixed on the present but images of Quent and her in this room—in this bed, kept intruding. They'd had a good marriage, hadn't they? Their sex life had been fulfilling, hadn't it? She'd been a loving wife, hadn't she? Yes, yes, yes. Then why had Quent left her? It was not because of Bootsie, she was sure of that. Bootsie had come later, an appendage to his new persona. As Derek had been for her.

Paula spread the pastel striped comforter, smoothed its edges. Derek, her friend, who had suddenly become her lover. Just thinking that word, lover, made her feel warm and shivery. She had spent the morning putting the house in order, refusing to face what had happened but she was going to have to deal with it. So what *had* happened? The actual details were blurred but she could recall asking Derek to make love to her. *She* had asked him, of that she was certain. Surely his lovemaking had not been as fantastic as she remembered it to be. She had never made love with any man except Quent until last night so there had been nothing with which to compare their intimate relationship. Had she been missing something all these years or was it that her abstinence since the divorce had made this seem so special? The chimes intruded into her thoughts and she hurried downstairs to open the door.

"Hello, girls, Holly, Pete. Come on in."

"I hope we haven't kept you waiting," Holly said as they followed Paula into the kitchen.

"No, I've just now finished with the house." She opened the refrigerator door, began removing jars and boxes.

380

"Good idea you had, sending all this stuff to Pleasant Acres." Holly gave boxes to Kathleen and Elizabeth as Pete picked up two gallon jars of punch. "Those old people will have a real party this afternoon, and it's not even anyone's birthday." She stacked one box on top of another. "It was a beautiful wedding, Paula. I was going to tell you last night but you disappeared before we left."

"I went for a drive with . . . to clear my head," said Paula quickly, not meeting Holly's inquisitive gaze as she felt her face grow hot.

"Why don't you come with us to Mother's house for dinner before you go? She said at church to ask you."

"Oh, I couldn't, Holly. I really need to—"

"Quent will be there."

"And Bootsie?" Paula asked quietly.

Holly shook her head. "Don't be too hard on him, Paula. He's lonely."

"So was I, Holly, when he walked out."

"Well, you seem to be doing all right now," Holly said stiffly, then added regretfully, "It's just not the same since you and Quent broke up. I wish things were like they used to be."

Paula reached out to touch her arm. "So do I, Holly, but we don't always get our wishes."

Holly looked hopeful. "Do you think there's

a chance you all could get back together? Lots of people do and—"

"No, I don't think so." Now it was Paula who sounded regretful.

"Because of that Vogel guy?"

"No," Paula shook her head, "Derek has nothing to do with it. Your brother wanted the divorce and from what I can see he's quite happy with his new life."

"He's so different, Paula. Pete says it's like Quent regressed to his late teens again." She shrugged, sighed. "Maybe we could just ground him until he comes to his senses." She looked at Paula intently, "And speaking of teens, you look about sixteen yourself today with your hair pulled back like that and wearing your cutoffs. I believe college life is agreeing with you."

"Holly, we'd better get the rest of these things to the car," said Pete as he and the girls returned to the kitchen. "Your mother'll have a hissy fit if we're late to dinner and we still have to stop at Pleasant Acres."

"Okay, Pete. We can get all that's left this trip." She pushed boxes toward the girls and picked up one of the remaining glass containers. "Don't give up on him, Paula. Think about what I said."

"Thanks for helping, all of you. We couldn't have done it without you."

"Glad to do it, Paula." Pete gave her a wide grin and winked. "Don't study too hard."

She stood watching them get into the car. That family could have been hers a few years ago. She and Quent, Amy and Jeff, Sunday church, dinner at Mother Howard's, the kids playing ball or going swimming in the afternoon. Where had time gone? Closing the door firmly on the relentless heat and her nostalgic thoughts she went upstairs to take a shower and pack.

Paula put her bags in the hallway and went out to the garden which seemed bare at first with all the chairs and wedding decorations gone. At the fountain she paused, stared regretfully at the broken stem where her first Christopher Columbus bloom had been. Last night's scene replayed in her head and she clenched her fists as she relived Quent's thoughtless act. He gave her what was mine, she said silently. Yes, Quent had given his sexy songbird much more that should have been hers. He gave her himself.

What about Derek? Why should she feel guilty for what had happened between them? Maybe because she had thrown herself at him. Or maybe because she still felt married to

Quent. Impulsively she broke off two nearly-opened rosebuds and left the garden. No one would see them blooming there anyway, so she'd take them with her and watch them open in her room at Winthrope Hall.

As soon as she arrived at the university Paula invited her friends for the wedding cake and punch that she'd kept chilled in a styrofoam chest en route. When they had each helped themselves from the buffet Paula had arranged on top of her desk, Ruth sat down on the bed near Paula and looked at her expectantly.

"So, tell us all about the wedding."

Sharon assumed the lotus position on the Dhurrie rug at Paula's feet. "I'll bet Amy was the most beautiful bride ever."

"What did she look like?" Louise asked as she settled herself on the bed opposite Ruth.

"Oh, radiant and absolutely angelic and—"

"No, no, I don't mean Amy. The *other woman*."

"Who cares about her?" Ruth interrupted before Paula could answer. "I want to know what the daddy of the bride, Mister Oatmeal For Brains, did when he saw you with your Paul Newman look-alike."

Paula laughed and raised both hands. "Why don't I just begin at the beginning and give you a blow by blow account of—"

"Oh dear, they came to blows?" Ruth looked comically alarmed, then told Paula, "Sorry, I got carried away, please go on."

"Well, I left campus about noon on Friday and—"

"Spare us the scenic drive, honey, and get to the good stuff," Ruth urged. "Can't you see we're wild with curiosity?"

"If you don't stop interrupting, she's never going to get there," Louise observed.

"Okay, I'll start with when I arrived at the house, which was more like Grand Central Station at the time. No, make that O'Hare Airport. Anyway . . ." they laughed as Paula took a deep breath and continued her story. She reiterated each event in sequence, describing the decorations, the food, and what everyone was wearing as her audience listened with rapt attention. She told them about Bootsie singing "The Rose", but not about Quent giving her one. And Greg sending a case of champagne, but not that she drank too much of it. And she didn't mention that Quent had spent Saturday night at the house on Northwoods Drive, and she hadn't. "And that about wraps it up," Paula smiled at them. "The chair will now entertain your questions."

"First, first," Ruth waved her hand. "Was Mister Ex shocked when you introduced your *friend* Derek?"

Paula looked thoughtful. "I don't really know. It's hard to tell about Quentin. He doesn't show his feelings easily."

"Mr. Stone Face, huh?" Louise asked.

"More like Mr. Stone Heart after what he did to our Paula," Ruth retorted. "Or Stone Head."

"Well, he certainly looks different." Paula poured more punch for each of them. "His hair is a lot longer, and the beard, and those western clothes."

"And the girl," Ruth added darkly.

"Yes, Bootsie." Paula sighed. "She's every man's fantasy personified, I guess."

"Not *every* man," Ruth said. "Some men have more mature tastes and can appreciate a real woman, not a—a—"

"Bubble head with more bosom than brains?" Paula suggested with a tinge of bitterness.

"Exactly," Ruth agreed. "And speaking of brains, we'd better get out of here and let you study for Monday's tests. The ogres of Oldham Hall will cut no slack for a weary mother of the bride."

"Do I look that bad?" Paula smiled wryly.

"Not bad at all," Louise assured her. "In fact I was going to tell you how much I like your hair pulled back that way—makes you look even younger."

"And who else do we know who looks like a movie star even without makeup?" Ruth asked as they walked toward the door.

"Thanks for the report and all the goodies," Louise said. "I almost feel as if I've been to the wedding."

"Me, too," Sharon added.

"As for going to the wedding, Paula," Ruth paused at the door, "aren't you glad Derek was there to show your ex and the others a thing or two?"

She hesitated briefly, then smiled brightly. "Oh, yes."

After Paula closed her door and Sharon stopped at her room, Ruth shook her head. "Why do I feel there was an awful lot of no in that yes? Maybe I'm wrong but I don't think Paula told us everything about the weekend."

"I'm sure it was a very emotional time for her."

"Yeah, and I don't like the way she sounded when she mentioned her ex. You don't suppose she might . . ." Ruth's steps slowed.

"She's probably coping with a lot of memories right now. And fighting possessive feelings after seeing him with someone else, but I think she'll be able to work through it."

Ruth opened the door to their room. "Well, Mrs. Freud, I hope you're right. I'd hate to think there's any chance that woman would ever take the rhinestone cowboy back again, especially when Mister Right is knocking at her door."

"The eternal matchmaker." Louise smiled at her, then asked innocently, "I presume you mean the paper mill magnate?"

"In a pig's eye! You know I mean that sizzling sex symbol of Rhodes Hall. Anyone can see they're perfect for each other."

"Then give it time."

"Time? They only have till summer ends. Who knows where they'll go then? If things don't move a little faster it surely won't be anyplace together."

Louise shrugged as she closed the door. "You can't rush love. The heart has its own seasons."

Ruth placed her tray on the table and sat down beside Paula. "Tell me, Derek, was Amy the most beautiful bride in the world like her mother says?"

"Absolutely."

"And I'll bet there's never been a more stunning mother of the bride either?"

"Ruth," Paula said before Derek could answer, "how do you think you did on that last essay question?" She was aware of the man who sat across from her in every inch of her body and it was difficult to breathe.

"Not too well, I'm afraid. I think I was still daydreaming about garden weddings and champagne."

"I thought it was a tough question myself." Derek took a long drink of tea. "But then the whole test seemed worse than usual."

Paula nodded. How could he sit there so nonchalantly? Didn't he feel anything of what she was feeling?

"Maybe you two still have wedding weekend hangovers." As four eyes bored into her, Ruth amended quickly, "Not literally, just a figure of speech. What I meant was you're probably still exhausted from the big night." Still under scrutiny she added, "And didn't have time to study very much."

Paula lowered her eyes and concentrated on her meal. There was no way Ruth could know what had happened between her and Derek.

She willed herself to speak in a natural voice. "Was Kurt okay last Friday?"

"He was a little put out because he had to do sight word drills instead of finishing his farm story."

Why didn't he look at her when he spoke? "He can finish it today."

"And he was a lot put out because he wasn't going back to the mill Saturday."

Had he always been this handsome, exuded this much pure masculinity? "I was afraid he would be," Paula sighed.

"And Irvin got all riled up because I'm not taking him out there again."

Is he sorry about Saturday night? Is this the way it's going to be now? "Sounds like you had a bad time with both of them."

"Nothing I couldn't handle."

"Well, obviously you two didn't talk shop at the wedding," Ruth commented dryly.

When they left the cafeteria with Ruth leading the way, Paula turned and spoke softly to Derek. "I don't believe I ever thanked you for coming to the wedding."

"You thanked me."

Paula looked away, feeling herself grow warmer than the outside heat could be blamed for. What had he meant by that? Did he consider their night together at the Coach House

Inn a thank you for coming? Keeping Ruth between them, the three walked silently to Oldham Hall.

"I tell you, something strange is going on between those two." Ruth shook her head. "Won't talk about the wedding. Won't look at each other. Stuck me between them when we walked to class so they wouldn't accidentally touch each other."

Louise looked up from her book. "Maybe they had a little misunderstanding."

"More like a major war."

Louise laughed. "Remember those bumper stickers, 'Make love, not war'?"

The words were no sooner out of her mouth than the two women looked at each other.

"Do you suppose . . ." Ruth began slowly.

"Uh-huh," they both nodded.

"But how, where, when?" Ruth asked incredulously.

"You left out why?" Louise added wryly.

"I know why." Ruth took a deep breath, let it out slowly. "But now they must be having second thoughts and I'd like to know the why of that."

"Maybe one was persuaded against her will."

"You said *her* will."

"Well, can you imagine Paula seducing *him*?"

"*I* certainly would." Ruth frowned. "But, no, not Paula, I guess."

"Then she's probably feeling guilty that she let him have his way, to put it nicely, and he's probably feeling guilty that he talked her into hopping into bed with him. So they're both having second thoughts and behaving awkwardly."

"Thank you, counselor, for all that enlightening information."

"Glad I could help." Louise returned her attention to her book.

"Question is, now what to do," Ruth mumbled as she opened her own book and settled back against her pillow.

"Can't help you there," said Louise absently, "but remember that old saw about fools rushing in."

"Yeah," Ruth nodded. "And when in doubt, don't."

It had been a terrible week, Paula admitted as she crossed the commons from Gaither Hall alone. Once the wedding was over she had expected to concentrate on her studies and tutoring and even have time to relax. But she had not expected to be on this merry-go-round of emotions. Ever since the weekend she'd alternated between what she felt for Quent and Derek and she was still confused. She knew she had not stopped loving Quent and she was hurt and angry that he had so easily replaced her with that showbiz sexpot. But she had to admit the powerful attraction she felt for Derek and she could not forget their exquisite night of lovemaking.

Still, his behavior all week had puzzled her. Their easy rapport was gone and in its place was a strange awkwardness. Was he resentful that she had practically forced herself on him or was he afraid she was reading some kind of commitment into what for him had surely been nothing more than a one-night stand? And she couldn't ask him, with him acting so friendly to Faye Browne. He was even going to her apartment for dinner tonight. Not that she would have known that if he hadn't made such a point of confirming his date with her when he'd turned in his material after tutoring today.

"Paula, Paula. Wait." She turned at the sound of Sharon Swafford's voice behind her. "Did you hear what happened last night?" She shook her head and Sharon went on. "A girl was attacked in one of the music practice rooms. They're soundproof, you know? And they're supposed to be locked from inside but I guess this girl forgot, and anyway, the guy got in."

"Was she hurt?"

"Yes, he beat her up and tried to strangle her. She's in the hospital and someone said she's on a respirator. They didn't catch him. He's still around here somewhere. Maybe just waiting to do it again."

Paula took Sharon's arm as they walked on. "We'll have to be extra careful." Sensing there was nothing to be gained by dwelling on it further, she changed the subject as they reached Winthrope Hall. "What have you heard from Todd?"

"He called last night. He's back on base now, but I think," she hesitated, "well, he just seems different, like something's bothering him."

Like father, like son, Paula thought wryly. "He's had a frightening experience, Sharon. Maybe it will take some time to adjust to it."

"I just wish he'd talk to me about it."

My sentiments exactly, Paula said silently. When they reached the top floor of the dorm Paula heard her phone ringing before she unlocked her door. Rushing in, she grabbed the receiver before it stopped.

"Paula, Greg again."

"Hello, Greg." He had called just last night to make a dinner date for Saturday. Was he calling to cancel?

"I want to ask you something and please don't say no until you hear me out."

"All right."

"I'm flying to Las Vegas tonight, a very sudden business trip. I'll spend a few hours touring a plant site in Henderson tomorrow and the rest of the weekend I'll be free to enjoy the city. I want you to come with me."

"Oh, Greg, I—"

"Let me finish, Paula. There are no strings attached. You'd have your own room. And you could sleep late and enjoy the pool or hotel shops, then we'd do the town and fly back on Sunday. Consider it a present from me, my apology for last weekend."

"I thought you said the champagne was your apology?"

"That was my apology to Amy. Have you ever been to Vegas, Paula?"

"No, and I've always wanted . . ." *So why don't you go, Paula,* she asked herself, *what's stopping you?* "How soon would we have to leave?"

"Not until eleven. The flight is at 12:05."

Yes, there would be time to shampoo her hair and figure out what to pack. "All right, I . . ." a sudden thought stopped her. "What about Kurt Yearwood? I told him today I'd pick him up at nine in the morning and take him to the mill."

"Well, he won't be able to help me in the gardens if I'm not here, Paula. Tell you what, I'll call his dorm and talk with him right now. And we'll see that he has a chance to visit the stables next weekend after a morning at the mill and one of Mellie's superb lunches. So I'll pick you up at eleven. And thank you, Paula."

Paula stood holding the receiver, unaware of the dial tone. What had she agreed to? Having dinner with Greg Winthrope was one thing, flying off to Vegas with him was something else. Well, why not? She was free to go anywhere she pleased with whomever she chose to go with. He had said no strings attached and she believed him. Greg Winthrope was a true southern gentleman, of that she was certain. And subconsciously she'd probably agreed to go because tomorrow was her birthday. She hadn't told anyone, hadn't planned to celebrate it but now she would indulge herself with this exciting weekend. Yes, the trip would be a present as Greg had said.

Paula wore her coffee-colored jumpsuit and had tied her hair back with a matching scarf low on the nape of her neck. Carrying her flight bag, she knocked at Ruth's and Louise's door.

"What's this, are you running away from school?" Ruth looked from Paula to the bag she carried.

"Sort of. I'm going on a weekend trip."

"Say, isn't this getting to be a habit? You did that last weekend." Ruth smiled at her. "Where to now? Nothing's wrong, is it?"

"No, I'm just going with Greg Winthrope to Las Vegas on a business trip."

"Really." Ruth's smile disappeared.

"It's not what you're thinking. We have separate rooms, and—"

Ruth waved her hands. "Don't explain to me, honey."

"But I don't want you to think—"

"What I think is that you don't know how you feel about your ex or *friend* Derek right now and I'd hate to see Mister Rich Guy win by default. So have fun but don't make any foolish commitments." She impulsively hugged her. "Now when can we expect you back?"

"Sunday evening. And thanks for the advice, Ruth."

"What was that all about?" Louise asked as Ruth stepped back inside.

"Trouble, I think," Ruth mumbled. "It's not enough he's got to compete with her husband's ghost, he's also got Mr. Rockefeller's money for competition. And what is he doing while Rome burns? Why, fiddling with that femme fatale named Faye."

Louise laughed. "Ruth, if you mix any more metaphors the whole thing is going to explode."

"Yeah, and me with it." She shook her head. "I just hope that guy doesn't sweep her off her feet before she knows what's happening. Anything could happen in that town."

Seventeen

There was a festive atmosphere on the DC 10 nonstop to Las Vegas which Paula and Greg had boarded in Nashville. Despite the late hour, every seat was filled and partying passengers enjoyed cocktails and cards, getting an early start on the weekend ahead.

"More wine, Paula?" Greg asked as the stewardess stopped beside their seats.

She hesitated, then nodded. "Yes, thank you." She was having white wine on the rocks, already more ice water than anything else, she reasoned.

"As I was saying," Greg continued, "this processing plant in Henderson has developed a new procedure for chemically treating waste water residue and after hearing about it last week I contacted the people there and asked for more information. So when they invited me to see it firsthand and talk with the engineer who conceived the idea I took them up on it." He smiled wryly at her. "I'm hopeful that with some modification we may be able to adapt the system to meet our needs at the mill."

"Which would mean cleaner air," Paula returned his smile, "though I must admit I don't notice the smell as much anymore."

Greg nodded. "People tend to get used to anything in time." He laid his hand over hers on the armrest between them. "Paula, I'm glad you came with me. It has turned a tiring business trip into a real holiday."

"I'm glad I came, too," she answered sincerely.

"If you'll excuse me now I think I'll try to get a little sleep before we land. Wouldn't want to fall asleep on the tour."

"I could use a nap myself," Paula told him as he reached to turn off the overhead light.

Paula twisted her body sideways in the roomy first-class seat so that she faced the window. Even with the effect of two glasses of wine she was wide awake. Although she had flown to Florida a couple of times to see her mother and Roger and had once accompanied the swim team to a regional meet in South Carolina, this was her first time to fly at night and it felt eerie and exhilarating to be cruising thirty-five thousand feet above the ground with patches of clouds visible below them.

She wondered what Quent would think if he could see her now. Probably that she had lost her mind. And how would Derek feel when he found out about her weekend fling? Well, what did she care what either one of them thought or felt about anything? Ruth's words came back to her and she had to admit she did have mixed feelings about both Quent and Derek right now. So maybe time away from all of it would help to clarify her thoughts.

The pilot's voice broke the monotonous hum of the plane's engines to request that all passengers place their seats in upright position and fasten their seat belts due to turbulence ahead. Paula was still loosely wearing hers and she tightened it now and glanced at Greg to be sure that he was wearing his also. She couldn't understand everything the pilot said because of static on the speaker but she made out the words "monsoon season" and "heavy storms" and "New Mexico."

Soon they were climbing and bumping into cloud formations in roller-coaster fashion. She could see bright streaks of lightning below them but the only sound was the plane itself. It was frightening to her but Greg was sleeping right through it so she watched this belated Fourth of July fireworks display with timid fascination. The pilot announced that they were swinging far south over Yuma to avoid the eye of the storm and finally leveled off, leaving nature's laser show behind them.

"We are now approaching Las Vegas. We will be landing at approximately 4:08 . . ." The speaker droned on but Paula didn't listen after she caught a glimpse of the lights in the valley below. As the jet engines whined on their approach to the landing strip she held her breath in awe at the larger-than-life kaleidoscope of flashing, turning, blinking neon.

Greg had rented an unpretentious Nissan Maxima and as they drove from the terminal down the spiral ramp to the street Paula stared at the city below.

"I can't believe this—it's unreal," she said.

Greg laughed softly. "Yes, unreal is definitely the word for it. And I apologize for not arranging a grand entrance for you in a limo but I have to drive out to Henderson later this morning and I thought it would save time to get a car at the airport."

"This is fine. I'd have been uncomfortable in a limo anyway," Paula assured him.

After driving several blocks, Greg made a left turn, then another and announced, "And here's the famous Strip. See, over there, that huge waterfall?" A little farther along he pointed out another landmark. "Watch, over here, the volcano is starting to erupt."

Paula gazed at the multihued frothing cascade of water. "Fabulous."

"And roll down your window. Recognize the scent?"

"Pina colada?"

He nodded and reached to touch her hand lying on the seat. "I've been here several times and it never ceases to amaze me."

"All these cars and people. I thought at this time of the morning—"

Greg laughed. "The city that never sleeps, thought it *will* be more deserted at noon than it is now."

"I've read about it, of course, but I never imagined all this."

"It is hard to imagine, isn't it?" As they inched along in the stream of traffic he pointed ahead of them. "Over there to your right, Paula, see those turrets?"

"A castle?"

"That's where we'll be staying." He smiled at her. "I guess it's every grown-up little boy's fantasy come true."

Paula smiled back. "And every grown-up little girl's, too. I feel like a princess already."

When a valet had taken the car, Greg led her across a drawbridge and into the cavernous stone-floored lobby. While he registered, Paula stood totally captivated by the troubadours and costumed maidens in their period regalia who strolled among the hotel guests. Greg took her arm and they followed a bellman past walls hung with crossed swords and heraldic banners toward the cluster of elevators and up to their third floor rooms. After assigning their luggage to its proper places and giving the bellman a bill, Greg stood at her door for a moment. "Would you like breakfast, Paula?"

"Oh no, thank you. I'd never sleep at all if I have breakfast now."

"Then I'll just shower and change first and get something on my way out." He touched her cheek lightly. "Sleep as long as you like. You'll need to be rested for our night on the town."

Paula smiled at him. "I'll try but I think I'm too excited for sleeping."

"You can always order room service when you're ready."

"All right."

"I'll leave word at the desk when I get back, so check on that after you wake up."

Paula closed the door and looked around the

room. The decor was elaborate, from the king-sized bed to the velvet loveseat and ornate lamps and tables. This must surely be an executive suite and have cost a small fortune. She experienced second thoughts about what she was doing. Would Greg expect something more than her company in return for all of this? Going into the enormous bath she marveled again at her luxurious surroundings. She smiled at herself in the stage-lighted mirror of the dressing table, took a deep breath and said aloud, "Happy birthday, Paula Howard."

After she removed her makeup and moisturized her face, she slipped out of her jumpsuit, turned back the heavy white woven spread, and crawled under the mauve satin comforter. The sheets were crisp and cool and she closed her eyes, savoring the feel of them, relaxing her taut body, and soon she slept.

Sunlight streaming through the blinds she had forgotten to close awakened Paula and for a moment she was temporarily disoriented. Then she jumped up and ran to the window and confirmed what she had seen earlier. Even by day the Strip was a spectacular sight with its bright colors and gigantic eye-catching signs. She took a quick shower and dressed in a peach silk blouse and linen slacks of a deeper peach, decided against room service and went downstairs. It was only ten and she felt certain Greg was not back yet but she checked anyway, then left a message in case he came before she returned to her room.

In the main lobby Paula drifted with the flow of tourists until she found herself in the hotel's enormous casino. She stood for a time mesmerized by the lights, the noise, the sheer confusion of it, then stepped closer to a row of slot machines and watched the people mechanically feeding coins and pulling handles. From time to time a machine spitting money back claimed her attention and she dug into her shoulder bag for change and sat down on the nearest vacant stool.

A costumed waitress stopped beside her. "Something to drink, ma'am?"

She took orange juice from the tray of assorted drinks and thanked her. Paula had only five quarters so she played one and received two back, played both and lost them. She dropped her remaining coins into the slot one at a time and was rewarded with ten on her last try. Deciding it was time to quit when she had doubled her money, she left the casino and wandered through the hallway where the hotel shops were located, stopping to look at window displays that caught her eye, browsing in a few of them. But it was the people, such a crowded collage of contrasts that held her rapt attention. At the back, doors led to a huge outdoor pool and cabana and she joined the bikini-clad guests who were relaxing there. Choosing a chair a little apart from the others, she put on her dark glasses and sat down in the sun for a while, wishing there was time for a swim.

Strange, she hadn't planned to do anything special on her birthday. With Amy in Hawaii on her honeymoon, Jeff in India doing God-knows-what, and her mother nursing Roger, she had not expected anyone even to remember the date. And now here she was in the most exciting place she'd ever been.

It was almost twelve so she went inside and called the desk. Yes, Mr. Winthrope had returned at 11:45, they told her, and rang his room.

"Paula? Just getting back?"

"Yes, I've been out enjoying the sights."

"Great. Give me time to change and then we can have lunch."

"Don't you need some sleep?"

"Sleep? Not when I plan to spend the rest of the day with you. I'll be at your door at 12:30."

When Paula opened the door for Greg she was surprised by his appearance. He wore a casual navy sport shirt open at the neck with white duck pants and looked much younger than sixty-two. He took her arm and said as they neared the elevator, "I thought we could eat at the garden restaurant next door then walk around a bit if you like." He glanced down at Paula's white sandals. "Will you be comfortable walking in those?"

"Yes, I'll be fine."

"Then afterwards I want to give you a car tour since this is your first time here. There's another whole world out there beyond the Strip and most tourists never know it."

"I want to see it all," Paula said, then changing the subject she asked, "How did your visit to the plant go?"

"Very well, actually. There is a lot yet to consider and I may have to come again and bring some of our personnel but I am hopeful it may be of help in our situation."

"Then the trip was worthwhile."

He looked at her meaningfully. "The trip was worthwhile even without that."

After a lunch of shrimp salad, coffee, and orange parfait, they wandered in and out of the nearby casinos, past nearly deserted black-jack and roulette tables and a few keno players among rows of empty seats. "Care to try your hand at craps or poker?" Greg asked, and when she shook her head, they moved on until they found themselves gaping up at a clown towering many stories high above them. Greg led her inside where the noise level was several decibels louder and they watched a high wire performance for a while and then stepped onto a carousel of slot machines.

Getting a bill changed, Greg gave Paul several rolls of coins and gestured toward the nearest machine. "Try your luck, Paula. And always play three at a time so if you win, you'll win big."

Paula glanced at the numbers on the garishly painted machine. Three dollars at one time? She hesitated, then shrugged and began feeding coins into the slot. Greg played the machine beside her, until winning a little, losing a little, they finally ran out of coins.

"Shall I get more?" Greg asked. "Or would you like to move along?"

"Let's go," said Paula. "It was fun but I don't like the way those monsters keep gobbling up your money."

He laughed. "They do seem insatiable today, don't they?" As he guided her off the still-turning carousel he asked, "Ready to see some natural wonders of the world now?" When she nodded, he led her back to the hotel to get the car.

As they drove slowly along Boulder Highway Paula leaned forward for a better view of the horizon. "You're right, Greg, I feel like I'm in a different world now. I hadn't realized the city was totally surrounded by mountains. And—that can't be snow in July even on those high peaks, can it?"

"Yes, it is. And if we had more time I'd take you to my favorite lodge near the top of that highest mountain, and you could see it up close." He smiled at her. "But for today you have to settle for Hoover Dam. That's a must on every tourist's agenda."

"I've never been in the West before," Paula told him. "Everything is so different here in the desert. It's so—so vast," she finished lamely.

"Yes," Greg agreed. "Makes one feel rather insignificant, doesn't it?" They were in the mountains now and as they rounded a sharp curve, he motioned to one side. "That's Lake Mead over there."

Paula caught a glimpse of vivid blue. "Everything seems more intense out here."

Greg parked the car between two minivans

and they walked to the overlook that offered a view of the spillway and the churning water far below. Paula stood silent for a long moment, then said, "It's magnificent."

"Isn't it? A real tribute to human ingenuity."

"I'm so glad you brought me here, Greg," Paula touched his arm resting on the railing beside her. "Thank you."

"The pleasure is all mine, I assure you." He covered her hand with his. "Perhaps we ought to go back to the car now. It's around 110 degrees out here."

"You're not serious?"

"There's almost no humidity in desert air, you know."

Paula took a deep breath. "That's why I feel so free, isn't it? No heavy air bearing down?"

"Perhaps." He looked at her thoughtfully. "Perhaps not."

They circled the dam and part of the lake before heading back to the city, watching the sandstone sides of the mountains change color as the sun moved. First magenta and rust, then mauve and orange, and finally lavender and peach superimposed with smokey blue shadows as the sun dropped from sight.

* * *

After a perfumed bubble bath in the luxurious Roman tub, Paula put on her cut-work embroidery dress that she had worn to the rehearsal dinner and arranged her hair in a French twist, fastening it with her pearl comb. She had no idea where they would spend the evening but she was sure it was going to be fun. She picked up her nearly empty bottle of Obsession, hesitated, then rummaged in her purse for the sample vial of Shalimar a perfume shopkeeper had given her this morning. She dabbed it on her ear lobes and wrists and sniffed. Yes, she thought, it was definitely lighter, and that was how she felt as she almost floated to the door at Greg's knock.

"Paula, you're absolutely breathtaking." Greg stared at her with frank enjoyment.

"You, too," she retorted, thinking that in his beautifully tailored dark suit he truly was the epitome of success.

Offering her his arm, he asked softly, "Shall we go out and dazzle this already-bedazzled town?"

She tucked her arm in his. "Of course. But will you tell me where we're going now? The suspense is killing me."

As they walked toward the elevators, he answered her question. "First we're going to dinner at the Hilton. Then I have tickets to the

Wayne Newton Show—not easy to come by on such short notice, I might add—and then we're going . . . wait, I have to save something for later."

An elevator door opened and they squeezed themselves in. Paula smiled at him. "I can wait." A prickle of apprehension made her shiver. Would he keep his no strings promise?

They had decided to have the elaborate buffet and Paula, in an adventurous mood, sampled things she had never seen before. A few of them she categorized as things she hoped never to see again.

After dinner they returned to the lobby where the evening was now in full swing. Paula noticed that people were two-deep at the blackjack and roulette tables and players filled every chair in the keno section as others waited for a vacancy.

As they joined the line to the show room Paula caught a glimpse of an adjacent area where several people sat playing cards at a long table and paused. There was something different about this. She turned to Greg. "What—?"

"Baccarat," he told her. "This is where the high rollers play."

She watched, fascinated by the scene before her, the faces showing all levels of tension as the expressionless croupier raked in the losses and paid out the wins. The line moved and Paula reluctantly allowed herself to be swept along until her view was obstructed. Then they were in the gigantic show room with its tiers of crowded tables and Greg gave a bill to the man seating them and he led them to a center table with a perfect view of the stage. A cocktail waitress appeared to take their request for drinks and Greg ordered a bottle of white wine.

In spite of the chilly temperature of the large room, the amount of smoke, perfume, and alcohol made it definitely seem stuffy, Paula noticed. And though the room was packed with noisy people now, no one had been seated at their table. She imagined the size of the bill she'd seen pass hands was responsible for that. Simultaneously, the lights dimmed, the music began, and the stage curtains parted bringing a hush, then loud applause from the audience. Then Paula gave her attention to the evening's famous entertainer until the last encore and standing ovation was over.

She turned to Greg as they joined the jostling crowd headed for the exit. "That was wonderful. I've always wanted to see him in person."

"I'm glad you enjoyed it, Paula."

As they waited for the car Paula looked around her. "It's almost as bright as noonday," she observed.

"And almost as hot," Greg added.

"Where are we going now?" Paula asked as Greg assisted her into the car.

"Caesar's Palace. How would you like to dance the rest of the night away on an Egyptian barge?"

"I can't think of anything I'd like more," Paula answered happily.

The entrance to Caesar's was the most ornate yet and Paula stood enchanted until Greg led her on inside where they went directly to the barge that floated on an authentic body of water. The undulating motion of the floor made dancing to the slow music almost hypnotic.

"I'd pinch myself to see if I'm dreaming but I'm afraid I'd wake up someplace else," Paula said.

"It's all real, Paula." Greg held her closer. "At least as real as Vegas ever gets."

They danced until early morning, then drove downtown to the Golden Nugget for a buffet breakfast, stopping in the casino to try their luck at the slot machines again. They played keno as they ate and had another go at the slots on their way out.

"Not my lucky day," Paula said as she poured another roll of coins into the bin in front of her and crumpled the brown paper wrapper.

Greg looked at her tenderly. "I hope it will be mine."

Here it comes, she thought. The proposition. But he turned his attention back to his own machine and groaned when a third seven slowed, then passed the winning position.

Back in the car, they drove slowly, passing gaudy wedding chapels on every block. At the Chapel of the Doves where larger-than-life birds fluttered on the chapel spire, Greg pulled to the curb.

"Paula, there's only one thing left to make this weekend perfect. Let's get married."

She looked at him quickly, expecting to see the humor in his eyes that would let her know he was joking but his expression was intense.

"Greg, surely you don't—"

"Yes, I do mean it, Paula. I've given this a lot of thought. We haven't known each other very long but I know all I need to know about you. We're not teenagers anymore. We're capable of making sound decisions."

"Yes, and that's why—"

"Hear me out, please. I . . . haven't been with another woman since before my wife died, haven't wanted to. Until now, that is." He smiled at her. "You excite me, Paula, in a way I haven't felt for a very long time. I know I'm older than you but I have a lot of years left. And I've got a lot to offer you—in other ways."

"Greg, please, I . . . I've just gotten divorced. I don't want to marry anyone just now. I'm flattered, of course, that you would ask me, but no, I just couldn't, not now."

"Then don't close the door on what I've said. I won't insist on now. And I'm of the old school of behavior so I won't ask you to go to bed with me before marriage. I have desires and needs but I'm also capable of controlling them," he smiled wryly, "after years of abstinence. You see, it wasn't *just* since my wife died. As you know, we had no children. We wanted a family and Rachel consulted a lot of doctors. It finally became clear that the problem was mine. Not impotence, you understand, sterility. And after that the relationship gradually became platonic, by Rachel's choice."

"I'm so sorry," Paula said softly.

He pulled her to him, kissed her tenderly. "I'm besotted with you, Paula," he whispered, "and if things work out between us, I would

417

like to think of your children as my family, too. Think about what I've said and don't make me wait too long."

He started the car and they drove in silence back to the hotel. From somewhere in the back of her head Paula heard Ruth's warning, "Don't make any foolish commitments." Had she guessed something like this would happen? Maybe a lot of people did foolish things here, or else why all those wedding chapels?

After a few hours sleep Paula and Greg were once more airborne headed back to Alabama. As the plane climbed she turned to the window for a last look at the city below and sighed. "Now back to the real world."

"And I hope you're taking a lot of happy memories with you," said Greg.

"Oh yes, a whole head full," she assured him.

They cleared the mountain range and she could see the entire panorama of Lake Mead outlined against the desert sand. "Look, doesn't that remind you of those sand tables we used to make in school? You know, sand on glass with blue paper underneath for the bodies of water?"

"I've never thought of that but, yes, it does," Greg agreed.

The plane leveled off and they seemed to be suspended motionless, then skimming over clouds that looked like bright snow fields with the brilliant blue sky above them. "It's so beautiful," she said.

"And so are you," Greg said softly. He reached out to cover her hand on the armrest with his. "And Paula, I just want you to know that proposal I made last night was not an impulsive whim. The offer is still open and I want you to give it serious consideration."

Before she could answer, a stewardess stopped beside them. "Coffee and croissants?"

"Paula?" At her nod, he spoke to the stewardess. "Yes to both, please."

He didn't return to the subject of marriage and Paula was relieved that she did not have to answer. A proposal from Greg Winthrope certainly deserved more thought before she turned it down. If she turned it down.

Eighteen

Paula set down her luggage and for a minute considered unpacking, then decided instead to share her weekend experiences with Ruth and Louise before her euphoria turned to fatigue.

"Well, if it isn't the world traveler." Ruth smiled and opened the door wide. "Come on in. Let's get a look at this sophisticated lady."

"Stunning," Louise pronounced as she noted Paula's navy slacks and sweater, her stylish navy and white pumps, white shoulder bag, and matching costume jewelry. "Simply stunning."

"Pull up a bed and sit down." Ruth waved toward the twin beds placed at angles on the far wall. "We're just having tea. You'll have a cup?" When Paula nodded, she prepared it as she went on, "How was your trip?"

"Fabulous." Paula sat down, slipped off her shoes and tucked her feet up.

"Don't stop there," Louise urged. "Tell us all about your short sojourn in sin city."

"Yeah," Ruth added as she gave a steaming cup to Paula. "Especially about the sin."

Paula laughed. "Should I wait until Sharon can hear this, too? I knocked at her door on the way over but she didn't answer."

"She's at the library. She'll be meeting us at Gaither Hall but that'll be ages from now and I can't wait," Ruth wailed. "Anyway, we won't mind hearing it again, will we, Louise?"

"Of course not," Louise closed her book, "so begin at the beginning and tell us everything. We much prefer armchair travel to studying as a Sunday afternoon pastime."

Paula sipped her tea, then smiled at them. "I see now why Sharon was so fascinated with the West. And Las Vegas . . . I don't know how can I describe that, but I'll try. Well, to begin, we got there about four, that was six here because of the time zone change you know, then Greg rented a car and—"

"Rolls-Royce?" Louise asked.

"No, Nissan."

"That cheapskate." Ruth grinned happily.

"He had to drive out to visit a plant site at

Henderson later in the morning and I'm sure he didn't want to appear ostentatious."

"Just one of the regular working guys, huh? How considerate." Ruth's smile faded.

"Anyway, when we got to the Strip . . ." Paula did her best to remember every vivid detail and share it with her friends and finally concluded with the return flight. "So here I am, home again, safe and sound."

"Didn't you leave out one thing, Paula? Like when Mister Rich Guy made his move on you, his proposition?" Ruth sipped her tea with studied nonchalance as she waited for Paula's answer.

"No proposition, Ruth," Paula said quietly. "Just a proposal."

Ruth spluttered, choked, coughed as both women fixed Paula with amazed stares.

"What did you say?" Ruth whispered when she could finally talk again.

"A proposal." Paula shrugged in an attempt to appear casual about the bombshell she had just dropped. "You know, he asked me to marry him."

"When?" It was Louise who spoke this time.

"Oh, last night."

"No, I mean when does he want you to—"

"I told you, last night. At one of those little wedding chapels."

Ruth looked at her with alarm. "Good Lord, you didn't . . ."

Paula shook her head. "No, I didn't. You advised me not to make any commitments, didn't you?"

Ruth's face relaxed. "Right."

"Imagine that," Louise said. "I never had Gregory Winthrope figured for such an impulsive guy."

"Me either," Paula agreed, "but he said he's thought a lot about it."

"Paula," Ruth set her cup down, cleared her throat, "I've already been warned about fools who rush in where they've got no business and this is a subject that's probably too hot to handle, no pun intended—"

"Ruth, I don't think we—" Louise began but the other woman went on.

"I couldn't help but notice the strange way you and Derek have been acting ever since Amy's wedding. Like you've had a lover's quarrel or something."

"No, we—"

"Let me say this," Ruth continued doggedly. "You can't have that kind of quarrel unless you're lovers first."

"But we—"

"And I've seen the way that dreamboat has looked at you for weeks, so I'd stake my ticket home on the obvious clues that you two finally got together. But what I can't understand is why you're both acting so weird now when you ought to be as happy as turtle doves," she paused, frowning, "unless I've missed something really vital, like maybe he's gay, or—"

"Oh no, he's a great—what I mean is, he's definitely not . . ." she stopped, blushing in her confusion. "I can't believe I'm discussing my love life in a college dorm, like an eighteen-year-old freshman." Paula paused, looked from one woman to the other, took a deep breath. "But as long as I've already admitted . . . it happened after the reception. I think we'd both had a little too much champagne. And we ended up . . . together." Her words were jerky, short. "At the Coach House Inn. And Derek keeps acting like the whole thing never happened so I guess he's afraid I'll read more into it than actually was, and he's going out of his way to be friendly with Faye Browne so I'll get the message, but I already have," now her words were tumbling over each other, "and if it hadn't been for Quent giving Bootsie my Christopher Columbus and me drinking Greg Winthrope's Dom Perignon I would never have asked him to do it, and now I'm really sorry I did."

Two pairs of eyes looked at each other in

astonishment. After a moment of stunned silence, Louise reached out to pat her arm. "Paula, can you slow down a bit? We're getting all confused."

Paula explained again, in sequence, and when she finished, Louise nodded. "Now it's beginning to make sense. But I'm not sure Derek Vogel's motives are what you think. If Ruth's intuition is right, he may be more afraid of himself than of you."

"Why?" Ruth and Paula asked at the same time.

"Well, maybe he *is* afraid of reading more into it than it was. A man burned once would be wary of having it happen again."

"But why the run on Faye Browne?" Ruth demanded.

Louise shrugged. "Fight fire with fire?"

"Well, it's very confusing to me, Mrs. Freud. And I wonder if we could get back to the current issue right now? Like, Paula, you didn't make any rash promises to Greg Winthrope?"

"I only said I'd think about it," said Paula.

"Good, but an outright 'no' would've been even better."

"Now, Ruth," Louise intervened, "Paula's just had an offer of marriage from this town's most eligible bachelor and I believe she ought to give it some thought—serious thought."

"Why?" Ruth demanded. "She certainly doesn't love him."

"There are many kinds of love," Louise answered quietly.

"Right," Ruth agreed. "But there's only one kind of man-woman love worth marrying for and that's the kind that snaps, crackles, and pops when you're on the same planet together," she paused, ". . . like I have with that wonderful man of mine."

"But I had that kind with *my* husband and look what it got me," Paula said.

"So it doesn't always last forever," Ruth shrugged. "It's not a one-time shot. You could get another chance."

"I'm not sure I ever want one," Paula said.

"You already got it, honey, want it or not," Ruth smiled at her. "You've got Derek Vogel who is obviously crazy about you. I think you're both a little mixed up right now but in time it should all work out. And then you've got this rich guy who keeps confusing things for you."

"But he's obviously smitten by you, too," Louise added.

"True," Ruth agreed, "but how do you feel about these two men, Paula? Look at it objectively. Could you have spent a weekend in Las Vegas with Derek Vogel without ending up in bed with him? Listen to your heart, girl. What does that tell you?"

"But what about *after* the weekend," asked Louise. "What then? Gregory Winthrope is offering you more than sex and there is a lot to be said for security after fifty."

"Sure, and die of boredom. I still say go with your heart, not your head. Why, he's ten years older than you are. If he didn't try to get you in bed this weekend, who knows whether his equipment is still functioning or not."

Paula laughed, then said seriously, "But I'm seven years older than Derek."

"When you were sixteen and he was nine that might have been a problem but once you're both past the age of consent, what's the big deal?"

"To begin with, I'm fifty-two years old—too old to be in college, too old to fall in love, and too old to start over."

"But you're doing all three," Ruth answered softly.

Paula covered her eyes with both hands. "I think jet lag just caught up with me. My brain has shut down." She stood up. "Thanks for the tea and therapy."

"You're welcome," Ruth told her as she took her cup.

"For the tea," Louise added. "We'll send a bill for the therapy."

Ruth followed her to the door. "And we'll be looking forward to our rerun of the trip at supper."

Paula waved and disappeared into her own room. Still thinking about what had just happened, she mechanically unpacked her bags. If she had expected the weekend trip to clear her mind she had missed the mark by a mile. And though she'd willingly participated in that confessional a few minutes ago and it *had* made her feel better to share, the same problems still remained. She loved her ex-husband, but she had no future with Quent. That left Greg, who had offered her a future. And Derek, who hadn't. She had sworn not to get involved with another man and now she was on a see-saw between two! One of them was willing to make a commitment and the other wasn't. Trouble was, she didn't know what she wanted from either of them.

Greg's attention made her feel appreciated and admired but Derek had a somewhat different effect on her. He made her feel desirable in a sexual way. And it was certain he would keep it confined to sex and not get emotionally involved with her or any woman. Why did her life have to be so complicated?

She looked at the books stacked neatly on her desk. Tomorrow there would be tests she was not yet prepared for. She would have to stay up late and study no matter how tired she was.

Two cups of coffee and one recounting of her Las Vegas trip followed the meal in Gaither Hall with Sharon, Ruth, and Louise. Their table was near the door and Paula had surreptitiously watched the students coming and going in hopes of catching a glimpse of Derek. She finally resigned herself to the fact that he was probably with Faye Browne.

"Paula, I almost forgot," Sharon said suddenly, "Derek Vogel called this morning and wanted to know where you were. I hope you didn't mind my telling him?"

"No, of course not."

Ruth, with a pleased expression on her face, looked at her watch. "Seven o'clock already? My, how time flies when you're having fun. But I've got lesson plans to finish." She stood up and the others joined her.

"So do I," said Paula, "and I haven't even begun."

As they started down the steps, Derek Vogel met them.

"Oh, hello." He was looking only at Paula as all of them answered. "Paula, you're back."

"Why . . . yes."

"Would you . . . come into the cafeteria with me while I get something to eat? I need to discuss something with you."

Ruth, grinning like a Cheshire cat, almost pushed Paula into his arms. "You go right ahead, honey. I'm sure Derek will see that you get safely back to the dorm."

"Yes, I'll do that," he answered quickly and the two of them disappeared through the double doors.

"I'll just be a minute. Grab a table somewhere and I'll find you." He took a step, turned back, "Can I bring you something?"

"A glass of water, please." Suddenly her mouth felt as if she'd been eating cotton candy and her knees were threatening to give way. Why did this man have such a crazy effect on her every time he fixed those penetrating blue eyes on her? Paula sat down at the nearest table and began tracing circles with her index finger on its shiny plastic top. Why had Derek wanted her to return to the cafeteria with him, she wondered nervously.

"Here," he set a glass in front of her and put his tray opposite and sat down but did not

430

begin eating. "Paula, there's something . . . I tried to reach you this morning."

She nodded. "Sharon told me a few minutes ago." Her heart beat faster. "What—"

"Uh, before you left, did you by chance talk with Kurt Yearwood?"

"No," she said quickly, "why?"

"Well, he . . . it seems he's not on campus. Maybe hasn't been here since yesterday."

"What? How—" she gripped her hands together to stop their sudden trembling.

"Nobody seems to know a damned thing. The last anybody saw of him he was headed to Oldham Hall to wait for his ride out to the mill."

"But he wasn't going to the mill yesterday, Greg Winthrope told him that Friday night." She swallowed the lump of fear in her throat, "Unless . . ."

"Then somebody needs to check with Winthrope."

"I could call him and see—"

"Yes, as soon as you get back to the dorm. A few minutes can't make much difference now, so let me eat something first. I've been driving all over town checking out likely places a runaway kid might be, ever since Faye called me this morning."

"How did she know about—"

"Somebody in the dorm finally missed Kurt at breakfast. There's supposed to be a bed check but the regular supervisor was off the weekend and the sub got careless."

"Have they notified the police?"

"Only the campus patrol so far. Don't want a lot of publicity about it."

"But what if something really bad—"

"Ben Colbert is calling the shots. At least, since he sobered up about noon and Faye got through to him." He took a large bite of his sandwich and washed it down with milk. "He's on a real rampage. God pity us all to-morrow unless Kurt turns up."

"Have they told his parents?"

"Faye's trying now. His dad is out on a job somewhere. He's a long distance trucker, you know. And his mother hasn't answered her phone yet."

"Kurt's run away before, but I thought he liked it here."

"Well, maybe the trip to the mill gave him the opportunity to get a head start on leaving before anyone missed him."

"But I just can't believe he's been fooling us."

"Who knows what goes on in a kid's head?" Derek swallowed the last of the food on his plate. "Come on, let's go make that phone call."

As they walked toward Winthrope Hall, carefully not touching, Derek asked as an afterthought, "How was your trip?"

"Very nice."

"Win any jackpots?"

"No, and I'm convinced the slots are rigged, but they're fun anyway."

"I, uh, hadn't heard you mention the trip before. Been planned long?"

"Oh no. Just a spur-of-the-moment thing."

"I see." They had reached the dorm and Derek paused inside the lobby. "I'll wait here. I want to know what was said in that phone call to Kurt."

"Okay, I'll be back down as soon as I can."

The phone at the Winthropes' rang several times before Mellie's soft voice answered.

"Mistah and Missus Winthrope be at church, Miss Paula," she explained, "and Mistah Gregory be gone out to the mill."

"Will you have him call me when he gets back, no matter how late it is, Mellie?"

"Yes'um, I surely will."

Paula went back downstairs and found Derek pacing the lobby while the girls at the desk gave him admiring glances.

After she told him about the call, he said,

"I've tried to think where a kid like Kurt might go. I figure he didn't have any money but I checked the bus station anyway. And all the fast food places, the video arcade at the mall, the park."

"But this makes two nights now that he's . . . wherever he is . . . alone." She shivered.

"You'd better get back to the phone. I'm going out and drive around some more. If you hear anything, let me know."

"But you'll be—"

"Call Faye Browne's apartment and leave word."

"Oh." Paula stood up, spoke sharply. "Are you staying there now?"

He gave her an amused look. "Faye has an answering machine. I check with her frequently for an update on the situation."

Paula felt her cheeks flame. She hadn't meant to say that. It was none of her business whether he was or wasn't. She was almost to the eighth floor before she realized his evasive explanation still hadn't answered her question.

Paula tried to study but finally gave up, overcome with worry about the small boy she had come to care for almost like her own.

It was after midnight when the phone rang. "Paula, I'm sorry to call so late but I have a note from Mellie that says to—"

"Yes, Greg, I told her no matter how late . . ." she stopped explaining. "You didn't ever tell me about your conversation with Kurt Yearwood before we left. Was he, did he seem upset when you told him about Saturday?"

"I actually never got to speak with Kurt." Greg paused. "Why do you ask?"

"I'll explain in a minute." Paula gripped the receiver. "Tell me what happened."

"I spoke with another boy in the dorm, I didn't ask his name. He went to call Kurt to the phone, then came back and said he was already asleep. It was late, you know, so I asked him to give Kurt the message. To write it down."

"Do you remember anything about the student you spoke with, an accent or something?"

"Well," Greg was silent a minute, "he had a sort of gruff way of speaking, sounded older than Kurt, and he called me man."

"Oh." Irvin Pendergrass. Greg had talked to Irvin, she'd bet money on it.

"Paula, tell me what this is all about."

"Kurt is gone. Missing. They think since Saturday morning. Somebody saw him heading for Oldham Hall to catch his ride to the mill. When I didn't show up, he must have felt like I'd let him down. So it's my fault he's missing, and—"

"Paula, Paula, listen to me. If anyone is to

435

blame for this it's me, not you. I'm going to hang up now and call Ben Colbert and tell him exactly what happened, and offer to do anything I can to help find the boy. Now stop worrying and get some rest. Everything will be all right. I mean, how far can one small boy with no transportation or money get in thirty-something hours? And Paula, stop feeling guilty. It's not your fault, sweetheart."

Paula sat for a long while staring at nothing while her mind pictured a young boy waiting eagerly for his Saturday trip to the mill. And waiting. Was this the kind of thing that had made him run away before? A sudden thought chilled Paula's heart. What if he hadn't run away? What if . . . No, she wouldn't think about that.

Later, still sitting numbly at her desk, Paula realized Greg would have to tell Dr. Colbert about their trip to Las Vegas, had by now in fact already told him. That ought to seal her fate as far as Dr. C's opinion of her was concerned. She sighed. What did it matter as long as Kurt was found safe? And if he wasn't, how could she ever forgive herself?

Dr. Colbert, looking harassed and haggard, appeared before his first period class with a brief statement about Kurt, then announced that Miss Browne would monitor the test and left. Faye gave no indication of her sleepless night as she paced back and forth in stiletto heels, wearing a gold coatdress with enormous black buttons.

Paula, after only a few hours restless sleep, stared at the paper in front of her, the questions a jumble of meaningless words. Finally she began writing, hoping her answers made more sense than they seemed to in her distracted state.

When the bell rang, Faye requested a word with Derek, who had gotten there late, and they walked to Faye's classroom together, amid the knowing smiles of the other students.

"They could be a little more discreet," Paula grumbled to Ruth as they trailed a short distance behind the striking pair.

Ruth looked at her slyly. "Do I detect a faint stirring of the green-eyed monster?"

"Absolutely not," Paula answered indignantly, "I just don't think Miss Browne should make such a show of favoritism, even if they're discussing Kurt."

"Maybe she just can't help herself." Ruth sighed. "He does have that effect on women, you know."

Paula pursed her lips and said nothing as she left Ruth and walked to her front row seat.

After second period Paula joined Ruth and Derek in the hallway. "Have you heard anything more about Kurt?" she asked softly as they walked upstairs.

"They called the police in on it last night," he told her, "and Faye told me they've finally contacted Kurt's mother."

"Is she on her way here?" asked Paula.

"Nope." He shook his head, "Didn't even seem alarmed, according to Faye. Said he'd done it before and always turned up okay."

Paula sighed. "Don't we just hope."

"I feel so responsible for this," Paula said sadly as she and Ruth walked from the cafeteria toward Oldham Hall. "If I hadn't gone with Greg it never would have happened."

"Paula, you had no way of knowing Kurt wouldn't get the message Greg left."

"The poor kid has had so many rejections in his short life and just when he thought someone really cared about him . . ." tears came in her eyes and she couldn't finish.

As they neared the building, Derek—who had left Gaither Hall early to seek more information—came out the door and walked toward them.

"Any word?" Paula asked hopefully when they were close enough to speak.

Derek looked grim. "They're putting it on the news now, and in the papers. And Gregory Winthrope has added private detectives and the mill's helicopter to the search."

"It's been two days now." Paula shook her head.

"I'd like to know who took that message and never delivered it," Derek said evenly.

Paula debated a moment before she told him what Greg had said about the student with whom he'd talked.

Derek drew his breath in sharply. "Do you think what I'm thinking?"

"I don't know," Paula answered. "It could have been Irvin but maybe not."

"Well, I'm going to find out." Derek strode purposefully toward a group of students near the building, Paula and Ruth behind him.

"Irvin," he said solemnly, "I'd like a word with you."

Irvin rolled his eyes. "What'd I do now, man?"

"You tell me. Like have you taken any messages lately—that you forgot to deliver?"

A look of guilt crossed Irvin's face but he

quickly recovered his cocky stance. "Yeah, man, I forgot. Ain't no law against that."

With one swift move, Derek backed the large boy against the wall, fists clutching his shirt, and glared at him, eyeball to eyeball. "Listen, punk, we're talking about another kid's life here. You know what you did and I know what you did. And you'd better pray that little guy turns up safe because if he doesn't I'm holding you personally responsible and I'm going to beat the hell out of you."

In the stunned silence that followed, Derek released the wide-eyed student and went back inside. Ruth looked at Paula and said in a low voice, "Lord, I hope Dr. C. doesn't hear about this. I don't think even the convincing Miss B. could save our friend's hide then."

"Miss Howard," Faye called as Paula and Ruth entered the building, "I'm assigning Irvin Pendergrass to you today. That will leave Mr. Vogel free to assist in the search for Kurt Yearwood."

"Smart move," Ruth whispered. "Those two don't need to be anywhere near each other for a while."

A subdued Irvin sat in Paula's cubicle, half-heartedly responding to words on a flipchart as she turned it. Finally he stopped and, not meeting her eyes, asked, "Miss Howard, do you think Kurt is gonna show up pretty soon?"

Paula put down the chart. "I don't know, Irvin."

"I saw him," his voice was so low Paula had to strain to hear it. "Headin' over to the place they got all the trucks selling stuff."

"You mean the fruit and vegetable market?"

"Yeah."

"Irvin," Paula stood up, "let's go tell Miss Browne what you told me. It may be just the clue they need to find him."

Tuesday's third period was almost over when a knock at the door interrupted Dr. Colbert's lecture. After he spoke briefly with Faye Browne he returned to the lectern and cleared his throat.

"Students, I'm pleased to announce that Kurt Yearwood has been found," a strained silence gripped the room as they waited for the crucial words, ". . . alive and well." A collective sigh of relief was followed by everyone talking at once. Dr. Colbert raised his hand for silence. "He was found in Michigan, on a tarpaulin-covered truck loaded with watermelons, thanks to a belated clue and some very good follow-up detective work." He took off his glasses, polished them briskly before he continued. "There is one other thing. I feel that I should reiterate here that our policy of no corporal punishment, or even threats of such, remains unchanged. We will tolerate *no* military-type tactics by tutors toward children." He paused, took a deep breath. "However, in some recent circumstances, the end has apparently justified the means."

The bell rang and Paula rushed to the back of the room and threw her arms around Derek who, after a moment of surprise, returned her embrace. "He's okay," she whispered.

"Thanks to you. If Irvin hadn't told you—"

"But he never would have if you hadn't," she paused and smiled at him, ". . . used military tactics on him."

It was a while before either of them realized they were still holding each other.

Nineteen

Saturday morning at the mill had passed quickly and lunch at the Winthrope dining table was almost over. Paula had been nervous about Kurt's possible behavior but he had seemingly made a good impression on the elder Winthropes.

"Mistah Kurt, would you like anothah of my raspberry tarts?" Mellie asked as she held the basket of hot muffins in front of him.

"I'm 'bout to pop already," Kurt told her as he wiped his mouth on a large linen napkin. Then he turned to Paula and asked in a low voice, "Why is she calling me mister? Can't she see good?"

Paula shook her head. "It's an old southern custom, Kurt. She's just being polite."

Lillian Winthrope looked at her husband

and smiled. "Remember when Greg asked exactly the same question, dear?"

He nodded, then spoke to Kurt. "I understand you can ride a horse, young man?"

"Yes sir," Kurt answered proudly.

"And speaking of that, it's time we were going to the stables, Kurt," Greg said. "Would you like to come with us, Father?"

"Why yes, I believe I would," the older man answered with obvious pleasure.

"Then why don't you stay here and chat with me, Paula?" Greg's mother asked graciously. "It's terribly hot at the stables this time of day."

Paula started to make her excuses but when she read Greg's wish that she oblige his mother, she said, "I would be happy to, if you're sure I won't be intruding."

"Not at all." She stood. "Let's go out on the sun porch where we can enjoy the backyard without having to endure the heat."

She presented her cheek first to her husband, then her son, and offered her hand to Kurt. He hesitated a minute, looked at Paula who nodded and smiled, then shook it vigorously.

"You must come to see us again soon, Kurt."

"Yes ma'am," he answered solemnly.

When the two women were seated in comfortable wicker rockers facing the sprawling well-landscaped lawn, she spoke again, "Gregory is very fond of that young man. He was quite upset that the . . . trip last weekend had such disastrous results."

"Yes, we all were."

"One simply can't be too careful. And things sometimes happen in spite of all your caution. Of course, Gregory had no idea the boy would resort to anything so . . . so . . ."

"I take complete responsibility for the whole episode, Mrs. Winthrope. The only part your son played was inviting me to go with him on the trip."

"Yes, well, Gregory has been almost a recluse since his wife died. And he has never done anything on the spur of the moment like that. You must have bewitched him, my dear."

Paula met her icy smile with a forced smile of her own. "Hardly."

"We were quite shocked that he would take a woman on a weekend trip. But he assured us it was all very proper. And," here she dropped her voice to a whisper, "he also confided to us that he has proposed marriage to you." She waited for Paula's confirmation, then continued, "Gregory has always wished for a son." She sighed. "Rachel couldn't have children and this was a great disappointment to him—to all of us. I had hoped when Rachel passed away that Gregory would marry again, and . . . perhaps it wouldn't be too late . . ." she stopped.

So Greg had allowed Rachel to take the blame for not producing a Gregory Winthrope V. No wonder she had decided to end the physical side of her marriage prematurely.

"Since Greg confided his proposal to you he must also have told you I didn't accept."

"He, ah, sounded hopeful that—"

"I haven't yet decided what I'm going to do when summer ends."

"I see." The woman looked pleased, "Frankly, I don't blame you for giving the matter very careful consideration before you accept this kind of responsibility. Gregory has a very important role in this city and his wife would have many obligations. There's the Charity League—Rachel served as chairwoman of the annual ball for years—and the hospital and library boards, the university social club, and . . . oh, I do hope I'm not intimidating you with all the obligatory duties that a family such as ours simply has to assume. It must sound terrifying to anyone who has never been involved in this sort of thing."

"Not at all," Paula answered confidently, "I

like a challenge." It sounded absolutely over-whelming and utterly boring but she was not about to allow Lillian Winthrope to scare her off as she was so clearly trying to do. Determinedly she changed the subject and resigned herself to a long afternoon of small talk until Greg and Kurt returned.

"Paula, may I come in?" Sharon knocked lightly at the partly open door.

"Of course." Paula marked her place and closed the book she was reading.

"I needed to talk with you about something."

"Sounds ominous." She patted the bed beside her desk. "Come sit down and tell me what your problem is."

She sat down on the bed and crossed her legs. "I just talked with Todd and I've found out what is bothering him."

"And?"

"He's not sure he wants to be a pilot anymore."

"He may feel differently a little later on."

"He says he thought a lot about it and he's more certain every day he doesn't want a military career."

"What does he want?"

447

"He isn't sure yet. Maybe go back to college," she paused, then smiled shyly, "and get married."

Paula raised her eyebrows. "At the same time?"

"Oh no, college first. But he doesn't really have the money for more schooling if he leaves the military. And he hates to ask anyone in his family for help, because he had the four years at Annapolis." She sighed. "We could get married right away if he stays in the Navy, but then we wouldn't be together much. And Todd doesn't want to be away from his wife like his dad was."

"Sounds like he has some hard choices to make." Paula looked thoughtful. "I hope he talks with his dad about this."

"He's already tried to talk about it with his mother and she thinks Todd would be making a terrible mistake to leave the Navy."

"How does she feel about him getting married?"

"He hasn't told her that. He wants to get married as soon as we can, but he has to work out this other thing first."

"Well, I'm sure he—"

"Anybody home?" called a voice.

"Come in, Louise. Where's Ruth?"

"Didn't she tell you? Her brother came this

448

morning to take her to see her family for the weekend."

Paula looked surprised. "You mean to Georgia?"

"Yes." Louise shook her head. "She called her parents last week and they wanted her to visit and offered to send someone to get her, so she went."

Sharon stood up. "Be back in a few minutes. Got to change for supper."

"How was your day with Kurt?" Louise asked as she sat down in the place Sharon had just vacated.

"Things went surprisingly well," Paula answered. "Greg and Kurt worked on the lily pond all morning. Then we had lunch at the Winthrope house with Greg's parents and afterward Greg and his father took Kurt to the stables while his mother told me all the reasons I shouldn't marry her son."

"She didn't." Louise looked shocked.

"I'm afraid so. She's very concerned that I wouldn't fit in," Paula said ruefully.

"Oh horsefeathers! A beautiful, charming woman like you?"

"But I don't have the right background. She made it very clear she didn't think I could handle the necessary social and philanthropic obligations that would be required of me."

"This isn't exactly the monarchy and crown prince we're talking about. The Winthropes are old money here I suppose, but you'd be an asset to any man. Sounds to me like Mrs. Astor is suffering from bats in the belfry syndrome."

Paula shook her head. "Just a typical case of our Deep South matriarchal society, I'm afraid."

"Well, don't you let Greg's meddling mama influence your decision about marrying him. I mean, she's got to be ancient already, so how much longer can she be around?"

"Probably longer than Greg," said Paula. "She looks indestructible."

"You mean even death would be afraid to approach her?"

"Right," Paula smiled, then grew serious. "But she and Greg's father were really sweet to Kurt. He had a wonderful day."

"Speaking of indestructible, it's amazing how he hid on that watermelon truck and survived on melons for three days."

"I was really afraid he'd done something worse than run away," Paula admitted.

"I worried about that, too."

"If only Irvin hadn't been so jealous of the attention Kurt was getting," Paula said, "but something good has come out of all this.

Irvin's really had a change of attitude. He's showing a lot more respect for Derek now."

Louise laughed. "Ruth told me about Derek manhandling him. Sometimes that's all guys like him can understand."

"Well, now Derek is trying a different approach. In fact, he took him fishing today."

Sharon appeared again and Louise said, "Let's go. Some of us, ahem, did not dine with royalty at noon, and we're starved."

As they entered Gaither Hall, Paula saw Derek in the line just ahead of them. No man ought to look that good in faded jeans, she thought, just as he glanced around and seeing them, threw up his hand.

He allowed the students between them to step ahead of him, then said to Paula, "How did it go with Kurt today?"

"He had a wonderful time, the mill, lunch, riding a horse, the works. How was the fishing trip?"

"Great. Irvin hooked a fish then stood up in the boat, which nearly flipped it over. We lost our picnic lunch and the fish ended up in Faye's lap."

He stopped and after an awkward silence Paula said stiffly, "I didn't know she was going."

"Me either, till the last minute. But she

wanted to observe Irvin in a nonscholastic setting."

A good excuse for spending the day with you, Paula said silently, as Sharon spoke aloud.

"Why don't you share our table, Derek? Ruth's not here so we wouldn't be a bit crowded."

"Sure, I'd like to. Where is Ruth?"

"Gone to see her family in Georgia," Louise explained.

"I had a call from Todd this afternoon," Sharon said to Derek.

Derek smiled at her. "How's he doing?"

"Fine," she hesitated, "and he said to tell you hello."

Derek shook his head. "Sometimes I still can't believe how lucky we are to have him."

"But there's always a chance it could happen again, and he might not be so lucky next time," Sharon said quickly.

Derek chewed thoughtfully, swallowed. "Life is a chance, Sharon. And a man has to do what he's happy doing."

"Well, sometimes people aren't happy doing the same thing forever."

Derek looked at her quickly. "That's true."

Louise changed the subject and they finished the meal without further mention of Todd or flying.

As they left the cafeteria, Derek touched Paula's shoulder lightly. "Paula, could we talk a minute? I'll walk you to Winthrope Hall later."

Nodding to Sharon and Louise to go ahead she fell in step with Derek, her skin still tingling from his touch. They slowed at the first bench near the sidewalk and he motioned her to sit down.

"What the hell was that all about?"

"What?" she asked while she tried to decide how much she should tell him.

"Sharon's remark about Todd's flying. Is she trying to get him to quit?"

"Oh, no, she's . . . I mean he's . . ."

"My son wants to marry the girl, right? So she's evidently holding out till she gets what she wants, which is probably a civilian husband."

"You've got it all wrong," Paula said angrily. "It's your son who wants to be a civilian. And Sharon is willing to go along with it even though it'll probably mean putting the marriage on hold."

"Oh." He sat in silence while her words sank in. "So that's what has been bothering him. And he afraid's to tell his old man. Keep up the family tradition and all that rot."

"Then why don't you just let him know it's okay? That is, if it is okay with you?"

"Okay?" He went on slowly. "It's about the best news I've heard in a long time. I've been having crazy dreams ever since his accident, only they keep searching and searching but he doesn't make it." Impulsively she laid her hand on his arm and he gripped it with his other hand. "I can't believe he wouldn't tell me. I thought he knew that he could say whatever he felt."

"Maybe it's part of becoming a man, Derek," she said softly. "Standing on his own feet."

"Hey," he looked at her appreciatively in the dim glow from the campus lights, "for a woman you're pretty savvy about man-to-man things."

He leaned toward her and she trembled as his lips brushed hers, then automatically wrapped her arms around his neck as he took her mouth in a hard, demanding kiss. After a long moment he disengaged himself from her and grinned crookedly. "You're not bad on man-woman things either."

He got up, pulled her up beside him and with an arm around her, set her feet walking. "Forget that happened, will you? I know how you feel about . . . fooling around. But some-

454

times when you look at me that way I get my signals crossed."

"But I . . ." she began, then stopped. There was no way to explain that she had wanted him to kiss her, that she ached for him. She had already told him that she didn't want a lover and even if she had foolishly asked him to be her lover once she hadn't changed her mind.

They walked in silence to the dorm steps, then stopped. The night air was hot, heavy, and Derek's masculine scent and sultry voice seemed part of it.

"Thanks for the insight, Paula."

"You're welcome."

"Good night." His fingers brushed her lips and before she could answer he had turned and walked away.

Paula had spent the morning finishing lesson plans and the afternoon relaxing at the pool, alternately swimming and napping. She was going to a movie with Greg this evening and they were stopping by an Italian restaurant near the theatre. Reluctantly she went back to the dorm to shower and get dressed.

As she entered the bathroom carrying her towel and basket of toilet articles, she saw Ruth in her emerald green jumpsuit leaning over a lavatory, rinsing her face.

"Hi! Welcome back," said Paula. She waited a moment for Ruth's response, then realized the running water had probably drowned out her words. She stepped closer and repeated her greeting.

Ruth raised her head and Paula could see that tears mingled with the water on her cheeks. "Ruth?"

"Oh, Paula." She made an effort to speak again but no words came.

"Ruth, are you all right? What happened?"

Ruth turned off the faucet with an angry jerk. "I went home—to Georgia." Paula nodded. "My youngest brother came to get me." Paula nodded again. "And they were all there, at my parents' house. Treating me like royalty." She smiled sadly. "They were so glad to see me. No recriminations. No accusations. Just love."

"Then what—" Paula began but Ruth shook her head.

"And after they'd all gone, Mama told me. Not feeling sorry for herself or anything, just like she was talking about what she'd cook for supper." She looked at Paula with stricken eyes. "Mama has cancer. She's already had surgery and she's starting chemotherapy next week, but there's not much hope. She's lost a lot of weight, but *I* didn't know because I hadn't seen her for so many years. It isn't fair, Paula. I find my way back to my family again after all this time and she's going to die." Her face crumpled and Paula hastily put down her things and wrapped her in a comforting embrace. As she sagged against Paula's shoulder she sobbed, "God is punishing me for turning my back on them. I want to . . . make it up but now . . . it's too late."

Paula patted her back gently. "No, Ruth. He led you back before she's gone so you could make things right. It's not too late."

"I've missed so much," Ruth struggled for control, wiped her cheeks with the back of her hands. "How can I bear to lose her when I've just found her again?"

"Maybe when classes end you could spend some time with her before you go back to Jamaica?"

"It won't be long enough." She shook her head again angrily. "If only there was something I could figure out to do. I'd like to take her home with me—her and my daddy. But of course, they couldn't go." She walked back and forth. "My brother said he'd come for me again any weekend but there's only three weeks left now and then I'll be going home—

only home suddenly seems to be in Georgia now."

"Ruth, do you think you might be able to take a few weeks from your job, maybe an extra week or two with Christmas vacation or something?"

"How do I know Mama will even live that long? She needs me now."

"Then ask for the time now."

"They could never manage with a sub, not with new classes starting." She straightened her shoulders. "Well, just look at me. Crying all over the place like I'm the only one who ever had a problem to face. I'll be okay, once I come to terms with this. And Paula, thank you for helping me take a look at my real feelings a few weeks ago. Otherwise I wouldn't even have this much to hold on to."

"I'm so sorry it turned out this way, Ruth," Paula told her softly. "Sometimes bad things happen and we just have to deal with them the best we can."

"Yeah, you know that firsthand, don't you, honey? I hope I can take a lesson from you on dealing with it gracefully." She managed a wan smile. "Now get on with your shower. I've already gotten you wet—all you need is soap."

* * *

"What a long day this had been." Ruth sighed deeply and shielded her eyes from the sun as she stepped outside Oldham Hall.

Paula, walking just behind her asked wryly, "Aren't Mondays always longer?"

"Cheer up." Derek closed the door and joined them on the sidewalk. "We're on the down side of the hoop and rolling."

"That's not much comfort to me at this point," Ruth said. "I'd been counting the days all summer till I could get back to my husband and now I'm torn between wanting to go and stay."

"Well," Derek said, "so far no one is clamoring to give me a job so I'll probably stick around this fall for a master's." He looked at Paula. "Have you heard any more about funding on the new Tuscumbia job?"

"Not yet."

"What will you do if it falls through?" asked Ruth. "Any alternative plans yet?"

Paula shook her head. "Not at the moment. I sent out a few résumés but I haven't had any response."

"Have you considered staying on here—getting your degree?" Derek asked. "Faye says it's much easier to get a job if you have it, and the pay is better, too."

"I couldn't, unless the house sells," Paula answered.

"You could have if you'd asked that ex-husband of yours for the alimony you deserved," Ruth said darkly. "And I think you really should consider staying on here. Maybe you could get an assistantship or something."

"Good suggestion, Ruth," Derek said as he turned away from them in the direction of Rhodes Hall. "See you tomorrow."

"Paula," Ruth looked serious, "do you think I'd be a fool to stay in the States instead of going back to my husband and job?"

Paula thought for a minute, weighing her words. "How would your husband feel?"

"He's the one who suggested it, bless his unselfish heart. And I really would like to take care of my mama. It would sort of make up for all the time we've missed together. But I want to be with my wonderful man, too."

"What about your job?"

"If I decide to do this, I'll ask for a leave of absence. And if they replace me permanently it won't matter financially, I don't have to work—for the money—but it's part of who I am, I *like* to work. So it's a chance I'll have to take, asking."

"Well," Paula shrugged, "all of life is a chance, isn't it?"

"You're right about that, honey," Ruth nodded, "and speaking of chances, Faye Browne is going to have a wide open field to move in on our Derek if he sticks around here past summer. Wouldn't surprise me if Miss Scarlett's intercepting his job offers just to make sure it happens."

"He sounded as if he'd like to stay," Paula said flatly.

"Yeah, and he suggested you stay, too." Ruth solemnly studied her as they rode the elevator to the top floor of Winthrope Hall. "So what does that tell you?"

"That he listens to what Faye Browne says and believes every word of it," Paula said as she stepped off the elevator and headed for her room.

Minutes later Ruth stood with her hand on the phone. "Well, I've done it."

"What did Mr. Cramer say?" Louise asked.

"That he was sure the Board would agree to a year's leave but he was going to have a hard time replacing me this late in the summer—especially for one year since the regular contract is for two."

"Say, does Derek Vogel have a job yet?"

"No, and I already thought of that, but I can't ask him."

"Why not?"

"Because he's thinking of staying on here and getting his master's. And if Paula's job offer doesn't come through, she might stay, too. Besides, Tuscumbia is only a short drive away but Jamaica is so far they might as well forget it."

"Ruth Valcourt, that's not a good reason! You know what they say about absence making the heart grow fonder."

"Yeah, it sure works for me but no, I just can't be the one who ruins their chances of getting together." She picked up her towel and robe. "I'm going to take a shower."

Louise stood looking after her for a long moment. "Well, my dear roommate, to quote your own intelligent reasoning on a recent occasion, *you* can't ask Derek Vogel, but *I* can," she said aloud and picked up the phone.

As Paula finished reading the assignment for Faye Browne's Thursday class, her phone rang and she reached for it quickly, wondering who could be calling at this late hour. "Hello?"

"Paula, this is Derek."

"Yes, I know." Her heart beat faster at the sound of his voice.

"Has Ruth talked with you about taking leave from her job?"

"Yes, she's just requested a year off to care for her mother."

"And they'll need someone to fill her place?"

"Yes."

"Louise Montgomery called me about it, said she wished I'd apply. But I don't know why Ruth doesn't ask me herself."

"Well, I guess she thinks you'd rather stay here, and—"

"No way. I'd jump at the chance for a job like that."

"Then just tell her," Paula said flatly.

"I thought maybe Ruth had asked you."

"She knows I'm waiting on a job already. In fact, Cynthia Gill called me earlier tonight and said the new class got funded. I've got an interview with the superintendent on Saturday but Cynthia says it's just a formality."

"Well . . . congratulations." There was an awkward silence before he went on, "I guess you'll be going back home again."

"Yes, if this works out."

"Then I'll probably mention the job to Ruth. Good night."

Paula slowly replaced the receiver. Saying the words to Derek had made it seem real for the first time. Yes, she would be going back home—at least back to Tuscumbia.

Paula undressed and put on her terry robe and scuffs. A hot shower might help her taut muscles. Getting soap and a towel, she crossed the hall.

There was something shiny lying on the tile floor inside the bathroom door. As she got closer she could see it was a pair of glasses, broken. Sharon's. At the same time the realization struck her she heard a muffled sound from the shower stall and ran toward it. She jerked open the door, saw the hulking body, the masked face, the hands closed around the neck of the limp girl trapped in the tiny space. She screamed, dropped her towel, and began flailing at him with her bare hands. For a brief space it seemed he was not even aware of her presence, so intent was he on the naked girl he was brutalizing.

"Stop it, stop it, you bastard!" Paula screamed, digging into his tee shirt with her fingernails. "Help, somebody, help!" she screamed louder.

He flung her backward with one heavy hand and she slammed against the metal door, swinging it open. She lost her balance and went sprawling, then quickly righted herself and rushed at him, grabbing one of his powerful hands and screaming again.

This time he let go of his unconscious prey and she slid to the floor in the stall. He turned toward Paula and jerked open her robe. With a guttural sound he reached for her as she clawed at his face, ripping the mask and drawing blood. He slapped her—hard—and she fell, her head hitting the slippery tile floor outside the shower stall. She opened her mouth to scream once more as he bent over her, his hand raised to strike her again, but the sound died in her throat as a dull thud sent his head lolling forward and then his whole body was sagging and she barely moved in time to keep his weight from crushing her.

There above him, looking fierce and wild, stood Ruth holding what was left of a rum bottle she had broken over his head. "Paula! My God, are you hurt?"

She shook her head as she half-crawled toward the shower stall. "Sharon—she's in there."

"Oh Lord," Ruth inched toward the stall, keeping her eyes on the unconscious hulk that lay crumpled on the floor. "See if she's breathing, Paula."

Paula reached for Sharon's wrist, searched for and found a weak pulse. "Yes, thank God."

"I've called security," Louise ran in, another rum bottle held high in her hand. "What—oh no, are you all right Paula?"

Paula nodded, pulling her robe together and reaching for her towel to cover Sharon, who was still slumped in the shower.

Just then the masked man stirred and groaned. He felt his head where blood and rum mingled in his long matted hair, then opened his eyes warily.

"Don't move, scum," Ruth took a step toward him, holding the jagged broken bottle in front of her.

The sound of the siren was closer now. He looked about fearfully, and tried to sit up.

Louise, hoisting a full bottle higher in her hand, moved in from the other direction. "Don't try it, buster," she warned.

With a whimper he ducked and covered his head, just as the elevator doors swung open and footsteps came pounding down the hall.

Two security guards handcuffed the man and took him away, then sent for an infirmary ambulance for Sharon and Paula. Louise and the remaining guard reassured the gathering crowd of frightened, curious students that everything was all right. As Ruth and Paula helped Sharon to her room to await the stretcher, Paula—feeling somewhat hysterical in the aftermath—began to giggle.

"Paula, what on earth—" Ruth began.

"I was just thinking, Ruth," she convulsed with laughter again, "How disgusting it was of you to talk like that. How crude."

Ruth smiled grimly and replied with a good imitation of Irvin's voice, "He had it coming, man."

Twenty

Paula sat in the empty waiting room of the university infirmary, holding a cold compress to her throbbing cheek. The fluorescent lights reflecting on the shiny floor were like snow-covered ground in sunshine and she closed her eyelids against the glare. "Paula, are you all right?"

Her eyes flew open at Ruth's touch on her shoulder. "Yes, just resting my eyes. Did you see Sharon?"

Ruth nodded and smiled reassuringly. "They've X-rayed and examined her and she's going to be just fine. Nothing broken, no internal injuries. The brute surprised her from behind as she went into the bathroom so she didn't have a chance to fight him off, which was probably fortunate."

"Did he . . ." Paula couldn't seem to say the

word aloud and Ruth, reading her thoughts, quickly put her mind at ease.

"No. He beats or chokes his victims into submission before he tries to rape them. But, Lord, if you'd been a few minutes later . . ." she shuddered and left the sentence unfinished. "Anyway, the police asked us both a few questions and then a nurse gave her a shot, so she's sleeping now. Did they talk to you on the way out?"

"Yes, and they said we'd have to testify against the guy when he comes to trial."

"Gladly. I'd like to have a part in putting the SOB behind bars for life." She gave Paula a wry smile. "I guess you know you're a campus celebrity now."

"But I didn't do anything. You were the one who—"

"Me?" Ruth looked incredulous. "It's easy to be brave when you've got a weapon. *You* attacked a monster twice your size with your *bare hands*. That took nerve. And you can be sure the radio and TV stations and newspapers will be clamoring for interviews tomorrow."

Paula's eyes grew wide. "Really?"

"This creep has been terrorizing the campus and security hadn't even told the local police. People are going to be asking some hard questions, like would he have to kill someone before the students were alerted, and—" she stopped in midsentence as the double doors swung open and Derek Vogel crossed the room in quick strides and knelt beside Paula's chair.

"Paula, are you okay?"

"Derek? How did you know—"

"Louise called me," he looked at her with concern and repeated, "Are you okay?"

"Yes, except for this." She indicated her face and he gently removed the compress to look at her swollen cheek.

"Christ, I'd like to kill the son of a bitch," he said between clenched teeth. "Have you seen a doctor?"

Paula nodded. "And he gave me something for the pain."

"Why are you sitting here?" he asked, looking at Ruth for the answer.

"She was waiting to hear about Sharon." Sensing his next question, Ruth went on. "And she's all right, too. But they're keeping her overnight for observation so I'll stay with her. And if you—"

"Of course." He reached to help Paula stand and continued to hold her. "I'll take you back to Winthrope Hall. Which brings me to another question. Don't they lock that place at dark? How in hell did this pervert get in?"

"The students keep the door propped open so they can come in from the parking area," Ruth told him.

"What a damn fool thing to do." Derek shook his head angrily.

Paula, feeling the effect of the sedative, swayed against him and he held her more tightly.

"We'd better go," Derek told her gently, "before you fold up like an accordion."

Ruth watched them make their way toward the door, a satisfied smile on her face. "Don't they make a lovely couple?" she said under her breath. "Even in the worst of times."

Inside the dark car, Derek pulled Paula to him, cradling her head against his shoulder with one hand, gently touching her wounded cheek with the other. "I wouldn't be surprised if you have quite a shiner tomorrow." Suddenly growing serious, he went on, "You could have been killed tonight, do you realize that?"

"I do now," Paula answered softly.

"You're a very gutsy lady in my book, Paula Howard."

"But Ruth—"

He put a finger to her lips, "I heard the whole story from Louise, and I know how you waded in bare-handed to fight him off. And if I don't get you back to the dorm soon you may have to fight me off, too." His lips brushed her forehead. "I'd hate to take advantage of you when you're under the influence—again." He released her and started the car.

All the way back to Winthrope Hall she tried to sort her thoughts. Did Derek think that he was the one who had initiated their night of passionate lovemaking, she wondered, but her head throbbed and her mind was too fuzzy to consider the question right now.

Derek had been right on the mark. It was quite a shiner. She gingerly touched the puffy bruised flesh over her cheekbone, traced the wide black smudge that circled the lower part of her eye. The photographer from the paper had insisted on shooting her so that it showed to best advantage and her face and Ruth's stared at her now from the front page of the *Alabama Herald* on top of her desk, beside the dozen roses Greg had sent. Under the headline "Coeds Capture Criminal" ran a two-column spread, detailing last night's ordeal.

The phone's shrill ring startled her and she

looked at it with trepidation for a long time before she answered.

"Mom?"

Her face registered shock, then disbelief. "Jeff?"

"Yeah, it's me, Mom."

"But where are you?"

"Right here in Alabama, looking at a picture of my mom the coed in the *Tuscumbia Times*. Jesus, what's going on down there?"

"Nothing—now," she reassured him. "And I never expected it to be in the paper there."

"And on the six o'clock news, too," Jeff told her. "You're famous, Mom. No kidding, are you really okay?"

"I'm fine except for one ugly black eye."

"Yeah, that showed up pretty good in the photo. Even better on TV."

"Oh, I forgot, you saw it already. It's hard to keep secrets anymore."

"They said the guy had a record, that he's already done time for hurting women. Try to be more careful, Mom, will you?"

"Okay, honey, I promise. Now let's talk about you. When did you get home and how come I didn't know you were coming?"

"Yesterday. And it was supposed to be a surprise, but seems like I'm the one surprised."

"Look, I'm coming to Tuscumbia Saturday for a job interview so can I see you then?"

"Sure, Mom, great. I'll be at Dad's apartment, so give me a call when you get in town." There was an awkward silence, then he went on. "Or better yet, tell me now where to meet you and I'll be there."

"Well, I could make it in time for breakfast—if you want to get up that early?"

"No sweat. Besides, in India it'd be late evening."

Paula laughed. "Okay, the Dutch Kitchen, nine o'clock."

"Got it. And I'll be the brown one carrying a big sign says 'My mom, the hero'."

"Go on. Flattery will get you a free breakfast. I love you, Jeff, and I'm so glad you're home."

"Me, too, Mom, the love stuff and home both. See ya. And hey, don't hang up. Dad wants to talk a minute."

Paula drew her breath in sharply. She hadn't realized Jeff was at Quent's apartment. She could hear Jeff calling his dad, hear muffled words being spoken.

"Paula? Jeff says you're all right."

"Yes, I'm fine."

"I never expected anything like this."

"Yes, well, things happen."

"The whole town's in a buzz about it. Phone's been ringing off the wall."

"The Howard family just can't seem to keep a low profile, can we?" The words slipped out before she could stop them and she could tell from the silence before Quent spoke again that they had stung.

"I guess not." His words sounded flat. "There is one other thing. We've got an offer on the house and we need to talk about it. Jeff said you'd be up here Saturday. Would you have time to stop by the house and go over the purchase offer?"

"Well . . . I guess so," she said slowly. "Sometime in the afternoon."

"One okay for you?"

"All right."

"See you Saturday then. And Paula, take care, will you?"

"Yes, Quent. Goodbye."

Paula slowly put down the phone. Jeff was home. What a wonderful relief that was. And they had a buyer for the house at last, so that meant she'd make it even if the job fell through.

She reached out to touch the velvet petals of a long-stemmed rose. So much was happening so fast. Nobody ever said college life was dull, but did it have to be this hectic?

The parking lot of the Dutch Kitchen was crowded as always on Saturday morning. Paula found a place for the Grand Am at the back and stepped out of the car just as Jeff raced around the building and caught her up in a fierce bear hug.

"My mom, the hero." He kissed her soundly.

"Jeff, put me down," she said breathlessly as she hugged him back. "Here, let me look at you. Say, you *are* brown."

"I look good, huh?" He flexed his muscles. "This is a real working-guy tan, too. Building houses, farming, repairing bridges, stuff like that."

"I can't wait to hear all about it," Paula told him sincerely as they walked arm in arm toward the restaurant. "And you do look great, a real sight for these sore old eyes."

Jeff grinned at her. "Well, I wasn't going to mention the eye, Mom, but you've done a good job with the makeup and shades. And you're pretty tan and fit, too. In fact, you look younger than you did when I left."

"Ah, go on, I'm buying breakfast already."

He held the door for her. "So where's the job, Mom?"

"Northwoods Elementary."

"How about that."

When they were seated and had given their orders for blueberry waffles, Paula smiled at her handsome son. He was a lot like Quent except for hair color and his dark tan accentuated his blondness. "So what are your plans, Jeff?"

"You mean short or long range?" he asked evasively.

She shrugged. "Whatever."

He dropped his eyes and began pleating his napkin as the waitress returned to fill their coffee cups. "I thought I'd just hang out with Dad—for a while."

Paula thought of Bootsie and wondered how Quent felt about his son's plans. "Does he . . . like the idea? I thought he had a very small place."

"Yeah, like only one bedroom, but I'm bunking on the sofa. And I've been sittin' in on practice sessions with the band. Their sound man quit and I'm taking his place."

"Why Jeff, that's wonderful."

"The pay's not too great, but hey, it's a few bucks to tide me over till something better happens."

"Like?"

He sampled the coffee before he answered. "I dunno, Mom. Maybe music, maybe not. But

Dad and I have been talking. Heavy stuff. I think he sees where I'm coming from now. And he says to take my time, no hurry. Whatever I decide is okay by him."

"Jeff, I'm so glad."

"And listen, Mom," Jeff cleared his throat, picked up his silverware, put it down, "I guess I've been too hard on Dad." When she started to speak he held up his hand to silence her. "Not that what he did was right or anything. And I know you didn't deserve it but hey, shit happens. Sorry, Mom. What I mean is, Dad just had to do what he had to do." He squared his shoulders, looked at her solemnly. "Men are that way. Like me, joining the Peace Corps. But I've got it out of my system now, the rebelling thing."

"And your Dad's over the controlling thing, too?" Paula asked softly.

"Yeah, I think he is."

The waitress brought their waffles before Paula could reply and they concentrated on adding butter and warm syrup, then ate hungrily. From the booth where they sat near the fireplace she could see familiar faces come and go. It seemed like other times for a moment, Saturdays when she and Quent had brought two children for a treat before swim practice. Now Amy was married and pregnant, she divorced and waiting for a job interview, and Jeff was bunking in a bachelor pad with Quent. How had her world turned so topsy-turvy in such a short space of time?

"Good morning, Paula." A cheerful voice interrupted her thoughts and looking up, she saw Cynthia Gill standing beside her.

"Hello, Cynthia. How nice to see you. Jeff, you remember Miss—"

"Sure do," Jeff said, rising quickly to his feet. "How are you, Miss Gill?"

"Jeff? Is it really you?" she looked astonished. "Last time I saw you I was the taller one and now look at you."

Jeff grinned self-consciously. "Yes ma'am. I've grown a little since fifth grade."

"Won't you sit down, Cynthia?" Paula asked.

"Oh no, thanks, I'm meeting a group of the teachers for breakfast." She smiled at Paula. "All ready for your interview this morning?" Paula nodded. "You look terrific, in spite of that ordeal you've been through. And I feel sure you'll get the job, but of course the Board has to approve it."

"How long will that take?"

"You should hear something by next week." She turned to Jeff who was still standing. "What are you doing these days, Jeff?"

"I just got back from a couple of years in

India—with the Peace Corps," Cynthia Gill looked impressed, "and now I'm doing sound, for the Confederate Cowboys at the Cabana Club."

"Really? I hear they're awfully good."

"Why don't you come out and see for yourself?"

"I just may do that. I love country-western music."

"Let me know when you're coming and I'll get you a good table near the front."

She shrugged and smiled, "How about tonight?"

"Sure. Will you be bringing anyone?"

"No, I'll be alone." She smiled at Paula, "Good luck on the interview. You know already you're my choice," then included Jeff, "See you tonight, and thanks."

Jeff sat down again. "She was one of my favorite teachers. Is she still at Northwoods?"

"Yes, she's the principal."

"No kidding? You mean, Miss Gill is gonna be your new boss?"

"If I get the job."

He looked across the room where Cynthia Gill was greeting a group of other women. "She's kinda pretty. Wonder why she never married?"

"I believe she took care of her parents and

maybe still lives in their big house over in Florence."

"Yeah, that sounds like something she'd do."

"So tell me all about your life in India until I have to leave for my appointment," said Paula.

Jeff motioned for the waitress to refill their cups, then sketched in the months that he had been away.

Finally, Paula looked at her watch. "I have to go now, honey," she said reluctantly, "and I want you to know I'm glad you decided to stay around for awhile."

He grinned, "I sure don't want to miss being here when I become an uncle."

"How did you find out?" Paula's face was puzzled.

"Amy wrote me."

"Does your dad know, too?"

"I'm not sure, maybe not."

"Well, I guess Amy will tell him soon."

"Yeah. When did she tell you?"

"When she came to see me at the university. Say, why don't you come down for a visit? There's still next weekend."

"Maybe, if I can borrow Dad's car."

Paula stood, kissed her son's cheek warmly. "Call me next week and let me know. I'd love for my new friends to meet you." She reached for the check but Jeff's hand got there first.

"My treat, Mom."

"But I invited—"

"And I'm paying. So go on to your interview and knock 'em dead."

"I'll do my best." She smiled nervously. "Can I drop you anywhere?"

"Thanks, but I'm just gonna head on back to the apartment. My turn to do the laundry."

On her way out, Paula stopped in the rest room to freshen her makeup. After she applied lipstick she looked at her image with a critical eye. White linen skirt and navy jacket over kelly green silk blouse, large white earrings and bracelet. Maybe she did look as Cynthia Gill said, terrific. She held herself erect and smiled, feeling surprisingly confident as she headed for her first job interview in thirty years.

The familiar feeling of coming home swept over Paula as she turned onto Northwoods Drive. Parking in the curved driveway, she walked slowly to the house feeling a sudden lethargy as though she were about to open a door to the past.

Inside the cool dim hallway she paused,

thinking of Amy coming down the steps in her wedding gown three weeks ago. A house had memories that were not for sale. It was half an hour until Quent would be here so she left her purse and jacket on the living room sofa and went from room to room saying goodbye to a period in her life. Going upstairs was harder. Here the baby crib had been. She made a mental note to ask Amy if she'd like it back from Holly, whose girls had used it last. Here the closets filled with baseball gloves, Barbie dolls. Here the marriage bed.

She retraced her steps and went outside. As always her garden comforted her. The roses spilled their fragrant blooms along the brick walkways as she made her way toward the fountain where the "Christopher Columbus" was now in full bloom. She forced away the image of Quent with Bootsie beside the arbor and remembered instead Amy and Chris saying their vows. She broke a pepper red rose and took it with her into the house, meeting Quent just inside the door.

"Oh, I didn't know you were here." She took a step backward.

"Sorry if I startled you." He smiled at her. "How do you feel?"

She returned his smile. "Fine."

"You're looking good. I thought you might be all black and blue after what happened."

"The media exaggerates." Her hand went automatically to her camouflaged cheek.

"How did the interview go?" he asked with interest.

"Very well, but I won't know for sure if I've got the job until the Board meets." She carried the rose to the kitchen, wet a paper towel and wrapped its stem.

Quent followed and sat down at the table. He placed a folder in front of him, opened it. She took a chair opposite him. "Here's the purchase agreement, Paula. The people are willing to meet our price, but they can't use the furniture. And they'd need possession in thirty days."

"Disposing of the furniture that soon may be a problem," she said thoughtfully. "Maybe Amy and Chris could use some of it?"

"Maybe." He closed the folder and looked at her intently. "Paula, could we talk?"

"I thought we were."

"No, I mean discuss something."

Oh no, she thought, heavy stuff. Maybe he wanted her to take an apartment big enough for Jeff so he could have more privacy with his bimbo. "Okay."

"Look, I . . . really don't know how to say

this. But I guess talking to Jeff these last couple of days has cleared up some things in my head. I don't know what came over me, Paula—walking out on you, I mean." He stopped but she remained silent and he went on more slowly. "I think I've finally figured out part of it. I thought I was getting old and I was in a rut. My marriage wasn't all that exciting anymore." At her look of surprise he added quickly, "That wasn't your fault—it was just living in the same place, doing the same things with the same people—"

"Including the same old wife?"

"I told you, Paula, I don't blame you," he said sincerely, "but I was bored and I hadn't done a lot of things I'd always wanted to do. Like playing in a band and driving a BMW."

"And bedding a bimbo with big bosoms?"

He sighed, hung his head. "Okay, I admit it was an ego trip to date a woman that young. But I wasn't looking for something like her. I was looking for myself—my younger self, maybe even the self I hadn't ever been."

Paula nodded, feeling more understanding and empathy for him than she was willing to admit.

He looked contrite, "I'm sorry, Paula, for how much I hurt you."

After a long silence she said, "Okay, apology accepted."

He stood up and she thought the discussion was over as he walked to the kitchen window, braced his hands on the sink and looked out across the garden. Then he turned and she saw the anguish on his face. "Paula, I made a terrible mistake. I can see now what a goddamned fool I've been. I love you—always have. It made me crazy when you asked that guy to Amy's wedding. And when you came in the next morning and—" he looked at her helplessly, "and I knew I'd lost you."

"I didn't like seeing you with someone either," Paula admitted.

"And then you got yourself half killed down there last week." He looked at her tenderly. "Paula, I don't want to sell the house. I want us to move back home, get married again."

Paula closed her eyes. Was she hearing clearly? Was Quent really saying this, or was she dreaming?

He crossed to the table, took her hand, pulled her up and into his arms. She automatically raised her head as he bent to kiss her. It was a long passionate kiss, his tongue probing, thrusting, as one hand caressed her throat, then her breast. Their bodies were still pressed together so that she could feel his growing arousal. And when he lifted his head and looked at her she was astonished at what she felt—which was absolutely nothing! "Will you marry me, Paula?" he whispered.

"No, Quent," she whispered. "I'm sorry, I can't."

His hands gripped her shoulders. "Paula, I know I deserve this. But, dammit, don't make us both suffer because of your pride. I said I was sorry, and God knows I am. I broke it off with Bootsie right after the wedding, if that's worrying you."

"It doesn't matter. I can't," she repeated regretfully.

"Is it him—the guy you brought here?"

"No. It's me."

"I know you've changed, Paula. I can see that. And you wouldn't have to be the same person you were before. I wouldn't expect it. You could work like you'd planned. You could have it all," he gestured toward the other rooms, "your house, your garden, a husband who loves you," he took a deep breath, played his trump card, ". . . and Jeff could stay here as long as he likes and we'd be a family again."

"I'm sorry, Quent," she said, and pushed herself gently away from him.

They stood facing each other in the quiet

room. "I'll give up the band. I'll sell the car. I'll—"

"Quent, I would never ask you to do those things. That's part of who you are now." She looked at his fringed blue denim shirt and tapered jeans, his long hair tinged with gray. "I wish for all our sakes I could say yes. But I don't love you anymore." At his stricken look she almost took the words back because she suddenly didn't feel like hurting him but she was helpless to stop.

He turned away from her, looked out the window, his hands gripping the edge of the cabinet, his shoulders shaking.

My God, she said silently, *he's crying.* She had seen him weep only once before in all the years she'd known him—at his father's grave. Perhaps it was fitting that he wept again today.

"Paula," he whispered hoarsely, "I need you. Don't do this to me."

She took a step toward him, willed herself to stop. "Goodbye, Quent. Do you want me to sign the papers for the house before I go?"

He shook his head.

I will put one foot in front of the other, she told herself firmly, and I will walk out of here and I won't look back. One slow step and she had reached the table. Another three, the door. She walked across the hall, picked up her purse and jacket. In the hall again, she heard the sound of Quent's quiet weeping and almost weakened.

The front door was open now and she could breathe the fresh air. She took another step, another, closed the door behind her. The car sat in the sweltering sun a mile away and there were concrete blocks tied to both her feet. But with herculean effort she lifted each in turn and by the time she reached it she had been stretched until she felt ten feet tall. Before she turned the ignition key, she looked back at the house and sighed deeply. Maybe Thomas Wolfe was right. Maybe you really couldn't ever go home again.

Twenty-one

It was after four when Paula returned to Winthrope Hall and went directly to Ruth's and Louise's room.

"I thought it might be you," Louise threw open the door and smiled warmly. "Come in and lower our anxiety level. You did get the job, didn't you?"

"Not officially. The Board has to approve but it's a pretty sure bet."

"If looking like a million dollars has anything to do with it, you've got the job," Ruth said emphatically. "You're absolutely glowing."

"Thank you." She crossed the room and sat on the bed with Ruth.

"So this means you definitely plan to go back to Tuscumbia?" Ruth looked grave.

"That's where the job is," said Paula. "The *only* job prospect I've got."

Ruth sighed. "Then I suppose I may as well ask Derek Vogel if he'd like to fill in for me this year."

"He hasn't mentioned it to you?" Paula asked with surprise. "He already knows about it."

"How . . ." Ruth looked first at Paula then at Louise who smiled apologetically. "Oh well."

"Did you have a nice visit with your son?" Louise appeared anxious to change the subject.

"Yes, we spent a couple of hours together this morning," Paula said happily, "and guess what?"

"What, what?" Ruth asked impatiently.

"You've sold the house?" Louise asked simultaneously.

"Jeff is doing sound for Quent's band and sharing his apartment."

"What about Miss Puss 'N Boots? Isn't it a bit crowded?" Ruth asked.

"Oh, Quent broke up with her," Paula said airily.

Ruth looked glum. "Could that be the reason for your glow?"

"There's more," Paula went on, ignoring the question.

"You've sold the house?" Louise repeated.

"Well, I guess so, if we want to."

"If?" Ruth looked alarmed.

"Quent and I had a serious talk today."

"Lord, I don't want to hear this," Ruth muttered to herself.

"He realizes now what a stupid mistake he made, and how foolish he's been acting and—" she paused dramatically.

"Lord, don't let this lead where I know it's going." Ruth closed her eyes tightly.

"He said he still loves me and he wants us to get married again."

There was a moment of silence following Paula's announcement, then Louise said with as much enthusiasm as she could muster, "Well, that certainly is a surprise."

"Yes, but not the biggest surprise." Paula shook her head in wonder. "I turned him down."

"You what?" Ruth shrieked, then slapped her hands together. "Hallelujah!"

"It was the hardest thing I've ever had to do," Paula went on. "All these months I've dreamed about getting back together with Quent, I've fantasized a thousand times about hearing all the things he told me today. And then it happened and I was given a chance to have my husband and my house and my son with even a new job thrown in. And," she said with awe, "I turned it down."

"Do you know why?" Louise asked softly.

"Because I don't feel anything for him anymore. Somehow without my being aware of it, the feeling died. Only I didn't know I was dragging it around like a dead weight." She took a deep breath. "Today I buried it."

"And you feel euphoric," said Louise.

"It's so strange to realize I don't love Quent. I still have feelings for him as the father of our children, of course, and eventually we may be able to be friends or at least tolerate each other. But whatever attraction was there just doesn't exist now. And on the drive back I kept trying to figure out why I was so upset with him at the wedding if I don't love him."

"Jealousy," Louise said with assurance. "He was like your property and someone else had taken him without your permission. It's human nature to guard our possessions."

"The dog-in-the-manger syndrome, Mrs. Freud?" Ruth asked wryly.

"Something like that," Louise answered, then looked at Paula. "So are you selling the house?"

"I think so, but Quent was too upset to discuss it when I left."

"Well, honey, I hate to sound vindictive, but

that man deserves what he's getting," Ruth said with satisfaction.

"I thought I'd like to see him suffer, too," Paula agreed, "but it really didn't make me feel good when it happened. In fact, I felt a little sorry for him."

"That's a sign of growth," Louise said.

Paula shrugged. "It's ironic, isn't it? He took away my life and I had to start over again. But now I have so much and Quent is the one who's suffering."

Ruth nodded. "Everything that goes around, comes around."

"And speaking of going," Paula looked at her watch, "I'd better. Greg is picking me up at six for dinner at Magnolia Manor."

"Now don't do anything drastic like agree to marry him just because you've exorcised your ex's ghost," Ruth warned.

"I promise," Paula crossed her heart, then smiled impishly. "But you have to admit two proposals in as many weeks is a pretty good track record for an old lady like me."

"Just remember, third time's charmed," Ruth called after her, then shook her head. "Wow, she had me scared there for a second. I thought sure she'd take the nightclub cowboy back if he ever asked her to."

"Paula's changed a lot since she came here,"

Louise said thoughtfully. "You know, she had everything going for her but she didn't believe in herself."

"Because that fool man had walked out on her."

Louise nodded. "But now I think she's beginning to find out she is a person of worth all by herself."

"Well, if she and a certain other guy I know would ever figure out the obvious, they could pool their worth and live happily ever after." Ruth put her hands to her head. "Oh me, oh my, how I wish I didn't feel I owe Derek Vogel a chance at my job."

"He's perfect for it, Ruth, and I know he'd like to do this for you. So ask him," Louise urged.

"Caught between the devil and the deep blue sea."

Louise laughed. "It's a hard life, being a matchmaker."

Paula stopped in front of a stately old white frame house surrounded by tall oaks draped in Spanish moss. Its black shutters and wrought iron fence looked newly painted and neatly trimmed ivy lined the sidewalk buckled from roots of trees on either side. What had seemed a good idea this morning caused her second thoughts in the oppressive stillness of the Sunday afternoon. But as long as she was here it couldn't hurt to check it out. She glanced again at the newspaper lying on the seat beside her to confirm the address and got out of the car.

A tall woman of indeterminate age answered the door. "Hello, are you the lady who called about the apartment?"

"Yes, I'm Paula Howard."

"Come in, I'm Patricia Taylor, but call me Trish." She led the way into a wide entrance hall with an ornately carved stairway. "The apartment's upstairs?" She made it sound like a question.

"Yes, you told me." Paula smiled.

The woman turned and walked up the carpeted steps, Paula following. A mahogany grandfather clock chimed the quarter hour as they passed it on the landing. "You'd have the whole floor," Trish Taylor said as she opened a transomed door and stepped back for Paula to enter. "I'm going to get it repainted— thought I'd wait and let the new tenant pick the color."

Paula nodded, walking slowly through the large room with its low windows and corner fireplace.

"Big bedroom has a fireplace, too, and a

window seat." She gestured toward the bay window that seemed to be supported by the leafy limbs beyond the glass.

The guest bedroom furniture from the house on Northwoods Drive would fit nicely, Paula thought as she looked around her.

"Here's the bath." A footed tub caught Paula's attention. before they passed into a smaller room. "Extra bedroom, or whatever you want. You alone?"

"Yes, I'm attending the university."

"Most of my tenants have been, it being in walking distance. Here's the kitchen. The stove and refrigerator are nearly new."

The wrought iron table and chairs from the patio would be perfect here, Paula thought, as she visualized them in front of the double windows overlooking the back.

"And you can use the washer and dryer downstairs. Here's the porch. And stairs leading up from outside if you want to use them."

Paula stepped onto the screened porch with its wicker swing and looked down at the neat beds of blooming perennials.

"The price I told you includes utilities, all but phone. Deposit's one month's rent plus first month in advance."

"I like it, Mrs. . . . Trish," Paula said when she had returned to the door leading downstairs, "but I would have to check on a couple of things first so I wonder if you could hold it a few days? If I make a deposit, of course."

The woman shook her head. "That won't be necessary, Paula. Just leave your name and phone number. I'm in no hurry."

"But—"

Trish Taylor shook her head as they reached the bottom of the stairs. "No, if we don't trust each other, we shouldn't live together. Now, would you like a glass of mint tea before you go?"

"I certainly would." Paula followed Trish Taylor to her old-fashioned kitchen with its round oak table and watched as she prepared refreshments.

"By the way, what color do you want the walls, Paula?"

Suddenly as certain of things working out as her new landlady appeared to be, she answered without hesitation "Sky blue."

Paula re-examined her options as she drove slowly back to Winthrope Hall. When she really thought about it, there was only one desirable choice. All of her life she had been trying to live up to standards set by someone else. Maybe it was time she asked herself what *she* really wanted and set about getting it.

Back at the dorm, Paula dialed Quent's number before she could reconsider and change her mind. "Quent, it's Paula."

"I know." His voice was warm, expectant.

"I've thought about the house. And I believe we can give possession in thirty days."

"You're sure you want to sell it, then?" he asked flatly.

"I'm sure." When he didn't respond she went on. "I'm going to take an unfurnished apartment. I can use the guest bedroom furniture, most of the things in the living room—and everything from the patio. I suppose we could store the rest until you or one of the kids can use it."

"Okay."

"And I'll need a few hundred advance until we get the money from the house—for the apartment rent."

"Jeff mentioned driving down next Saturday. I suppose he could bring the papers for you to sign. And he can bring a check, unless you need it sooner."

"No, Saturday's fine."

"Or I could take it by if you tell me where—"

"Oh, didn't I mention . . . no, I guess I didn't. The apartment is here."

After a long silence he spoke again. "What about your job?"

"I'm not going to take it. I've decided to stay on at the university and complete my master's."

"I see."

"So tell Jeff to let me know what time he's coming Saturday." She took a deep breath. "Quent, this really is the best way—for all of us. I don't belong in Tuscumbia anymore. I couldn't ever be happy there now, or make you happy. I'm sorry. Goodbye."

She hung up and called directory assistance. Better get it all done, burn the bridges behind her so there'd be no going back.

"Cynthia? This is Paula Howard. I'm sorry to bother you on Sunday, but—"

"Paula! I'm glad you called. I talked to the superintendent yesterday afternoon and he has assured me you'll be the one he'll recommend to the Board."

"That's what I'm calling about, Cynthia. I really appreciate all you've done for me and I know I would enjoy working with you but—I guess I was also hoping to come back to my old life again—and now I know that's not what I want. So I'm staying here to finish my degree."

"Well, I was looking forward to having you

at my school but I understand that circumstances change sometimes." After a short silence, she asked, "Paula, are you sure you're doing the right thing?"

"Yes, I'm doing what's right for me."

"Then I won't try to change your mind. And I wish you all the best."

"Thanks, Cynthia, especially for helping with the university grant. It's changed my life."

"For better, I hope?"

"I think so."

"When you're up this way again, Paula, give me a call. I'd love to hear from you."

"Thanks, I will. Bye." As Paula replaced the receiver, she said to herself, No, Cynthia, I don't just *think* it is for the best. On second thought, I *know* so.

The week dragged interminably and for some reason she could not explain Paula told no one of her tentative plans. Ruth recommended Derek to fill her job and he sent a resume, then waited anxiously for a response.

On Friday afternoon as the three tutors left Oldham Hall, Irvin Pendergrass yelled after them, "See ya tomorrow, man—uh, Mister Vogel."

"Okay, Irvin. See you."

"Going fishing again?" Paula asked.

He nodded. "Last Saturday we'll be here." He looked glumly at Ruth. "And still no word on the job. What could be taking so long?"

"Government red tape. Have patience," said Ruth.

"I'll let you know if I hear anything over the weekend."

"I won't be here till Sunday evening. My brother is taking me home again tonight," Ruth answered. "Good luck."

"I'll need it." He left them and Paula and Ruth walked on together.

"Have you noticed how Miss Scarlett and our handsome friend have scarcely spoken all week?" Ruth asked as soon as Derek was out of hearing range.

"Maybe he's made another conquest and lost interest," Paula suggested tartly. "That seems to be his modus operandi."

"Well, I'm not so sure about that." Ruth looked thoughtful. "I heard a rumor today that the sexy Miss Browne was leaving."

"For where?"

"The girl didn't know. Just said she knew a secretary who overheard Faye tell Dr. Colbert she was ready for a change of scenery and she'd never have a better chance."

"Like maybe go to Jamaica?"

"Don't be silly. She'd never give up what she has here to follow a man."

"Strange things happen. Maybe that's why they've been acting so cool. She wanted him to stay here and he wanted her to go."

"Paula, she is not his type."

"Try telling him that. He seems to like her fine."

"Why, she's so organized she'd probably schedule her orgasms," Ruth spluttered.

Paula smiled grimly at Ruth and retorted. "Well, maybe an ex-rear admiral would like that."

Jeff arrived a little before noon on Saturday, bearing an armful of Christopher Columbus roses. "Dad sent them," he gave the flowers to Paula. "Said something about you forgetting them last weekend."

"How thoughtful." Paula led the way to the elevator and as they went up she buried her face in their fragrant softness remembering when Quentin gave one of her treasured blooms to Bootsie. Somehow this generous bouquet made that careless gesture a less painful memory.

She unlocked her door. "So, here's my

digs," she said as she went to the chest and put the roses in a pitcher of water.

"Looks like a palace compared to my last place of residence," Jeff told her. "But Dad says you're moving."

"Yes, I wanted a place where I could cook and have company sometimes."

"Oh, and Dad said to tell you that if you want to rent a van with pads and stuff, that he and I could get the furniture down here for you."

"Maybe I'll do that," Paula answered. "And say, I'll drive you by to see the apartment after we eat lunch if you like."

"Sure, Mom." Jeff walked to the window, looked down. "Dad and I may be moving, too. We've looked at a condo."

"Condo? I didn't know Tuscumbia had any."

"Over in Florence, in a nice complex Cynthia—Miss Gill told us about." Paula raised her eyebrows. "I took her out for coffee after the show last weekend and Dad went, too."

"How nice," Paula said sincerely.

"Anyway, the condo has two bedrooms, so Dad said we could use the den furniture and kitchen table, and I could take the stuff from my old room."

"Why doesn't he take the master bedroom furniture?"

"He's getting a waterbed, Mom. Said he'd always wanted one of those real sloshy kinds. Besides, Amy and Chris are gonna take the king-sized bed."

"Really?"

"Yeah. She called this week and said they're buying a little house out in Marietta after the baby gets here."

"Did she tell your dad that?"

"Yeah, and he nearly lost it he was so excited."

Paula had always imagined how thrilled she and Quent would be when they became grandparents and now they would not be sharing this special event. She swallowed past the lump in her throat, said, "Shall we eat in the cafeteria or would you like to go someplace else?"

"Cafeteria's fine." He grinned at her. "I want to get the whole picture of my mom, the coed."

Paula pointed out the library and Oldham Hall as they crossed the commons, telling Jeff a little about her classes and the tutoring program. They were still engrossed in conversation when they reached Gaither Hall and neither saw Sharon and Derek coming down the steps until they spoke.

"Hello," Paula smiled at them, then turned to her son. "Jeff, I'd like you to meet two of my friends. This is Sharon Swafford who lives in the room next to mine."

"Hi, Jeff." Sharon held her hand out. "I've heard a lot about you."

"And Derek Vogel is a classmate."

"Good to meet you, Jeff." They shook hands, appraising each other as they did.

"Derek has some news," Sharon said to Paula.

She looked at him quickly. "Have you—"

He nodded. "You're looking at the new learning disabilities teacher of The Priority School in Kingston."

"Well, congratulations," she said and tried to hide her disappointment. To Jeff she explained, "Derek's going to teach in Jamaica for a year."

"That's great," Jeff said and looked truly pleased.

"Have you heard anything about the Tuscumbia job, Paula?" Derek asked.

"I . . . I'm staying here." She didn't meet his eyes.

Sharon said happily, "I'm so glad."

Paula glanced at the younger girl with puzzlement. Why would she be glad about that?

Derek was looking at her intently. "When did you decide this?" he asked softly.

She shrugged, acutely aware of his intense scrutiny which left her feeling flustered and breathless. "Oh, I've been considering it for some time," she answered evasively, then looked at her watch. "We've got to be going now before the cafeteria line closes."

"Wouldn't want to rush in late. That causes collisions," Derek said in obvious reference to their first meeting, and Paula smiled.

"See you all after lunch back at the dorm?" Sharon looked at Jeff.

"Mom's taking me by to see her new apartment," Jeff told her. "Maybe after that."

Paula saw the surprise registered on Derek's face at this new revelation, but he said nothing.

As they walked up the steps, Paula regretted not having told Derek about her job earlier but she hadn't wanted him to think she'd stayed on to be with him, not when he was trying so hard to get Ruth's job in Jamaica. If he'd cared about her he wouldn't have wanted to go at all.

"Mom," Jeff's words punctuated her thoughts. "That's him, isn't it?"

"Who?" she felt color rise in her face.

"The guy you invited to the wedding, the one Amy told me about."

"Yes, it is." She felt something more was called for. "Derek has a son about your age who dates Sharon."

"Oh. I thought maybe these two were hanging out together."

Paula laughed. "That's the impression your sister got, too, when she first met them."

"Well, she doesn't think so now," Jeff mumbled as they went inside.

It was just after Jeff had gone that Amy called.

"Poor timing," Paula told her, "Jeff was here until a few minutes ago."

"Sorry I missed him," Amy answered.

"So how are you, honey?"

"Wearing maternity clothes and feeling super. And how's my mom? Has the black eye gone away?"

"Yes, it finally faded."

"Mom, what I'm calling about is Dad said you'd turned down the job at Northwoods. And" she hesitated before she added "him."

"Amy, did he ask you to—"

"No, Mom. I'm butting in all by myself. So did you?"

"Yes, Amy, to both."

"Mom, why? It would be so great to have you two back together, especially for the baby's sake."

Paula took a determined breath. "Honey, I know this would be wonderful for the *family's* sake. But it wouldn't be good for *me.*"

"But, Mom, I thought you wanted Dad back and—"

"I thought so, too, but I was wrong. Look, I'm not rejecting you—none of you. I'm just accepting myself and trying to be myself in the way that feels right to me. Can you understand that, Amy?"

"Well, I'm not sure, Mom. But I'll try." After a short silence she asked, "And you're going to stay at the university and get an apartment?"

"Yes, honey. And you and Chris can visit me here. And if the baby is born during Christmas break as you expect, I'll still come and help you."

"Mom, does all this have anything to do with Derek?"

Paula made an effort to steady her voice. "Derek is leaving for Jamaica—to fill in for Ruth this year."

"Well, I just thought maybe—anyway, he's a great guy and I wouldn't mind if you two—if you and Dad can't—hey, I think I'm in over my head, Mom."

"I know what you mean, and I love you for caring. And give my love to Chris, too."

After they said goodbye, Paula walked to the window and looked across the commons toward Rhodes Hall. Amy and Derek were very fond of each other already but both Jeff and Todd would have to be won over gradually. For what, she asked herself crossly. One night stands required no family approval or support.

The lights from Magnolia Manor sparkled like crown jewels against black velvet as they approached and Paula felt nostalgic remembering the first time she had come here at the beginning of summer. They left the Jaguar with the valet and were shown to their favorite table by the maître d' who now recognized Paula as well as Greg.

After ordering their usual wine, Greg smiled at her. "I'm sure you get tired of hearing me say this, but you are a beautiful woman, Paula Howard."

"A woman never gets tired of hearing those words." She gave him a dazzling smile.

When the wine had been poured, Greg

lifted his glass to Paula and said, "This evening marks the end of summer, doesn't it? Shall we drink to new beginnings?"

She touched her glass to his, then sipped the pale liquid. His words were more prophetic than he knew, she thought. She looked around the room, no longer intimidated by its elegance and sighed. She had become accustomed to dining in fine restaurants and she would miss the pleasures Gregory Winthrope had given her, but after tonight it would be back to basics.

The waiter brought menus and she studied hers for a moment. "I'll have the filet of sole, wild rice and Waldorf salad."

Greg added his own order, then asked, "Did you have a nice visit with your son?"

"Yes, I did. And how did the day go with Kurt?"

"Quite well. You know, he's really good with horses for such a small fellow."

"I thought small fellows were always the best with horses. Are you thinking of training him as a jockey?"

Greg chuckled. "Not a bad idea. I'll give it some thought." He suddenly became more serious. "I have some news to share with you. Kurt is going to stay on this fall and attend the university school. He can continue his tutoring when Ben finds a suitable tutor." He looked at her regretfully. "I wish it could be you, but I understand about your job in Tuscumbia."

"But where will Kurt stay when—"

"With me. I've talked with Ben about this and he's working out the details. A sort of foster home arrangement." He shook his head. "Neither of his parents want him, you know, and I'm sure both were relieved to have this solution offered." He shrugged, "And who can tell, adoption may be a possibility later on. My parents would be pleased if that happened. And Mellie adores him."

"How wonderful. And I have a surprise for you," she paused dramatically, "I *will* be on campus so I'm available to continue as Kurt's tutor after all."

"Then your job didn't—" Greg looked sympathetic.

"I decided to turn it down."

"Well, their loss is certainly our gain. Especially Kurt's. And mine," he added meaningfully.

She would have to tell him now, Paula decided, then changed her mind. It could wait until after dinner, there was plenty of time.

Paula entertained Greg with anecdotes about the week's tutoring sessions as they ate and he updated her on the progress being made on the mill's pollution problem. When they finished their lemon chiffon pie and coffee, he said, "Isn't it time we danced? I need an excuse to put my arms around you." He stood and pulled out her chair.

Paula was wearing a white eyelet halter dress with her hair upswept, her only jewelry large white earrings and a wide bracelet. She was aware of many admiring eyes on her as she walked through the restaurant toward the veranda.

"Greg, over here," a familiar voice called out and she turned to see Dr. Colbert and his wife seated near the piano. Another couple sat at the table and even with their backs toward her she knew instantly it was Derek and Faye. Greg stopped to exchange greetings and Derek turned and met her startled eyes.

"Greg, I'd like to introduce my assistant, Faye Browne and her escort, Derek Vogel."

Derek rose to shake Greg's hand and remained standing. Ben Colbert rose and half bowed to Paula. "Paula, you've met everyone I believe?"

"Yes, Dr. Colbert." She smiled around the circle. Faye looked stunning in a very short black coatdress that showed her long black-stockinged legs to full advantage, and even

Shirlene Colbert looked fashionable in a turquoise silk.

"We're celebrating Faye's acceptance into the doctoral program at Yale, so tonight is a sort of farewell party. And," he gallantly offered her his hand, "I was just about to ask her to dance with me."

Faye stood and sensuously followed him toward the open French doors. Shirlene looked nervously toward Derek then up at Greg in a way that was impossible not to understand. Greg glanced apologetically at Paula, who nodded slightly.

"Shirlene, want to dance with me for old times' sake?"

"Yes, I'd be happy to, Greg." Her face dimpled into a relieved smile as she stood and took his proffered arm.

Derek looked at Paula. "Shall we?"

They were standing only inches apart and she could feel his body heat even before he took her arm and guided her toward the dance floor. On the veranda they turned and moved together in one graceful motion and when his hand touched her bare back, Paula shivered and moved closer without conscious thought. She felt she should say something but no words came to mind and Derek made no effort to break the electric silence between them as he expertly led her between and around the other couples on the crowded floor. Paula moved in a dreamlike trance, her body as pliant as a willow in wind, her eyes melded to Derek's whose message eluded her.

She was distantly aware of the music changing and Greg taking Derek's place, and then the spell was broken. Ben and Shirlene Colbert bobbled by, then she saw Faye and Derek glide past cheek to cheek. Greg pulled her closer. "Why so pensive, Paula?"

She missed a step. "Could we talk, Greg? Now?"

"Of course." He led her down the steps and toward the lighted gazebo. They sat in silence for a moment listening to the strains of "Moon River."

"Greg, you asked me not to wait too long before I gave you an answer to your question." He nodded, his piercing gaze expectant. "And since I'm staying on at the university, I don't want to leave you with the wrong impression." She took a deep breath. "I *have* considered your offer very carefully and although I do admire and respect you very much and enjoy being with you and am flattered and grateful to you for everything, I can't marry you— ever." She stopped, out of breath from her long speech.

After a moment of silence, Greg said in a low voice, "I'm not surprised by this, Paula. I saw the competition and realized it was formidable."

"But there's no—"

"The heart can't be programmed. I want you to be happy, Paula." He bent to brush her lips with his.

"I hope we can still be friends but if you don't want that I'll understand."

"Nothing's changed in that area."

"I'm moving into an apartment when summer ends. Would you come for dinner if I invite you sometime?"

"Only if you'll allow me to reciprocate."

"Deal."

"Come dance with me." He stood and held out his hand to her.

Gratefully she took Greg's hand and smiled at him.

The dance floor was more crowded now and she didn't see any sign of the Colberts or their guests. And when Greg led her back to their seats for a nightcap, the table where the others had been was occupied by strangers.

"There was something different about Dr. Colbert tonight," said Paula. "He seemed unusually . . ."

"Sober?" Greg asked with a wry smile.

"Yes," Paula said with surprise, "That was it."

"He's joined AA, according to Shirlene, who is understandably elated over it," Greg explained. "When Kurt disappeared that weekend and he was unable to function effectively in an emergency situation, he was pretty upset with himself. And for the first time, she said, he's come to terms with his problem."

"I'm really glad. He's a brilliant man and I've learned so much from him, but he seemed to think I was just here to have a good time. I'm not sure I've ever convinced him otherwise."

Greg looked at her thoughtfully. "I wasn't aware Ben had the wrong impression of you. And going out with me must have reinforced his false ideas. Why haven't you mentioned this before?"

Paula shrugged. "It wouldn't have changed anything. And it doesn't matter to me anymore. *I* know why I'm here, and that's the important thing."

Twenty-two

Sharon announced that it was Friendship Day—time for a celebration. By the time Ruth returned from Georgia the others had made the plans and they piled in Paula's car and headed for the Inn of the Paper Moon.

"We all like Chinese food so it seemed to be the perfect choice," Sharon explained to Ruth on the way downtown.

"Besides, it's dark in there and we wanted to bring our own bottle of Jamaican rum," Louise giggled, "which some people, ahem, have a knack for wasting."

"Don't remind me," Ruth groaned.

Inside they cajoled the hostess into seating them at a large corner table in the back and then ordered.

"How was your visit, Ruth?" Paula asked as

Louise poured dollops of rum into the Cokes they had just been served.

"Wonderful. My son came over from Emory and met all our family for the first time."

"Did they like each other?" Sharon asked.

"It was love at first sight," Ruth said softly, "on both sides. And he's coming back every weekend he can after I settle in."

"Hear, hear." Louise held up her glass. "I propose a toast to families." They touched glasses and drank.

Sharon looked at Ruth. "But you are going to Jamaica first, aren't you?"

"Oh my yes. I couldn't stand not having a couple of weeks R&R with that man of mine. And the R's stand for romance."

"Besides, you'll need to show Derek the ropes so he doesn't hang himself," Louise added.

"He'd do all right without any help from me," Ruth smiled. "It's such a relief to know he's the one who will be filling in."

"I have some news," Sharon announced. "Todd is leaving the Navy, and" she stopped, smiled at the group who waited expectantly, "coming here to enroll in the university."

Ruth groaned. "And his dad and all of us will be gone. What a shame."

"*I* won't be," Sharon continued. "I'm staying on as grad assistant and working on my master's here."

"I'll drink to that good news and how glamorous you look in your new contacts," Ruth said, and the others agreed and joined her.

"So that's why you were pleased I was staying," Paula said.

"What?" Ruth looked at her quickly. "What *is* this? I thought the Tuscumbia job was a sure thing. How could they—"

"They didn't." Paula laughed at Ruth's fierce scowl. "In fact, I was assured it was mine when I called to turn it down."

"But why," Ruth asked, "when Derek is leaving, and—"

"Because I decided I'd rather be here. And I've already rented an apartment in one of those lovely old houses on Oak Street."

"Neat," said Sharon. "Let's toast Paula now."

"I'll make this one," Louise said. "To the lady who's picked up all the pieces and put them back together even better than before."

"I'll drink to that, too," Ruth said sincerely. "Looks like our Paula has come out of her cocoon and is ready to test her wings and fly."

Paula smiled. "Thanks for the vote of confidence."

"Well, after all these exciting announcements my news will seem pretty bland," Louise said slowly, "but Derek Vogel will be staying at our house this year while he's on the island."

"Oh, to live in the same house with that gorgeous man," Ruth moaned. "Some people would kill for the chance." She looked pointedly at Paula and raised her glass. "To Paul Newman II." As the waitress returned to the table with egg rolls and steaming bowls of soup, Ruth looked at Paula and Sharon. "Since you two will be staying on here, you can drive over some weekend and visit me. I'd like you to meet my family."

Paula's face brightened. "We surely will. I'm going to miss all of you terribly. Of course, Sharon will be on campus but I'm sure she'll be spending time with Todd and it won't be like all of us together in the dorm."

"It's been a great summer," Louise said seriously. "I've missed my family but I've really enjoyed the time I've spent with all of you."

Ruth shook her head. "I thought I'd never make it through the summer without my husband. And now look at me, planning to stay away from him a whole year. But it's going to be worth the sacrifice to make amends to my family."

"And make peace with yourself," Louise added quietly.

"Yes," Ruth nodded, "especially that. You can run away from your problems but not from yourself."

"If I hadn't come here I never would have met Todd, nor all of you." Sharon smiled happily, "I guess it was just fate."

They laughed together, then Paula added, "I can't even put into words what this summer has done for me. It's given me a whole new life, and goals, and friends who are like a second family."

"So here's to friends," Ruth raised her glass again.

"To friends," they all repeated as they touched their glasses to hers and drank a final toast.

After she got back to the dorm on Sunday evening Paula lay awake, unable to sleep. She had burned all her bridges now, her ties with Tuscumbia and the house, Quent, and her job at Northwoods Elementary. And she had said a final no to Greg Winthrope's offer of marriage. There was no need to think about her feelings for Derek Vogel, because he was leaving and whatever relationship they might have had was history. If she could just get past the next five days, he would be gone and that would be the end of it.

A soft knock interrupted her thoughts and she opened the door to find Sharon standing there in her sleep shirt.

"I came to tell you something." She sat down on the bed, looking serious.

"Okay." Paula sat down beside her.

"I wasn't going to tell anyone yet, but since you're staying on . . . Todd and I, well, we're going to share a place when he comes."

"I see."

"We do plan to get married, but not just yet, and we want to be together so we . . . we're going to live in Faye Browne's apartment. She didn't want to give it up and she's subletting it furnished at a real good price. Derek took me over there last Saturday to look at it and it's very nice."

"Yes, I've seen it."

"I talked to Derek a long time about what Todd and I were planning to do, and he told me not to do it just to please Todd. He said I should do what *I* felt like doing, and if Todd loved me enough, he'd accept it and if not, why then I didn't need a guy like that anyway."

Paula nodded. "Very good advice."

"And this *is* what I want to do. I'm not ready

to tell my family just yet but I wanted to explain it to you so you'd understand, Paula. I hope you won't be offended, but I've thought of you as kind of like a mother this summer—especially since you saved my life."

"Well, I hope you won't be offended either, but I've come to think of you sort of like another daughter." She hugged her warmly and added, "And I'm going to keep my eye on you, so if things don't work out with the arrangement you're making you can always come home to Mother Paula."

The third test of the morning was almost over and Paula flexed her numb hand and went on writing.

Just before the bell, Dr. Colbert's voice cut through her thoughts. "Miss Howard," she looked up quickly, "I'd like to see you in my office after class, please."

The bell rang and Ruth and Derek were standing beside the door when she reached it. "Would you like us to wait for you?" Ruth asked quietly.

Paula shook her head.

"If you don't make it over to Gaither Hall we'll bring you a care package," Derek said in a low whisper.

She shook her head. "Thanks, but I'm not hungry."

He grinned encouragingly at her. "Good luck."

Paula walked slowly down the stairs to the first floor and by the time she reached the door marked Dr. Benjamin Colbert, he was already seated at his cluttered desk.

"Come in, Miss Howard, and close the door." He motioned toward a chair directly in front of his desk. "Sit down."

She wasn't sure if she sat or her knees buckled but she found herself in the chair, staring across the stacks of books and papers into Ben Colbert's impassive face.

"I've read your term paper, Miss Howard. Very competent." He reached out, took a folder and gave it to her.

She could see the "A" in large bold print under the clear plastic cover. "Thank you, sir."

"Your weekly test grades have been above average and your work in the tutoring program has been very creative and consistently dependable." Another hurdle passed. She thanked him again. "I understand you will be staying with us at the university this year working on your master's from this department?"

"Yes, sir."

"Then you will be available to continue tutoring Kurt Yearwood?"

"Yes, I'll be happy to."

"You know that I've arranged for him to live with the Winthrope family?" Paula nodded and he cleared his throat. "And my friend Greg has told me that he, uh, offered you marriage and you, uh, have turned him down?" Paula nodded again. He took off his glasses and polished them. "In view of all this I, uh, find that I may have misjudged your intentions, Miss Howard—Paula. And I'd like to apologize for that."

Understanding began to dawn then. Greg Winthrope must have talked to him about what she had said. She smiled graciously. "I accept your apology, Dr. Colbert." Expecting to be dismissed now, she was surprised when he spoke again.

"As you also know, my assistant is leaving." He looked at her intently. "I wonder if you'd be interested in taking her place?" Paula opened her mouth but no words came out and he went on. "You'd teach one class per semester and help with grading papers, that sort of thing. There is a small stipend, and free tuition, of course."

"Why, I'd . . . it's . . . well, yes, if you think

I can do it," Paula stammered, ". . . but I'm not at all like Miss Browne."

Dr. Colbert smiled at her. *"No one* is like Miss Browne. She's unique, but I suppose we shall bumble through somehow without her." He sighed forlornly, then said with a determined air, "Since we'll be working together you might as well call me Benny."

Paula suppressed a smile with effort. "Thank you, but if you don't mind, I would prefer to address you as Dr. Ben, out of respect for your position."

"Fine." He stood up. "Well, Paula, it might be helpful for you to talk with Faye one afternoon before she leaves, if you can arrange it." He stuck his hand across the desk. "Welcome to the team."

Paula left Ben Colbert's office and softly closed the door.

Paula hesitated in front of the office next door, wondering about making her appointment with Faye now. Behind her, elevator doors opened and she recognized the familiar click of Faye's high heels before she spoke.

"Waiting for me, Miss Howard?"

"No, I . . . yes, I was going to see if you would have time to talk with me later this week about—"

"My job? You said yes?" When Paula nodded she went on, "Good. Come on in and I'll check my calendar." Faye flipped open a date book on her desk. "How about Wednesday after tutoring, say 3:45?" Paula nodded again and Faye scribbled hastily on the page.

"I'd like to congratulate you on your acceptance at Yale," Paula said sincerely.

"Thank you," Faye smiled wryly. "I guess I owe this move to Derek Vogel." When Paula looked surprised, she went on, "You see, I've always believed what my daddy said about men being intimidated by smart women."

So that explained the Scarlett O'Hara act, Paula thought, and made a mental note to tell Ruth.

Faye shrugged. "Derek has helped me finally come to terms with my intellect and I've decided to make the most of it, but to be honest, if he were staying, I'd stick around instead and give you a run for your money."

Paula felt the color rise in her face. "But I don't—"

"Paula, *I'm* aware of why Derek didn't respond to my best efforts to seduce him, even if he isn't. But given a little more time," she shrugged suggestively, "who knows?" She sat down at her desk. "Anyway, on Wednesday I'll give you ten easy steps for coping with Benny the Bear and the tremendous work load he'll try to pile on you."

"Thank you," Paula said and turned to go.

"Don't thank me," Faye said wryly. "Whatever you've got, you earned it."

Paula stood at her window, staring pensively at the commons dappled in late afternoon shade. It seemed so short a time since she first looked down on the familiar scene but summer was at an end now. She would miss all of her summer friends—Ruth, Louise, and especially Derek, but she would survive because now she knew she was a survivor.

When the phone rang, she reached for it expecting to hear Derek's voice. "Hello?"

"Paula?"

"Hello, Mother. I've been meaning to call again and check on Roger. How is he?"

"Roger's fine. But I'm wondering if *you* are."

"Why, yes, I—"

"I've just talked with Jeff and he told me you turned down your job in Tuscumbia. Paula, how do you ever expect to get your husband back if you aren't even in the same town with him?"

"I don't expect to, Mother," Paula said.

"There's still a good chance—"

"Apparently Jeff *didn't* tell you I also turned down Quent's proposal to marry him again."

"Paula!" Jeanette's tone was shocked. "I can't believe you would do this. What about Amy and Jeff?"

"Well, Amy has a husband and home of her own now, and Quent's buying a condo large enough for Jeff to share."

"But he needs a mother. And Quentin needs a wife."

Paula smiled to herself. "Jeff managed to survive in India without me, so I think he'll be okay in Tuscumbia. And as for Quent, he should have thought about what he needed before he walked out."

"Don't be vindictive, Paula. It's a woman's place to forgive."

"I have, Mother, but I don't want a rerun."

"Jeff told me about some violent person hurting a girl in your dorm. And he said you were involved and got your picture in the paper. I should think you'd be glad to leave that place as soon as you could."

"I am leaving the dorm, Mother. I've rented an apartment off campus."

"You'll live alone?" Jeanette's voice was incredulous.

"Yes, and I'll be working as a graduate assistant to the head of my department."

"But it can't possibly pay as much as the real job in Tuscumbia."

"I'm sorry I can't talk longer, but I have to go, Mother. I'm meeting a friend for a picnic at the lake."

"A man friend?"

"Yes."

"Paula, I can't believe . . . what on earth has happened to you at that university?"

"Well, Mother, I think what has happened is that your little girl has finally grown-up."

She put the phone down with more force than necessary. Her mother's conversation had shown clearly the priority of her concerns. Mend the marriage. Make a home for the children. And as an afterthought a passing mention of her risking her life. Never a word about what she needed to be happy or what she wanted to do. She sighed. Her mother was a victim of her own programming by society and she was trying to make her daughter fit the only mold she saw as acceptable—the woman's place, as she'd called it.

Paula finished buttoning her navy denim skirt, tied her long hair back, and bent to pull on her espadrilles. She spritzed herself generously with Shalimar, grabbed her patchwork denim bag and went downstairs.

Summer school was over and the hallways were crowded with students moving from Winthrope Hall. Tomorrow she would be in the midst of it but tonight she'd been invited by Derek Vogel to a picnic at the lake.

When she stepped outside she saw his Firebird double parked at the front entrance and hurried down the steps.

Reaching to open her door, he grinned at her appreciatively. "Hurry and get in before someone else grabs you and takes you home with them."

Paula laughed. "It could easily happen by mistake. Isn't it awful? I had no idea there would be this mad rush to leave."

"Life is short and every moment counts," Derek answered ruefully as he concentrated on maneuvering through the heavy traffic. On University Boulevard he glanced at her and asked, "Plans all made for your own getaway tomorrow?"

"Yes, I'm taking Ruth and Louise to the airport before noon, then Sharon to the bus station about three. I'll drive on to Tuscumbia from there."

"And?"

"And spend the night at the house, getting things sorted out and packed for moving the following day." She looked at his handsome profile and felt a foolish urge to unfasten her seat belt and move closer to him. "Will you be leaving early?"

"Probably. I'm going to have to push to make it out in three days, but bringing Todd back will be easier."

"It worked out well for him and Sharon to use your car while you're gone."

"Yes. Given enough time, all things seem to have a way of working out." He looked at her and smiled, then shoved a cassette in the tape deck and the soft notes of Joe Henderson's saxophone filled the car. They were silent, listening to the music until they reached the lake.

Derek parked the car in a secluded cove and spread a blanket near the water, then opened the box of picnic supplies he'd brought. When Paula offered to help, he shook his head. "I'll do this," he said firmly.

He set out paper plates, napkins, and plastic cutlery, then carryout containers of Chinese food. "Compliments of the Inn of the Paper Moon—complete with fortune cookies," he told her, then took a bottle of California Chardonnay and two paper cups from the box. "Compliments of Lindsay's Package Liquor."

Paula laughed and kicked off her shoes. "This is what I call wining and dining a lady in style."

"It's not that I didn't want to take you someplace nice for dinner." He shed his own loafers and joined her on the blanket, then popped the wine cork and filled their cups. "I just wanted to have you all to myself."

Paula felt a shiver of anticipation as Derek raised his cup. "We made it, Paula. Nobody ever said it would be easy and it wasn't. But we persevered and look at us now. You, a university grad assistant, me a sub in Jamaica." He grinned at her and touched the rim of his cup to hers, "To the future."

"To the future," she repeated and they both drank.

"And now may I serve you?" When she nodded, Derek opened boxes and prepared Paula's plate, then his own. They ate, sitting cross-legged on the blanket.

"Are you apprehensive about the job?" Paula asked as she finished an egg roll and wiped her fingers.

"Dread it more than combat duty."

Paula laughed. "If tutoring was any indication of what it will be like, then it *is* combat duty."

"What about you? Any second thoughts about being Benny's girl Friday?"

"Scared to death," Paula admitted, "but he does seem different lately. And he did admit he'd been mistaken about me and apologized."

"He owed you."

"I . . . think I understand him a little better now. And Faye Browne, too." She looked at Derek solemnly. "Faye said you'd helped her come to terms with her intellect."

He looked embarrassed. "Faye said that?"

"And Sharon said you encouraged her to put her own feelings first—before Todd's?"

"What is this? Are all the women I know in a conspiracy against me?"

"In praise of you. And I wanted you to know I admire you for it."

"Then all's not vain, or whatever the expression, if it raised my standing in your eyes, Paula."

He looked so earnest Paula smiled. "You didn't need the boost," she assured him.

"I think I did." He put down his empty plate. "I took advantage of you in a weak moment, Paula, and I'm not proud of myself for that."

"My weak moment or yours?" Paula asked lightly.

"You know what I meant," he told her solemnly.

"Well," Paula lifted her chin defiantly, "I'm not sorry. About what happened that night, I mean. But I do regret that when I gained a lover, I lost a friend."

"Is that what you think?" he regarded her intently.

"What else could I think? After that night all our easy camaraderie was gone. And you've made it plain you prefer Faye Browne to me."

"You believe that?" he asked softly and when she nodded he went on. "Then I guess I'd better explain a few things. After Marsha, I swore I'd never love another woman, and I've steered a wide course from any real emotional involvement ever since—until now." He stopped, sighed deeply, then went on, "From the first time I saw you I've wanted you, but at the same time I also wanted to protect you from guys like me. And when I finally made love to you I knew I was the one who needed protecting. I've been running like hell ever since."

"There was no need for that," Paula said quietly.

"When I saw you at Magnolia Manor with that Winthrope guy I knew what an idiot I'd been. And as for Faye, I admit she was a diversion. But it didn't work, and she's been a damned good sport about it."

More like she's biding her time, Paula thought, as she remembered Faye's challenge and the way she'd contrived to keep in touch with Derek, subletting her apartment to Todd.

"Ruth told me you'd turned down the chance to marry this rich guy?" Paula nodded. "And that your ex-husband asked you to come back and you said no?" She nodded again. "I never thought I'd say these words again but the truth is I love you, and if I'd had any idea you'd be staying on I wouldn't have left the university now. Because I want us to be together—for always. Paula," he took her hand, "will you marry me?"

She lifted her eyes to his. "I love you, Derek, and I will marry you—when the time is right." He made a move toward her but she held her hand between them and he kissed her open palm. "I'm going to miss you terribly but I think we need time apart before we're ready for commitment."

"I hate leaving you in the same town with a man who obviously adores you. And an ex-husband who's helping you get settled in." He glowered at the thought.

Paula laid a gentle hand on his arm. "That's

part of the reason we need this separation. Trust is important—for both of us."

"I'm flying back at Thanksgiving."

"I'll cook a turkey with all the trimmings. And invite Todd and Sharon. And Jeff and Amy and Chris."

"I'll help. Will your landlady let me stay with you?"

"We'll see. If not, there's always a motel."

"The Coach House Inn?" he leered at her playfully.

"I'm sure we could find something closer."

"And you can fly to Jamaica for Christmas vacation. I'm sure Louise would enjoy having you visit, too."

"I'd love that, but I can't, Derek. I've promised Amy I'd be with her when the baby comes and it's due Christmas Eve."

"Then I'll come here. We could have a couple of days before you leave, then I can drive you to Atlanta, spend some time here with Todd and Sharon, and come back for you, if you like."

She smiled at him. "Sounds good to me."

"How about spring break? Any prior commitments then?"

"None."

"Good. Put a week in Jamaica on your calendar."

"I'll look forward to that. Lately I've been thinking I might check on a job in the American Schools someplace myself."

"We could explore the possibilities together, Paula. There have to be locations with opportunities for both of us, and I'd be happy to live and work anywhere you are." He looked at her intently, "Now, my love, one more question. How do you feel about premarital sex?"

"Well," she pretended to study the question carefully, "as long as two people really love each other and feel committed to the relationship I have no problem with it."

"Lady, you have just made me the happiest man around."

She laughed. "That was easy. You're the *only* man around."

He slowly took the scarf from her hair, loosened it to fall about her shoulders. Then he reached for her, took her face in his hands and lowered his mouth to hers in a kiss that blotted out all thoughts of past or future leaving only now. When he lifted his head, he shuddered and pulled her into his arms, holding her to him in a possessive embrace that left her breathless. Once more he separated himself from her and slowly unbuttoned her white knit blouse, his eyes caressing hers as his fingers worked their way from her throat to the smooth plain between her sensitive breasts and below. He pulled the soft material away from her body, reached behind her to unfasten the clasp of her lace bra and let it fall with a sharp intake of his breath as he looked at her with yearning. He carefully laid her back against the blanket, his hands burning the cool flesh of her shoulders. He kissed her eyelids, temples, throat, and she gave herself to the pleasure of his lips. His mouth blazed a sensuous trail of desire down the valley between her breasts, finally scaling the peak of each taut mound to bring a wave of longing to the very core of her being. He claimed her mouth again, the sensual motion of his tongue writing a message on her mind which she answered with mounting passion.

Derek knelt in front of her and with gentle hands unfastened the large buttons of her denim skirt. Pushing it open, he memorized the curve of her hips, the flat surface of her belly, the firm flesh of her thighs and she writhed and moaned softly. He removed the wisp of nylon that remained between them and caressed the center of her desire until she arched toward his stroking and clasped her hands behind his head and brought it down to whisper, "Derek, please, now."

She tugged at his shirt, and he impatiently

tore it off. She groped for the buckle of his belt and when it was undone, felt for the fastener of his tightly stretched jeans.

"Wait," he fumbled in one pocket, then with a low groan shrugged off the rest of his clothes and flung them aside. She knew that he had not been celibate for all the years since his divorce and she was grateful that he protected her without asking.

Kneeling above her once more, he lowered himself and entered her and she took all of him, reveling in the feel of him in the innermost part of her. Then he began to move, slowly at first, then more rapidly, so deep within her that she felt as though he were part of her. And she knew the full meaning of the words "And the two shall be made one."

He tried to hold back as she moved with him but she urged him forward into a final explosion that left them exhilarated and awed at the depth and breadth of their feelings.

"Ah, Paula, Paula, how I do love you," he said as he lowered himself beside her and pulled her against his chest so that she felt the pounding rhythm of his heart match her own.

"And I love you," she told him softly as she wove her fingers through the silken hair of his chest.

As they lay, lazily fondling each other, he

asked, "Did you bring a swimsuit like I asked you to?"

"Uh-huh, did you?"

"Yes, but I don't think we'll need them now."

Paula looked around her and realized that dusk had given way to darkness except for the full moon suspended over the lake.

"Let's go for a swim in the moonlight." He stood and his silvered torso was so beautiful she caught her breath. He pulled her to her feet and held her against him, then said huskily, "Come on, before I change my mind."

Taking their beach towels to the edge of the water, they waded in holding hands, then broke apart to swim languidly near the shore. The water was cool in the sultry night air and Paula turned and floated dreamily on her back, gazing at the star-studded sky. Two arms enfolded her from behind, two hands cupped her breasts.

"My silver goddess," Derek whispered. "We're moon lovers, did you know?"

"Yes," she whispered back and turned to kiss him deeply. He caught her against him and with joyous abandon she mounted him and in the hypnotic motion of the lake water they danced the age old dance of lovers—point to counterpoint, a minuet merging gradually to a tango.

With a throaty laugh she said, "You make me feel wanton."

"Good, because I'm wantin' you again, too."

She playfully slapped the water with the flat of her hand, spraying him with droplets and he set her down. He caught her arm and pulled her toward the shore.

"Come on," he whispered urgently. He grabbed a towel, wrapped it around her and draped the other at his waist.

"I would have taken you there in the water except for one thing," he growled as he groped again for his jeans. This time they went more slowly, learning the unique paths to one another's greatest pleasure, touching, tasting, teasing, until his need demanded release in spite of his efforts to maintain control. With one fluid motion he pulled her astride him and together they reached the summit and soared beyond anything they had ever imagined.

She lay atop him, exhausted from their ardent coupling. "It's never been like this for me before," she said softly.

He stroked her damp hair. "Nor me, though it's not the act itself but how two people feel about each other that makes the difference."

"I feel as though I've been traveling a long way and just come home."

"Home is where the heart is, my darling Paula." He kissed her forehead gently.

"When do we have to go?" she asked drowsily.

"Not yet," he answered. "Let me hold you for awhile."

"Yes," she whispered, "hold me." After a little while she said, "Derek, we forgot the fortune cookies."

"Never mind," he told her indulgently, "We already know our future."

"Yes, we know," she answered, thinking that she must remember to tell Ruth tomorrow that she had been right: the third time was charmed.

The moon sank lower over the dark water, making a silver path from shore to sky. In the silver silence the night sounds rose in symphony. Summer was at an end, but after summer would come a glorious autumn, and beyond that a serene and beautiful winter. With Robert Browning, she could believe now with certainty that the best was yet to be.